2/09

D0457046

STAR TREK®
GATEWAYS

WHAT
LAY
BEYOND

STAR TREK®
GATEWAYS

WHAT
LAY
BEYOND

Based upon STAR TREK® and STAR TREK: THE NEXT
GENERATION® created by Gene Roddenberry,
STAR TREK: DEEP SPACE NINE®
created by Rick Berman & Michael Piller,
and STAR TREK: VOYAGER®
created by Rick Berman & Michael Piller & Jeri Taylor

POCKET BOOKS
New York   London   Toronto   Sydney   Singapore

POCKET BOOKS, a division of Simon & Schuster, Inc.
1230 Avenue of the Americas, New York, NY 10020

STAR TREK is a Registered Trademark of Paramount Pictures.

This book is published by Pocket Books, a division of Simon & Schuster, Inc., under exclusive license from Paramount Pictures.

ISBN: 0-7434-3112-X

First Pocket Books hardcover printing November 2001

10   9   8   7   6   5   4   3   2   1

POCKET and colophon are registered trademarks of Simon & Schuster, Inc.

For information regarding special discounts for bulk purchases, please contact Simon & Schuster Special Sales at 1-800-456-6798 or business@simonandschuster.com

Printed in the U.S.A.

Contents

STAR TREK

STAR TREK
CHALLENGER

STAR TREK
DEEP SPACE NINE

STAR TREK
VOYAGER

STAR TREK
NEW  FRONTIER

STAR TREK
THE NEXT GENERATION

STAR TREK®

ONE GIANT LEAP

Susan Wright

Chapter 1

Captain Kirk was suspended in the gateway, floating between the countless dimensions. The interstellar transport lasted for only a few seconds, but the flashing light seemed to freeze every thought and feeling he had.

Then he was falling out the other side, rolling to his feet and unsteady on the soft surface. He was standing on the edge of a small platform, suspended near the top of a giant crevice. The sheer parallel cliffs extended for miles to either side.

Holding his arms out for balance, Kirk could only look down. The cliffs descended out of sight. The bottom was obscured by mist or smoke that was rising, softening the sharp edges of the cliffs. The rocks on both sides looked as if huge sections often sheared off and fell forever into the center of the planet.

Backing away from the edge, Kirk looked around and saw the two Kalandans. "Tasm! Stop!"

Commander Tasm was on the other side of the platform, trying to wrest away the large cylindrical unit from her errant officer, Luz. The blue neutronium cylinder was the key component of the gateway, and they were waving it around between them at the edge of an abyss!

Kirk briefly considered stunning them, but they were too close to the edge and he was afraid they would be knocked over by the impact. So he ran forward and grabbed Tasm around the waist, pulling her away. Luz hung on to the cylinder and came with her.

The soft ground gave Kirk plenty of traction, and he was able to drag both women closer to the wall of the cliff. There was an arched doorway there leading to a tunnel. Apparently that was the way off the platform.

Tasm struggled against him, but Kirk took hold of the cylinder with one hand, expertly twisting it away from her. The Kalandans were thin and frail even if they were tall.

But Luz hung on, kicking at him and jerking on the cylinder as if she were crazed. It swung wide and hit Tasm in the head, driving her down to the ground with an agonized cry. The commander rocked crouching on her knees, her head in her hands.

Glaring at him, Luz managed to push Kirk closer to the sheer drop. The streaks of green and blue on her eyelids suddenly looked right. He hadn't seen such a display of outright passion from any of the Kalandans.

"It's mine!" Luz screamed. "Let go!"

Kirk stayed calm. "Stop fighting me or we're both going over."

In response, she swiped a leg at him, catching him behind the knee. Kirk stumbled, and her momentum carried her forward, taking him right to the edge of the platform. Kirk wasn't letting go of the cylinder. He meant it—if he went over, then he was taking her with him.

Their brief struggle showed that she didn't know anything about hand-to-hand combat. But she fought in a frenzy, nearly knocking him off the platform.

Kirk got his feet under him and spun away from her, back toward the doorway in the cliff. As she fell back, he grabbed hold of her wrist. She tried to wrench it away from him, but he twisted her arm down, forcing her to take one hand off the cylinder.

With a quick turn, he stepped behind her, bringing her arm behind her back. Now that he had leverage on her, he had the advantage. She didn't have enough brute power to shake him off.

He jerked the cylinder from her grasp and bent her arm up until she went to her knees. Her cry didn't stop him. He hung on to her long enough to make her realize there was no way she could win in a fight. "Had enough?"

Panting, she continued to struggle to get away from him. But she knew she couldn't beat him.

Finally Kirk let go, pushing her away to roll on the ground next to

Tasm. Tasm was still on her knees, groaning from her head injury. Her eyes were bleary as she tried to focus on him.

Kirk pulled his phaser from his belt and trained it on them both so they didn't get any more ideas. Then he quickly assessed his situation. They were standing on a platform hardly six meters square. But what he had mistaken for soft sand was really some kind of plush rubbery material that coated the rock.

He took a few steps inside the tunnel, getting a better look at the thick beige stuff. It ran up the sides, covering it completely. Farther in, the tunnel ended. When he poked at the stuff, it felt like a dense block of suede.

Back outside, Kirk looked in both directions up and down the crevice. He had seen two metal-plated buildings on top of the cliffs before jumping through the gateway. Now he had to strain to see them. They were much farther up on the opposite side. The sun in the orange sky was so bright it made it hard to focus on the dull metal.

One look at the cliff behind him, and he knew it couldn't have been a tougher climbing challenge. Kirk was willing to bet he could make it with hands and feet alone, with the gateway cylinder strapped to his back by his uniform jacket. But that was his last resort.

Still holding the phaser on the two women, Kirk demanded, "Where are we?"

Tasm was moaning and clutching her head, so he jerked his phaser at Luz. "You brought us here. What is this place?"

Luz's lips drew back from her teeth, a desperate expression. "This is our birthing world."

"You aren't Kalandans."

"We're Petraw!" she spit at him. "You're such fools! Such trusting fools . . ."

Tasm was struggling to stand up. "Silence, Luz! You've betrayed your pod—"

"*I* saved the interstellar transporter!" Luz let out a high-pitched shriek, rushing at Tasm.

With surprise on her side, Luz managed to shove Tasm toward the edge. Tasm fell flat to stop herself from going over. Luz sat on top of her, grabbing her around the throat, screaming inarticulately.

"You never learn, do you?" Kirk dropped the cylinder to go to

Tasm's defense, but he wasn't exactly willing to risk his own life for her. Aiming his phaser, he hesitated as they rolled over, Tasm on top, then on the bottom again.

Before he could fire, he was surrounded by people. Hands grabbed his arms and took away his phaser. They were rough, their manner abrupt. It was like they appeared out of nowhere.

Kirk stopped struggling immediately. When they realized he was giving them no trouble, they let his arms free so he could stand among them. He couldn't see what had happened to his phaser, but it was gone.

They separated Tasm and Luz, taking them to opposite sides of the platform. Kirk counted eight humanoids crowded onto the platform, dressed alike in whitish-transparent bags complete with enclosed hands and feet. The loose hoods over their heads slid forward.

Kirk settled his uniform, reaching down for the cylinder. But one of the strange people picked it up first.

Kirk had to look up to see his face. It was like melted wax, with his nose, eyes, and chin softened and flattened.

"I'm James T. Kirk of the *Starship Enterprise*." Kirk pointed to the cylinder, holding out his hand. "I believe that belongs to me."

Luz cried out, stumbling forward. Kirk couldn't understand what she was saying, something about completing an engagement . . . Tasm was speaking to others, still holding one hand to her injured head. Clearly these were her people.

The androgynous Petraw held up the cylinder. "This is for the matriarchs to deal with."

"Are those your superiors?" Kirk asked. Getting an affirmative in response, he agreed, "Lead the way." He was more than ready to talk to someone in charge. Tasm had clearly lied to him about everything.

Tasm and Luz were herded into the tunnel behind him. It had somehow become unclogged and continued much deeper inside the cliff. It curved ahead, so he could only see a short way, and the top was within reach of his hand. It was cramped, but better than climbing that towering cliff freehand.

Kirk could hardly see a thing. There was no obvious light source, but the pliable material covering the walls was so pale it seemed to glow like amber under a light.

It wasn't long before the tunnel ended in a slightly more bulbous section. Straight ahead were six hexagonal openings stacked three across and two high. Each opening was about a meter wide.

"In there." The Petraw holding the cylinder gestured to the first hexagonal opening on the bottom.

Kirk peered in, but he couldn't see out the other side. "This is the way to the matriarchs?"

Several of the Petraw crowded close to him, trying to push him inside. Their baggy coveralls rustled as he resisted.

"What's the rush?" Kirk tried to regain his footing on the mushy floor.

They still nudged him forward, pressing down on his shoulders. He realized he was being given no choice and he began to fight back.

Without hesitation, the Petraw seized his legs and arms, subduing him by sheer numbers. Before he knew it, they were tossing him into the hexagon.

They slapped something on the end. Kirk scrabbled at it with his fingers. The covering was hard and peach-colored, almost opaque. He could see the shadows of the Petraw outside, but even when he kicked hard against it with both feet, he couldn't budge the seal on the end.

After a while Kirk couldn't see any more shadows. It was pitch dark inside. He kept kicking against the plug, but it held firm. He crawled to the other end, checking it for openings, but it was sealed tight as well. He was trapped.

It didn't take long to search the place. Kirk could sit up inside the cell if he hunched over, his hair brushing the ceiling. He could also lie down and stretch out to his full length, but both ends touched his feet and outstretched arms. It was a tiny, claustrophobic place. A sarcophagus buried in the rock.

He wasn't sure where the fresh air was coming from. Feeling around, he found nothing but smooth, slightly damp walls that were cool to the touch. Too bad his phaser was gone. But they hadn't taken his communicator.

Operating the communicator by touch, Kirk checked each frequency, listening for activity. There might be a Starfleet vessel in the area, or an allied planet that had diplomatic ties to the Federation.

"This is Captain James T. Kirk of the *Starship Enterprise.* Can anyone read me? I'm being held prisoner. . . ."

He repeated his distress call on every frequency. If the Petraw didn't like it, they could come stop him.

But there was no response. The static was extremely high, crackling on the lower frequencies, leading him to believe that a shield could be interfering with the subspace channel.

Kirk grimly kept trying.

His voice was raw from speaking into the communicator when he finally gave up. No one could hear his calls.

A different course of action was required. Kirk flipped the cover up and felt the screen mesh. No sharp edges on it or on the smooth black body of the unit. He tried wrenching the cover from the communicator, straining with both hands to twist it out of its hinge.

The mesh cracked at one corner, breaking free and leaving a jagged edge. He winced when it cut his probing finger. The other corner slid out of the hinge.

Kirk dug the broken cover into the seal on the end of the cell. It reacted like some kind of polymer. The jagged edge left a small slice in the flexible stuff.

He hacked away at the seal. The polymer wouldn't tear, but successive jabs cut deeper into it.

Satisfied that he was finally making some progress, he worked faster.

It took a while for Kirk to break through. At first only one hand could push out of the cell. He continued to dig at the polymer to enlarge the slash.

Getting his shoulders through was the hardest. He struggled with the polymer as if the cell were alive and determined to keep him inside. When he finally slid through, dragging his legs after him, he rolled onto the soft ground.

Only to find himself trapped again. The tunnel was exactly the same as before, nearly dark with no way to get out. But the Petraw were gone.

Kirk carefully retraced their steps, and found the tunnel once more clogged at the end with a dense mass of tan polymer. But now he knew that it could be opened.

He plunged his hands into the center, feeling them sink deeper and deeper. It was powdery dry. The stretchy texture reminded him of the thick rubber bands he had used as a kid for makeshift slingshots. He pushed harder on it.

The walls slowly started drawing back, opening up to reveal the platform where the gateway had deposited him. It was darker outside now, and Kirk went forward to see the blood orange sky looming over the parallel cliffs. It was densely spangled with bright white stars. Everything inside the crevice was ruddy, including the cliffs and the tunnel.

The Petraw could have taken a transport from the platform up to those metallic structures. But why did Luz bring them here instead of directly to the top? The last thing she had expected was for Kirk and Tasm to come along with her.

Kirk crouched down and went right to the edge of the platform to look over again. The crack seemed to descend forever, cleft deep into the planet. It was completely dark down there, and would likely be even in the brightest daylight. Plus there was that odd smoky mist. It didn't look very inviting.

No, the answer must lay inside the tunnel.

Kirk went back inside, returning to the six hexagon cells.

He didn't have much time before the tunnel began to close behind him, shutting out most of the light. But he searched the walls quickly, pushing and poking, trying to find another place where the polymer would open up.

Right next to the cells, his hands sank into the wall. Kirk leaned in, pushing his arms into the center. The barrier began to give way, irising into an opening tall enough for him to step through. It was not much brighter inside this tunnel, with the ambient light coming from a warm glow within the walls themselves.

The tunnel finally widened as it ended in a cross-tunnel. This passageway was apparently well trodden, with the tan polymer floor roughened and pitted by use.

Going down this tunnel, Kirk paused to listen to the echo of odd mechanical noises. Light slanted out of a doorway ahead. Edging closer, he could see a brightly lit, cavernous space filled with various large pieces of equipment. They were interconnected by ductwork and conduit junctions. The walls and floor were bare rock rather than being covered by the beige polymer.

A shadow crossed the doorway as several Petraw approached the door from inside. Kirk pulled back, pressing against the wall. He sank in deeper and deeper until it almost covered him. His muscles strained to keep him inside, and he wondered if he could bury himself completely. But there was still a stripe down his front that wasn't covered.

But the Petraw passed by in the gloom without noticing him. Kirk finally managed to pull away from the wall, which took as much effort as sinking into it. Then he looked around the doorway again. The machinery appeared to be pumps and some kind of a hydraulic press. They were being operated by Petraw in the baggy coveralls.

Kirk waited until none of the Petraw were in view before vaulting across the opening. He wasn't ready to take on a dozen Petraw by himself. Not yet.

He felt very conspicuous in his gold and black uniform. If anyone came down the tunnel, he would be spotted instantly. But he continued on. Far ahead, light was slanting out another door, and beyond that was another door.

Kirk made the same careful approach. Each large chamber held different types of machinery. In every one, the rock was left exposed and work lights gave adequate illumination for the Petraw.

His luck changed when he found the factory where the coveralls were made. Inside the door were racks of drying coveralls, shining and smelling strongly like a brand-new spacesuit. They were translucent when wet, drying to nearly a solid white.

Kirk slipped in among the racks, going deeper to avoid the Petraw who were conveying the garments out of a mold and hanging them up to dry. Some of them were miniature, probably for babies, while others were bigger than he was. They were designed exactly the same; bags with legs that started at the knees and arms that started at the elbows, ending in booties and four-fingered gloves. The hood was attached to the neck.

He found one his size, but he wasn't sure how to get inside it. After some experimental testing, he realized the neck stretched if it was steadily pulled on. By the time his shoulders got through, it was hanging open wide. But when he pulled up the hood, the elasticized stuff began to shrink back into shape. What little shape it had.

With the hood up, Kirk felt much better. His black pants could vaguely be seen through the near-opaque polymer. But in the darkness, no one would notice.

Finally feeling free to roam, Kirk slipped out of the garment factory and began briskly walking down the center of the tunnel. He didn't have to sneak up to every doorway, and could take more time to examine the unusual machinery. It had the same hodgepodge construction as Tasm's ship, as if different materials and technology had been jumbled together to form one functioning unit.

No one paid any attention to him, even when several Petraw passed close by. They kept their eyes cast down as they walked, and their movements seemed somewhat slow to Kirk.

He grew bolder, ranging through the corridors. His general direction was up, figuring that would be the way to get out of the complex. Yet the tunnels went on and on, making him pause as he tried to remember his route. No sense getting lost in the maze. It appeared to be laid out in concentric rings, with short, steeply sloping tunnels up to the next level.

Though it had long underground corridors like the Kalandan station, everything else was different. The Kalandan passageways were large and kept sparkling clean like the space station it was. This place was cramped, dark, and dirty, like an underground mine. The Petraw, especially the smaller ones, were bowed down with work. With their melted faces, he couldn't tell any of them apart.

Kirk didn't want to feel sorry for Tasm, but for some reason he did.

It took hours before Kirk found what he was looking for—a docking bay for spaceships. Keeping his elation in check, he passed a few of the larger vessels the size of Tasm's ship. They filled the underground bunkers from one end to the other. Then he came across several hangars for the smaller shuttlecraft-type ships, the kind that a single man could operate.

Kirk was grinning in relief. That hadn't been too difficult. Now all he needed to do was get hold of the interstellar transporter and steal a ship to return to the *Enterprise.*

It took a while to explore the extensive hangars to find the right ship. Most were being worked on round the clock by the silent wax-work Petraw.

At this point, he didn't hesitate to go right up to them. They were so intent on their jobs that as long as he appeared to be doing a task of his own no one paid attention to him. They coordinated with each other with a minimum of clipped words, almost a technocode.

The one time Kirk was asked a question, he made sure his hood hung over his face before grunting and shaking his head. The worker accepted his ignorance and asked someone else.

Finally Kirk found a small ship that appeared fully operational. He slid into the pilot's seat and examined the controls. The panel was activated, but it was like nothing he had ever seen. Spiky symbols scrolled down one side, with triangles and diamond patterns on the other side.

"Uh-oh," Kirk muttered. "Maybe not so simple . . ."

His other problem was how to get the ship out of the hangar. There were large recessed doors in the ceiling of each bunker, but he couldn't see a control panel that operated them.

I might need a native guide, he thought. Not that Luz or Tasm seemed predisposed to help him.

Working at the panel, Kirk managed to call up the navigational chart. The pattern of a galactic star map was clear in any language. He felt a rising hope that he would manage in spite of any obstacle—

Then he realized what he was seeing. Amid the multitude of stars, there was one that coincided with a red stationary indicator. It was near the center of the galaxy, in the spiral arm at the base of the Beta Quadrant.

Kirk froze. In the center of the galaxy . . . if that red indicator meant what he thought it meant, then he was there! At least forty thousand light-years away from Federation territory . . .

Dazed, he tried to do the math. At top warp speed of 9.9—and no ship could go that fast for very long—it would take him over twenty years to get back to the *Enterprise.*

Chapter 2

It was a shock, no doubt about that. Kirk kept thinking about the orange sky outside. It was filled with stars just as the sky would be on a planet close to the galactic core.

But Kirk wasn't completely convinced until he checked two other navigational arrays on different spacecrafts. Each one showed the location indicator positioned over the same star near the galactic core.

Well, that certainly changed things. Much as Kirk liked space travel, he didn't intend to spend the better part of his life dashing through unknown space trying to get home. Who in their right mind would do something like that?

His only hope was the dimensional transporter. If he could get hold of the cylindrical unit, hook it up to a self-diagnostic subprocessor, then somehow build an archway out of solid neutronium . . .

Even Spock would consider that an impossible task. Kirk had no idea how neutronium could be made or shaped since it was supposed to be impervious to heat and pressure.

He was almost delirious after so much searching, then hours of examining spaceships. He hid out for a while in the fresher of one of the ships as he tried to consider his dilemma, but he didn't want to be discovered or, even worse, be on board if the ship took off to points unknown.

Cautiously, he emerged in time to see at least a dozen Petraw heading toward the door of the hangar. Kirk tagged along behind. He kept thinking of the millions of stars between him and the *Enterprise.* Was his crew looking for him now?

But the silent workers commanded his attention. Kirk wondered what sort of terrible hardships must have befallen these people to make them so downtrodden and subdued. He kept his own head down, too, to cast a shadow over his well-defined features.

But when they emerged onto a ledge, he forgot himself and looked up in frank amazement. They were at the bottom of another crack, a miniature version of the crevice outside. These parallel walls were much closer together. The inner wall was lined with hexagonal cells, just like the one he had been sealed into by the Petraw. These cells were open; a honeycomb of thousands of cells stacked at least a hundred rows high.

The edges of each cell glowed, making a latticework up one side of the narrow crack. The other wall loomed close in the darkness.

The lattice was crawling with Petraw, climbing up or down, easily gripping the open sides and stepping on the staggered rows. But it was completely, eerily silent.

The Petraw from the hangar started climbing, so Kirk did too. His gloves and booties were skid-resistant, helping him keep a grip on the edges of the cells.

Inside most of the cells were Petraw, lying down. They were on their backs, their heads concealed in the darkness at the other end. Their encased feet stuck toward him.

Kirk climbed very high where more of the cells were empty. He didn't want to take someone else's spot, though he wasn't sure how anyone could find a certain cell among these identical units.

Crawling inside, he sat on the edge and looked down. He was about seventy-five meters high, but it seemed higher because of the nearby opposite wall and the many levels between him and the floor.

Kirk stretched out, lying down with his head at the inner end to hide his face in the shadows. He was still trying to think of a way out of this mess when he passed out.

Kirk was dreaming. It was a nightmare replay of the events leading up to their leap through the gateway. But this time it was different, as if he were watching it outside of himself, seeing details he hadn't noticed before: Luz's snarling mouth as she fought, the flare of the protective shield over the crevice, and the arrival of the defenders on the platform. . . .

That drove Kirk nearly to wakefulness, making him roll over. But he let sleep pull him back in.

Then he was dreaming about Tasm. She was being praised by the matriarchs. But he could only see a waxy-looking Petraw dressed in baggy coveralls. Then something in the way she moved and inclined her head as she acknowledged their praise made Kirk realize it was Tasm!

His eyes opened wide as he was jolted out of sleep. But he could still see Tasm in her new guise. Only now it seemed to fit her constrained and sexless manner. That's why he had rejected her kiss. His subconscious mind had detected the forgery, and had recoiled from a false intimacy with her.

Tasm will be rewarded with our highest honor. She will take her place in the birthing chamber and will be fed the royal gel. She will make a fine addition to our birthing world. . . .

Kirk sat straight up, his heart pounding. Now he couldn't hear anything. But somehow the words had formed in his mind.

His hands felt the slight curve on the floor at the end of the cell. It was made to fit his skull. The concave surface felt warm.

It was an information feed. He wasn't sure how he knew that, but he did. Just as he knew the matriarchs used it to distribute their orders and information to Petraw throughout the galaxy.

Kirk hesitated for only a moment. Then he lay back down, placing his head in the curve. He breathed deeply, trying to relax. If this thing provided information, that's exactly what he needed.

His fatigue helped. In spite of his surprise, his mind started to drift. Then he saw Luz. Her face had been transformed, too. Now she had mere dips for her eyes, with an abbreviated nose and a bump for a chin. She was fully Petraw.

Apparently Luz had already given her version of events. Kirk was disappointed; he wanted to know what had possessed her to steal the interstellar transporter from her own commander. He was certain now that Tasm had been surprised and appalled by Luz's betrayal. Apparently that was the consensus.

15

Luz is defective and must be put away from the Petraw. The defenders will put her into the deep.

Kirk could see Luz crying out, her gloved hands reaching up to something he couldn't see. She was apparently protesting her innocence. But he couldn't hear what she said.

Two of the larger Petraw took her by each arm, and Kirk couldn't see her anymore.

He lay there for a few moments longer, but he got no other information. It seemed like a haze hung over his thoughts.

Kirk resisted, sitting up. They were going to kill Luz. If this was happening in real time, they were going to do it any moment. Not that he had any affection for Luz. Quite the contrary, it was because of her that he was trapped so far from home. But the Petraw defenders had made the first move against him by sealing him in that cell. Their enemy was his potential ally.

Tasm was clearly out of the picture, now that she was a favored member of the ruling clan. He would never trust her again.

Kirk slid forward to the edge of his cell. He had slept for a while, to judge from the cramp in his shoulder. *Now where, in this huge complex, is Luz?*

It would be easier to figure out where they were taking her. *The deep . . .* He was sitting at the edge of what was certainly a deadly plunge, but he wouldn't call this the deep.

It had to be the giant fissure outside. They were going to throw Luz off the platform.

Kirk rapidly climbed down the cells. There was still a lot of movement over the latticework. After sleeping in the information feed, it made more sense. As if he had been listening to routine orders given throughout the night. He now knew there were thousands of workers in this one block who kept the factories and shipyards functioning. Other vast blocks of cells catered to the guards they called "defenders," and the scouts in training.

Kirk hurried through the tunnels, slowing down only when he spotted a Petraw ahead. He had been careful to memorize the tunnels he had used, and was able to find his way back with only one wrong turn.

After pushing through the first barrier, he knelt down to check on the cell where he had been sealed in. It was difficult to see that the seal had been broken unless you got close. So they might not know yet that he had gotten away.

Feeling his way along the wall, he went toward the outer barrier. It opened for him more easily this time, and he was outside again. The orange light was bright.

Kirk leaned over the edge. The beige polymer sort of dripped over the edge, but it offered no strategic advantage.

As the barrier closed again, he took up a stance behind it, against one wall. He would jump the Petraw when it opened. Assuming that they hadn't already marched Luz through here and over the edge. In that case, there was nothing he could do for her.

The barrier started to open, and by the time the Petraw stepped through, Kirk was clinging to the wall near the top curve of the tunnel. His hands and feet were buried in the soft polymer, giving him the perfect ambush position.

They didn't see him. As the Petraw passed underneath, Kirk dropped down on the first one. His feet kicked out to catch the other Petraw in the face. They let go of Luz to fight back, but with a few well-aimed chops from Kirk, they were both lying unconscious on the floor. He wished he could learn how to do that Vulcan neck pinch. It would be easier on his hands.

Luz looked completely different now, with smoothed features that left her expressionless. Except for her thin-lipped mouth, which was perfectly round in horror. "You!"

Kirk grabbed her. "Come on! Run!" he shouted at her.

Jerking on her arm, he pulled her after him. After a few stiff steps, she finally got going. She must have been in a near-trance, unable to resist being taken to a plunge to certain death.

The second barrier was too slow in opening for Kirk's comfort. But then they were through and running toward the factories. "Where to?" Kirk asked.

She looked at him blankly, her steps faltering.

Kirk stopped and gave her shoulders a commanding shake. "You better snap out of it and start helping me! The first thing they'll do is announce that you've escaped. If you don't *want* to take a dive into nowhere, you'll have to find us a safe place to hide."

"Yes!" she gasped out, clutching at his arm. "Yes, I think I know where we can go."

Luz hurried down the tunnel, passing the doorways to the factories until she found the one she was looking for. Kirk ducked inside after her, wary of other Petraw. But Luz beckoned him to follow her behind a bulky ion generator before anyone noticed them.

It was very dark behind the generator, though the polymer coating on the wall continued to glow. Luz crouched down near an obstruction. Kirk shifted until he could see that it was the wall itself, stretched out and attached to a large round collar in the side of the generator. It was nearly a meter in diameter.

Touching it, Kirk discovered the wall material was taut, pulled to its maximum extension. It was amazing, the uses the Petraw found for polymer.

Luz glanced up, her eyes shining with a fierce intensity. But she didn't speak.

"This isn't going to be enough cover." Kirk crouched down, too, but the junction wouldn't hide them if anyone walked behind the generator.

"Everyone always underestimates me," Luz retorted scornfully.

Placing both hands against the wall next to the junction, she pushed. An opening appeared in the wall, widening to about a meter in diameter. It was low to the ground, so Luz stuck her head and arms inside, and with a wiggling motion, disappeared inside.

Kirk scrambled closer. There was faint warm light glowing in the walls of the small tube. "Can't you open it a bit wider?"

"Nothing satisfies you, does it?" Luz shot back over her shoulder. She started to crawl away.

Kirk shook his head, knowing he'd be a bit caustic, too, if his own people had just tried to throw him off a cliff. Bending his arms, he crawled inside after her.

The opening slowly began to close behind him. "What is this?" he called up to her.

"Access tubes for maintenance and repair." Her own voice was low. "Be quiet, will you? There's other Petraw in these tubes."

Creeping through the tiny space, bumping his head and elbows with almost every movement, Kirk swore he would never again complain about the size of the Jefferies tubes on board the *Enterprise*. If he ever got back to the *Enterprise*.

At least the polymer offered padding for his knees, even if the tube was too small. But it also took extra effort to move since he sank into the stuff. It was like crawling through sticky clay.

Kirk caught up with Luz as she reached an intersection. Another tube crossed theirs. She listened for a few moments. Kirk wasn't sure how any sound waves managed to carry in such spongy surroundings. There was nothing for them to bounce off.

But Luz seemed satisfied. She turned right, scuttling away again as Kirk slogged after her.

Luz was pushing on the ceiling when Kirk caught up again. Another round opening grew in the top of the tunnel to nearly a meter wide.

"How did you know where that tube was?" If she was going to keep leaving him behind, he needed to be able to navigate on his own. He didn't trust any of these Petraw.

Her rapidly blinking eyes and nervous twitching indicated she was about to crack under the strain. "I can see it," she snapped.

"Be more specific. What is it you see?"

Luz ignored him. She stood up inside the tube, lifting one foot to dig it into the lip. Her toes sank in, giving her a grip. Her legs disappeared up the tube.

Kirk couldn't see what she was holding on to. So he stood up in the tube, feeling around with his hands. There was nothing but the pliable wall. He figured she was clinging to the polymer the same way he had ambushed her captors.

So he followed her, planting one foot into the tube and pushing until his back braced against the other side. Using that for leverage, he dug the heels of his hands into the wall next to him. It was faster going up than forward.

Luz led him through a long series of tubes, climbing a number of levels and heading deeper into the complex. Kirk was panting from fighting the rubbery walls when she finally turned in to a side tunnel that terminated in a dim cul-de-sac.

"Is there another way out?" Kirk asked.

"Yes," she said shortly.

Kirk waited, but she didn't offer anything else. "Listen, we're in this together, whether you like it or not. I asked you a question, and I expect an answer."

Luz sullenly gestured to the end of the wall next to her. "This takes us into one of the waste reclamation chambers. Nobody uses this tube because the opening is so high up. But if we have to, we can jump down."

Satisfied, Kirk sat down next to her, straining to see the wall at the end. It looked no different from everything else. He knew he would have trouble finding his way through the access tubes without Luz. And she was not being cooperative.

Kirk had learned that when all else failed, make friends with your enemy. "Why did you do it, Luz? Why did you take the gateway?"

She glanced over at him. Her face was so different that he kept having to remind himself that he knew this person. If only Dr. McCoy hadn't stopped him from interrogating her inside the Kalandan station. Luz was obviously unstable. If he had ordered McCoy to stay out of it, he might have cracked her cover. But at the time he had nothing concrete on which to base his doubts. The Petraw were competent con artists, if nothing else.

Luz tried sarcasm to fend him off. "Why would anyone take the gateway? Who wants to transport thousands of light-years in an instant?"

"I wish I could," Kirk replied. "What I don't understand is why you betrayed your own people. Surely Tasm was planning on taking the gateway for the Petraw."

"Tasm!" Luz blurted out, unable to restrain herself. "This is all *her* fault. She made the wrong decision at every point. *I* was trying to save the gateway!"

Cannily, Kirk agreed, "You did bring it back to your people."

"That's what I told the matriarchs! Tasm is so inept she would have lost it. She was going to try that Klingon ruse herself, to scare you away. It was a inane idea."

"You used it," Kirk had to point out.

"Yes, to gain time to secure the station. It worked perfectly for that." Luz looked proud of herself. "But Tasm doesn't have a shred of originality. *She* didn't think of using the gateway to return home. *She* would have sent it back on an automated drone, making the Petraw wait another generation before we had this technology to use."

"So you did help your people." Kirk added, "Now they'll find out how the gateway technology works."

"Thanks to me!"

"Where do you think they'll take the cylinder to analyze it?"

Luz drew away from him slightly. "I'm not telling you anything! I'm a loyal Petraw."

"Yeah, so loyal they almost killed you."

Luz closed her burning eyes. "That's because *Tasm* came along and ruined everything! I would be the one accepted into the birthing chamber if *she* wasn't here. Another cron and I would have been gone before you arrived!"

Luz put her hands over her face, curling into a ball. Kirk knew it would be useless to try to get information out of her right now. It was depraved the way these people lied and cheated, even their own crewmates, to get what they wanted.

He no longer felt sympathy for any of the Petraw. To think, this selfish greed was what had brought him so far from his own ship. Kirk turned away from Luz, propping his head in his hand. He almost wished he hadn't rescued her.

Time blurred together for Kirk, with no way for him to tell when each day had passed. They snatched sleep in the tiny access tubes, leaving only to go to one of the cell blocks where Luz showed him the feedtubes deep inside.

Kirk needed to eat, but it was a strange experience. He had to pull on the strawlike tube until it straightened and dripped a golden liquid. It tasted tart and was rather thick and syrupy. According to Luz, it supplied the nourishment needs of the Petraw in this complex. He was thirsty enough to drink deeply every time he could, but after a while he wished there were some other flavor. He wasn't used to eating the same thing all the time.

Whenever they left the narrow access tubes, they saw scores of defenders, the bigger Petraw who were searching for him and Luz. At first Kirk thought he had made a tactical error by rescuing Luz, alerting the Petraw that he was on the loose. But Luz knew a great deal about the complex that enabled them to avoid the defenders.

At one point, the search teams were going through the access tubes meter by meter. Luz kept trying to dodge them. They were forced to keep moving or be caught.

"I didn't want to do it, but I guess there's no other option," Luz finally said, huddled in the tube in front of Kirk.

"Now what?" It looked as though their time was running out.

"We'll have to go into the web. That's the network of tubes that link a block of cells close to here."

Kirk had become more comfortable with the towering cells, but he wasn't prepared for the tangle of access tubes that filled the space behind. He crawled after Luz, sighting workers here and there in the dim light. They kept making sharp turns, climbing up, then down to get away.

Kirk was exhausted from the climbing when Luz uttered something in exasperation. "They're all around us."

"I don't see them," Kirk protested, looking behind.

"I can feel it in the tube," she said vaguely. "We'll have to make a dash for it."

"For what?" he asked doubtfully.

Luz didn't answer, opening a tube above them and starting to climb even faster than before. Kirk didn't try to talk to her, saving his breath for the effort.

After a long ascent, Luz finally paused. She appeared to be listening before she cautiously pushed on the wall next to her, opening the tube. Then she slithered through headfirst.

Kirk emerged into a much larger room. Without hesitation, he lifted his arms up, stretching as tall as he could. He felt as if he were turning into a scurrying bug that inhabited the woodwork.

Luz was kneeling over something. Another tube was opening up.

Kirk sighed, but when she pulled back so he could look inside, it wasn't a tube as he expected. Below the hole in the ground, it opened up almost as large as the chamber they were in. About four meters down, there was a smooth flat floor. It was a deeper golden color and lacked the inner glow of the surrounding walls.

"Hold on to the edge," Luz told him. "We'll hang from here until they pass through."

"What is it?"

"A nutrient sac, holding the nourishment for distribution to the cells."

Kirk swallowed. How could he miss that smell of the sweet syrup they drank every day?

Luz swung over the edge, digging her gloved hands into the lip of the sac. Kirk thought he heard voices, and he quickly slid over himself, making sure his grip was good. The opening was already slowly squeezing shut.

He swung slightly next to her. "Can't we just tread water—or, whatever you call it?"

"The walls are stretched taut. We wouldn't be able to climb back out."

She shifted as the opening shrank back to nearly its closed position. Kirk also had to regrip. He hoped none of the defenders would see their fingers digging into the pliant edge.

The smell was overpowering. He didn't want to imagine what would happen if he fell into it, stuck swimming until he couldn't stay afloat any longer, then finally sinking under. . . .

This time he could feel the slight vibration of people walking around. Maybe because his entire weight was supported by his fingers. He was in agony, trying not to make a sound.

After a while, the vibrations ceased.

"Are they gone?" he whispered, aching to get back out.

"A bit more. They'll have to check the other sac rooms."

Luz hadn't said a word about the interstellar transporter since Kirk had first questioned her. But as they dangled uselessly from the lip of the sac, she finally said, "Tasm is completely inept. You would never have let her take the gateway, would you?"

Kirk looked at her in surprise. "You want to talk about that *now?*"

"Why not?" Luz was staring morosely down at the nutrient fluid.

Kirk considered the question. "My orders were to keep the gateway from falling into enemy hands. I didn't trust Tasm, so I don't think I would have let her take it."

"I thought so." Luz shifted, getting a better grip. "Tasm would have destroyed your ship to take the gateway."

Kirk remembered the ease with which Tasm had disintegrated the Klingon cruiser with their quantum torpedoes. "The *Enterprise* has been in worse situations and survived."

"Then it's too bad you didn't bring your ship with you," Luz retorted.

"I like a streamlined mission every now and again." Kirk smiled, showing his teeth. He was not about to indulge in useless worry or let Luz know that this was a particularly tight spot he was in. Confidence was the key to success. If he didn't make it back to the *Enterprise,* he would have plenty of time later to think about failure.

Chapter 3

Kirk tried various tactics to make Luz cooperate with him. He was desperate enough to single-handedly hijack a starship, but he wasn't leaving without the gateway component. Luz refused to tell him anything that would help him locate it.

They continued to elude the searchers, forgoing sleep to keep on the move. Kirk was amazed anew at the size of the complex.

Every time they had to go into a block of cells to get some nourishment, Kirk placed his head in the information feed, trying to hear news about the gateway. But it was hard for him to access the feed because he had to be nearly asleep to hear anything. He was so wary of searchers checking the cells that it was tough to relax.

Needless to say, despite his attempts he didn't discover anything useful. But he did get the sense that the search for him and Luz was easing off and valuable workers had been returned to their regular duties. He wasn't surprised. They would eventually be found, and there wasn't much they could do to harm the Petraw while they were on the run. Especially with Luz still fanatically loyal to her own people.

Yet the countless days of constant companionship, forced to struggle together to survive, had an impact on Luz. Kirk could understand it would be hard to stay faithful to people who were out to kill you. Gradually, Luz's rants against Tasm shifted against the matriarchs and the other Petraw. Her most scathing comments were reserved for her own podmates.

They were sitting in yet another narrow access tube, with Kirk trying to ignore the closeness of the walls, when Luz muttered for the hundredth time, "No imagination. No insight. Just because Tasm was the leader, they rewarded her and tossed me away. Even though *I* was right. Now Tasm will breed a bunch more idiotic Petraw to bumble around out there, making a mess out of their engagements."

"You're obviously not meant to be with these people." It was a habit now for him to try to flatter her. "Why don't you leave here? Surely there are other Petraw who would appreciate your talents."

Luz frowned thoughtfully. "I thought about that. Petraw territory is far-flung. There are birthing worlds far removed from here."

"You think you could get a ship out of this complex?" Kirk asked with deceptive lightness.

"Possibly." She seemed wary of telling him more. "The shield generators on top would have to be disabled."

Kirk felt a leap of eagerness. "Disabling shield generators is my line of work."

Anything would be better than skulking around in the dark. But what if he did get off this planet? Then what? Stranded far from Earth, possibly never seeing another human being again . . .

Not if he could help it.

Luz was shaking her head. "But even if I was allowed to stay on another birthing world, I'd be relegated to cleaning waste tubes for the rest of my life. Only those born in the complex are accepted into the birthing chamber."

"Didn't Tasm earn that by giving the matriarchs the gateway?" At her sudden interest, Kirk added, "Valuable technology like the interstellar transporter is worth something."

"But our matriarchs would spread the word against me," Luz protested.

"Do you really think anyone in their right mind would give up the gateway? They'll want to back-engineer it for themselves."

She searched his face. "That's true. I could take it to one of the distant worlds where it would take time for the feed to spread. And once I was made a matriarch, it would be too late to change it."

"I'll make a deal with you, Luz. I want out of this place. I can't stand it anymore." He give a realistic shudder, hoping she would think his human sensibilities were overwhelmed by the alien culture. "I'll help you get the cylinder for the gateway if you get me out of here. Once we're off this planet, we're both free to go our separate ways."

"You said your orders are to keep the transporter from falling into enemy hands," Luz pointed out. "Why would you let me take it?"

His grin twisted. "If you help me get out of here, then that makes you my ally."

Luz hesitated, then shook her head. "I don't believe you."

Kirk almost sighed. It had been worth a shot.

"But," she added, "I think you're right that taking the gateway is the only way I'll earn my proper place among the Petraw. I've got to get it back."

Hiding his elation was not easy, but Kirk simply nodded. "Then we can both get out of here."

Her shallow eyes and smooth skin were like a mask, hiding her true feelings. "I know where it may be."

Kirk didn't want to risk upsetting his tenuous agreement with Luz, so he contained his anticipation as he followed her through the tubes. They kept going down, and were heading toward the side of the complex adjacent to the cliffs.

They descended lower than Kirk had ever been, when they reached a long tube that slanted downward. "This is different."

"It's one of the access tubes for the conduits supplying the experimental stations." Her voice was muffled, facing downhill in front of him. He could only see her rounded behind and her feet pointing back at him. "That's where we work with technology we don't understand. It's safer that way."

"Safer? Why?"

She paused to look back. "The cliff has been rigged with charges so that in an emergency, each experimental station can be dropped into the chasm. It's molten rock at the bottom, so anything dangerous is swallowed up before it can damage the rest of the complex."

Kirk could appreciate their caution. He would have taken care to protect his ship before attempting to crack open that neutronium cylinder. It would take an incredible amount of energy to penetrate the seal on the gateway's secrets.

The search began. There was a long row of chambers that held experimental stations, and Kirk doggedly crawled through each tube after Luz. There were Petraw workers in these access tubes, but Kirk just kept his head down and pretended to be intent on his duty.

The tubes were attached only to the inner walls of the rooms. To check each station, they crawled forward and opened the wall, usually next to some conduit, while Luz peered around. These rooms were solid rock except for the inner wall. They were brightly illuminated by pole lights.

Kirk couldn't recognize most of the equipment they saw, but Luz only needed a glimpse to dismiss each station. It made him uneasy, but he was convinced that she truly wanted to find the dimensional transporter. She was focused in a way he had never seen before, intent on her objective. Finally he could see the determination that had enabled her to fool everyone, including himself. She had almost succeeded in getting away clean with the gateway.

Luz leaned forward on yet another opening. She barely pushed, allowing the tube to iris only slightly. She got very close to look through, blocking Kirk's view.

"There's the magnetomotive," Luz exclaimed. "It's fully operational."

"Let me see." Kirk squirmed up next to her, putting his eyes to the hand-sized opening. They were about four meters above the floor with a conduit running out from the wall next to them. It was attached to a scaffold tower. The interlocking bars seemed too delicate to support the enormous black rings. Each ring was at least twenty meters wide and five tall. Kirk counted fifteen rings stacked on top of one another, separated by suspension units on the scaffolding.

"What is it?" Kirk asked.

"A series of magnetic circuits that focus the electromagnetic field of this planet."

The light glanced off a microthin coil wrapped around the magnet rings. Spock would have been able to tell him exactly how much magnetic flux was being generated.

Kirk guessed it might be enough to power the dimensional transporter. "You think they're trying to activate the gateway?"

"Naturally."

"But there's no archway, no computer . . ." Then he remembered Tasm's pouch, probably conveniently stuffed with all the information Spock and her officers had obtained while working on the gateway.

The bulk of the room lay beyond the dull black tower of magnets. Determined to discover the truth, Kirk pushed open the tube so he could see better. The floor between the magnets and the inner wall was smooth rock. But the door was down to their left, and he would be in full view of anyone entering or leaving.

"Will that conduit hold my weight?" he asked Luz.

She also looked down, then at the wide duct next to them. In answer, she swung her leg over the duct, using her hands to balance on the shaft. Kirk kept an eye on the doorway, hoping no one would come in at that moment.

Hitching herself forward, Luz crossed over the gap so she could step onto the scaffolding. Kirk swiftly followed.

This close to the magnetic flux, Kirk could feel his hair rising on his body. A subsonic hum rattled his bones, filling his ears with an endless thrumming. It sounded as if the circuits were powering up.

Their scaffolding tower was connected to the others on either side by narrow catwalks that circled the open sections between the magnets. Squat round suspension units were spaced along the catwalks, holding up the incredible weight.

"Higher," Kirk whispered, gesturing up. If there was anyone in the room, they wouldn't be as apt to notice them if they were in the darkened area near the ceiling. Most of the light was concentrated low.

The tower swayed under their climbing, seemingly too weak to hold up the magnets. But that work was really being done by the suspension units. The entire framework would crash to the ground if enough suspension units failed.

Near the top, Kirk stepped onto one of the catwalks. He went in the opposite direction from the door so he wouldn't be seen.

As he started out, it was impossible not to look down. His arms stretched out for better balance, but he instantly pulled his hands back in. The magnetic field was strong enough to cause a burning sensation against his skin.

It was tough to balance on the narrow metal grate as he walked. At the next tower, he eased forward, looking further around the magnets. The only thing he could see was the next scaffolding tower. Luz was already starting to cross the catwalk after him.

It took two more nerve-racking trips across the catwalks to reach the scaffolding tower one-quarter of the way around the magnets. Then Kirk saw a Petraw standing against the far corner in the attitude of a guard.

Kirk pointed down, gesturing to Luz to keep quiet. She stayed at the back of the scaffolding, gazing fearfully at the hooded head of the defender. Kirk went forward to the front end of the scaffolding. A mere two meters made the difference. Now he had a view of everything in front of the magnetomotive.

The arch was the first thing he saw. It was standing in the center of a ring of lights, highlighted like a rare piece of art. It was an identical replica of the one they had found on the Kalandan station. The neutronium gleamed in blue-black highlights, and the impenetrable alloy was even molded into the same pattern. He knew he shouldn't be surprised at anything the Petraw were capable of. Though they looked like simple underground dwellers, their technological capability exceeded that of almost every other culture he had encountered.

That arch changed everything. Kirk couldn't begin to imagine the terrible things the Petraw would be capable of with an operational interstellar transporter. These people were ruthless and would use this technology to their own advantage. It was his fault the gateway had fallen into their hands.

Kirk was determined to change that. Staying very still to keep from attracting the attention of the guard, he searched for the cylindrical unit. In the very front of the magnetomotive, the huge rings were open, with a segment at least five meters wide cut out, indicating it was the more powerful open-flux system.

But he couldn't see the key component of the gateway from his position. It wasn't attached to the new arch, which meant he couldn't steal it the same way Luz had done. Instead, there were a bunch of cables that snaked along the floor toward the magnetomotive.

Luz joined him, keeping a wary eye on the guard. Her sharp intake of breath indicated she saw the gateway, too.

A voice came from below. "You two get back to the door. Just because we're holding a test run doesn't mean you can leave your posts."

Kirk couldn't see who was talking, but he recognized her voice. It was Tasm.

A hooded Petraw strode up to the arch and knelt to check the cables. From nearly sixty meters up, Kirk couldn't see much other than a sharply foreshortened view of her head and shoulders. "Is the flux stabilized yet?" Tasm asked.

Another Petraw somewhere down below and around the curve answered, "It has reached optimum level."

"Proceed with the test run," Tasm ordered.

She pulled back to the corner of the room, standing next to the defender who was posted there. If she looked up, she would see Kirk and Luz. He hardly breathed.

A different Petraw stepped up to face the gateway. Kirk clenched his hands around the scaffolding. They were at the point of testing the gateway? Those long days of dodging through the tubes and snatching naps in cul-de-sacs took on new meaning. The Petraw must have worked continuously to pull the gateway together.

The Petraw standing in front of the gateway let out a slight cry. "I see it!"

Inside the gateway an image had formed of windblown sand nearly burying two metallic structures. The orange sky looked fluorescent in the blazing light. Kirk recognized the surface near the fissure.

"Now go through," Tasm urged from her safe spot across the room.

The Petraw eagerly stepped forward. Kirk leaned out as far as he dared to see the hooded form enter the gateway in a flash of brilliant light. The magnetomotive shook the scaffolding as power was drawn at a phenomenal rate.

Nothing came out the other side. The Petraw was gone.

The subsonic hum of the magnetomotive made Kirk's head pound.

Tasm was staring down at a handheld communicator, rigid in concentration. "Anx made it! He's next to the shield generators."

The unseen Petraw exclaimed, "The gateway is functional! I'll inform the matriarchs at once."

Tasm tapped into the communicator. "I'm ordering Anx back. We'll try a long-range test this time. Keep the magnetomotive on full standby."

Her underling acknowledged, pride in his voice. *They should be proud of themselves,* Kirk thought. They now possessed a weapon of unbelievable strength.

Kirk was determined to make this work for him. The gateway offered him the chance to cross those troublesome forty thousand light-years in an instant. But he couldn't allow the Petraw to keep the gateway. The responsibility would be his if they used the gateway to harm others.

Tasm went to the base of the magnetomotive, disappearing from view. Kirk carefully withdrew to the back of the scaffolding, where he could no longer see the guard.

Luz seemed goaded to dreams of glory. "How are we going to get everyone out of here?" she whispered.

"We'll have to create a diversion." Kirk reached into the top of his boot to retrieve his broken communicator. The sarium krellide power cell was too small to cause much damage if he made it overload. But there must be something he could do in a neighboring chamber that would draw Tasm out. It would have to last long enough for the gateway to read his mind and cut through the light-years between him and home—

Luz tried to snatch the communicator from his hand. "What are you doing?"

Kirk managed to hang on to it, but the broken cover flew off the hinge, arching down and falling sixty meters. Both of them drew back as far as they could before it hit bottom, uselessly trying to hide in the shadows.

"Now who's the idiot?" Kirk shot at Luz.

"You were going to sabotage the gateway—"

"You've just proven my point."

Gritting his teeth, Kirk hoped the cover wouldn't make too much noise on the rock floor. But it bounced erratically, hitting corners and edges, before spinning slowly into a stop.

The movement caught the defender's attention. He instantly alerted the other Petraw in the room with a loud shout.

Kirk wanted to push Luz off the scaffolding. Only someone who thought they were smarter than everyone else could do something so lame-brained.

He tried a strategic retreat as the defender went to inspect what had fallen. He made it to the next scaffolding tower while Luz was still inching over the catwalk, but it didn't take long for the defender to light up the entire tower and detect them both. Kirk couldn't see any way to escape with Petraw climbing up the scaffolding on either side of him. With visions of the chasm dancing before his eyes, he slowly climbed down to the floor.

Luz was dragged from the scaffolding as well, and in the shrieking melee she caused trying to break free, Kirk made a dash for the arch. All he could think about was the misty terrace next to the commandant's office at Starfleet Academy, overlooking the glorious arch of the antiquated Golden Gate Bridge. He could almost taste the salty ocean air, he wanted it so badly.

But Tasm stepped between him and the archway, stopping him short by pointing his own phaser at him. One look in her eyes and he could see Tasm even through her dissolved face. "Don't move, Kirk, or I'll put you away for good."

Chapter 4

Kirk froze. "You'd use my own phaser on me, Tasm?"

She was as coldhearted as Kirk always believed. "Yes."

Kirk kept his hands out. "It's set to kill."

"I know."

She didn't flinch, and he didn't doubt she would fire if he made a threatening move. He did nod toward the distinctive blue cylinder that was mounted on a large computer unit. It was sitting next to the magnetomotive. "The gateway doesn't belong to you."

"Now it does. I earned it."

Kirk couldn't see anything left of the woman he had kissed in the Kalandan station. Her unformed features were softened and flattened like the other Petraw. Except for her eyes, fierce with Tasm determination.

The big Petraw defenders weren't taking any chances this time. With each of his arms held by a defender, Kirk was marched out of the experimental station. He cast one longing look back at the gateway. So close. He had almost made it home.

Tasm took the lead, overshadowed by the defender next to her. Kirk was half-carried, half-dragged up a long slanting corridor. As they went up, Kirk wondered if they were being taken to the exterior platform where they would be summarily tossed off the cliff to smash into the molten rock at the bottom. At least the heat would burn him to a cinder before he hit the lava.

But after going up a few levels, they began to move deeper into the complex. Kirk kept track of every turn they took, optimistically intending to use the knowledge to find his way back to the gateway. That was the spirit. He only needed to get Tasm and the defenders to cooperate by turning their backs and ignoring him for a few minutes. . . .

They picked up more defenders along the way who seemed eager to pound him into a pulp if he so much as twitched. He wasn't sure how he knew that when they didn't say a word. Maybe it was because they all looked alike, and something about that uniformity was unnerving.

A couple of times Luz started yelling past Kirk at Tasm, venting the frustration that had been boiling inside of her for days. Kirk wasn't sure how Tasm kept her steady pace. Some of the insults about her intelligence and command abilities were enough to make him wince on her behalf. He supposed Luz wasn't counting on leniency from her commanding officer. She hadn't gotten it the first time.

They finally reached their destination. Kirk could tell by the way Tasm glared at him, cautioning, "One wrong move and I'll shoot you."

Kirk raised his hands slightly to indicate he didn't want any trouble. "You could just give me a ship and let me go right now, Tasm."

"That's for the matriarchs to decide."

Luz was panting, infuriated. She hardly looked Petraw compared to the others, with her face contorted in anger. "*I* saved the gateway! I brought it back."

Tasm actually smiled. "Perhaps the matriarchs will thank you before putting you away, Luz."

"You don't deserve to join them! It should be my honor . . ." Luz lunged against the defenders holding her, but she couldn't shake them. She swung there, a fighting slip of a woman.

Tasm didn't touch the wall, but an opening began to grow slightly larger than the others. The Petraw herded them inside. There must have been a dozen defenders around them now, along with Tasm holding the phaser.

Kirk looked up and kept on looking. They were at the bottom of a cylindrical well that rose very high into the rock, at least ten times higher than it was wide. In the very center, a long slender tube dangled down to a bulbous gold sack that nearly brushed the floor. It was shaped like a ripe pear, and swayed slightly as the air was disturbed by their entrance. Its rounded sides were shiny taut.

Looking up, Kirk saw that the surrounding walls, starting about ten meters above them, were dotted by hundreds of small protrusions. The curving wall was so dark that it took him a moment to see they were moving.

They were Petraw. At least, each one was the head, arms, and chest of a Petraw. Kirk shifted so he could see the lowest one better, and gulped. Where its legs had once been was a swollen mass that stretched wide, bulbously attaching to the lumpy, moist wall.

"What is this?" he asked incredulously.

"This is the birthing chamber," Tasm said reverently.

"Joining the birthing chamber is our highest honor," Luz snapped. "*She* doesn't deserve it!"

Tasm glared at Luz, but saved her words for those who mattered. "Beloved matriarchs, we have brought you Luz and the invader."

Kirk didn't think it was a good idea to be considered a nameless antagonist. "Matriarchs! I am James T. Kirk and I come in p—"

One of the Petraw defenders belted him in the stomach. That dropped him to his knees, and they withdrew to a watchful two paces.

Kirk coughed and choked, trying to catch his breath. Luz landed next to him, on her knees, looking up the well of matriarchs. Heads turned on the wall, and arms gestured in various attitudes of distress or condemnation.

Tasm stood next to them, with the phaser still aimed at Kirk. "Matriarchs, we found Luz and the intruder near the gateway while we were testing it."

Kirk had to put his hands to his ringing ears. Something about the well amplified their voices, but it was pure sound with no articulated words.

Gradually, there seemed to be streams of consensus within the tones, as threads of their comments rose to near-audibility. Kirk relaxed to hear what they said, much the same way he did inside the cells. He realized this was the source of the information feed in action.

Luz is defective. Luz must be put away immediately.

Luz's mouth opened wide. "But I'm the one who brought you the gateway! Ask him! He wouldn't have let Tasm take it. She would have lost it!"

Like an implacable river, the thoughts droned on: *Luz is defective. Luz must be put away immediately.*

Rather than be condemned without a hearing, like Luz, Kirk lifted his hands to appeal to them. "Matriarchs, it was an accident that brought me to your world. I'm no invader! Surely we can come to an understanding—"

He could hear their rising agreement even as he spoke, buzzing through the bones of his ears. *The invader must be put away. The invader must be put away immediately.*

Tasm finally looked satisfied. "I knew it. I'll make sure it's done properly this time."

Kirk started to protest, but a new sentiment began rising from the matriarchs. It was filled with something like warmth of feeling.

Tasm is exemplary. Tasm will soon join us.

Kirk was nonplussed by the idea of what must happen for Tasm to be transformed and joined to the wall of the birthing chamber. She would be stuck somewhere up there among the hundreds. . . .

Tasm took another step closer to the sack that hung in the center of the birthing chamber, raising her empty hand toward it. Her body trembled in eagerness. "The royal gel is almost ready."

That's when he understood. The polymer substructure of the Petraw complex was the living body of the matriarchs. It was one vast organism that was growing in the tunnel-riddled cliffs. This well was their brain center. The matriarchs supported their children in their own body, using their own life systems to distribute nourishment and remove the waste.

Kirk refused to let his own cultural bias affect his judgment this time. What concerned him most was the monolithic nature of these Petraw. He would never be able to admire a society that forced all individuality out of its people.

One thing was clear, there was no reasoning with these Petraw. Kirk made his decision and acted instantly.

He knocked against Tasm, grabbing for his phaser. She was so absorbed in gazing at the sac that he twisted it from her hand. The defenders leaped at him, but he bounded up the slight rise and jumped onto the hanging sac.

It swung widely. Cries rose around him, with Tasm's outraged wail the loudest. The defenders hesitated, pulling back as the sac swung toward them, as if it was taboo for them to touch the royal gel. Kirk scrabbled higher up the side, feeling the tension in the full sac like it was going to burst.

He got to the top. "Nobody turns my own phaser against me, Tasm."

"You can't touch the gel!" she screamed.

"Oh, no?" Kirk stamped on the bag, hanging on to the slender tube as it swayed sharply.

Tasm shrieked as the defenders gathered around the base of the sac, cutting off any avenue of escape. The waving arms of the matriarchs and the buzzing of their thoughts warned him that more defenders were being dispatched from the blocks of cells. They would be here shortly. Luz backed toward the door, seeing a chance to escape.

Kirk aimed his phaser down at the sac and fired as he jumped. It was set to kill.

A geyser burst straight up in a spray of yellow blobs of goo. Kirk was propelled higher into the air as the sac exploded in a boiling gush of sticky liquid. Tasm and the defenders were covered.

His feet slipped in the ankle-deep stuff, as he landed. But he was instantly up and heading for the door, phaser firmly in hand.

Matriarchs were protesting in shrill voices, echoing through the well. Tasm was also crying out, but it sounded like ecstasy as she flopped around on her side. The baggy coverall over her legs began to swell.

The defenders were gasping in agony, writhing on the floor. Apparently only females reacted well to the royal gel. Kirk kicked to try to dislodge the rancid stuff from his feet, but it didn't seem to be bothering him.

He reached Luz in time to pull her away from the edge of the splattered gel. Her eyes were glazed, and she was shaking with desire to dive in.

"Make your choice, Luz. I don't have time to fight you."

Her straining toward the gel eased, and her eyes focused on him. "They would kill me before they let me join the birthing chamber."

"Then let's go!"

Kirk set off down the corridor at a flat run. It would be a race to see who got to the gateway first.

When he had a moment, he adjusted the phaser setting back to stun. He wouldn't be reduced to the ruthlessness of the Petraw. But he freely stunned workers and defenders who spotted them. There was no way they would have gotten through the complex without the phaser. If they were faced with a large enough attack force, he could be overwhelmed by numbers. It depended on how long it would take the matriarchs to rally the defenders and send them down to the gateway.

Kirk stunned several more Petraw in the long corridor to the experimental stations. But there were no defenders posted at the door to the gateway room. They had been too eager to accompany them to the matriarchs.

Inside, the magnetomotive was running at full standby. Ready for the final test.

Kirk hit Tasm's assistant with a phaser beam before she could say a word.

Luz went to the cylinder and grabbed hold of it, trying to wrench it from the metal computer unit.

"No!" Kirk demanded. "This gateway is our only way out."

Luz protested, "But I need it! No other birthing world will take me without it—"

"There's no time! It's either die here or come with me. *Now.*"

She hesitated, glancing at the door where defenders would arrive any moment. Then she looked at the phaser held loosely in his hand. He could point it at her to force her to agree, but his innate sense of decency wouldn't allow it.

Maybe that did it, or else Luz finally saw the wisdom in his words. She went over to the controls of the magnetomotive and adjusted the dials. "There. It's ready to go."

Kirk went to the gateway. The image of the terrace overlooking Starfleet Academy was bright in his mind's eye. But his hands were busy with the phaser. He clicked it to level ten, then set the energy feed wide open. It was the same way the Kalandan defense computer had overloaded his phaser back on the station. A whine quickly began to grow as the power cell cycled faster.

"What are you doing?" Luz demanded. "You can't—"

"I'm keeping them from following us."

He took a deep breath and concentrated on the terrace. Voices were coming from the corridor outside as the moist flagstones appeared. The cloud-filled sky loomed over the craggy hills of San Francisco. It was just as Kirk remembered.

Without another thought, he pushed Luz through the gateway. It blinded him for a moment as she stumbled over the threshold. Then the light faded while she fell onto the flagstones, looking around in surprise as if she could no longer see him.

Several Petraw burst into the room and rounded the magnetomotive. As Kirk jumped through the gateway, he flung the overloading phaser sideways, directly into the gap of the magnets where the flux crossed.

The flash as he passed through the gateway was brighter than he remembered, but this time the light didn't stun him. He looked back as the Petraw running toward him were caught in the explosion of the phaser. It broke the delicate hold of the suspension units, and the magnets began to crash to the ground, falling directly toward the gateway.

A push of air seemed to propel him through the gateway faster than his own momentum.

The last thing he saw, the walls of the chamber shuddered and began to fall. It disintegrated, taking everything in it down into the chasm and the molten rock below.

Kirk's heart was pounding in reaction, feeling as if he were also sliding to certain death. But the flagstones were firm under his hands, and he could hear Luz's gasping cries. They were on the terrace overlooking Starfleet Academy, forty thousand light-years from the destruction of the gateway.

It was done. He had buried the gateway in the fiery heart of the planet. And he had managed to return home at the same time. He couldn't stop grinning. "Welcome to Earth!"

Commodore Enwright and the other Starfleet officials eventually let Luz go after she and Kirk were fully debriefed. She didn't know much more than Kirk had already figured out during his visit to the Petraw birthing world. Luz claimed that it was against Petraw laws when Tasm had made them pose as Kalandans to steal the gateway. Kirk didn't believe a word of her testimony, knowing that Luz would say whatever it took to get her way. But Starfleet was satisfied.

On the last day, when the *Enterprise* was finally due to enter orbit, Kirk went to say good-bye to Luz at the orbital space station.

She was subdued to suddenly find herself alone without any of her people. Kirk hadn't heard a word about how stupid they were since they had passed through the gateway.

"Do you plan to try to return to the Petraw?" he asked. "It's a long way back."

"No," Luz said flatly. "The Petraw would never accept me. I'm heading out on my own now."

Kirk was sure she would be fine. After all, she had almost succeeded in getting everything she wanted. "The Alpha Quadrant is a remarkable place. It may offer more opportunities than you think." Kirk had to shake his head. "There's a lot to admire in your people, but I don't see how their totalitarian regime could satisfy your needs."

She looked at him oddly. "You never did understand the Petraw, did you? Our unity is what makes us magnificent."

"You violated that unity," Kirk pointed out.

Luz finally smiled. "Well you heard the matriarchs. I'm defective."

"Lucky for me."

Luz gazed out the observation window, looking toward the core of the galaxy. "But the other Petraw are strong. And they're coming, I know it. We haven't seen the last of my people yet."

STAR TREK®
CHALLENGER

EXODUS

Diane Carey

The free dancer was dying. Its enormous lunglike body inflated one final time, but not enough. The creature wailed as its microbrain struggled to remember the path to the skies.

Where would it land?

Alarms rang through the city trails. Despite the danger, steel shutters clanked open on the north side of many domed huts. Brutish winds scraped by, unable to get a grip on the oystershell domes. Slowly the giant descended from the biohaze in a shroud of parasitic life-forms. The parasites puffed outward from the free dancer and raced upward to the stormy atmosphere, their abandonment clear proof of the animal's doom. The free dancer twisted its long tendrils of shock floss upward as if beseeching its little riders to come back.

When they didn't, the free dancer almost seemed to understand. It gave off a last sad crackle, buckled like an accordion bellows, and quite sharply dropped the last fifty feet to the ground.

Tanggg! Tang-tang! Tangggg—shutters closed all over the quarter, just in time. The harsh sound echoed and continued longer than any reasonable echo, into the city, onto the plain, to the mountains, and rang there awhile.

Like a cattleprod touching flesh, the planet came up to meet the dying free dancer with a sharp slap. At the first inch of contact the creature heaved, then flattened to the trail's surface and there gushed

45

out its life. Electric-blue neon crackles engulfed the corpse in a violent coccoon.

Again Nick Keller found himself reminded of old newsreels—the crash of the dirigible *Hindenburg*—a giant lung collapsing into a single great mercurial transfer of matter to energy, as all the animal's stored power shot directly into the planet.

What a waste.

"Close the shutter! You'll be burned by the blast wave!"

"I need to see it."

Raw energy strobed between the huts. The uncontrolled natural death of a free dancer could take a hundred people with it in a population complex, or go without witness on some distant open tundra.

The whole planet was a tundra. A metal tundra. Soot on silver on pearl on ingot, with leaden shadows and pewter hills. The only natural life was in the skies, and it came down only to die.

This animal grounded on the outskirts of the City of the Living, the oldest settlement on the planet, a cluster of knobby buildings and dome huts secured with pylons rooted twenty feet into the planet's mantel. Out there, in the "suburbs," were six or seven scattered huts out by themselves. As Keller watched in morbid fascination, the free dancer flattened right on top of one of the huts. The energy transferred back into the planet, and an instant later the blast wave blew through the city with a single deafening bark.

The echo bonged like a big doorbell. Blinding disruption blossomed across the open terrain.

Keller let the heavy iron shutter drop closed just in time, and ducked. The dome thundered around him.

When the shaking subsided, he bolted to his feet and grabbed his tricorder. "Come on! It landed on a hut!"

"Keller, why do you do these things?"

He didn't wait. Braxan would follow him. She always did.

Heat from the dead free dancer radiated through the metallic streets and buildings with a vibrating thrum of harp strings. Though he felt the heat, he was protected by the chain-mail sheath over his own clothes and his tightly woven mail footwear.

The primary structural shape in the Living city was a dome. The city looked like a huddle of shellacked mollusks. They were built by inflating a free dancer's float gland, then spraying a composite—which Keller's tricorder analyzed as some chemical soup that hardened when mixed, along with a bunch of unreadable adulterants—over the balloon frame. The result was, on average, a six-hundred-ton house. The curvature could absorb hundreds of pounds' pressure per square centimeter, which the weather frequently tested.

Otherwise, there were a few towers and a few large storage facilities. That's all.

The free dancer's dropping on a house with its shutters open caused an implosive charge. Curiosity had gotten the better of somebody. The people inside had made a bad bet—a free dancer could die a half mile away, then in its final convulsion flip over and land right on some poor slob's head.

Could've been me. Next time maybe I'll close the shutter. It's just such a sight!

The carcass was now a huge pile of placemat-sized ashes crudely recalling the shape of the dead animal, thickened by the spilled and stir-fried contents of its guts—hundreds of pounds of candleflies, now cooked to a paste. Keller plowed right into the mess. Giant black flakes blew out of his way, then began to clog around his knees as he went deeper into the fried remains. His feet were gummed up in the candlefly paste. Behind him, hundreds of people swarmed out of the domes to watch. A few helped push the cooked flakes away from the imploded dome, but most held back.

As he pushed through the hesitant people, Keller cast a glance behind for Braxan.

She was there, right behind him. Her narrow shoulders shifted back and forth under the shimmering foil tunic she wore. What it would be on the other side of the gateway, he had no idea. Here, everything was silver, ferrous, bullion, and plate. The planet was one big ingot, hammered, pocked, or polished by constant storms. Some unknown inner force had formed jagged inorganic mountain peaks in the distance, but Keller's tricorder offered only basic statistics and couldn't read beneath the planet's surface. Like a pet dog in a strange house, it didn't act very happy here.

Braxan stayed with him until he began climbing the dome's ash-entombed ruins.

"Hold this!" He handed her his tricorder just before climbing out of arm's reach.

"When will you understand?" she warned. "They've been Anointed!"

"Don't be silly. Come up and help me."

"I shouldn't."

He glanced around for someone who might help and spotted two of their neighbors, a pair of brothers. "Donnastal! Serren! Climb up here! Help me pry this thing open."

The two teenaged boys looked around at the others, scouting for disapprovals. Excitement got the better of them. They broke with traditions and swam through the ashes toward Keller, who was now about ten feet up on the crumpled dome, straddling the nearest shutter.

The shutter wasn't latched, but only bent by the force of the free dancer's frying-pan act. The hinges were crimped.

"Ready . . . three . . . two . . . haul!"

Though his hands weren't strong enough, his foot behind the shutter and the two boys pulling on the sides did the trick.

Donnastal and Serren were young, but on Metalworld a teenager was a mighty commodity. Serren was wiry and Donnastal, though only sixteen, was built like a shuttlecraft. Against all the precepts and rules of their planet, these boys would take chances and do what the stranger ordered. Keller wasn't beyond making use of a little teenager hero worship.

The iron shutter rasped a god-awful honk and bared the glassless window. Keller swung around on his hip and dropped into the hole.

Inside he dug through what was left of the house and came up with three people right under the shutter—one unconscious, one moaning, one dead. The shutter was a skylight. Probably they'd been sleeping and hadn't heard the alarms in time. Any minute they'd be crushed by the weight of the shifting rubble. The Living called it destiny, fate, random order. Keller didn't buy it.

He got the moaning woman up on his shoulder and called, "Donny, reach down! Pull these people out and hand them to Serren. Good boys."

He hoped they wouldn't hesitate. The Living carried fatalism too far. An unintelligible mutter of protests squabbled outside, but Donnastal appeared over his head and reached down. One by one, the victims were hoisted out of Keller's arms and into the open.

"Braxan, hand down my tricorder. Can you hear me?"

The instrument had a terrible time operating on this side of the gateway. Half the readings were scatterbrained and silly. He'd learned to take notice of sick blips that otherwise he would ignore and to expect huge skips in data. The terrible moment came when the instrument figured out what he wanted it to do, and reported, clearly, nothing.

Keller turned off the tricorder. He leaned back against one of the bent steel braces and closed his eyes. No one else buried under this jagged, electrocuted mess . . . around him, the ruined dome structure groaned. Metal scratching against more metal. Unsupported, it would soon collapse under the very weight of its own materials.

Metal and more metal and more. For the first six weeks he'd hardly slept a wink from the weirdness of the noise. Simple footsteps made the ring of chains. A falling tool made not a thump or bonk, but a *jannnngggggg*. He was living on a giant tuning fork.

No wonder these people dreamed of trees and moss.

What about *Challenger?* What were his shipmates thinking after so long? He'd left them with the order to keep the gateway open to the last Anointed.

"Are you returning?" Braxan's voice threaded from outside. "The dome will crack and you'll be a legend. How would you like me to tell the story of you?"

He looked up. Donnastal was reaching down for him.

"Thanks, butch," he said, and accepted help out.

Donnastal bit his lip. Neither of the boys talked much—mostly they were waiting to see just how far their culture could be pushed.

And I'm counting on that, Keller thought.

The three victims had already been taken away, two to be tended, one to be Anointed. Cold wind scratched across Keller's skin and pulled at his hair, which, as it batted in his eyes, reminded him again why so many of the Living wore their hair clipped very short. In defiance he hadn't cut his. In fact, it lapped at his shoulders—a ridiculous state of being for a good ranch hand. He thought of his brothers and how they would hoot at him. Shave, but no haircut.

Before him a throng of brush-cuts and slick-downs clustered around the dome, waiting to see what the mysterious stranger would do next. He was still enough of an oddity that the people liked to watch him. Good entertainment was hard to come by.

Overhead, lightning and long neon storm clouds skated the biohaze. When he slid down the dome into the sea of warm ash, Braxan came quickly to him.

"By saving them, you've gone against random order," she told him. "If you stay here, you must learn to accept these decisions."

"These aren't decisions," he countered. "And I'm not staying here. And neither are you."

His words disturbed the people around them. Braxan noticed, even more than Keller did, or a least cared more.

"Get your Grid mats," she said. "Spread the word for all hunters to meet at the Feast plain."

The people broke up and hurried back into the city to prepare for the hunt. *Ring-ring-ring-ring-ring-ring-ring*—their chain-mail moccasins were like jinglebells anyway. Vibrations couldn't be muffled here.

Braxan was uneasy giving the order to hunt, or any order. It wasn't in her nature. She reminded Keller some of himself when he had been suddenly spun into charge of a ship in crisis and a colony in trouble, without the people he had come to depend upon. She was alone too, without family. Braxan had lost all her relatives in the last few hunts, a group of people who hadn't been blessed with many children. Most women Braxan's age had a half-dozen children. Braxan had none. Apparently the luck of the draw.

So Braxan was alone, except for the injured traveler she had nursed back to health.

This would be the fifth hunt since Keller came through the gateway and crashed the spinner out on the plain. Through weeks of Keller's recovery, Braxan had provided both nursing and information. She had wanted to go through the gateway more than either Riutta or Luntee, and for that reason she had stayed—one of those old-order quirks of caution.

"When you appeared in one of our spinners," she said, "we didn't know what kind of being you were or why you came. You told us we must use our stored energy to power more ships, to cross over before the gateway closes . . . that it is still time to go. Still, there are many fears to this."

"Braxan, you have to keep believing." He clasped her arms and bothered to look deeply into her eyes, hoping she would find the truth in there. "This side doesn't want people. It never did. On the big scale of time, eleven thousand years isn't that long. The time of the Living is running out on this big ball bearing. Lightning, rain, ice—on the other side of the gateway you can do more than just survive. You can grow. You won't have to give up thousands of people to the hunts. It's better there. It wants life."

"I believe it's wonderful," she said. "I believe you. We'll keep storing energy, and keep trying to convince Kymelis. If her voice is with us, then we'll all go."

He smiled at her, but not because she was telling him what he wanted to hear. She wasn't the youngest nymph on the planet or the prettiest, but he liked looking at her. Her harsh features—a sharp nose, thin eyebrows, high cheekbones, thin lips, and a chin that came to a dimpled point—were offset by worshipful eyes like two balls of hematite in a setting of platinum skin. She was a very simple person, content with small comforts and controlled hopes, yet she had warmed to Keller's tales of life on the other side in a way that made him feel valuable.

Though she had no unique talents or wisdom or skills, she was special because she had survived more hunts than all but two others of her people. That made her the third Elder, the one Riutta and Luntee had left behind. After so long with no word from Riutta and Luntee, the Living had accepted two new elders. Braxan was now in a new triumvirate of leaders for the Living.

There were Braxan, a one-eyed woman named Kymelis, and a man named Issull, in that order of seniority. Braxan wanted to go through the gateway. Issull intended to go through, but didn't think this was the time. Since there was trouble in space on the other side, perhaps another ten thousand years of preparation was needed.

The middle Elder, one-eyed Cyclops, hadn't made up her mind about what random order "wanted."

Three elders—a leadership in turmoil. One for Keller's way, one against, and one vacillating. Kymelis knew hers was the swing vote, but also didn't know whether to trust Keller, a stranger who had soared through the gateway after the signal from the Anointed was silenced. Was Keller the one who had stopped the signal? What had happened to the Anointed? These many troubled months hadn't been smooth skating for Keller or his message of welcome from the other side.

Of course, one key factor was that Issull *did* want to go through the gateway, as all their histories planned, but he didn't think this was the time. That meant he could eventually be convinced. Keller only needed two Elders to go his way.

"Time's running out," he murmured, more to himself than Braxan. "If my multiplication's right, it's been almost thirty hours on the other side. They can't hold the gateway open much longer."

"I think you'll prevail," she said quietly. "My people listen to you."

"Well, the Living don't waste. I'm a stranger, but I've got special knowledge and skills. They can't ignore me . . . it's not exactly the same as listening."

"You are a champion of many here, especially the young ones like Donnastal. He defies everything for you."

"Mmm . . . that's because I'm the suave foreign substitute teacher. What I am is the focus of conflict, really."

"Our first leader, Ennengand, meant for us to go through. We have invested generations in this. I still believe."

"But is Nick Keller the messenger?" he asked. "Ol' Cyclops isn't sure."

Braxan's glossy eyes regarded him warmly as he came out of his thoughts. "There are some who say you treat me gently for the sake of influence. So I'll go with you."

"Hey, hey . . . don't blame the messenger." Keller grinned, caught her hand, and pulled her up close. In a cold world, she was his only warmth and therefore all the more precious. "You always wanted to go to the other side. I didn't change your mind, did I?"

"Random order sent you to us to tell us it's time to leave. Why would you be here otherwise?" Like a silver bell on a cord she swung in his arms, and appreciated him with her eyes.

"I'm glad you've survived," he murmured, "even if you have to bear the burdens of an Elder." Usually he tried not to be so candid. But for this moment, would a little selfishness hurt? "How do you stay so nice in a place like this? You don't even realize how much death breathes on this place, do you? It'll always be a subsistence living here. If more resources appear, the population expands just enough to make it subsistence again."

"We have enough to survive," she said.

"You have metal. Nothing else. No help from others, no neighbors in space, no way to make medicine . . . you live on candleflies and legends of better places. People are afraid to form relationships, children are pushed away by their parents, nobody dares to care too hard . . . there's complete insecurity. You lose everybody you love, or they lose you. The only thing in my culture's history, the only parallel I can think of . . . is the Black Plague."

"You always speak of other colors," she said, steering him away from his morbid subject. "We have darkest dark, this 'black' you've shown me. I like to hear about the others. Red and green. Cobalt and pumpkin . . . very exotic names."

"They're exotic." He twiddled his fingers through her coppery hair. "Not quite as exotic as you, I don't think." With his eyes out of focus he hugged her and gazed at the silver dome over their heads. "I wish I could remember . . . sometimes I dream in colors . . . but I'm afraid I might be forgetting what they really look like. Seems to have been an awful long time . . ."

"Time—" She pulled away, her shiny eyes bright. "It's time for the hunt. I have to be there."

"I know." He sighed. "You, me, coupla hundred other hunters, and my trusty tricorder."

She smiled. "Again you'll take it onto the plain?"

"I have to reset it just before the capture. You know that."

"You reset at the last hunt, and the one before, and before that."

"Oh, I s'pose," he mumbled as he palmed the instrument. "Clears the head . . . electrical interference is my hobby now. I can compare certain electrical readings. Y'know—research. Data acquisition. Fun with numbers."

"On our world there is not enough electricity for you already?"

"Hon, on your world there's enough electricity for dang near everybody, dang near everywhere. If we could box it—"

He stopped himself, held back from telling her too much. These people had survived in an impossible place by holding to some kind of purpose. Civilizations had been doing that for a long time, but this one took the method to an extreme. Keller knew he had to work within their system. They wouldn't accept too much rebellion.

"Stand right in front of me. Let me use you for—"

"A sensor anchor," she completed. "I know. You will 'read' me now, and you will 'read' yourself on the plain, and later compare the information. I shall stand better than anyone ever has stood."

She squared her shoulders, spread her hands out, drew a deep breath and closed her eyes, still smiling. Her hands, less a little finger on each, were slim and feminine. Even the bitterness of evolution and of life on this rugged world hadn't taken the girl out of this girl. She didn't have much of a figure, but the simple foil sheath made an enchanting envelope.

"Mmm, you're good at standing," Keller commented wryly. He finished scanning her and turned the tricorder on himself for a quick sweep. "Ought to do it . . ."

Braxan pressed her hands to her gold-leaf pixie-cut hair. Her hair looked brassy to him here. What it would look like on the other side— he had no way to guess. All he knew was that her smile was friendly, her heart forgiving and unsuspicious in a place of inclement legend, and she had started to look pretty to him.

"I wish I could have you give the commands." She sank against him, pressing her chin to his shoulder. "Why would random order select such as me to be made an Elder?"

"When we go to the other side, you can be whatever you want. There's no 'random order' there. You can be lots of different things. All at once, if you want." He gazed at her. "What do you want?"

It was like asking a cloistered novice to describe Mardi Gras. Her lashless eyes tightened with the mystery he put before her.

"I would like to see trees," she said.

"We have trees on Belle Terre. We're sowing sod too. Grass. I think you'll take to grass between your little stubby toes down there."

She smiled, but he had awakened a cautious streak. "Does color hurt?" she asked.

Her innocence filled him with a whole new kind of responsibility. Cupping her neck, his own hands were a bizarre computer-generated pearly texture instead of their normal shade of Santa Fe. Everything here seemed artificially animated. He'd almost forgotten what a human really looked like or the kind of world he and all life like him was meant to occupy. Was some inner part of him expecting to be trapped here?

He slid his hands down her shoulder blades and solemnly promised, "Color is one of the best things."

"Hunt! The hunt!" Cries from the streets shook them out of their private moment. Local heralds were running through the streets, summoning all those qualified to hunt. The same thing would be happening in the other settlements.

Keller looked up and sighed. What a shame—a free dancer had just landed here, but all its energy was lost. Hundreds of people would soon die a horrific electrical death to tempt down more free dancers in a controlled environment, so one could be killed and its energy taken into storage.

"It's time to hunt," Braxan said, and pressed back, breaking their quiet communion.

"Right," he acceded. "Let's buckle on our swash and participate in chivalry at its weirdest."

The hunt plain was nothing more than miles of ferrous flats, brushed to a dull sheen by wind and storms constantly battering this planet. Lightning flashed overhead and the skies growled. The biohaze, a shroud of primordial life surviving in the atmosphere, flickered and swam and tumbled.

There were twenty thousand people or so on this planet, by Keller's best reckoning. The low number was a sad clue. According to the "old records," there had once been upward of a hundred thousand, all descendants of the crews and passengers of those first two ships to pass through the gateway, one Blood, one Kauld.

Nature was intolerant here. The planet couldn't support a population. The Living were more devolving than evolving. Families had fewer children, even though they produced as many as they could. Women dutifully produced babies their entire adult lives, by several men, to keep genetics from singularizing. They had developed an Eskimo-like manner of cooperative tribal structure, to be sure children were cared for if their adult relatives didn't survive the hunts, and to make sure nonhunting families were fed. There was food sharing and a strict hierarchy of distribution, the top of which involved the families of people who had been "chosen" in the hunt. Perfect, to the dreamer's eye.

Reality was far less kind. Several times, the histories told, this system had broken down. Communalism would support only the very smallest of communities. This inhospitable planet was a test case. When there proved no other way, communalism's answer had been to make the community smaller, not bigger.

They survived, but didn't thrive. Starvation, competition, failure. Generation after generation, the pattern repeated itself. The population surge to five hundred thousand had only happened once, and like a flare quickly collapsed. Now they were on their way to another wave of harsh limitation. Their numbers were shrinking. The metal planet would never let them flourish. It didn't want them.

So they clung to their legend about going home. It was their single enduring plan. They *wanted* to go. They *planned* to go. Unless they were "chosen" in the hunt of a free dancer or "Anointed"—killed by accident or illness—they worked toward the goal of eventually leaving this tin pot.

The plan's most recent leg had been a mighty monumental one—to take thousands of Anointed home, then send a signal for the rest of the people to follow. That signal had never come. Instead, quite another signal had been sent. The Anointed had been summoned down from their pedestals all at once, not by destiny but by Nick Keller in his determination to save his side of the gateway first.

Taking the unexpected "destruction" of the Anointed as a message, the Living had hunkered down once more to the business of collecting energy from the free dancers, but this time with the idea of another ten thousand years of work before trying again. They had used up almost all their stored energy to open the gateway and hold it open, then power Riutta's spinner fleet. They had to hustle now, hunt more and more often, to gather enough energy to go on surviving.

But Keller had come. He wanted them to use their new power stores in a different way—to go through the gateway en masse, as they had originally planned.

He was the only one who knew the clock was ticking to a much nearer alarm. *Challenger* and the grave ship could hold the gateway open only a few hours on their side, more than a year on this side.

A year . . . sounded long, but wasn't. The Living had been waiting years on this side for Riutta and Luntee to send a summons, then instead received a cutoff. They supposed the Anointed had met with tragedy in space. After hundreds of generations, nothing had come of this. They had accepted two new Elders, along with the one left behind, and they had begun again. More than half of these people would die in a stepped-up schedule of hunts, to provide enough energy for the other half to keep existing on this brittle ferrous ball.

What could Keller do? Send a pigeon through the gateway and tell Shucorion to throw another dead guy on the fire?

The gateway was still open. He clung to that.

He clamped his lips on his thoughts as he and Braxan worked side by side, along with hundreds of hunters from all the settlements, to fit woven gum segments into place and seal the seams. The heavy mats, woven with patterns and messages and tributes, would prevent a grounding. Ironically, the mats protected the free dancers from the planet, but didn't protect the Living from the free dancers. The Living had learned long ago that they had to let the free dancers . . . well, there was no nice way to say it . . . let them *feed*.

Rather quickly, the mats were puzzled together into a gigantic circle of a size perfect for its task, big enough that the free dancers would be able to sense the Living crowded upon it, but not so big that the Living couldn't race for the edges when the time was right. Keller had seen four other hunts and had participated in three. A more ghastly spectacle he had never witnessed.

He got a shudder up his arms as he remembered, and fully realized again what was coming. Hundreds of healthy innocent men and women would strip down to their birthday suits and plunge out onto the plain, then wait for the free dancer herd to "see" them—whatever that meant—and come to the trough. Against all instinct, the Living had learned to simply stand there and be "chosen" in an electrical feeding frenzy that defied description.

The mental pictures alone turned Keller's stomach. The people would stand with their faces up, fear clearly shown, as the monsters came down, and wait for the Elders to decide the free dancers had eaten enough that they would return next time. Finally, the scramble back to the perimeter while the slaughter went on . . . desperate hunters would pull on their silky chain-mail tunics so they would be protected from the pyrotechnics, snatch up their arc spikes, pulpers, clamps, nets, and race back to harvest one free dancer for the reservoir of energy and the gizzard full of candleflies it provided.

Not exactly Home on the Range.

Overhead, enormous shapes painted shadows upon the hunt plain. Heat blew downward from the skies, a sure sign that the free dancers were clustering above. A fine hail of ice particles bitterly pummeled the back of Keller's neck, his head and arms, as he worked on the gum mats, so hard that he fell to both knees. His hands were cold, but as much from the inside as the outside. Courageous people would be dying soon, and horribly.

But not him, and not Braxan. He needed to live, and he needed her to live—

"Look!"

"What is it?" someone shouted.

"A spinner!"

Keller raised his hand to shield his face from the ice particles and scanned the ugly sky. Beside him, Braxan hunched her shoulders and turned her unprotected face upward.

In the sky a tiny dot grew quickly larger, a bug-shaped metallic vessel with forward mandibles and a bulbous stern. A spinner from Riutta's fleet on the other side of the gateway—and quite literally the last thing Keller expected to see.

Who was piloting it? Was someone bringing a message for him? Had Riutta abandoned the gateway? Had one of the Living crew broken away? A hammer blow of worry hit him.

To a planet that hadn't entertained a visitor in ten thousand-plus years suddenly came the second visitor in a matter of months. Things were changing here—a harbinger now landed upon the plain, a much better touchdown than Keller had managed when he came through.

"Uh-oh . . ." he uttered. "This can't be helpful."

"Perhaps it's one of your friends," Braxan suggested.

"Bet it ain't."

At first Keller didn't recognize the man who stepped from the spinner. The smooth silvery skin and dark eyes threw him off. On the other side of the gateway, the skin of the Living revealed its mottled pattern and their eyes were—different.

"It's Luntee, alive!" Braxan chirped, pushing on Keller's shoulder. "This will put to rest the idea that you may not have been honest with us! There were rumors that Riutta and Luntee had died on the other side!"

"They're fine," Keller hoarsely confirmed. "I told you they were fine . . ."

He found his feet and pushed his way through the crowd of hunters. They knew him and were curious, so eagerly they parted before him and Braxan, until he was face-to-face with Luntee.

Though they both appeared like Halloween versions of themselves, they recognized each other.

"Couldn't take it, huh?" Keller flatly asked.

Luntee squared off with him, unsurprised and obviously prepared. "You don't belong here. We don't belong Outside. We should never have gone."

Aware of the hundreds of people staring at them like a swarm of bees waiting for a flower to open, Keller held himself in check and went for information.

"What's the status on the other side?"

"They think you're dead," Luntee announced. "Almost all the Anointed are gone. Time is running out."

Keller held up a hand. "We've been getting ready. We've been storing energy to power the transport ships. All the Living will be able to go through the gateway and settle in the Sagittarius Cluster."

Braxan appeared beside him, almost between him and Luntee. "The plan is troubled now."

He looked at her. "Why?"

She and Luntee watched each other as lightning flashed on their faces. "Luntee has returned to us and he is an Elder. There can only be three Elders. Luntee is senior to Issull. Issull is no longer Elder. Luntee's voice will now be heard with the voice of Kymelis."

She might've been trying to be kind or cautious, but everyone here knew what she meant.

The matter broadcast itself when Luntee spoke up again. "We will not go through," he declared. "We will destroy all the transporting vessels and we will live here, as we are meant."

"Meant?" Angry, Keller flopped his arms. "Nobody's 'meant' to live on this pie plate! There's no natural life here at all!" He turned to the crowd and implored, "The gateway is still open. That's a clear message. My friends and Riutta are holding it open. They're still waiting for us!"

Luntee held up his hand and pointed to the skies. "It remains open because his friends are forcing Riutta to push Anointed after Anointed into the processor! Wasted!"

Keller spun back. "Don't talk like that. They're not being wasted. They're saving you, all of you, all you people, if you'll just go through. Riutta knows that now—"

"Riutta is ill in the mind!" Luntee gasped. "You made her weak. The Anointed are almost gone. The gateway is soon and forever to close!"

"And you didn't want to be trapped on the other side," Keller accused. "Why not? Tell your people the truth. *You* couldn't adapt. You didn't like it over there, you found it uncomfortable, and you like being an Elder. Riutta wanted you to spend your life in space and you can't stand the idea. Here, you're a big fish in a small pond." His finger leveled at Luntee's chest, at the chain-mail shirt he couldn't punch with a phaser. "At least admit that this is about you, and not about your people."

Braxan started to say something, then looked at Keller and asked, "What's a fish?"

"What's a pond?" Luntee asked, but in a mocking way. "I hate it there. I'm saving my people—"

"You're saving yourself. You won't take the time to adjust or let us help you. Did Riutta know you were escaping back through the gateway?" Keller plowed on, "Or did you break away on your own? I'm surprised Shucorion didn't knock you out of the sky."

Luntee's expression turned hard. "They think you're dead! Take the spinner! Go away from us and put their fears to peace! And leave us alone!"

"That's exactly what you'll be," Keller said. "Alone."

The crowd was nervous, doubtful, and suddenly scared. Their fear crackled as clearly as the electrical frenzy high in the sky, and just as palpable.

Push!

"You like that, don't you?" he pressed on, and actually stepped closer to Luntee, to put the focus where he wanted it. "The difference between you and all these other people is that you want to stay here. Everybody else is debating *when* to go through. You don't want to go at all. Tell them the truth."

"I speak truths," Luntee said. "I know how long you've been here. We have enough to go, but only if all our energy is used. Is this not also true?"

Keller started to speak, but all he could do was agree. Better not to do that.

Luntee took the silence as a cue. "If we go to space and the gateway closes before we go through, then we all die. All our energy will be used up. We'll freeze and starve by thousands. We have a fresh store of energy, to be used in powerful vessels to go through the gateway to that place of horrors, or to be used to make life better here. More heat, more building, new ways to hunt—"

Feeling his influence slip, Keller took care to keep desperation out of his tone of voice. "But most of the Living want to go through the gateway, as Ennengand intended. Isn't that true? Braxan, isn't it true?"

Her eyes were solemn, communicating to him that his argument was pointless now. "There are three Elders," she said. "If Kymelis decides to stay—"

"The old rules are too old," he argued. "Three people shouldn't be making decisions for tens of thousands of others—not *this* kind of decision. All of your people—*each* person has the right to decide whether or not to go."

"No one knows how to make this kind of choice."

"I do!" He turned and met the eyes of as many individuals as he could. "I surely do. This place is appalling. The best you can ever do here is make life barely bearable. Your legends came down of a wondrous place polluted by people who struck off into space. Okay, I'll tell you the truth—things aren't perfect on my side. It's not all wonderful, but it's *mostly* wonderful. The other things—we're working on all of it. You folks, you're right to stop looking for simple ways to live. You have a spectacular technology here, your metallurgy and your free dancers, and how you've learned to use them . . . what a gift! You could improve life for billions of people, and you won't have to suffer anymore. You can be warm and have food—no more hunts, no more orphans—growing, breathing planets, flowers and grass and color— think of it and brace up!"

He paused, and watched the crowd. They were like a pack of gray wolves staring down a deer that wouldn't run. They had all the power and possibility, but didn't know what to do.

"Keller speaks with the voice of Ennengand," Braxan defended. "We should go through. I have always said it and I'm very smart."

He glanced at her, charmed by her ability to find a joke at these kinds of moments. Suddenly he felt stronger.

"The Elders speak with separate voices," Luntee reminded. "If no two Elders agree, then random order will declare which voice shall be final."

"Hold it," Keller snapped. "What's that mean?" His own question gave him a shiver.

Lowering her chin, Braxan watched Luntee cannily. "It means there must be a hunt decision."

A rumbling ball hardened in Keller's stomach. "What's a hunt decision?"

*   *   *

"Watch the biohaze! When the first free dancer descends, all hunters will retreat except for the two challengers. One will be chosen. The other, the voice left behind, is meant to be heard."

Luntee, who had been reserved, skittish, and overwhelmed on the other side of the gateway, boldly addressed the gathering of hunters—numbers well into the hundreds. He spoke up sharply, and something about the acoustics of this metallic world carried his voice almost to the horizon. Keller had found that out the hard way.

Since all the hunters were gathered anyway and there were free dancers in the sky, the hunt decision would happen here and now. Just as well, wasn't it? To get all this over with? No time to think twice?

The judge would be Cyclops—Kymelis—the impartial Elder. Impartial? Vacillating, really. She was a stocky woman with many children, her right eye and right ear destroyed in some hunt catastrophe. Whether or not she coveted control or just accepted it was a mystery. Since becoming an Elder involved nothing more than surviving more hunts than any but two others, there was no political parrying or ambition in play. Being an Elder, status-wise, was nothing more than jury duty or a rotating chairmanship, except that big decisions were made for big numbers by these entirely random leaders.

Of course, until very recently, the decisions hadn't been so very big.

Kymelis was also dangerously superstitious. She was waiting for a "sign" that this was the right time to abandon their ridiculous planet.

As if there hadn't been enough signs lately! Belle Terre Trail, Blood Junction, Crossover Crossing, Keller Corners—

"What if both die?" Keller asked. "If both are chosen?"

"Then neither is meant to be heard," Kymelis explained. Her bulky shoulders changed shades with the violent storms overhead as the free dancer herd noticed the hunt plain and began to gather. "There will be two new Elders."

"Wait—wait a minute. What do you mean by 'two new Elders'? If I'm chosen, Braxan still—"

"You will not be on the hunt plain. Braxan will be."

"This is between Luntee and me!"

"You're not an Elder," Luntee said. "Braxan is the dissenting Elder."

"Yeah, but you're not taking her out there."

"Yes."

"No. This is between *you* and *me*."

Luntee shrugged. "Braxan is your voice. A hunt decision is made with Elders."

"There's got to be something better," Keller insisted, "something involving me. I should be able to stand for my own purpose and take my chances."

Around them the hundreds of hunters shifted and bobbed with anxious curiosity. None dared cheer his words or even speak up, though he saw cheers in many eyes. Rules were rules and a lenient crowd wouldn't change them, but the effect wasn't lost on any of the three Elders. After all, if none of these people wanted to go through the gateway, there wouldn't be a problem, would there?

Kymelis's remaining eye shifted back and forth, as if scanning the old records and laws and rules and their details.

How could such a crowd be so quiet? It was like being watched by owls in the night woods.

"She can select a surrogate," Kymelis concluded.

Keller went up on his toes. "Great! Perfect—" He swung to Braxan. "Pick me. Come on, hurry up. I'm right here."

She looked at him, at Kymelis and Luntee, and back at Keller.

"Come on," he urged, twitching like a kid. "Let's go. Pick me."

"I can't," she murmured. "You are the next Ennengand. You'll find a way."

"But if you—if you're chosen, Luntee's side wins!"

She gazed at him with miserable adoration. "And if you are chosen, there will be no one strong to speak for going. I'm not strong enough to lead. Whatever happens, you must remain to lead the Living. I will stand on the plain."

So she did believe in him. Too much.

"Braxan will go onto the hunt plain for the decision," Kymelis judged.

"No—oh, no!" Keller's head started to pound on the inside and down the back of his neck. He pushed forward toward Luntee and might've hit him—he might have—except Donnastal and Serren held him back.

Maybe they were smart. Maybe there was some little law about hitting an Elder.

What about insulting one?

"You're devious, Luntee," he tempted. "All right, you don't like me—fine. You want me to pay—that's fine too, but don't make me pay with *her* life!"

"These are our laws." Something had stabilized in Luntee's voice. He sounded much more confident than he had on the other side of the gateway. "You have come here and must live within—"

"I will," Keller blurted, "if you go out there with me, not with her. Let me be my own voice!"

A light came on in Luntee's eyes. "Very well," he complied. "You will be on the hunt plain."

Why had that gone so well?

Braxan shook her head frantically, suddenly overtaken by a new horror. Why?

A groan rose in Keller's throat. "What a low-down trick."

Eminently satisfied, Luntee spoke again to him, clearly enough to be heard well around.

"You, Nikelor, will go out as my surrogate. Braxan will represent the voice to go. You will represent me and the voice to stay. Random order will decide which voice remains to be heard, as it has for five hundred generations."

Keller fought his own inner arguments and tried to add up the situation. If Braxan lived, her "voice" remained and Ennengand's ideal of going through the gateway would prevail. But Luntee could easily muddy the waters, play on Kymelis's doubts, and make the clock run out. He could stall enough to let the last Anointed go into the processor and the gateway to finally close, locking the Living to their fate on this side. Braxan wasn't the type to fight him hard enough.

In fact, Luntee had Keller better than even Luntee realized. Keller had only his one ace, his big secret. He could arrange for one or the other to survive on the Feast Grid. He could do it artificially.

Now what? Admit to these brave hunters that he'd been hedging his bets, immunizing himself and Braxan with tricorder scans? Tell them how different the energy acted on either side of the gateway? Just as the grave ship's power wouldn't read in conventional sensors, the tricorder acted differently, and had different effects.

Cheating . . . His own actions left as bad a taste in his mouth as the scans did in the free dancers', but he had a lot to stay alive for. If he didn't influence them, didn't complete his mission, these people would stay here, would probably shuffle along for a few more generations trapped in this hellish place, and probably die off. Without Keller, there would be no one to speak for going to the other side, right now, while they had the chance, while the gateway was still open.

He had to at least *appear* to be playing by their rules. He had to participate in their society, or they wouldn't respect him.

Now he couldn't even play his one ace. If he did, the free dancer would descend, but wouldn't choose either him or Braxan. He could save both their lives. Then what? Another hunt decision? And another one, until random order was satisfied?

Or if random order defied a choice, then the Elders would decide. By now Keller knew Kymelis well enough—she wouldn't decide. She would want to wait for a sign or a clue that would never come. Luntee would win, because time would run out.

A sly glint lit in Luntee's eyes as he watched Keller. On the other side of the gateway Luntee had seemed a minor player, hesitant and unclever, hovering on the sidelines as Riutta made the decisions. On this side, all that changed. He was not only playing the laws, but daring to make hunches about his adversary and doing it with the rocky nerve of a riverboat gambler. If Braxan were chosen and Keller lived, representing Luntee, then Luntee's voice was *meant* to be heard. Luntee's trick was flawless. It left Keller no good way out, no way to win.

The wind tore at Keller, at them all. The sky began to crackle and grow lower. Giant shadows moved across the grid mats.

"All I have to do is throw myself before the free dancer, and Braxan's voice remains," Keller announced. "I swear to do that, Luntee," he vowed. "I won't let your voice be heard."

A singular moan swelled through the crowd at this shocking declaration. Approval . . . shock . . . everything. He had to push.

He'd guessed right—nobody had ever said such a thing among the

Living. He was glad to shock them. He needed their respect. All of the people here, and on the other side of the gateway.

His hand was on his tricorder, but he dared not use it now.

Around him, Luntee, Braxan, and Kymelis a sea of hunters rounded their shoulders against the bitter wind, their soft link shirts ablaze with reflected lights from overhead.

So the free dancers would decide. Except that the tricorder would have more influence. Braxan was already immunized. Keller hadn't done himself yet.

And now, he wouldn't. Braxan had to live. Luntee's voice couldn't be allowed to prevail. Keller would stand on the hunt plain, and take his chance the hard way. No tricks.

"Crackle!" one of the hunters called. "There's crackle above! We have descent!"

The hunt plain turned gunmetal gray under snaggletoothed sparking from overhead as a blizzard of candleflies panicked and shifted in giant tides. The free dancers had begun scooping them up, causing the biohaze to boil. A sense of imminence crawled over every shoulder.

"Descending!"

The cry was picked up and transferred through the hunters all across the plain. It rang like an echo.

Overhead, the first free dancer released its heat and floated down toward the Grid to take its meal. Above it came others, also sensing the crowd of hunters.

Nick Keller's fingers were stiff with cold, his neck stiff, teeth gritted, legs aching. The hunt was a perfectly nightmarish experience, both physically and mentally. Everything hurt.

Around them, the hunters began to scatter, to fill out the Feast Grid in the way determined by centuries of desperate efficiency, the best way for the dirigibles above to spot them and be tempted down. Billions of candleflies caused a sparkling cloud to fog the Feast Grid.

With his mind racked at the probabilities—dying out here right now, for one—Keller moved away from Braxan. When they were alone on the field, when the free dancer came for him, he didn't want to be anywhere near her. Strobe lightning and candlefly fog damned his vision. The nearest free dancer must almost be down!

He closed his eyes and stripped the tricorder strap off his shoulder. His fingers were cold, slow. Fear balled up in his stomach. He hadn't bet on this as his last act, but it would have to write its own poetry later. Maybe he'd be a legend someday, like Ennengand.

Suddenly he stumbled and fell to one knee, yanked hard by a force on his left arm. His tricorder flew from his hand, its strap raking his arm as he grabbed for it.

"Hey—hey!"

He twisted, still on his knee, off balance. Over him, Luntee was aiming the tricorder directly at him.

"Hey!" Keller shouted. He lunged, but fell short.

The tricorder *chirrrupped* and set up the electrical interference, with its short-range focus aimed at Keller. A few seconds . . . the deed was done.

Now he would never be chosen! He would give the free dancers a burning mouth.

Too far away to change anything or know what to do, Braxan called through the curtain of panicking candleflies. "Keller! What are you doing! The free dancer is descending!"

With a shove Keller vaulted to his feet, knotted his fists, and would've struck Luntee if they had been two paces closer. "How'd you know? How could you possibly know about that?"

Luntee held the tricorder as casually as a Starfleet yeoman. Somehow he seemed to regret what he was being forced to do. "I have lived here a lifetime. Energy is our tonic. Now I've been to the Outside and I know all things behave in strange dances."

He dumped the tricorder on the mats, turned, and raced away from the center of the Feast Grid. He didn't realize Braxan was already immunized.

But now Keller was immunized too. If the free dancer chose neither of them, time would run out before another decision could be hammered into place. Luntee would still be able to keep his people here.

Pretty simple. One-dimensional, like this pewter pot they lived on.

"I'll be damned," Keller grumbled. "All right, I can play too." He turned and shouted over the noise from overhead. The free dancers were getting closer. "Kymelis! Kymelis, wait!"

In a clique of hunters, some of whom were her family, the stocky Elder squinted her one working eye at him. "More? But we have descent!"

She pointed to the sky, to the giant bulbous animals growing larger and larger.

"This decision is too important!" Keller called. "There's only one way to really be sure. Luntee will stand on the plain with Braxan and me. All three of us take our chances."

"Why should this be?" Luntee demanded. "Order has already been established!"

Keller turned to Luntee and suddenly there was no one else in the universe but these two men and their challenge. "If your voice remains, there won't be any doubts. Braxan will do what you want. I will too. That's my promise to the Living."

Through the haze of heat waves and candleflies, Kymelis and several hunters hurried back toward the center of the Grid. She was already thinking. Her one eye was crinkled with puzzlement. "What is this way of thinking?" she asked.

"Why should I stand with you?" Luntee demanded. "You are my surrogate. Braxan represents the hunt challenge. All is correct!"

"Don't be so tied to your rules that you make a big mistake." Keller peeled off his mail shirt and tossed it to Donnastal. It flushed and eddied like water between them. "I'm ready."

Luntee hunched against the flash and wind and turned to Cyclops. "I reject this! He uses our rules against us!"

"He's afraid of real random order," Keller pointed out.

Cycl—Kymelis looked up at the lowest free dancer, a truly horrifying sight no matter how many times experienced. "All things come from random order," she said, and looked at Luntee. "If you're afraid, then I side with Braxan and we will go tomorrow."

Her single eye fixed on Luntee.

Rain began to pummel the confused crowd. The hunters were nervous, glancing up. Pellets of ice were melting in the heat of the first few free dancers as they came down directly over the hunt plain, long strands of electrical floss snapping like a woman's hair in the wind.

All the hunters were on the plain, with Keller, Braxan, and Luntee at dead center. They had left their nonconducting mail shirts behind and thus would be unprotected from the savage tendrils of floss.

"Clear the plain!" Kymelis's shout was carried dutifully through the throng, and the hunters raced for the perimeter to pull their mail shirts back on—there to stand and watch as a great decision occurred on the Grid. For a woman who had trouble making a decision, she was done with this one.

"What happened?" Braxan called. With Luntee still standing on the plain, she didn't understand the change. She was afraid—that showed clearly enough through the tides of candleflies.

"Stay there!" Keller called. "It's the three of us now!"

"Why!"

"Just stay put!"

Luntee had no choice but to stand his own ground as the first free dancer came down and the hunters flooded off the Grid. As far as anyone else knew, this was a fair fight. Only Keller and Luntee knew otherwise.

The shock floss moved toward Braxan, a maneuver which Keller had to battle in his own heart. He wanted to run and protect her, but he'd already done all he could, with his tricorder. Luntee never bothered to look at Braxan.

Of course—he must assume Keller would already have immunized her.

Yes. Of course.

The tendrils snapped around Braxan, but quickly retracted at the "taste" of her.

Luntee knew, for sure now, that he was the only vulnerable person here. "I thought you were not so brutal," he charged. "You know who is chosen now."

Just between the two of them, Keller offered a nod of understanding. "Yes. But it's your life against all these others. One person's life—one selfish person—against a whole community of lost souls."

"Then you sentence me?"

"One more death in this place?" Keller told him bitterly. "You know, it's almost a joke. That's the way it is. I'm sorry for it. I'm sorry!"

He was shouting. No choice now.

The free dancer came down, confused because a moment ago it had seen a herd of hunters and now it was searching for any at all. An easy target—but this time there was no call to ready the arc spikes, nets, pulpers, reactor clamps, or other equipment to reap a harvest of candleflies or to transfer energy from the captured free dancers. All those had been left behind, on the perimeter of the Feast Grid. Today the free dancer would descend to feed and instead be the jury in a very strange case.

Keller summoned all his resolve to stand firm while everyone else was running off the Grid. The emotional suction was overwhelming! Despite a year in this place, despite the work of the tricorder, he had to fight hard against the pressure of self-preservation.

He drew power from Braxan's determined face and narrow hunched shoulders as she stood her own ground thirty paces in front of him. His thoughts were lost under the scream of shock floss and the puffing of the giant over his head.

Several paces from him, Luntee squinted and raised his arms to shield his face, but he was doomed.

Floss snapped and sizzled around them, between them. Keller couldn't see Braxan. In his mind he knew she was immunized and that he was too, that the free dancer would taste them and bully them, but probably leave them alone and snap up Luntee into its electrical processors. Even so, instinctive terror overrode what he knew in his mind. As he gritted his teeth and tried to see Braxan, perfect panic rose in his guts and he pushed up all his resolve to keep from bolting. If nothing else, these people needed to see him *not* running away.

He couldn't see Braxan anymore. His only duty now was to move away from Luntee and let fate take its course. He had to live, to take these people home.

A step, another step—he began to shift sideways away from Luntee. A dozen feet over their heads, the lowest free dancer roared and screamed and flapped its floss. Tendrils slapped the Grid mats viciously.

Luntee closed his eyes, gritted his teeth, and prepared to lose. But he never ran, never even attempted to protect himself or change what had been choreographed either by random order or by Keller's manipulation.

Keller ducked the tendrils and the electrical crackle and watched Luntee a couple more seconds before he finally snapped.

"Aw, hell, why aren't I rotten? Braxan, down! Braxan!"

"Where are you!"

"Never mind! Get off the Grid! Get off! Run!"

He swung around, cupped his hands at his mouth, and shouted to the crowd on the perimeter. "Donny! Arc spike!"

Donnastal was ready. The boy seized the nearest spike, raised it to his shoulder, and heaved it like a Roman pilam. The fifteen-foot spear flew poorly, but enough to sail over Luntee's head toward Keller. In a maneuver that would've been impossible a year ago, Keller bunched up his body and propelled himself into the air. With his high hand he knocked the spike out of its path. It cartwheeled once and thumped to the mats ten feet from him.

He came down—it seemed to take a month—on one knee, and rolled until his hands made contact with the spike. The long device leaped into his grip. He hugged it, rolled again, and turned the spear-end upward. With one hand he found the bitter end, cupped it, and gave a mighty shove.

The body of a free dancer was fifty percent guts and fifty percent hot air. The long spike punched through the hide with skill honed of thousands of hunts over thousands of years. Like a fish scaler, it knew its job to perfection. Oily glue poured over Keller's hands, but he didn't stay to receive the rest of the spillage.

Rolling to his knees, he kept a grip on the end of the spike and endured the deafening whine of the injured free dancer over his head while he plunged at Luntee. He caught the other man with the point of his shoulder and drove him down. Once on top of Luntee, Keller dug his fingers into a seam between the gum mats until his fingernails scraped metal.

The planet's surface!

With all the strength in his lean and muscled arm, he hauled back on the woven gum. With the other hand he grounded the arc spike's blunt end into the now-bared spot of surface metal and rolled for his life.

A conflagration erupted over them. The gum mats coiled around him and Luntee. Keller kept rolling until the mats were tight around them both in a rubber coffin.

Crushed against him, Luntee made a strangled shout and hammered his fists against the gum.

"Stop it! Lay still! I mean *lie* still!"

He couldn't hear himself over the giant frying pan that sizzled around them. The free dancer was grounded. All its stored energy flashed into the planet in a single, instant, roaring display of pyrotechnics and raw voltage.

The gum mat became instantly hot. From outside the lightning flash was so bright the opalescence even penetrated the layers of woven rubber. Keller crammed his eyes shut. His skin was burning! Luntee's body jolted against him. They were frying!

Cramped tightly against him, Luntee let out a long cry of panic. His elbows tucked tight, Keller buried his face in Luntee's body and determined not to make a noise. The rubber box vibrated and jumped with them in it, slammed down, jumped again, rolled, as they were nearly cooked inside. Every hair on Keller's body stood up and spun. His back and legs tightened inside the rolled mats, trapped, yet every muscle contracted as if he were running full out.

Grounded!

What he felt on his skin, though his body, he saw as an ultimate picture of destruction in his mind. The free dancer had made direct contact with the planet—instant, complete energy transfer.

Indescribable heat had soon filled up his brain and broiled away his thoughts. Time lost meaning. He was aware only of a terrible hammering from outside, as if the rubber roll and its pathetic inhabitants were instead the head of a mallet.

The planet surged up under the great electrical bladder and sucked back what it had once given in some weird ancient trade. When the last crackle sounded, Nick Keller had stopped trying to handle the moment and simply allowed himself to be slaughtered. All the more surprise when he found himself alive.

With his aching hips he changed the balance inside the coiled mats and forced himself and Luntee to roll free. Like Cleopatra falling out of the carpet, the two men suddenly sprawled free.

Keller tried to move his legs, but his arms shifted instead. For five or ten seconds he worked to retrain his brain on the use of limbs. When he found his legs, he crawled to Luntee. Hot, alive—and not melted. The worst they each suffered was a bad sunburn.

Around them and rising several stories on one side was the cooked mess that had once been the free dancer that nearly killed them, now a mountain of blackened flakes.

"Why—why did you—" Luntee's gasp ended in a weak cough.

Keller crawled to him, pushed him flat on the still-sizzling gum, and sat on him. "Shut up a minute. Braxan! Braxan!"

She didn't answer . . . then, she did.

"Keller? Keller! Where are you!"

He couldn't see where she was through the flying ashes and powdery remains of billions of toasted candleflies.

"She's alive," he growled down at Luntee. "So are you, chickenhawk."

"Why?" Luntee choked. "Why would you save me?"

Possessed with sudden ferocity, Keller grinned and snarled at the same time. "Because I don't have to accept the verdict of random order. Those aren't gods in the sky. They're animals. The free dancer chose you to die, but I choose for you to live."

Luntee stared up at him. Behind the frothing hiss of the barbecued free dancer they heard the cheer and rave of the hunters who were just now coming to understand what had just happened. Donnastal was the first to appear. Braxan came behind him, her narrow face crumpled with fear. Next were Kymelis and her family, Issull and his brothers, Serren by himself, and two by two, three by three the rest of the hunters pushed through the mountain of ash and fibrous smoldering flesh until there were hundreds crowded on the melted segment.

Shaking with aftershock and satisfaction, he managed to stand up. With Donnastal on one side and Braxan on the other, he glared down at Luntee.

"Random order is finished here," he announced, without any particular force. The word would spread itself. "I'm in charge now. We don't belong here and we're not staying. Finally, blessedly, we're gonna saddle up and leave this moodless world."

*   *   *

74

Frigate *Challenger,* Bridge
The twenty-ninth hour

"This is like waiting for somebody to come out of a coma, except with every hour there's less brain activity. You know what's coming, don't you?"

"Clam up, Ring. Just clam up."

"Flirt."

"Both of you . . . this is unhelpful." Shucorion didn't enjoy interrupting Ring and Bonifay in their prickled communion, or in particular conversing at all. On the main screen, a view of the grave ship and the gateway's flicker had become a torturous mock, and somehow worse than anything he had ever endured. A large statement, considering all.

Nick Keller was in a horrible place and to their nearest calculation he had been there more than a year. What could possibly take so long? Was he dead? Was he trapped?

On the sci-deck, Savannah Ring maintained constant contact with Riutta on the grave ship, monitoring the energy output to the gateway. As Shucorion watched her shoulders tighten and her body shift from foot to foot with nervousness, he realized how deeply this tragic decision dug into them all.

"We're down to the last chamber of zombies," she reported, sensing his gaze. "Any one of those corpses could nourish a power system on our side for months. But to keep that gateway open, we're pouring them in like penny candy."

She didn't look down at him, or acknowledge that he heard her.

Shucorion clasped his hands tightly, very tightly. What should he decide, and when?

He crossed the deck to the starboard rail. At the impulse/mule desk, Zane Bonifay indeed made a pathetic sight, his face hot and wet, throat tight, his hands dug halfway through his black hair, both elbows planted in frustration upon the pulpit's wrist roll. His reddened eyes were fixed on one of the dozen small screens, each of which was crammed from frame to frame with numbers, several of them running complex data in some kind of computer panic.

"I can't do it . . ." His voice caught in his throat. He was a child again, helpless to affect what he saw. "There's no way to replicate or match their power levels. It's . . . it's time-compressed somehow. This is like cramming a whole year's worth of starship power into one day. The grave ship's still working on other-universe time."

"We can't keep the gateway open then," Shucorion concluded.

"Not a chance," Bonifay mourned on a sob. "We have the energy, but we can't time-compress it." He slumped further, and pressed his hands to his face and fingerpainted with his own tears. "Can't we go after him?"

"No."

Bonifay pivoted sharply. "Why not? Because you won't take a risk?"

"Because he ordered us not to go."

Perhaps Bonifay saw the misery in Shucorion's own expression, for he retracted his contempt and went back to simple suffering.

Shucorion pressed his elbow to the rail, leaned there, and peered at the gateway. "I should never have let him go."

Behind him, Bonifay mumbled something in a dull tone. The words were lost.

Shucorion turned. "Something?"

With an agonized sigh, Bonifay slumped back against the useless readout board. "I said . . . it's not your fault."

"My thanks. I don't know my role here yet. Thus, I fail."

"You're in command now. That's your role." Bonifay gathered his emotions somewhat and turned back to his miserable attempts to widen this narrowing tunnel they were in.

The turbolift hissed. When Shucorion turned, Delytharen stood on the quarterdeck, unhappy and stern.

"Avedon," Shucorion greeted.

"I have come for the criminal," the Blood commander announced.

"Mr. Keller has not yet returned."

"He never will return. The gateway has consumed him. I offer my sympathies."

"Your sympathies!" Grief boiled out of Bonifay. He pushed up from his chair.

Shucorion raced to the aft steps and got between them in time to block Bonifay's charge. Delytharen, though missing an arm and twice

Bonifay's age, would easily have turned the bosun to pulp. In fact, the other avedon did not even flinch at the attempted threat.

"He is in my custody," Shucorion said, holding Bonifay behind his arm. "The agreement will be satisfied."

Delytharen tilted his head and scolded, "You know better than this . . ."

"I do, but I'm stalling."

Bonifay relaxed his pressure on Shucorion's arm. "Subtle."

"You must realize Keller is wrong to protect him," Delytharen attempted. "Belle Terre needs Blood Many, and we will not help them if Keller refuses to punish this man."

"Questions have arisen," Shucorion said. He heard uncertainty come out in his tone and knew Delytharen heard it too. "Flexibility may be required from Blood Many."

"Never." Delytharen shifted and gazed at him. "You will topple us all with these caprices. You should be the bulwark here. Instead, you flex."

"He's a rebel," Bonifay commented. "Rebels flex." The anger seemed to have gone out of him, or something else had taken over. He moved back, away from Delytharen and Shucorion, folded his arms, and sadly leaned against the burbling consoles at the communications station.

"I will take him," Delytharen quietly claimed.

Shucorion shook his head. "Not until—"

"Activity!" On the sci-deck Savannah Ring bolted to the forward rail. "Oh, *please!*"

At the helm and nav stations, Creighton and Quinones popped to renewed life, to new tension. Zoa stood up at tactical, staring forward.

"Sir, I'm readying metallic objects!" Creighton cried. "Could it be ships?"

At the helm, Quinones blurted, "Should we go and meet them? Should we?"

Dropping from the quarterdeck to the main arena, Shucorion felt his chest tighten. "I will never doubt him again if he has done this thing . . ."

No one else spoke as they watched the gateway's insides smolder, brighten like a spotlight behind smoke, and ultimately spew a single bulb-shaped ship made entirely of brass. The new ship was alone for only seconds before four more ships came behind it, then four more, and more and even more after those, until a swarm of brassy ships crowded space around the frigate.

"Those are transports if I ever saw one!" Creighton said, shivering with excitement. "Bet there's a thousand people on every one!"

The crew rose in a singular cheer that charged Shucorion to the depths of his being, but he could not react himself except to stare with a daring anticipation at the oncoming ships.

"Should we hail them?" Quinones asked.

"No," Shucorion countered. "We'll give them—"

A dot of light appeared on the port side.

"Stand back!" he snapped to Quinones at the helm, then wasn't satisfied and physically pulled her out of the way.

From the dot of light, a micro-gate spun itself into presence, a hole in the air that led to heavily draped surroundings of silver and brass curtains.

"No, stay put."

It was Keller's voice! Nick Keller's voice speaking inside the micro-gate!

Shucorion almost stepped through, so magnetic was the sound of that voice. Only the greatest self-control prevented such action.

And to the good—a hand appeared on the edge of the micro-gate. A moment later, Nick Keller himself appeared—or a frazzled version of Nick Keller.

His hair, once sand-brown and casually tidy, now was beaten to a crispy shag about his shoulders, blackened at the ends as if burned. His friendly face was leathery from exposure, his clothing a perfect nightmare. He wore his regular trousers and burgundy crew sweater, but they were gaudily patched with interwoven segments of chain mail where some catastrophe or other had torn them. The left sleeve was entirely mail now, and it had brass patches on the silverwork. More than one catastrophe, apparently. What must it be like through the gateway?

Fighting thoughts of his father's last years, Shucorion's heart hammered as he forced himself to stand still, to let their prodigal regain his bearings.

Keller seemed to be having trouble with his eyes. He blinked around, put out a hand to steady himself, and stepped onto the bridge. Shucorion reached out to him, to offer help if he needed it. Now Keller stepped more confidently forward. He seemed to know who had him.

The micro-gate withered and winked away behind him. He didn't give it so much as a glance.

"That you up there, she-devil?" He peered up to where he knew the sci-deck was. Perhaps he recognized the shape of Savannah Ring, or could see the dark red of her hair.

"Right here, sheriff," she managed, controlling herself valiantly.

"Tell Riutta to stop powering the gateway. There's nobody left on the other side. We'll need the grave ship's system to move these freighters. There's no more power coming from the other side. Just let the damned hole close up for good."

"Sure," she rasped. Relief poured out. "Good idea. I can cure interstellar post-nasal drip—why not?"

"That's the spirit." Keller inhaled deeply and seemed to be tasting the air. He shielded his eyes with one hand for a moment, then focused on Shucorion.

"Hey, shadow," he greeted.

On a ragged breath Shucorion asked, "Where are . . . the . . . others?"

"They're all over on those ships, pretty much panicking." Keller pressed a hand over his eyes to block out the blaze. "And I don't blame 'em . . ."

Shucorion grasped his arm. "Are you all right?"

"Uh-huh, but you wouldn't believe what I'm seeing! What senses forget in a few months . . . I'm just . . . dazzled!"

"I understand. I once went to the mountains on my planet to search for ore vanes. When I returned, the land looked *so* flat . . . I could scarcely breathe."

Keller held up a finger. "That's it, you got it."

He lowered his hand to Shucorion's arm and they held on to each other as if they might stumble without support. He looked around, adjusting, and reveled in what he saw—the quatrefoil-cut spark shield on the sci-deck, the cobalt-obsidian dome overhead, the multitude of flickering data screens, the carpet, the rail.

"This bridge is . . . beautiful!"

Now he turned his fatigued gaze to Shucorion, to Savannah, Quinones, and Creighton, and finally to the quarterdeck at Zoa and Zane, and even Delytharen, indulging in a moment's communion with each. After all, he hadn't seen them in more than a year.

"You're all beautiful," he sighed.

Suddenly overcome, Zane Bonifay skipped down the deck steps, shot past Shucorion, and flung his arms around Keller. He tried to speak, but couldn't. The embrace spoke well enough. He had been lost to them, and they knew how long the time had been and how small the chances for this moment to have arrived at all.

"Aw, the famous Bonifay true-blue cryptomorphic gypsy campfire bearhug," Keller murmured. He smiled genuinely. The reddened skin on his cheeks and around his eyes crinkled into patterns. "Home on the Range."

"Delytharen, how are ya?"

"Mr. Keller. My congratulations on your mission."

"Thanks."

"We have an agreement."

"I know we do. Give me another minute."

"I have already—"

"You can wait another minute. Zane, come here."

Nick Keller stepped forward on the bridge, away from everyone else, to a place near the stunning visions on the main screen where a bit of privacy could be culled off. He brought Zane Bonifay with him, and motioned Shucorion back.

Zane swabbed his eyes with his sleeve and made a heartwarming effort to regain officer demeanor. He wasn't too great at it, but he tried. He wasn't the type to care much about who saw his emotions when they bared themselves.

He leaned back against the end of the quarterdeck rail and took a couple of steadying breaths. "You look different," he commented.

"Bet I do."

Keller marveled briefly at the wonders of Bonifay's doeskin complexion and navy blue sweater, but also controlled himself to say what had waited a year to be said.

"There have to be laws. You did understand your rank and obligation. It was disrespectful to act on your own. What if there'd been a hundred crewmen on that Plume? Would you have left?"

"No, course not," Zane admitted.

"The decision wasn't yours to make. We can't have two people on a ship making the same decision. For every man who acts on his own, there are a hundred more who think about it, and don't. We can't have crewmen rushing to escape when we ask them to stand. If every deck acts on its own, the ship falls apart."

Zane simply folded his arms and nodded. Apparently he had been thinking about this too.

"We live in what amounts to a logging town," Keller told him quietly. "Small towns are different from other places. We need help from Shucorion's people. They have to be able to trust me—"

"I get it, Nick." Offering a gaze of surprising candor and maturity, Zane unfolded his arms and stood straight. "I said I wouldn't die for nothing. I never said I wouldn't die for *something.*"

The bridge winked and murmured its faint electrical song around them, so different from the disorderly crackle of Metalworld.

Deeply moved by this gallant change, Keller took a moment to appreciate Bonifay, and silently let him feel the admiration. *That's the spirit.*

He took Zane's arm and escorted him in some kind of personal propriety to the quarterdeck, to Delytharen.

"Avedon," he addressed, "your prisoner."

"My thanks." Delytharen reached down with his one remaining hand to draw Bonifay up the steps, but Bonifay pushed the hand away.

"Don't touch me. I'm a Starfleet officer and I'm coming with you. My word's good, and so's his." He nodded toward Keller.

Delytharen seemed to respect that. "Very well. Our thanks."

Keller turned to Shucorion. "You're going with him."

"I?"

"Yes." He jammed his finger into Shucorion's chest and warned, "Make sure it's fair. Make sure it's *quick.*"

There was something in his eyes that rattled Shucorion to the bone, and made the others cold around them.

Keller knew he had come back changed. He just hadn't quite figured out which changes were permanent.

"What will you do with the Living?" Shucorion asked.

"I'll decide that later."

With all his crew watching him, he found his way to the command chair and ran his hand along the studded forest-green leather, which looked to him as if it actually glowed.

"Whatever happens," he said, "you can bet they'll hear the ring from hell to Belle Terre."

STAR TREK
DEEP SPACE NINE®

HORN AND IVORY

Keith R.A. DeCandido

Chapter 1

The ax nearly took her head off.

Its wielder was large by the standards of the Lerrit Army, but she still stood half a head taller. The plate armor he wore on his chest was too small for him, and it slowed him down, making it easier to anticipate his movements, and therefore just as easy to duck the attack.

That it still almost decapitated her spoke to how long she'd been fighting. How many hours had they clashed on this grassy plain just outside the capital city? She'd long since lost track, but however long it was, the fatigue was taking its toll. Her muscles ached, her arms and legs cried out for respite.

She ignored the pleas of her limbs and fought on.

The ax-wielder probably thought the sacrifice of movement was worth the protection his armor afforded. The problem was, it only covered his chest and groin, leaving his arms, legs, and head exposed: still plenty of viable targets. So as she ducked, she swiped her staff at his legs, protected only by torn linen. She heard bones crack with the impact—the staff was made from a *kava* tree, so it was as hard as they came—and the Lerrit soldier went down quickly, screaming in pain at his broken leg.

She stood upright and surveyed the battlefield. The smell of mud mixed with blood combined with the faint tinge of ozone left from the morning's rainstorm to give her a slight queasy feeling, but she fought it down with little difficulty.

As they'd hoped, the Lerrit Army's formation had been broken. *As last stands go,* she thought, *this is pretty weak.* The war had been all but won on the seas, after all. Lerrit had lost all control of the port, and without the port, there was no way they could hold the peninsula, even if they somehow were able to win today.

Based on the number of Lerrit Army bodies on the ground, that wasn't going to happen.

She caught sight of General Torrna Antosso, the leader of the rebel army for whom she fought, and who looked to be the victor this day. As she ran toward him, one man and one woman, both much shorter than her, and both unarmored, came at her with swords. She took the woman down with a swipe of her staff, but the man was able to strike, wounding her left arm before she could dodge the blow.

Gripping the upper part of the staff with her right hand, she whirled it around so that it struck her attacker on the crown of his head. He, too, went down.

Tucking the staff under her injured arm, she put pressure on the wound with her right hand and continued toward Torrna.

As she approached, she heard the reedy sound of a horn.

Torrna, a wide-shouldered bear of a man with a full red beard and bushy red eyebrows that encroached upon his nose ridges, threw his head back and laughed. "They retreat!" he cried.

She came up to his side, and he stared her in the eye—easy enough, as they were the same height. "We've done it, *Ashla,*" he said, his yellowed, crooked teeth visible in a smile from behind the beard. "We've driven the last of them off!"

"Yes, we have," she said, returning the smile with her perfect white teeth. The nickname *Ashla*—which meant "giant"—was given to her shortly after she joined the rebel army, since she was taller than all the women, and as tall or taller than most of the men.

Torrna's words were prophetic: the horn was indeed the sound of retreat. The Lerrit soldiers who were able ran as fast as they could northward. No doubt they were returning to the base camp the Lerrit had set up on the other side of the hills that generally demarcated the border between the peninsula and the rest of the mainland.

Raising his own ax into the air, Torrna cried, "Victory is ours! At last, we are free!"

The remaining soldiers under Torrna's command let out a ragged cheer.

Next to him, Kira Nerys did the same.

Chapter 2

The meeting room needed a paint job, but at least it didn't smell like a charnel house anymore, Kira mused. A particularly brutal battle had been fought here when the rebel army took over the capitol building. Even with the tide of war turning, the building was still the most heavily guarded, and the fight to take it was a brutal one with excessive casualties on both sides.

But someone had done their job well enough to make the place habitable, if not aesthetically pleasing. The meeting table had been scrubbed, the chairs repaired, and the floor, walls, and ceiling washed.

Looking around at the assorted happy-but-tired-looking faces in the meeting room, Kira wasn't entirely sure what she was doing here. It was, after all, for the high-ranking members of the rebel army. At best, she was a soldier—hardly what anyone would consider important.

And she didn't want to become important. She'd done enough time-traveling—both voluntary and involuntary—to know the risks.

Flexing her left arm, Kira winced slightly. The wound from the sword had been long, but not deep, and was proving maddeningly slow to heal. Unfortunately, Deep Space 9 and Julian's infirmary wouldn't be built for many millennia, leaving Kira to heal naturally, just like when she was in the resistance. Her tendency to scratch at her wounds and not give her body a chance to heal properly hadn't changed with age. In fact, she remembered a snide comment Shakaar had once made about how symbolic it was that Kira always picked at her scabs. . . .

Kira had met most of the people in the room only once or twice. The ones she'd gotten to know thus far were Torrna and the tiny, short-haired woman who entered the meeting room last: Natlar Ryslin.

"Thank you all for coming," she said as she approached the seat at the head of the table. "Please, everyone, be seated."

It soon became apparent that there were far more people than chairs, by a factor of two to one.

With a small smile, Natlar amended, "Or stand, whichever you prefer."

Soon enough, many were seated around the table, with the rest standing against the wall. Kira was among the latter—Torrna, though, sat in the seat opposite Natlar, at the foot of the table.

Her expression serious, Natlar said, "I hereby call to order the first meeting of the government of the Perikian Republic."

A cheer, much less ragged than the exhausted one Kira had participated in on the battlefield, met that pronouncement. Periki Remarro had first agitated for independence against the oppressive Lerrit regime years earlier. The nation of Lerrit had ruled the peninsula with an iron fist and a hefty tax burden, and, though she was not the first to desire the removal of their yoke, she was the first to say so publicly.

Periki had died soon after she began that agitating, hanged by Lerrit authorities. Her cause had lived on, and was now, finally, victorious.

I always wondered how the Perikian Peninsula got its name, Kira thought with a smile.

As Natlar went into the details of what needed to be done next, Kira found herself tuning out. She had been to plenty of meetings just like this—hell, she'd *led* meetings just like this. But those meetings were far in the future and, paradoxically, in her own subjective past. She saw no reason to involve herself now.

She stared out the window, seeing the people of the capital city—which would no doubt also be renamed at this meeting—rebuilding their homes and places of business. The window faced south, so she could also see the docks and the large port beyond the city—the true heart of the peninsula.

Docked there were several warships, armed with massive cannons, that carried the flag of the nation of Endtree.

Kira turned back to the table just as Natlar was saying, "Admiral Inna, once again, we thank you for all you have done for us."

Inna Murent, a short, stout woman with salt-and-pepper hair severely tied back and braided, nodded her head. Kira noticed that she gripped the edges of the table—no doubt a habit from a life aboard a seafaring vessel where the surface beneath her feet was never steady. "We simply followed the road the Prophets laid out for us," she said.

Kira's eyes automatically went to the admiral's right ear, which was adorned with an earring. Though it was nowhere near as elaborate as those worn by Kira's time, Kira knew that it symbolized devotion to the Prophets—a way of life that had not become as widespread in this era as in hers. Kira wasn't completely sure how far back she had gone, but, based on the clothes and weaponry, it had to be over twenty thousand years in the past. *Which means,* she thought, *the first Orb won't even be found for at least ten thousand years or so.* Still, though no Lerrits she saw wore earrings, a few from the peninsula did, as did most of those from Endtree.

And, of course, Kira, though a believer herself, didn't wear one either, thanks to a decree by a religious authority that did not yet exist.

The admiral's comment elicited a snort from Torrna. "I doubt that the Prophets were the ones who put those cannons on your ships, Admiral."

A chuckle spread around the table.

"Be that as it may," Natlar said before Inna could reply, "I am afraid we have more business with our neighbors in Endtree."

Inna seemed to shudder. "With all due respect, Prefect—" Kira blinked; she had missed Natlar's assumption of that title "—I'd rather leave any other business to the diplomats and politicans. I was happy to aid you in casting out those Lerrit leeches. Their shipping tariffs were an abomination. But whatever further relationship there is to be between our governments, it is not for me to arrange. I would simply like to return home and await new orders."

"I, however, would rather you did not return home just yet." Natlar folded her hands together. "While General Torrna has assembled a fine army, and one that I would pit against any other nation's in the world, we are still vulnerable at sea. Lerrit does have a navy of their own, after all, and the moment we lose the protection offered by your fleet, they will return and take us back with little difficulty."

"Perhaps," Inna said cautiously. Kira knew that tone of voice. The admiral knew that Natlar was absolutely right, but to admit it would mean going along with something she did not want to do.

"I therefore would like to request that Endtree leave a delegation of five ships behind to protect the port."

Torrna slammed his fist on the table. "Prefect, no!"

"Is something wrong, General?" Natlar asked, her tone never changing from the reasonable calm she'd been using all along.

"We've just fought for our independence."

"With our help," Inna added with a small smile.

Sparing the admiral a glance, Torrna said, "For which we thank you, Admiral. But if we allow them to stay here, we become as dependent on them as we were on Lerrit! We'd be exchanging one oppressor for another!"

"My people do not 'oppress,' General," Inna said sharply. "The Prophets—"

"I'm fully aware of your people's religious beliefs, Admiral. They don't change the fact—"

"Many worship the Prophets," Natlar said. "It is not a reason to dismiss Endtree as a potential ally."

"I still think—"

"General, can we adequately defend the port with our current forces?"

Torrna grimaced. "Given a few months, we can assemble a fleet that—"

"And until that fleet is assembled?"

Kira winced in sympathy for her friend. She understood all too well the difficulty Torrna was having.

Some things never change, she thought.

Inna was speaking now: "One of my ships is setting out for home with a full report at first light tomorrow. I will include your request, which will be put before the Council."

Nodding, Natlar said, "Thank you, Admiral. General Torrna will serve as your liaison to me—and, should the Council see fit to honor our request, he will continue in that duty."

Torrna stood up. "What!?"

Before Torrna could argue further, a young girl came in. "Excuse me, but three men are here claiming to represent the Bajora."

Kira blinked. *Just when I thought this couldn't get more interesting.*

Natlar barely hesitated. "Send them in." To Kira's ear—well used to the nuances of politicians—the prefect sounded relieved that her argument with Torrna had been interrupted.

For his part, the general sat back down, but glowered at the prefect. Kira knew Torrna well enough to be sure that he would pick up this argument sooner rather than later.

Three men entered. They wore red robes that reminded Kira a bit of those of a vedek in her time, though these were shorter and tighter about the sleeves.

They also wore earrings in their right ears.

"Greetings to you from the Bajora," said the one in the middle, the oldest of the three. "Do we have the pleasure of greeting Natlar Ryslin?"

"I am Prefect Natlar, yes."

All three bowed their heads. "We would like to extend our respects to your provisional government, and—"

Torrna stood up again. "There is nothing 'provisional' about our government! We are the Perikian Republic, and we will be treated with the respect we deserve!"

The envoys looked a bit nonplussed at the general's outburst. *Good,* Kira thought. They seemed a bit too obsequious to her.

"My apologies for my imprecision in speech. Regardless, we do come to you with an offer."

"Really?" Torrna said with a laugh. "The battle has been won less than three days, and already the Bajora have sent their envoys. Were you flown here by *remla* bird with this offer?"

"General, please," Natlar said in her usual calm tone, but it was enough to induce Torrna to take his seat. The prefect then turned back to the envoys. "General Torrna's point is well taken. You cannot have received word of our victory and composed any offer in so short a time."

The envoy smiled a small smile. Kira noted that the envoy had yet to provide a name for himself or his two aides. "You are correct. We have been in the city for several weeks now, awaiting the outcome of your war. If you were victorious, as our intelligence reports indicated you likely would be, then we were prepared to offer you entry into the Bajora. If you lost, then we would simply return and await a more felicitous time to add this region to the glory of the Prophets."

"The Prophets?!" Torrna's voice was like a sonic boom. "You wish to make us part of your theocracy?"

In a snippy tone that Kira recognized from certain vedeks back in her time, the envoy said, "We are not a theocracy, sir. The Bajora is a democratic government of the people of this world. Our goal is to unite the planet once and for all."

"Really?" Torrna's tone was dubious.

"For too long," the envoy said, and now he was addressing the entire room, not just Torrna or Natlar, "we have squabbled and bickered in conflicts much like the one you just finished."

"That was hardly a 'squabble,' " Torrna said angrily.

"True," the envoy said, sparing the general a glance, "many lives were lost. And they need not have been, for if we were a united Bajor, there would *be* no such conflicts. Sister need not fight against sister, blood need not be spilled recklessly—we would all be free to follow our *pagh* without worrying about who rules us or who we will fight tomorrow." He turned to Natlar. "I urge you, Prefect, to consider our offer. The Bajora can only bring benefit to you in these difficult times. You would have the service of our navy to guard your port, you would have the benefit of our assistance in repairing your soil—"

"And all we'd have to do in return is worship your Prophets, yes?" Torrna said. "A small price to pay, I'm sure."

The envoy turned to the rest of those gathered. "And does this man speak for you all? Will you let one man stand between you and progress?"

Natlar suppressed a smile. "General Torrna does not speak for us all—he simply speaks loudest." A small chuckle passed around the table at that—though Torrna looked even angrier at the barb, and Kira couldn't blame him.

"The point is," the envoy continued, "you have been weakened by this conflict. True, the Lerrit have as well, but they have greater resources. The Bajora, however, have even greater resources still, and we're expanding. It is only a matter of time before we have united the entire planet—we urge you to aid in that process."

The envoy went on for quite some time, outlining in more detail what joining the Bajora would involve. Kira found her attention wandering. It reminded her a bit too much of the meetings with Federation dignitaries when they carried on about the joys of joining them.

Another parallel . . .

Finally, Natlar said, "You have given us much to think about." She signaled to one of the guards who was standing at the door, who sent the young girl in. "We do not have the finest accommodations, but Prilla will show you to a chamber where you may refresh yourselves while we discuss your proposal."

Prilla came in as the envoy nodded. "We thank you for your hospitality and your indulgence, Prefect." Then he and his two aides followed Prilla out of the conference room.

Silence descended upon the room for several seconds, before Torrna's booming voice, predictably, broke it. "You can't *possibly* be considering their request, can you?"

Natlar sighed. "Of course I am *considering* it, General. I would be a fool not to."

Torrna slammed a fist down on the table. "No, what would be foolish would be to accept their offer! We'd be trading one oppressor for another!"

One of the other people at the table, an older man, said, "You keep saying that, Antosso. What, you're saying the Bajora, Lerrit, and Endtree are all the same?"

"That's *exactly* what I'm saying."

"Then you're even more naïve than I thought."

Again, Torrna slammed his fist on the table. Kira half expected to see a dent in the wood at this point. *"I'm* naïve? *I* have been fighting for our lives out there, Morlek! Don't you *dare* tell me—"

"No one is doubting your accomplishments," Morlek said, "but the truth is—"

"The truth is, *we are free!*" Torrna looked at each person at the table as he spoke. "But we are not going to remain free if we just let someone else do exactly what Lerrit did! So many have died so that we could shape our own destiny—*not* so we can let someone else do the same thing. No matter who it is—Bajora, Lerrit, Endtree—we cannot let *anyone* direct our paths!" He turned back to Morlek. "You're right, Morlek. Lerrit, Endtree, and the Bajora are *not* the same. But from our perspective, they are all outsiders, and *that* is what concerns me—and should concern all of us. If we are simply going to allow ourselves to be subsumed by the next power that comes along, then I have to wonder what, precisely, we have been fighting for all this time."

Torrna strode purposefully toward the exit. "I will abide by whatever you decide in this room, Prefect," he said as he walked, "but I will not sit here and listen to any more foolish ramblings. Just remember this one thing." He stopped and gave the table one final glance. "Periki Remarro did not die so we could become part of the Bajora. Or part of Endtree. She died so we could be *free.* If we are to name ourselves for her, then we should *never* forget what she stood for."

And with that, he left.

Chapter 3

Kira found Torrna two hours later in his quarters. He was sitting on the windowsill, staring out the window at the port. Kira noticed that his quarters were clean, which was a first. *Guess that's how he spent the last two hours,* she thought with amusement.

"You want the good news or the bad news?" Kira asked as she entered.

Torrna didn't even look at her. "I find it impossible to believe that there is good news."

"Well, there is. Natlar rejected the Bajoran offer."

Shaking his head, Torrna said, "Amazing. I wouldn't have given them credit for thinking that clearly."

"Why not?" Kira asked angrily. "You think you're the only one who was fighting out there?"

Torrna sighed. "I sometimes wonder." He shook his head. "No, of course, you're right, *Ashla.* I simply don't want to see everything I—*we* fought for ruined by shortsightedness."

"Give Natlar a *little* credit, Antosso. She's not about to throw everything out the window."

"I suppose not."

Kira wasn't finished. She moved closer to Torrna and went on: "But give the Bajora some credit, too. What they're trying to do is important. I know you don't believe in the Prophets, but what they're doing is bringing—bringing the world together." She had almost said, "bringing Bajor together," but that word would not be applied to the planet as a whole until after the Bajora succeeded in uniting it many years hence. "Don't let a little bit of agnosticism blind you to that."

Chuckling, Torrna said, " 'A little bit of agnosticism.' What a wonderful way of phrasing it. I may not be the most spiritual person in the world, *Ashla,* but—" He hesitated. "Perhaps you're right. But even if I thought the Bajora were the most wonderful people in the world, I wouldn't want to become part of them. Someday, maybe, but not today. Not after all we've fought for."

Kira put a soothing hand on Torrna's shoulder. "I know, Antosso. *Believe* me, I know. But you can't blind yourself to a good thing just because *you* don't like it."

"I know that." He smiled. "Well, at least, I sometimes know that."

Taking in the newly cleaned room with a gesture, Kira asked, "That why you had the cleaning frenzy?"

Torrna laughed. "It was either that or punch through the walls—and I do have to live here."

Wincing, Kira said, "Well, actually, no, you don't. That's the bad news—the prefect wants you to relocate to the port and set up your office there to serve as liaison to the Endtree fleet."

It took only a second for Torrna's face to go from amused contriteness to vicious fury. "An *office?* Inna hasn't even asked her government's permission yet, but Natlar wants me to set up an *office?* "

"She's hoping for the best," Kira said with a shrug. "Besides, after your performance today, I think she wants to keep you far away from the capitol building."

"Yes," he said bitterly, "to keep my voice from being heard."

Kira smiled. "Antosso, even from the port, *your* voice is going to be heard."

Torrna whirled on her, then let out a long, hissing breath that sounded like a deflating balloon—apt, since the crack seemed to deflate his anger. "How do you do that, *Ashla?* "

"Do what?"

"All of this."

"I haven't done anything, Antosso."

"You may not think so, but you have been a most valued right hand. And one I am reluctant to lose. If I am to be exiled to Natlar Port—"

"What?"

He smiled. "The resolution to pass the name change has been postponed until the prefect isn't in the room, since she'd never let it come to a vote otherwise. In any case, if that is where I am to be sent, I want you by my side. To guard my back and to keep me from making a complete ass of myself."

Kira hesitated. "Can I think about it?"

"Of course. Let me know tomorrow. It will take me that long to pack up my own belongings and inform Lyyra and the boys that we'll be moving."

"Moving where?" came a voice from the doorway.

Kira turned to see a large, stout woman with a mane of red hair to match Torrna's own standing in the doorway to Torrna's quarters. She had met the general's wife only once, but she was probably the only person who could stand up to Torrna and not be killed for their trouble.

"I am to be the new liaison with the Endtree fleet that will be occupying the port."

"Good. The change in climate will do some good. The humidity opens your pores, you know." She turned to Kira. "How are you, Nerys? Is the arm healing well?"

Lyyra was an apothecary, and the first time Kira had met her was when she'd given her a remedy to help heal her arm faster.

"Well enough," she said neutrally. *I'd kill for a dermal regenerator, but this'll do.*

"I still want to know what you've done to keep your teeth so perfect."

"Nothing special." Not wanting to pursue this line of questioning, she said, "I need to get going—and think about your offer. I'll talk to you tomorrow. Good to see you, Lyyra."

Chapter 4

Kira Nerys lay on the bunk in the barracks that she shared with a dozen other soldiers. It had been surprisingly easy to readjust to sleeping in uncomfortable beds or no beds at all. Since arriving here—

Whenever that was . . .

—she had either slept on cold ground or on uncomfortable beds, either way crammed into a too-small space with dozens of other soldiers.

Just like the good old days, millennia from now.

Kira's memories of arriving in Bajor's past were hazy. She often didn't bother trying to think about it, simply accepting what her senses told her as reality.

Tonight, facing the end of the conflict that had raged since she arrived here—

However that happened . . .

—and the start of something new, she once again cast her mind back to see how she should proceed forward.

The last thing she remembered with any clarity was that arid desert planet in the Delta Quadrant.

Everywhere she looked on the ground was sand, broken very rarely by bits of plant life, and the one freshwater lake that she had made sure to land near. It was flat land, with the only variations being the curvature of the planet itself. Not even any hills or mountains or sand dunes in sight.

She'd gone there and abandoned her runabout in order to block a gateway, a portal in space through which deadly theta radiation was flowing into orbit around the inhabited planet of Europa Nova, in the Alpha Quadrant. Kira's actions had prevented one lethal piece of radioactive waste from going through the gateway, thus saving the lives of the Europani as well as the task force she herself had assembled to evacuate the planet.

But to do that, she'd also had to abandon her companion, the Jem'Hadar named Taran'atar, who had stayed behind to fight a Hirogen hunter, keeping him occupied while Kira blocked the gateway.

After that, she couldn't recall what happened. She knew that she found a gateway on the planet where there had been none before. She knew that the theta radiation on the planet had grown to fatal levels.

And she knew that she was now many thousands of years in Bajor's past, fighting in a rebellion that the history of her time had long forgotten. She wasn't even sure how long it had been since she'd arrived in this time. All she was sure of was that she no longer had the radiation sickness she'd been afflicted with—

—and the Prophets had something to do with her sojourn to the past. Maybe.

The gateways weren't built by the Prophets, after all, but the Iconians—in fact, there weren't any gateways within ten light-years of the Celestial Temple. Based on the reports she'd read en route to Europa Nova, the gateways had not only come in all shapes and sizes, but types. Some even seemed to work interdimensionally—so it was quite possible that they could move through time as well.

(Of course, the Orb of Time had that capability, too, as Kira knew from more than one firsthand experience . . .)

Still, she hadn't questioned her odyssey, simply because it felt right. Once before, during the Reckoning, she had served as a vessel for the Prophets. That same feeling she'd had then, she had now.

Well, okay, she thought wryly, *it's not exactly the same—then I couldn't even control my own actions. But I can't shake the feeling that They're the reason I'm here, somehow.*

She lay awake on her pallet, listening to the sounds of the other slumbering soldiers. Some snored, some mumbled in their sleep, some simply breathed heavy. Until the Cardassians pulled out of Bajor, Kira Nerys had always slept in large groups of people, so tuning out the sounds came easily to her. In fact, when she'd first been assigned to Deep Space 9, one of the hardest things had been learning to sleep in a room by herself.

But sleep eluded her, not because of the noise, but because she wrestled with her conscience. Fighting with the rebels had been an easy choice. Agreeing to accompany Torrna to his new duties at the Natlar Port was somewhat less so.

On the one hand, she was concerned about altering the past. On the other, very little was known about the history of this region.

If the Prophets had sent her here—and she felt at the core of her *pagh* that they were involved *somehow*—then they'd done it for a reason. She needed to continue down the path that was set before her.

Dying didn't concern her. She had accepted the reality of her own death in the Delta Quadrant. As far as she was concerned, any living she did from this point forward was a gift. That was why she had no compunction about fighting alongside Torrna with weapons far more primitive and, in their own way, more brutal than any she used in the resistance.

Besides, she thought, *I have to believe that I'm here for a reason. There are far too many similarities to my own life for this to be a coincidence.*

She resolved to accept Torrna's offer first thing in the morning.

Within minutes of making that resolution, she fell into a deep, peaceful slumber, unbothered by the breathing and snoring around her.

Chapter 5

"Look, Torrna's *not* going to bite your head off if you take this complaint to him."

"Are you *sure?*" The merchant looked dubious. More than that, he looked scared to death. "I've heard about how he drove off the Lerrit Army by breathing fire into their camp and setting them alight!"

Kira tried not to laugh, but she did at least keep an encouraging smile on her face. "I can assure you that his days of breathing fire are long in the past. Just go to him and tell him that you object to the inspections. I can't guarantee that he'll do what you ask, but he *will* listen. Just give him a chance."

The dubiousness did not leave the merchant's face. "If you say so."

"I say so. He should be back in the next day or two, and I'll make sure you get to see him, all right?"

"Fine. Thank you, ma'am."

Nodding, Kira excused herself from the merchant, leaving his quarters and going out onto the deck of the docked merchant trawler. It never failed to amuse her, this fear that people had of Torrna. Mainly because she knew that his bluster was worse than his bite.

She also had to wonder, though, if this was what people thought of her after the Cardassian withdrawal. Did people fear that she would breathe fire? Was that why she had been sent to Deep Space 9? After all, she'd been assigned as first officer and Bajoran liaison before the discovery of the wormhole turned the station into a major port of call. She'd never had any illusions that it had been done to get her out of the way of the provisional government, who found her intemperate ways to be too much for them to handle—at least nearby. So they sent her into orbit.

Natlar had all but done the same to Torrna. The disruptive influence he could have in the council chambers—as evidenced by the way he all but took over the meeting shortly after the Lerrit Army's final retreat—was probably seen by the prefect as an impediment to actually getting anything done.

Kira walked down the gangplank of the merchant's ship to the marina and took a deep breath of the sea air. She'd lost track of how long she'd been serving as Torrna's adjutant at the Natlar Port, but she'd been enjoying it immensely—particularly now that the weather was warmer, the sun was shining, the Korvale Ocean was a clear green, and a lovely breeze was pretty much her constant companion every time she walked outside. She hadn't spent much time near the sea prior to this, and when she did, it was during her days in the resistance. She had other things on her mind, then.

She nodded to the assorted dockworkers who passed her by, then whirled around when someone cried, "Look!"

The Perikian Peninsula jutted out into the Korvale Ocean along the southern end of the coast of the continent. Any ship that came down the coastline from the west would have to, in essence, come around a corner and therefore would not come into sight from the marina until it was almost ready to dock.

Right now, one of the largest and most impressive ships that could be found on the planet was coming into view around that bend. It stood at ten meters above the surface of the ocean, with the green-and-black flag of Endtree whipping in the breeze from the mast.

Kira peered more closely and noticed that there was a second flag under it: the flag of the Perikian Republic. *Interesting,* Kira thought. *That wasn't there when they left.*

The ship was Admiral Inna's flagship, the *Haeys,* returning a day early from their investigation of the reports of pirate activity.

Several people on the marina stopped what they were doing to see the flagship approach the dock. As it settled into port, a cheer started to break out, which spread all the way across the marina. Kira found herself joining in the cheer—and she wondered how much of it was general goodwill toward Admiral Inna's fleet and how much was the new presence of the Perikian flag.

Within half an hour, Inna and Torrna had extricated themselves from the admiring crowd. Kira noted that they had been chatting amiably as they approached the gangplank before they were set upon by the admirers. *Quite a switch,* she thought, *from all the sniping they've been doing.* The admiral went off to consult with the captains of the other fleet ships in dock, and Torrna walked with Kira back toward their office in the rear of the marina.

"So what happened?" Kira asked.

"We found the pirates and took care of them in fairly short order. They didn't have anything to match Murent's cannon."

Smiling, Kira said, "'Murent'? That's new."

"I beg your pardon," Torrna said, a little indignantly.

As they approached the office, nodding to the sergeant at the desk, Kira said, "It wasn't that long ago that the only way you referred to her was as 'the admiral' or 'that damned woman.' "

To Kira's surprise, Torrna actually blushed, his skin turning the color of his hair and beard. "I suppose so. But she showed me something on this trip that I didn't expect. She was efficient yet merciful with the pirates, she was very effective in questioning the pirate leader without being unnecessarily brutal, and she agreed to fly the Perikian flag."

"I was going to ask you about that."

They entered Torrna's tiny office. The general sat behind his rickety wooden desk, which was cluttered with assorted pieces of paper that required his attention. Torrna ignored them and instead poured himself a drink from the small bar that sat under the window looking out onto the mainland. Torrna had specifically requested a north-facing office so he could look out on, in his words, "the republic that I fought for, not the ocean that is controlled by someone else."

He offered Kira a drink, which she declined. *They liked their drinks a little less smooth in the old days,* she had thought after the first drink she had shared with Torrna, and she made it a point to avoid the stuff when possible.

"It took surprisingly little argument," he said as he sat down. "I pointed out that her fleet was there at the invitation of the Perikian government and was there to protect Perikian interests, so it made sense that they should fly our colors. Not that she gave in completely, of course . . ."

"Let me guess, you wanted the Perikian flag on top?"

Kira had spoken with a modicum of facetiousness, but Torrna leaned forward and said gravely, "These are *our* waters, *Ashla*. We must never forget that."

"I haven't," she said with equal seriousness.

She also noted that she'd said "the Perikian flag," not "our flag." Perhaps a minor point, but, even though she had fought for the republic's independence, even though she now worked for Torrna, she still couldn't bring herself to think of this as home. She knew this was the right place for her to be, but in the back of her mind was the constant feeling that this was not her new home, that she was only visiting. It made no sense to Kira on the face of it, and she wasn't sure what to think of these feelings.

Deciding not to dwell on it, she leaned back in her chair. "So what did the pirate leader say when Inna questioned her so efficiently?"

Taking a sip of his drink, Torrna said, "Actually, the most interesting intelligence we received wasn't from the pirates, but from their slaves. The most recent conscriptions they picked up were refugees from a disaster in the fire caves."

Kira blinked. "What?"

"Apparently the entrance to the fire caves collapsed—and completely destroyed Yvrig." Yvrig was a city on another peninsula west of Perikia but on the same continent; it, too, had a thriving port.

Torrna snorted as he continued. "Some of the slaves claimed there was some kind of blue fire when the caves collapsed, but I don't put much stock in that."

Kosst Amojan imprisoned . . . the Pah-wraiths banished to the fire caves . . . Shabren's Fifth Prophecy . . . the Emissary going to the fire caves to stop the Pah-wraiths from being freed . . .

Kira knew exactly what had happened, remembering her experience channeling the Prophets during the Reckoning, and now knew precisely *when* she was. Some thirty thousand years before she was born, the Prophets banished the Pah-wraiths to the caves, sealing them in there forever. Only their leader, Kosst Amojan, was imprisoned elsewhere, on a site that would one day be the city of B'hala. The others remained in the fire caves, until Winn Adami and Skrain Dukat attempted to free them only a few months ago, subjective time. Only the sacrifice of the Emissary—Benjamin Sisko—had thwarted the scheme.

Or, rather, will thwart it. I hate time travel. We need new tenses . . .

Until now, though, it never occurred to Kira that the Prophets' actions at the caves might have had harmful consequences for the people near the site.

"We've got to help those people. There may be—"

"Sit down, *Ashla,*" Torrna said, which was when Kira realized that she'd stood up. As she sat back down, Torrna continued. "This happened over two weeks ago. There's very little we can do."

Right. Of course. There is no instant communication here. Kira nodded in acknowledgment.

"However, this does mean that we're going to see a significant increase in traffic in the port. Without Yvrig, we're the only viable port on the southern part of the continent."

Kira nodded. "Traffic's going to increase."

"That's an understatement." Torrna broke into a grin.

Yet another parallel, she thought. The discovery of the wormhole transformed Deep Space 9 from a minor outpost to a major port of call. This wasn't quite on the same scale as that, but Kira did remember one important thing from those early days on DS9.

Torrna continued speaking. "We'll need to work on expanding the marina to be able to accommodate more ships. Maybe now Marta won't close her tavern down the way she's been threatening to. For that matter, we'll probably need a new inn. Plus—"

"We'll need more ships from Endtree—or we'll have to start building some of our own."

Frowning, Torrna said, "What for? I mean, we'll need more people for the Dock Patrol, obviously—the number of drunken louts on the docks will increase dramatically—but I don't think we'll need—"

"We're going to need more ships to hold off the pirates—and the Lerrit Navy."

Torrna snorted again. "The Lerrit Navy is barely worth giving the title."

"Don't be so sure of that. We just got another report from Moloki." Moloki was one of the spies that the Perikian Free Army had observing the goings-on in Lerrit. In fact, the PFA had many such operatives, more than even Torrna or Kira knew definitively about. "He says that they've employed shipbuilders from Jerad Province to completely rebuild their navy from scratch. Within the year, they may well be a legitimate naval power—or at least legitimate enough for us to worry about. And with this change in the geography, they're going to be more interested in taking us back, not less."

Torrna frowned. "Isn't Jerad part of the Bajora?"

Kira nodded.

He shook his head. "Wonderful. We don't join their little theocracy, so they help Lerrit take us back."

"You can't blame them for taking on a lucrative contract like that," Kira said, trying not to examine how much that sounded like Quark.

"I can damn well blame them for anything I want!" Torrna stood up and drained his drink. "Damn it all, I was actually enjoying the good news."

"I'm sorry, but—"

Torrna waved her off. "No, that's all right. That's why I keep you around, *Ashla*. You have the knack for dragging me back to reality when I need it most." He turned to stare at the view from his window. "There is a great deal of work that will need to be done."

Kira got up and walked to Torrna. "Then we'd better get up off our butts and do it, shouldn't we?"

"Definitely." Torrna smiled. "What else did Moloki have to report?"

"Nothing different from his last few. The official word is that the Queen is dying, but she keeps showing up at official functions. She hardly ever says anything, but she's there and smiling a lot. Moloki seems to think that Prince Avtra is doing all the real work."

Shaking his head, Torrna said, "That woman will *never* die. You know, she swore that she would live long enough to see the peninsula brought back under her rule. She's probably the one who contracted the Jeradians to build her a navy so she could fulfill that promise. I daresay she's clinging to life solely for that reason."

"Maybe." She hesitated. "I'm glad you and the admiral are getting along better."

"Yes, well, her tiresome insistence on giving those silly Prophets of hers all the credit for her work aside, she's quite a brilliant tactician." They both sat back down in their seats after Torrna poured himself another drink. "She was able to deal with those pirates with a minimum of fuss. You should have seen . . ."

He went on at some length, describing how she stopped the pirates, and her ideas for curtailing some of their activities in the future. Kira smiled and nodded, but naval battles were not an area of great interest to her—her tactical instincts for vehicular combat of that sort tended to be more three-dimensional.

She was just glad that Torrna and Inna were getting along. She had a feeling that that would be vital in the long run . . .

Chapter 6

The worst thing about the dungeon was the smell.

True, Kira had spent most of her formative years living in the caves of Dakhur Hills and other less-than-hospitable places. But even though she had been roughing it by the standards of her culture, it was still a world that had replicators, directed energy weapons, faster-than-light travel, near-instant communication over interstellar distances, and other luxuries that Kira had always taken for granted. Such a world did not include a dungeon that smelled of dried blood, infected wounds, and the feces of assorted vermin.

She looked over at Torrna, sitting in the corner of the cell. The wound on his left arm was growing worse. If it wasn't treated soon, the gangrene would probably kill him.

Just hope our capture did some good, she thought.

Kira had no idea how long the war with Lerrit had been going on. At this point, she couldn't even say for sure how long it had taken the re-treating troops to bring Kira and Torrna to Lerrit's capital city and the dungeon where they'd been languishing. On the one hand, in a world where communication and transportation was so slow, the pace of life was much slower than Kira was used to—on the other, it seemed like the rebellion had only just ended before this new war with Lerrit had begun.

Kira had been fearing this very thing since the collapse of the fire caves meant more business for the Natlar Port. The port had indeed thrived, giving the Perikian economy the shot in the arm it so desperately needed in order to truly start building itself into a legitimate power in the region, instead of an insignificant nation lucky enough to have a nice piece of real estate.

What she had not expected was the sheer strength of the Lerrit Army. The same army that Kira had helped repel had doubled its numbers and was much better armed. The navy was giving the Endtree ships a run for their money—and the war had been declared on both Perikia *and* Endtree, so there was also fighting in Endtree's territory, both on land and sea.

Still, they had won a major battle at Barlin Field, driving the army completely out of the Makar Province.

All it had cost them was their best field general.

The door to the dungeon opened, and Kira winced. The place had no route of escape (Kira had spent the first six hours in the cell scouring every millimeter for just such a thing), and only one window, which was fifteen meters above them—just enough to provide a glimmer light and hope for escape without any chance of that hope being fulfilled. A (very small) part of Kira admired the tactical psychology that went into the dungeon's design.

The flickering torchlight from the hallway, however, was far brighter than the meager illumination provided by the faraway window, so it took several seconds for Kira's eyes to adjust. When they did, she was confronted with the guard who brought them their food and waste buckets (not replacing them nearly often enough to suit Kira). The guard wore the usual Lerrit uniform of gray and blue, with the addition of a shabby black cloak that probably served to keep the stink and filth of the dungeon off the guard's uniform. Standing next to him was a very short man dressed in a white jacket and white pants, both with shiny gold fastenings, and a white cape that served the same function as the guard's cloak—and, being white, was more noticeably the worse for doing so.

Kira recognized him, barely, from the coins that sometimes changed hands on the docks: this was Prince Syba Avtra of Lerrit.

"You look better on your coins, Your Highness," Kira said.

The prince looked up at her. "Very droll."

Then he glanced at the guard, who rewarded Kira's comment with a slap to the face. All Kira could think was, *I've known some Cardassians in my time who would eat you for lunch.* She gave the guard a contemptuous look in reply.

Avtra, meanwhile, had moved on to Torrna. "You will rise in the presence of royalty, General."

Torrna looked up at Avtra with the one eye that wasn't swollen shut. "As soon as I'm in the presence of some, I'll consider it."

Again Avtra gave the guard a glance. Since Torrna was seated, the guard elected to kick the general in the stomach rather than bend over to slap him.

After coughing for several seconds, Torrna said, "I'm disappointed. I was hoping that Her Royal Highness herself would come to gloat over our capture. It is, after all, the only true victory you have won in this war."

The prince laughed heartily at that.

"Something amuses you?" Torrna asked the question with contempt and with a few more coughs, diluting the effect of the former.

"My 'dear' mother has been dead for some time, fool! Do you truly think *she* engineered this war? Or our alliance with the Bajora?"

This time Kira felt like she'd been kicked in the stomach, though the guard had made no move toward her. *The Bajora? No* wonder *they're so well armed!*

"I can see by the look on your face that you appreciate the position you're in, General. With the Bajora behind us, we will destroy Endtree, squash you upstart rebels and finally control the entire southern coast." He moved toward Torrna, looking down on the general's dirty, bruised, swollen face with a sneer on his own clean visage. "Now I don't suppose you'll tell me what the troop movements are for your little band of spear carriers?"

"If I thought you were worth wasting the spit, I'd spit on you right now," Torrna said. His voice was more subdued than usual—not surprising after the ordeal they'd been through—but the tone was abundantly clear.

"I assumed as much. Besides, I can't imagine that even your soldiers are so stupid as to retain the same battle plan after one of their generals have been captured. Still, I had to ask. And I wanted to see the infamous General Torrna in our dungeon for myself. You will be publicly executed at dawn tomorrow. It was going to be yesterday, but the demand for tickets is simply outrageous, and we had to postpone so we could put in extra seating in the stadium."

Kira wondered if that was the same stadium that had been unearthed in this region during the Occupation. After the Cardassian withdrawal, Bajoran archaeologists had speculated that sporting events had been held there as long as fifty thousand years prior to its rediscovery. That it was used for public executions was a fact of which Kira could happily have remained ignorant.

Avtra finally turned back to Kira. "As for this one—I suppose we should let Torrna have one final night of companionship before we take her to the front lines. She'll make fine arrow fodder."

With that, he turned and left, saying, "Enough of this. I need to get the stink of this dungeon off my person."

The guard closed the door, leaving Kira wishing she could get the stink of the prince off herself as easily.

"We have to get out of here," Torrna said.

Kira snorted. "I'm open to suggestions. The only ones who have free rein in and out of this cell are insects and rodents."

Torrna tried to stand up, but made the mistake of bracing himself with his left arm, and he collapsed to the floor.

Kira moved to help him up, but he waved her off. "I'm fine. Just forgot about the damn wound. Stupid arm's gone numb." He staggered to his feet. "Damn those foul Bajora—I hope those Prophets of theirs strike them down with lightning."

The Prophets don't work like that, Kira thought, but refrained from saying it aloud.

"We *have* to—argh! I'm fine," he added quickly, again brushing off Kira's offer of help. "We have to get this intelligence back to the prefect and to Inna. If the Queen is dead, and the Bajora are helping . . . You were right, the fire caves' collapse definitely made our land more attractive."

"I don't think that matters as much as we thought. From the way that kid was talking, he's been wanting to start a war with us for years, but his mother's been holding him back. The collapse of the caves probably made it easier for him to justify it, but I'm willing to bet that we'd have had a war on our hands as soon as the Queen died no matter what."

Torrna nodded, and Kira could see him wincing in the dim light. *He's more hurt than he'll admit, and the stubborn bastard won't let me help him.*

"We've got to find *some* way out of here! If we can get back, tell them about this, we can change our strategy, try to hit the supply lines the Bajora are using. . . ."

Sure, no problem. I'll just tap my combadge, order the runabout to lock in on our signal, and then we'll beam out of here. Then we can transmit a subspace message with our intel. That'll work . . .

The door opened suddenly again. A guard—a different one—came in with two buckets.

Then he closed the door. *What the hell—?* The guards *never* closed the door.

The guard dropped the buckets, then reached into his cloak and pulled out a set of keys. "C'mon, c'mon, we haven't got much time. Take these, take these."

"Who the hell're you?" Torrna asked.

"Right, right, the password." The guard then uttered a phrase in Old High Bajoran that Kira only recognized two words of.

Torrna's eyes went wide. "Moloki?"

"In the very frightened flesh, yes."

"We thought you dead."

"I probably will be after this stunt, *believe* me. Don't know *what* I was thinking coming up with this ludicrous plan. They'll use my guts for building material, they will."

Kira took the keys from Moloki. "What happened to you?"

"Nothing happened *as such.* I simply couldn't get any messages out. The moment Her Royal Senility dropped dead, all hell broke loose. Truly, a spy can no longer make anything like an honest living in this environment."

"Can you get us—" Torrna started.

"*Yes,* yes, I can get you out of here, just give me a moment to collect myself. I've never been much for impersonations, and I had to pull off being one of those imbecile guards that the prince likes to employ.

Stomping 'round all day, bellowing at the tops of their lungs so loud you can't *think.*" He shuddered. "No style at all, more's the pity." He reached into his cloak. "In any case, here's a map that'll show you how to get out of here once I bring you to the surface, as well as a map that shows the supply lines the Bajora are using. Assuming you get home alive, that should be fairly useful." He put his hand on Torrna's shoulder. "Let me make something abundantly clear, General—it will *not* be easy to get home. It will involve going through a swamp and then across a mountain range. Deviate even slightly from the route I've mapped out, and you're guaranteed to be captured."

"And if we stay on the route?" Kira asked.

"Then you're just *likely* to be captured."

"I was afraid of that," Torrna muttered.

Kira looked at Torrna and winced. "He's not going to make it with his arm in the shape it's in."

"He has to, dammit!" Moloki said sharply, in marked contrast to his more affable tone. Then he composed himself. "Listen to me, and listen very carefully, because I'm only going to say this once. Years ago, I offered to help Periki Remarro in whatever way was necessary—not because I have any great love for that silly peninsula of yours, but because I want to see Lerrit great again. That isn't going to happen as long as those inbred mutants are in power."

"So you've been working to undermine them from within?" Kira said.

"Something like that, yes. It's been a bit of a chore, but I thought the end was near. Avtra is sterile, you see, and so can't produce any heirs. I had hopes that the Syba dynasty would *finally* end its pathetic chokehold over my home." He sighed. "This ridiculous alliance with the Bajora changes all *that,* of course. The Bajora know damn well that Prince Idiot is the last of his moronic line, and they plan to use this alliance to gain a toehold so they can take over once the Crown Imbecile dies." Moloki unsheathed the sword he had in a belt sheath. "You'll need this more than I will."

Kira took it and hefted it. It was a pretty standard design, average balance, nothing spectacular. *But it beats being unarmed.*

She looked at Torrna, who was now sweating rather more than was warranted by the temperature in the chilly, rank dungeon. "You okay?"

"No," Torrna said honestly, "but it doesn't matter. Moloki is right, we *must* return with this news or everything we've fought for will be lost!"

Chuckling, Moloki said, "You're as much of a crazed zealot as I suspected, General." He held up a hand to cut off Kira's protest. "I meant it as a compliment, my dear, believe me. I can say that as the craziest of crazed zealots. Now come, let us go over this map quickly before someone decides to check up on us . . ."

Chapter 7

In over thirty-three years of life, Kira Nerys had been sure many times that she was going to die.

Thus far, she'd been glad to have been wrong each time, but as she crouched in the half-meter of snow, sweat pouring from her brow even as she shivered uncontrollably, checking to see if anyone was coming up behind them, she was starting to wish she would die, just so her present hell would end.

First they had spent two days trudging through a swamp. She had done what she could to keep Torrna's arm from getting worse, but it was an uphill battle, and she was no medic. Plus, they had no food— Kira had many skills, but foraging had never been one of her best. They'd scavenged a few animals here and there, but most weren't anything larger than a *paluku*.

Resistance had been less than expected, but as Moloki had explained, the castle itself was not very well guarded. Support from the Bajora notwithstanding, in order to fight, in essence, a three-front war—on the ground against both Periki and Endtree, on the sea against their combined navies—the prince had limited resources to keep an eye on things at home. Kira and her newly acquired sword had been able to take care of the few guards they had seen with little difficulty.

Then they'd gotten to the mountains.

From humidity and high temperatures to snow and frigidity. From her old wound feeling just fine to her arm stiffening up from the cold. And now, quite possibly, coming down with pneumonia.

If Julian were here, he'd give me a shot of something, and I'd be fine. Of course, I'd have to listen to a lecture about not taking better care of myself.

She shook her head. That part of her life was over now. She was here, and she had a duty to perform. The Prophets sent her here for a reason.

Right. To die on a mountain with a blowhard general who got himself captured, and was only able to escape imprisonment thanks to a spy. Makes perfect sense.

Sighing, Kira satisfied herself that they still weren't being pursued, despite the five corpses they had left behind in the castle and the obvious trail they had made through the swamp. She got up, hugged herself with her arms (wincing in pain from the wound), and, shivering all the way, went back to the small inlet where she'd left Torrna.

"Dammit!" she yelled when she saw that Torrna had fallen asleep. He'd been fading in and out for quite some time. Kira's medical knowledge was limited, but even she knew that going into shock would be deadly.

She slapped his face a few times. "Torrna. Torrna! Dammit, Antosso, *wake up!*"

He blinked a few times. *"Ash—Ashla?"* he said in as weak a voice as she'd ever heard him use.

"Yes, it's me," she said, plastering an encouraging smile to her face, hoping her teeth weren't chattering too obviously. "We're still not being followed. And we've only got a few more kilometers to go. Think you're up to it?"

He nodded. "I think so. I just—*arrrrrgh!*"

Torrna had started to rise, then collapsed back to the snow-covered ground. "Sorry," he said through clenched teeth. "Keep forgetting that the arm doesn't really work."

"Let me take a look at it," Kira said, moving as if to pull back his cloak—stolen off one of the guards they'd killed on the way out.

With his good arm, Torrna grabbed Kira's wrist. "No!" He took a breath. "I'm sorry, *Ashla,* but you fussing over it isn't going to change

117

the fact that it feels like someone's driven a flaming hot poker through my shoulder."

"Once we get back home—"

"It'll be too late, then. *Ashla*—I need you to cut the damned thing off."

Kira laughed derisively. "Antosso, I'm not a surgeon. And I don't have anything to staunch the bleeding or cauterize the wound with. If I cut your arm off now, you'll bleed to death." *Not to mention that I'm shivering so much that I'll probably cut off your head by mistake . . .*

"And if you don't, I'll die from the infection. You yourself said that was a risk."

"A risk means the possibility of success. If I just hack your arm off right now with no alcohol, no bandages, no cauterizing agent—"

"All right! You've made your point." Smiling grimly, Torrna added, "I suppose this means I'll just have to make it back to Perikia, then."

Kira just nodded, and helped him to his feet.

They trudged their way through the snow-covered region, climbing over outcroppings, under crevices, and through chest-high snowdrifts.

She didn't know how long it was before she drained the water supply. Or, for that matter, when the blisters started breaking out all over her skin. She didn't have the wherewithal to check her tricorder to see how bad the radiation was. Every fiber of her being was focused on the overwhelming task of putting one foot in front of the other.

How long ago was it that she had been trudging through the hot, arid wasteland of that theta-radiation-racked planet in the Delta Quadrant? Days? Months? Years? Now she was engaged in the same mindless task, staying focused solely on moving forward, ever forward, in the hopes of reaching her goal. Then it was to reach a gateway. Now it was to make it back to Perikia.

Of course, the gateway took her to Perikia. *Is there some kind of symbolism here?*

Or maybe it's just nonsense. Maybe all of this is. Maybe I'm just here because it's where the gateway sent me. There's no purpose, no road the Prophets have put me on, I'm just here because some portal built by a bunch of aliens hundreds of thousands of years ago happened to show up when I needed it to get off a planet.

She closed her eyes and then opened them. *Focus,* she thought. *Just put one foot in front of the other and try not to think about the fact that your internal temperature is skyrocketing while your external one is plummetting. At this rate, I'll explode by nightfall . . .*

Kira trudged her way through the snow, willing the feeling to stay in her feet even though they were starting to numb again—the last time they did, they had stopped in the crevice.

"Yet your gods cast you out."

"Not my gods. Only a few men and women who claim to represent them."

Kira had no idea why the conversation she and Taran'atar had had in the *Euphrates* was coming back to her, but she tried to banish it from her head. "Shut up!" she cried.

"What?" Torrna asked from behind her.

"Nothing," Kira said, embarrassed. *Great, now I'm yelling at the voices in my head.*

"We will make it, *Ashla.* We *must.* There is no other way—if we do not, Perikia will be lost. It's *our* land—the Lerrit do not belong there, and I'll do everything I can to keep them out! But we can't do it if we don't get Moloki's information back to the prefect."

Kira looked back at Torrna, and saw the look of determination on his face even through the snow and facial hair, through the bruises, and through the pain he felt.

And she felt ashamed for doubting.

"We'll make it," she repeated.

One foot in front of the other, she thought. *You can do it. We can do it. We'll make it back.*

Half an hour later, she collapsed face-first into the snow.

Chapter 8

"Major?"

"Sir?"

"Tell me another story."

. . .

"While you had your weapons to protect you, all I had was my faith—and my courage. Walk with the Prophets, child. I know I will."

. . .

"I was there."

"Sir?"

"B'hala. It was the eve of the Peldor Festival. I could hear them ringing the temple chimes."

"You were dreaming."

"No! I was there! I could smell the burning bateret *leaves—taste the incense on the wind. I was standing in front of the obelisk, and as I looked up, for* one moment, *I understood it all! B'hala—the Orbs—the Occupation—the discovery of the wormhole—the coming war with the Dominion . . ."*

. . .

"A people can be defined by where they come from. Who the Bajorans are is shaped in part by our world. It's part of what ties us to the Prophets. The Cardassians didn't belong there, so I fought them. All my life, I've fought for *Bajor because that is* my *unit."*

"You believe caring for your home brings you closer to your gods?"

"I suppose that's one way of looking at it."

"Yet your gods cast you out."

"Not my gods. Only a few men and women who claim to represent them."

. . .

"Why have you taken this woman's body?"

"This vessel is willing. The Reckoning—it is time."

"The Reckoning—what is it?"

"The end, or the beginning."

. . .

"But what do the locusts represent? And why Cardassia—?"

"You were dreaming—and dreams don't always make sense."

"This was no dream!"

. . .

"The captain is not going to die. He is the Emissary, the Prophets will take care of him."

"With all due respect, Major, I'd rather see Julian take care of him."

"Chief, I know you're worried, but the Prophets are leading the Emissary on this path for a reason."

"Do not attempt to convince them, Major—they cannot understand."

"Since when did you believe in the Prophets?"

"What I believe in—is faith. Without it, there can be no victory. If the captain's faith is strong, he will prevail."

"It's not much to bet his life on."

"You're wrong—it's everything."

. . .

"Major?"

"Sir?"

"Tell me another story."

. . .

"Nerys?"

Kira's eyes fluttered awake. "Where—where am—?"

"You're back home."

She didn't recognize the face. "Who—who are you—where—?"

"You're in the infirmary—"

Julian?

"—at Fort Tendro."

No, Fort Tendro's on the outskirts of the peninsula—practically the front lines. That's where Torrna and I were headed.

She looked up to see a pleasant, round face, partially obscured by a wispy white beard and equally wispy white hair. "I'm Dr. Maldik," he said. "How are you feeling?"

"Thirsty. And warm."

Maldik smiled. "That's good. Both very encouraging signs."

"Wait a minute!" Kira cried out as Maldik started to walk away. "What about Torrna? We were in the mountains, and—"

"Yes, you were in the mountains." Maldik turned back around. "Almost died there, too, based on the shape you two were in when you got here."

Pouncing on the words "you two," Kira said, "Antosso—General Torrna. Where is he?"

Tugging on his beard, Maldik said, "He's already gone back to the capital. You and he had been declared dead by the Lerrit, you see— they claimed to have executed you. It therefore came as something of a surprise to see him stumbling into the fort, carrying you on his right shoulder."

That bastard, Kira thought. *Avtra must've been annoyed that he didn't get his stadium receipts, so he decided to get some propaganda value out of pretending to kill us.* Musing over her present condition, she thought, *Of course, he came pretty close to calling it right that we were dead. . . .*

"In any case, he left immediately to pass on some news or other about the Lerrit, and also to let his wife and children know he was alive."

Letting out a breath, Kira said, "Lyyra must have been devastated."

"I wouldn't know. Oh, the general did ask me to pass on a message."

Kira gave Maldik a questioning glance.

The doctor tugged on his beard some more. "He said, and I think I'm quoting this precisely, 'Thank her for me.' "

Snorting, Kira said, "He's thanking me? What did I do, besides fall on my face?"

"Well, from what he said, you didn't actually come out and tell him you were dying of pneumonia while you were stupidly trudging through freezing mountains after wading hip-deep in a swamp."

In a weak voice, Kira said, "I didn't want to worry him."

Another beard-tug. "No, better to wait until you fall unconscious and then completely frighten him. Yes, good point, much better than simply worrying him."

Kira ignored the barb, instead asking, "What about his arm? Were you able to save it?"

"Barely. You did a good job of keeping the wound clean. If you'd continued your summer stroll for much longer, it would've been infected, but he got the two of you here in time." One last beard-tug, then: "Enough gossip. You need your rest."

"I'm fine," Kira said, and she started to sit up. The room proceeded to leap around, whirl in circles, and generally behave insanely—until she lay back down, and then everything was fine. "On the other hand, maybe rest isn't a bad idea."

In a tone that sounded irritatingly like Julian at his most smug, Maldik said, "Soldiers make such *wonderful* patients. Try listening periodically, it'll do you wonders."

Chapter 9

Kira spent what felt like an eternity on her cot. Every once in a while she was able to sit up, but never for very long.

As time went on, news from the front lines, and from the capital, came in the form of messengers. Admiral Inna led a convoy of ships to the Kendra Valley River in an attempt to cut off the Bajora's supply lines. Natlar also sent an envoy to the Bajora, asking them to cease their support of Lerrit.

It turned out that the battle at Barlin Field had been more decisive than Kira and Torrna had realized, busy as they were being captured. It had been a major victory, and led to the complete reclamation of not only Makar Province, but also most of the Lonnat Valley.

By the time Kira was well enough to travel, a ship was coming down the coast—the fort was located near the Korvale Ocean—to bring injured troops home. Being, in essence, an injured troop as well, Kira went along.

The captain of the ship was a *very* short, no-nonsense woman named Tunhal Din. Kira noticed that she wore an earring in her right ear. "Who the hell're you?" was her way of introducing herself.

"Kira Nerys. I'm General Torrna's adjutant."

"Didn't know he had one. Well, find yourself somewhere to sleep. If you get sick, do it over the edge or clean it up yourself."

"How's the fighting going?"

Tunhal shrugged. "We haven't surrendered yet."

Kira had never traveled much by sea. Her initial assumption that it would be much like flying in an atmospheric craft turned out to be optimistic. She managed not to throw up, but that only through a supreme effort of will.

When they came around the bend into sight of Natlar Port, she had other reasons for being ill.

The port was on fire.

She stood at the fore of the ship, next to the wheel, watching in shock. Tunhal was next to her. "Well, that was damn stupid o' them Lerrits."

Kira looked at her. "What do you mean?"

"Port's what makes this land so damn desirable. Why'd they cannon it to smithereens like that? If they're trying to win back the land, why screw up the most valuable part of it?"

"It depends on your goal," Kira, who had spent her formative years as a terrorist, said after a moment's thought. "If you're trying to take land from the enemy, you're right, it is stupid. But if you're trying to do damage to your enemy where it hurts the most, that's the thing to do."

Tanhul looked at her like she had grown a second head. "That's insane."

Kira had to bite back her instinctive response: *You say that because the tactics of terrorism haven't really been invented here yet. They haven't needed to be. And you should thank the Prophets for that every night before you go to bed.*

Instead, she said, "It's actually a good sign, believe it or not."

"How's that, exactly?"

"They wouldn't have attacked the port directly if they had any intention of taking it. This was the final defiant act of a navy that knows it's lost. A kind of 'if I can't have it, no one can' gesture. This probably means the war's going well for our side."

"Your definition of 'well' differs from mine," Tanhul said dryly.

There were no obvious piers available for docking—half of them were damaged beyond usefulness, and the rest were occupied. The marina itself was a mass of chaotic activity, with small fires being put out and people coughing from the smoke.

Someone noticed them eventually, though, as a small rowboat approached the spot where Tanhul had dropped anchor. Kira recognized its occupant as the assistant dockmaster, Hiran. As he pulled up alongside the ship, Tanhul ordered a ladder lowered for him.

"Good to have you back, ma'am," he said upon sighting Kira as he arrived on deck. Then he turned to Tanhul. "I'm sorry, Captain, but as you can see, we're a bit shorthanded."

"I've got wounded here."

Hiran frowned. "Let me see what I can do. I might be able to get a few skiffs over to offload the worst of them." He turned to Kira. "Ma'am, you should know that General Torrna's in his office. You might want to see him."

Kira didn't like the tone in Hiran's voice. "Is he all right?"

"I really think you should see him, ma'am." Hiran's tone was more urgent. Kira also knew him well enough to know that he was unlikely to say anything else.

She accompanied him back on the rowboat to the marina. As Hiran stroked the oars, Kira asked, "What happened here?"

"Lerrit's last stand, you could say, ma'am," Hiran said, almost bitterly. "General Torrna pretty much beat them on the land. See, on his way back from Fort Tendro, he came across General Takmor's regiment—but Takmor'd been killed."

Damn, Kira thought. *She was one of the good ones.* "I'd heard that she was the one who reclaimed Sempa Province."

"Actually, that was General Torrna, ma'am. The general, see—well, he just plowed on in and led them to victory. They were ready to call it quits, but he rallied 'em, and they took Sempa back. Meantime, Admiral Inna came back here when she found out that the Lerrit Navy was gonna throw their whole armada at us."

Kira looked at the smoky, ruined port. "Looks like they did."

"Oh, the admiral, she threw back pretty good, too. Cost her her life, mind, but—"

"Inna's dead?"

Hiran nodded. "Just what we needed after everything else."

"What everything else? Hiran, I've been laid up at Tendro, and obviously I haven't been getting all the news."

"Oh, ma'am, I'm sorry," Hiran said in a sedate tone. "I guess you didn't hear that Prefect Natlar was killed, too. See, same time the Lerrit Navy did their last stand here, the Lerrit Army did likewise in the capital. Didn't work, of course—thanks to the blockade, they were underfed, understaffed, and underarmed. We beat 'em back mighty good, truth be told, but—" He sighed. "Not without a cost, if you know what I mean."

Kira shook her head. "So we won?"

"Yes, ma'am, if you can call this a victory."

They arrived at the marina. Kira disembarked from the rowboat, and couldn't help contrasting this with the last time she set foot on the dock. Then, the sun was shining, a stiff breeze was blowing, carrying the smell of fish and seawater, with the Korvale Ocean a sparkling green in contrast to the dull-but-solid brown of the dock's wood. Now, the sun was obscured by billowing smoke, and the wind carried only the smell of that smoke, occasionally broken by the stench of blood and death.

Then she saw the bodies.

They were arranged in a row just past the marina in a ditch that hadn't been there before. Many wore Perikian uniforms; many more wore Lerrit uniforms. A few—though even a few were too many—wore civilian clothing.

Nerys walked into the other chamber, Furel right behind her. Kira Taban's body was laid out on the pallet. She had seen far too many dead bodies not to know one now.

Her father was dead.

"He died calling your name."

It took an effort for Kira to pry her horrified eyes away from the array of corpses and continue her journey to the office where she and Torrna had spent so much time together.

The small wooden structure had held up remarkably well during the attack—only a few scorch marks differentiated it from Kira's memory of the building. Several familiar faces greeted her hastily; others ignored her completely. One person, a merchant who had set up a shop specializing in merchandise from Endtree, muttered, "Thank the Prophets she's here. Maybe she can talk some sense into him."

Nobody sat at the sergeant's desk.

She entered Torrna's tiny office. The general sat behind his rickety wooden desk, which was piled top to bottom with enough refuse and detritus to be a serious fire hazard, given the conditions outside. The small bar that sat under the window was full of empty, overturned, and broken bottles. Kira was therefore not surprised that the smoky stench that had filled her nostrils since Tunhal's ship came around the bend was now being overpowered by several different types of alcoholic beverage. At least three more bottles were visible on the desk, not to mention the large glass that Torrna Antosso clutched in his right hand.

The smoke obscured the view of the mainland, as it obscured everything right now.

The general looked like a zombie. His eyes stared unblinking, straight ahead. If not for the smell of alcohol—not to mention Torrna's atheism—Kira would have thought he was in the midst of a *pagh'tem'far* vision.

"They're *dead,*" Torrna said without preamble, his voice barely more than a monotone. "Dead dead dead *dead.*"

"I know, Hiran told me about the prefect and Admiral Inna. But—"

Torrna made a sweeping gesture, knocking over one of the empty bottles. "No! Not them. I mean, they're dead, too, but tha's not who I mean."

"Who's—"

"Lyyra! She's *dead!*"

Kira found herself unable to reply at first. She had been prepared to console Torrna on the deaths of Natlar and Inna even as she herself struggled with the fact that the serene prefect and the no-nonsense admiral were gone.

"What about the kids, are they—"

"They're dead, too. All of 'em, dead dead dead dead *dead.* An' they didn' know."

Frowning, Kira prompted, "Didn't know what?"

"Th'I was alive! B'fore I could get home I found Takmor's regimen'."

"I heard."

"By time I got home, they were dead—an' I never got to tell 'em I was alive!"

"They probably found out from the dispatches," Kira said, not sure if, in the chaos of the end of the war, anyone would have the wherewithal to contact Lyyra about so trivial a matter as the fact that her reported-dead husband was still alive. *Especially if she and the kids*

*were close enough to the fighting to be killed. Hell, knowing Lyyra,
she was right in the midst of it. She was always a healer at heart.*

"Doesn' matter. Nothin' matters. They want me to take over now't
war's over. Ain't gonna do it."

"What do you mean?"

"Gonna drink m'self to death. If that doesn' work, I'm gonna cut
m'throat. Don't wanna live in this world without 'er."

*. . . Odo "putting on" the tuxedo for the last time before descending
into the Great Link . . .*

"Listen to me, Antosso, you can't just give up."

"Why not?" He pounded his fist on the desk, rattling the bottles and
knocking several papers off. "Haven' I done enough?"

*. . . Bareil, his brain barely functioning, slowly fading away on the
infirmary biobed . . .*

"No, you haven't! You've spent all this time fighting, you *can't* give
up now! Perikia *needs* you! They couldn't have fought this war without you, and they certainly wouldn't have won it without you."

"Doesn' matter. Without Lyyra—"

*. . . Captain Sisko—the Emissary—traveling to the fire caves, never
to be seen again . . .*

"There are still hundreds of people out there who fought and died
for Perikia—including Lyyra. Without Natlar, without Takmor, without Inna—they're going to need your strength. They need the man
who beat back the Lerrit Army. They need the man who trudged
through the swamp and the mountains to get home. They need *you.*"

. . . her father lying dead in the caves of Dakhur Hills . . .

Torrna shook his head. "Can't do it. Jus' can't."

Snarling, Kira got up and went to the other side of the desk. She
grabbed Torrna by the shirt, and tried to haul him to his feet.
Unfortunately, while they were the same height, he was quite a bit
larger—and, in his drunken state, so much dead weight.

*. . . Opaka lying dead after a shuttle crash on some moon in the
Gamma Quadrant . . .*

"Get up!"

"Wha' for?"

"I said get *up!*"

. . . Furel and Lupaza, only on the station to protect her, being blown into space by an embittered, vengeance-seeking Cardassian . . .

Torrna stumbled to his feet. Then he fell back into the chair. Kira yanked on his arm, which seemed to be enough to get him to clamber out of the chair again.

She led him outside. She propped him up on one of the wooden railings that separated the small office building area from the main marina and pointed. "You see that?"

"I don't see anythin' but—"

Losing all patience, Kira screamed. "The bodies! Look at the bodies! Those people died fighting for Perikia! So did Natlar, so did Inna—and so did Lyyra. You have no right to give up now—because if you do, Lerrit has won. There's no one else who can unite these people the way you can now—you're a hero! Without you, they'll fall apart, and either Prince Avtra or the Bajora wil be able to come right in and take over."

Torrna stared straight ahead for several minutes. Then he turned back to Kira.

When she first entered his office, Torrna's eyes were glazed over. Now, they were filled with sadness.

In as small a voice as he'd used when they were traveling through the mountains, Torrna said, "I'm sorry."

Kira remembered that the ground-based gateways tended to do one of two things: jump randomly from vista to vista every couple of seconds, or, like the one at Costa Rocosa, stay fixed on one location. This one, however, was different: it jumped back and forth between only two destinations.

The first was ops on Deep Space 9.

The other was the comforting light that Kira Nerys knew in her heart belonged to the Prophets.

As she stared at the pathetic, drunken figure of Torrna Antosso standing in the midst of the wreckage of Natlar Port, Kira at once realized that she made the right and the wrong choice in stepping through the gateway when she did.

This, she thought, *is me. And whether or not Torrna decides to drink himself into oblivion or takes charge of the Perikian government— doesn't matter.*

Kira walked away, then. Away from Torrna Antosso, away from Natlar Port, away from the Korvale Ocean, away from the Perikian Peninsula.

Or, more accurately, under it.

She'd been in these caves before. The last time was when the Circle had kidnapped and tortured her thirty thousand years from now. She had no idea why she came down here, and yet she was never more sure of anything in her life.

Despite the fact that the Denorios Belt's tachyon eddies prevented any gateways from being constructed within ten light-years of Bajor, Kira was not surprised by the fact that an active gateway was present in the caves. She didn't know where it would lead her, but she felt supremely confident as she stepped through it, ready to face what lay beyond . . .

Chapter 10

Kira Nerys stared at the galaxy.

She had to look up to see it in its entirety, its bright face filling half the sky. She'd seen images of the galaxy before, simulations and holos taken from deep-space probes launched centuries ago by any number of worlds. But nothing prepared her for the sight before her now.

The galaxy stared back down at her, a still and silent maelstrom that seemed to scrutinize her as she stood beneath it, and she knew that it was no simulation. She was as far from home as she'd ever been, and might ever be, and under the unblinking eye of the immense double spiral, Kira Nerys felt very, very small.

She was only partly aware of her surroundings: the smooth circular floor beneath her feet, the central console with its brown-and-blue color scheme and alien markings that registered dimly as matching the known designs of the Iconians.

And no walls. Only sky. She stood in a room without shadows, lit by a hundred billion suns.

Must be a forcefield, but—

"Ah, there you are."

She felt the voice more than heard it, as if it came from within her. Kira wanted to turn around to respond, but found herself transfixed by the starscape.

A finger seemed to appear from nowhere and point at a spot in the lower left quadrant of the vista spread out before Kira. The voice said, "It's here."

Kira finally tore her gaze away from the view and followed the finger back up the hand and arm it was connected to, and finally to the body. The figure was huge, though definitely bipedal and apparently humanoid, standing at well over two and a half meters tall, dwarfing even the immense Hirogen hunter that she and Taran'atar had faced in the Delta Quadrant. He—the voice *sounded* male, at least—wore a maroon cloak with a hood that obscured his features.

"Wh—what?"

"The world you come from is here. I believe you refer to it as Bajor."

"Who are you?"

The figure hesitated. "You might say I'm an emissary of the people who built this outpost, but that might have unfortunate connotations for you. Suffice it to say that I am the custodian of this place."

"You're an Iconian?"

There was a movement inside the cloak that Kira supposed could have been a nod. "You'll be pleased to know that I was able to cure you of that unfortunate energy."

Energy? It took Kira a moment to realize that he was referring to the theta-radiation poisoning. She had been on that arid desert of a planet in the Delta Quadrant, theta radiation eating away at her, when the gateway beckoned. Her tricorder had told her that the radiation levels were fatal. . . .

Of course, the rational part of her brain said as she looked down and saw that she no longer wore the ancient clothing of Bajor's past *(did I ever?)* but was instead in her sand-soiled Militia uniform.

It was some kind of dream, she thought, *that's all. Or maybe a* pagh'tem'far. *That would certainly explain—*

She cut the thought short as she felt a mild stiffness in her left arm. Looking down, she saw the badly healed wound she'd received the day they drove the Lerrit Army out of the capital city. "How did—how did this get here?" She pointed to the wound.

The hood tilted a little to one side. "Presumably you received it at an earlier date."

"You're a big help," she muttered.

"I assume that you wish to take the gift that has been given to you and then go home?"

Kira almost asked the figure what he meant by that. But duty took over. Like Torrna Antosso, she had a role to play, a duty to perform, and a planet to defend—regardless of what obstacles had been placed in her path.

"Actually, I need to return to Europa Nova. I made a promise that I would do everything I could—"

Before she could finish the sentence, the custodian drifted—*walk* was too clumsy a word to describe how he moved—over to the center console.

"Ah, I see. One of our *hezlat* gateways is in orbit of that planet," he said after touching one of the triangular controls.

"*Hezlat?*" Kira asked as she approached. Two small holographic displays hovered on either side of the blue globe atop the console, each showing a star system. The sizes and magnitudes of the two stars matched those of Europa Nova's star and the star where they'd found the tanker in the Delta Quadrant.

"Many different types of gateways were constructed over time," the custodian said, "some large and inelegant, some small and functional, others that could be held in the palm of one's hand. The *hezlat*s were among the first, and also among the largest. Let's see, this one is stable—it links System X27πL with System J55ΔQ."

The custodian seemed to be just staring at the display, so Kira helped him along. "Someone decided to dump theta radiation into that—that *hezlat* of yours. We had to evacuate everyone from the planet on the other side before the radiation levels became fatal."

"Yes . . . I see that now. But there is something blocking part of the gateway."

Thank the Prophets, the Euphrates *is still there.* "Yes, that's one of our vessels. That's how we travel, by ship—and I used mine to block the radiation from coming through and—"

"I understand, Colonel. I observe your ships traversing the galaxy all the time from here. It is not a pastime shared by all my people."

"There are more of you, then?"

"Yes. Some of them are dealing with this crisis now. I have faith in the Sentries."

Kira had no idea what that meant, but she didn't want to get off topic. "What about Europa Nova?"

"Hm?"

"System—" She peered at the console screen, but couldn't read it. "X2-whatever," she said. Finally, she pointed at the holographic display. "That one!"

"Oh, yes. I am searching now. Ah, there we are. System O22ψT has a star that will suffice for the purpose."

A third star-system image appeared in the holographic display. From the brightness and magnitude, it had an O-type star.

"I can reprogram this particuar *hezlat* gateway to transport the matter that is emitting the energy on both sides into the star in System O22ψT. The star there will render the energy inert." He turned to Kira. "I will also remove the object blocking the gateway. Would you like it in System O22ψT, System X27πL, or System J55ΔQ?"

"Uh, the second one," Kira said. "Is the place where you're sending the waste uninhabited?"

"Of course," the custodian said as if the answer were self-evident. Kira had no such assurances, though. After all, according to most of the legends, the Iconians were conquerors.

The custodian made some adjustments on the panel. "I assume by the state you arrived in that your species is vulnerable to this type of energy."

Assuming that he meant theta radiation, Kira said, "Yes, very vulnerable."

"In that case, you must be careful. The gateway can remove the matter, but some of the energy will remain around that planet you were concerned with. You say it was evacuated?"

Kira nodded.

"Repopulating it will be a challenge."

"Like I said—I made a promise."

Again, the custodian made a gesture that might have been interpreted as a nod, then said, "It is time for you to leave." The Iconian touched a series of triangular panels. A blue light shot out from the globe and then a gateway opened near the edge of the floor. Through it, Kira could see the bustle of ops, with Dax giving orders to Sergeant Gan.

She looked at her host. "We thought there was a natural phenomenon preventing your gateways from functioning in the space around my planet," Kira said. "That isn't completely true, is it?"

"No," the Iconian confirmed. "But we respect the beings who watch your worlds. And we long ago promised never to interfere with them."

"Worlds . . . ?" Kira asked.

"Farewell, Colonel."

A million questions on her lips, it took a conscious effort to turn toward the gateway. Taking a deep breath, Kira walked around the console.

Before stepping into the gateway, she took one last look at the immense galaxy above her.

She once again found the spot where the custodian had indicated that Bajor was. From there she traced an imaginary line to the region she knew was the Delta Quadrant, and wondered whether or not Taran'atar had survived his battle with the Hirogen. Then her eyes drifted to the Gamma Quadrant, to the expanse that contained the Dominion, and the Founders' world.

You don't look so far away from here, Odo.

The custodian waited patiently while she took it all in, and eventually she turned away from the sprawling mass of stars.

Enough self-indulgence. It's past time I went back to work.

But as she approached the gateway, it seemed the custodian had one more thing to tell her. "One of the things that doomed the Iconian Empire, Colonel, was that the gateway technology meant that we could no longer travel. We lost sight of the journey in our desire to achieve our destination. Don't make that mistake."

Kira smiled at the cloaked figure. "I won't. And thank you."

Then she stepped through the gateway, knowing full well what lay beyond.

Chapter 11

Ezri Dax had, Kira knew, centuries of life experience thanks to the Dax symbiont, and she also knew that, among her nine lifetimes, she had probably seen everything.

So seeing her jump up, scream, and drop the padd she was holding when Kira walked into ops made for a fairly amusing sight.

As usual with the gateways, there was no feeling of transition from one point to the other. It was as if ops had been the next room over from the extragalactic outpost. The only change was that the Iconian outpost's gravity was a bit lighter than that of DS9, so Kira stumbled a bit upon her arrival.

Dax blinked several times. "Colonel?"

"Yes, Lieutenant, it's me."

Gan said, somewhat redundantly, "You're alive."

Kira resisted the obvious rejoinders. "Report."

"Europa Nova has been completely evacuated. Most of the refugees are on Bajor. The station's also filled almost to capacity. Lieutenant Ro, Sergeant Ychell, and Quark have returned, and Ro says she's got some good news regarding the Orion Syndicate. And Taran'atar's in the infirmary."

Kira's eyes widened. "He's all right?"

Dax winced. "I wouldn't go that far, but he'll recover. Whatever he fought gave him quite a beating." Then she smiled. "Apparently enough to cause delusions, since he reported that you were dead."

Probably didn't read my life signs on the planet and made assumptions, Kira thought. *Given the radiation levels, I can't really blame him.* "Let's just say I was able to make the gateway technology work for me. Go on."

Dax continued with her report, including the fact that the *Defiant* had gone off to rendezvous with the *Marco Polo* to help implement a plan to deal with the gateways; that the *Trager* was attached to Upper Pylon 1, Gul Macet having been invited to stay for a bit by Vaughn; the continued presence of Councillor Charivretha zh'Thane on board the station; and the fact that Lieutenant Bowers had taken the *Rio Grande* back to Europa Nova to keep an eye on the gateway there.

"It's been taken care of," Kira said. "There won't be any more anti-matter waste in orbit of Europa Nova at all. Send a message to Bowers; tell him to do a full sensor sweep to determine how much contamination is still there. If we're lucky, it's little enough that we can work on repopulating sooner rather than later." She smiled. "And tell Bowers when he's finished to tow the *Euphrates* back. It should be in orbit." *With,* she recalled, remembering the shield enhancer she had salvaged from the tanker, *a nice piece of new technology.*

"Yes, sir," Dax said, moving toward a console. Then she stopped, and smiled. "It's good to have you back, Nerys. I don't think this place could've taken losing another commanding officer."

"Good to *be* back, Ezri. Don't worry, I'm not going anywhere. I've still got too much work to do."

Chapter 12

Kira sat in her office, looking over the historical records she had been able to scare up from the Perikian region. There was distressingly little from as long as thirty thousand years ago. She had found no record whatsoever of the Lerrit, aside from some archaeological indications of some kind of empire from that time period that looked Lerrit-like to Kira.

Kira had taken care of a variety of administrative duties—not to mention assuring everyone from station personnel to First Minister Shakaar that she was, in fact, alive, contrary to reports—and also been sure to visit Taran'atar in the infirmary. He was fairly weak, but recovering quickly, though Julian had made noises about even laboratory-bred supersoldiers needing their rest when they have the stuffing beaten out of them. For his part, Taran'atar had only one thing to say: "It is good that we have both reclaimed our lives."

"You don't know the half of it," Kira had said.

Afterward, she returned to her office and tried to find out what she could about the Perikian region thirty thousand years ago.

The name of Torrna Antosso did come up in several texts, as did that of others with that family name. Historians had debated just who Antosso was and what form his apparently tremendous influence had been in the peninsula, but given the number of landmarks and streets and such that had been named for him or other members of the Torrna family, it was obvious to Kira that he had taken her advice.

Assuming I was ever really there, she thought, as she rubbed her left arm, which still had the scar. Julian had offered to remove it, but she had refused.

Shutting down the computer terminal, Kira stared straight ahead for a moment, then picked up the baseball.

Benjamin Sisko had always kept that baseball on his desk. The central element of a human game that he'd been inordinately fond of, the white spheroid with red stitching was a symbol of Sisko's presence. When the station had been taken by the Dominion during the war, Sisko had deliberately left the baseball behind as a message to the occupying forces that he planned to come back—a promise he had fulfilled.

Even though the station was now hers to command, Kira had not been able to bring herself to remove the baseball. She wasn't sure why she had left it there.

No, I know why. I kept thinking in the back of my head that the Emissary was going to return—hoping that he'd return and take the burden off of me, that he'd take the station back just like he did two years ago, and everything would be back to normal.

But that's not going to happen. This station is mine, now. I may have lost the Emissary, Odo, Jast, and the kai, I may be Attainted—but I've got responsibilities, just like Torrna did.

And dammit, I'm going to live up to them.

She opened a drawer in the desk and placed the baseball in it.

I'll hold it for you, Benjamin, for when you come back.

But I need this to be my office now.

She got up and went back into ops, knowing her journey was far from over.

Two gates for ghostly dreams there are: One gateway of honest horn, and one of ivory. Issuing by the ivory gate are dreams of glimmering illusion, fantasies, but those that come through solid polished horn may be borne out, if mortals only know them.

—Homer, *The Odyssey*

IN THE QUEUE

Christie Golden

Chapter 1

"Intruder alert!" The voice was rich, deep, and oh so wonderfully familiar.

Janeway stared, almost unable to bear the joy of it, at the familiar surroundings of a starship. Not just any starship, either. With Barkley/Fluffy still wriggling in her arms, she turned and beamed at Captain Jean-Luc Picard.

"Captain Kathryn Janeway requesting permission to come aboard," she stated in a voice that, despite her best efforts, quavered. "Belatedly."

That patrician mien softened and melted into a warm, surprised smile.

"Kathryn," Picard rumbled, rising and staring at her. "My God. You are literally the last person I expected to ever see on my bridge." He strode to where she stood beside the turbolift, hand outstretched. "Welcome home, my dear. Welcome, welcome home."

Janeway let Barkley jump to the floor, where he obediently plopped his behind down in a formal sit/stay right beside her left foot. She moved forward quickly and gratefully took the extended hand, feeling it close, warm and strong, about her own slender fingers. Tears welled in her eyes, and for once, she let them come.

"I can't believe this," she stammered. She heard voices talking in murmured excitement, felt rather than saw the strong presence of Will Riker loom up beside her. She had met him once before, when Q had transported him to *Voyager* as a witness in the trial of the alien who later took the name Quinn . . . and not long after that, took his own life. Riker, of course, would have no memory of the encounter. She turned to address him. She'd forgotten what a large man he was. Shaking and laughing, she wiped at her wet eyes while extending a hand.

"Captain Kathryn Janeway. We've met. I'll tell you about it later. I can't believe this," she repeated.

"So, Captain, I'm delighted that you're here, but I'd like to know why and how," said Picard, stepping back and letting her regain control. "The last we heard, you were still in the Delta Quadrant. Operation Pathfinder has only just reported making contact with you. We'd hoped that you'd make it home one of these days, but I confess, manifesting on my bridge like some sort of ghost was not what I had expected."

He eyed the small animal. "And I see you've brought a friend," he added, a hint of disapproval creeping into his sonorous voice.

Fluffy barked and wagged his tail.

"It's a long story," said Janeway, clearing her throat and trying to recover her usual decorum. "A very long story."

"One which I and Starfleet Command will be very eager to hear," said Picard.

Janeway took a breath, preparing for a debriefing, which, if she knew Picard, he'd want to hear immediately, if not sooner. Instead, he did something which took her completely by surprise.

"Whatever it is, it can wait until you've had a chance to freshen up and eat something." She frowned and began to protest, but he held up a commanding hand. "I won't hear otherwise. I'm certain that whatever journey you and this creature have been on, it's been arduous and long."

She stared at him. Her "journey," or at least this most peculiar leg of it, had been approximately five minutes—most of which had been spent on Picard's own bridge. Mentally, she shrugged. Who was she to contradict Captain Picard on the bridge of the *Enterprise?*

"I'd consider it an honor if you would use my quarters," Picard continued. "Take all the time you need to refresh yourself. I'll meet you there in an hour or so for a bite to eat and I assure you I will be all ears, eager to hear about your adventures."

144

With that, he turned and resumed his seat. Will Riker was still standing beside her. With a grin, he made a mock bow.

"You're almost legendary in this quadrant now, Captain Janeway," said Riker. "I hope you'll afford me the honor of escorting you to Captain Picard's quarters?"

Janeway hesitated. She had no wish to appear discourteous, but she would have been much more comfortable sitting with Picard in his ready room, sipping coffee (he'd probably order that nasty Earl Grey tea he was so famous for drinking) and telling her fellow captain all about the gateway. Who knew how long it would be open? All the others had closed. Starfleet would certainly want to hear about them, and precious time was ticking by.

"Captain, I have no wish to appear ungrateful for your hospitality, but—"

"Then don't," said Picard, a touch irritably. "Go to my quarters, have a bit of a rest and a bath, and I'll meet you for dinner."

"Captain Picard—"

"Has spoken," said Riker smoothly. "Trust me, you won't do well to question him." Playfully he extended his arm. "Come on. Put aside the trappings of command for a little while. After more than five years lost at sea, you could use a little break and some pampering Starfleet-style."

Janeway was at a loss for words. There was no way she could continue contradicting Picard, certainly not in front of his crew. Finally, she nodded, and, uncomfortable with the gesture but not wishing to appear rude, took Riker's arm. They entered the turbolift, Fluffy trotting obediently beside her. As the doors hissed closed, she kept wondering why Picard hadn't debriefed her at once, especially after so extraordinary a materialization on his bridge. It was out of character for him.

But then, she had been gone a long time. She knew how people can and did change.

And frankly, a hot bath sounded wonderful.

"So what's this about you meeting me before?" asked Riker, breaking her reverie.

"You were on my ship. Courtesy of one Q," she said. Riker's blue eyes widened, and he laughed.

"That Q. Up to his old tricks, is he? I suppose he's gotten bored with dour old Jean-Luc."

Janeway raised an eyebrow at the familiar, almost condescending tone Riker used. She knew his reputation; "fun-loving" wouldn't be an inaccurate term to describe him, but she had expected more respect from a first officer toward his captain, especially in front of someone who outranked him.

"You were a key witness in a trial," she continued, trying to overlook Riker's faux pas. "Q brought you to my ship in order to testify for his side. Afterward, he returned you and wiped your memory of the incident."

That, she thought, ought to ruffle him. Instead, Riker laughed aloud. "Doesn't that bother you? That you were snatched against your will, transported halfway across the galaxy, and you don't even have a memory of it?"

"Not really. I mean, that's Q for you, isn't it? He's not all that bad. He always means well, even if sometimes he doesn't understand how things bother us humans."

She stared at him, then shrugged. "I guess I have been away a long time, if the first officer of the *Enterprise* harbors warm and fuzzy feeling toward Q."

Riker merely grinned.

Janeway had often lamented the fact that all other Starfleet vessels were equipped with sonic showers. The only bath that had been taken aboard *Voyager* had been indulged in by Neelix when he first came aboard her ship. He had been overwhelmed by the proliferation of water and had simply had to try the experience of actually immersing his entire body in the liquid.

She personally hadn't had a real, hot water bath since she and Chakotay had been left on that planet together, when they had been infected by a disease the Doctor couldn't cure and the only way to save both their lives was for them to remain on the planet where they'd been infected. He'd built her a bathtub, and my, how she had enjoyed it. There had been much about that time together she had enjoyed, and regretted leaving.

Janeway was surprised to discover that Picard's quarters had a tub. *Well,* she thought, *the* Enterprise *is the flagship. I would imagine Starfleet would think it a minor luxury for their esteemed Picard if he asked for it.*

There was even a bottle of bubble bath perched on the side. Janeway stifled a laugh at the thought of Picard in a bubble bath, but who was she to judge? She certainly had no compunction about using up a bit of his supply. She liberally poured the liquid into the hot water, shed her uniform, and stepped into the tub.

"Oh," she breathed. The pleasure was keen, almost painful. She lay back and enjoyed the hot water penetrating to her bones, and played lazily with the mounts of white, frothy bubbles. Laying her head against the tub's edge, she closed her eyes and drifted. . . .

"Mustn't stay in there too long," came Picard's booming voice. "You'll get all wrinkled."

Gasping, Janeway started awake. To her utter shock, Captain Jean-Luc Picard stood in the doorway to the bathing room, a smile on his lips, holding two glasses of wine. He was clad in loose-fitting white pants and a matching shirt that revealed small curls of gray hair. Comfortable-looking slippers adorned his feet.

Intellectually, Janeway knew the mound of bubbles shielded her body from his gaze, but that didn't matter.

"Captain, this is improper and inappropriate behavior. Please close the door." Her voice was icy, summoning all the dignity and confidence she could muster. Which, at this terribly awkward moment, wasn't a lot.

"All right," he said affably, stepped inside, and closed the door behind him. He stepped toward her, extending a wineglass. "This is a lovely merlot. I think you'll enjoy it."

Janeway snatched the nearest towel. Heedless of how wet it would get, she immediately wrapped it around her. "What the hell are you doing? I'm going to report this to Starfleet Command!"

"Oh, no, I don't think so," said Picard, leaning against the door and grinning.

"I do," Janeway stated. Dignity in every movement, she rose, clutching the sopping towel around her, and stepped for the door.

"You're late again, cadet."

Janeway blinked. She was no longer standing, naked save for a dripping wet towel, in Captain Picard's private bathroom, but in the doorway of a classroom. Standing at the desk was Professor Kerrigan, the woman who had become Janeway's personal bête noir. Janeway stared, first at Kerrigan, then at the sack full of padds she carried, then down at her own smaller, younger body.

"What's happening?" she whispered.

Kerrigan cleared her throat. The young Janeway looked up at her. "I said, you're late again, cadet. Do you *want* to add more homework?"

"S-sir, yes sir. I mean, no sir. . . ."

"Which is it, Janeway? I've told you before, just because your father is a notable figure in Starfleet doesn't mean you're going to simply ace this class."

"I—I'm late, yes sir, and no sir, I don't want to add more homework."

"Then take your seat." Kerrigan, all height and muscle and frosty blond hair, returned to her old-fashioned podium while Janeway stared aghast at the array of seats. Familiar faces stared back at her. Eddie Capshaw made his famous rubber face, crossing his eyes and sticking out his tongue. She had always thought it terribly immature behavior for a nineteen-year-old cadet, and it seemed even more so seen from her true forty-something perspective.

Which seat was hers? She'd be in for a special project if she kept standing in the doorway like an idiot—

"I'm a starship captain," she said softly, to herself. But Eddie Capshaw had heard the murmured comment and gaped.

"What was that, cadet?" Kerrigan's voice cut through her fog.

Fluffy. Where was the little animal? "Barkley. Fluffy," she called, and the class erupted in laughter.

"Silence!" ordered Kerrigan. The cadets tried to comply, but couldn't quite manage to completely eliminate a few stray snorts and snickers. "Cadet Janeway, take your seat. Now. And report to me after your classes today. I've got something special lined up for your detention."

At that moment, with a snicking sound of claws on smooth flooring, Fluffy/Barkley skidded around a corner and rushed up to her. Dropping the bag of padds, she scooped the animal up and felt him lick her face. Even though she clasped him to a petite, nineteen-year-old body, the memories of the true years were emblazoned in her mind. *Voyager.* Chakotay. Tuvok. All the rest of her incredible crew. The journey they had undergone, the losses, the tragedies and victories that had kept them going. That was what was real, was true and important, not this false classroom.

She turned to face Kerrigan. "You're a petty tyrant, Wendy Kerrigan. You were abusing your power for years before I got here and you're still doing it even in my imagination."

Kerrigan straightened to her full, imposing height of nearly six feet. "I hope you like civilian life, Janeway, because you're about this far from getting yourself expelled."

"I graduated with honors," Janeway retorted, warming to the task. "I have my own command, a crew that's as loyal and true to the ideals of Starfleet as you are bitter and false to them. I don't know why I haven't acted earlier. I'm going to see to it that you're fired. I'm going to tell them everything. The last thing impressionable young cadets need is someone like you beating all the life and enthusiasm out of them."

"You may leave, Janeway." Hate blazed in those eyes. Janeway lifted her chin and stared right back.

"I'll leave, all right. But I'll be back. You won't."

She turned and—

—stood at the front of the room. Twenty-six faces gazed up at her with rapt attention. Janeway smiled a little, then touched the holographic display unit.

"Who can tell me what this is?"

Twenty-six hands shot up. Janeway picked the shy little girl in the back. "Cadet Anson?"

"That's a Borg cube," the girl whispered, barely audible.

"Correct. And what is this?"

It was a loaded question. The image of Seven of Nine appeared, looking the way she had when she was still part of the collective. The bald head, the arrogant gaze, the fit body tightly swathed in black. More hands shot up.

"Cadet Garcia?"

"That's a Borg," he replied with confidence.

"You're right . . . and you're not right. Can anyone tell my why Garcia's identification is only partially correct?"

Now there were only a few hands. Janeway picked Cadet Bedony. "Yes, Cadet?"

"It's a Borg, but it's also your crew member Seven of Nine. Before you liberated her from the collective."

Janeway smiled. "That's right." She touched another button and a holographic Seven of Nine, most of her humanity restored, stood beside the image of her former self. Janeway had to chuckle at the reaction of some of the male cadets, and one or two of the females. Seven of Nine was indeed a strikingly attractive woman. She was almost unrecognizable as the drone she had been. Even though these cadets were familiar with her—who wasn't? Seven was the biggest celebrity of all of them from the minute they returned home— Janeway wasn't surprised that most of them had found her unrecognizable.

She continued her talk, showing images of Neelix and Kes, the Hirogen, the Vidiians, the Caatati, the Malons, and several of the other races *Voyager* had encountered during its amazing trek. Her mind drifted back to the day when she and her entire crew had been feted with a glorious parade in the heart of San Francisco.

Janeway frowned. Something was not right. She could remember the parade, but not preparing for it, nor what had happened afterward. She glanced down at her notes. They were all gibberish scribblings. There was not a single recognizable word on the padd. And beside the podium at which she stood sat a small doglike creature. When it caught her gaze, its tail began to thump happily.

"Barkley," she whispered.

Hands shot up. She looked up, confused. "What?"

"Reginald Barclay. The one who made contact with you through Pathfinder. He was the one who brought you home." Cadet M'Benga looked very pleased with herself.

Feeling somewhat dizzy, Janeway looked down at the creature. No, she hadn't been talking about Reginald. She'd been talking about this creature. Barkley. Fluffy. Tom and Neelix had argued about naming him, and as far as she had heard, they never had decided. . . .

Her hand went to her temple. A vein throbbed there. She tried to concentrate.

"Admiral Janeway?" It was young Cadet Anson, standing beside the podium. Concern was on her face. "Are you all right?" Tentatively, the girl stretched out a hand and placed it on Janeway's arm.

Janeway, moved by Anson's gesture, reached to pat that hand. She froze in midmotion.

"You're not real," she said, quietly, but with conviction. Cadet Anson stared back at her, her blue eyes wide with confusion and hurt. Slowly, lowering her gaze, the girl withdrew her hand from Janeway's arm, curling the fingers closed and hiding it behind her back as if ashamed. Her soft cheeks turned fiery red.

"Admiral?" The voice belonged to Cadet M'Benga.

Janeway tore her gaze from Anson to regard M'Benga steadily.

"I'm not an admiral. I'm Captain Kathryn Janeway of the Federation starship *Voyager.* We're still lost in the Delta Quadrant." As she stated the words, she knew in her heart the truth of them. Her mind knew it, even though the evidence of her eyes might suggest otherwise. She was missing parts of the homecoming parade day because there never *had* been a homecoming parade, nor even a homecoming.

Fluffy/Barkley barked.

"We were leading a caravan through dangerous space," she said, continuing to speak aloud. The cadets had fallen silent and now stared at her as if she had gone mad. Which, she supposed, to their way of looking at things, she had.

Except they weren't real. None of this was real.

"I stepped through a gateway," she said, her voice growing louder. "With Fluffy. And I'm not here teaching or attending an Academy class, I'm not on the bridge of the *Enterprise,* I'm on the other side of that gateway and someone is pulling the strings."

She picked up the dog, felt the reassuring warmth, the thump of its heart.

"I don't take kindly to being controlled," she said aloud to whoever was listening. "Show yourself and let us open a dialogue. I don't know if you're trying to make me feel more at home or are simply toying with me. Either way, it's not working. I can see through it."

The cadets disappeared. The room remained. Janeway took a deep breath and strode out the door.

It was the fragrance that registered first. She breathed in the scent of freshly cut grasses, the sweetness of flowers she could identify—apple blossom and roses, honeysuckle and freesia—and some achingly wonderful smells she couldn't. The light was bright, but her eyes adjusted quickly to behold one of the most tranquil scenes she'd ever had the good fortune to witness.

Green grass, waving in the gentle breeze that had carried the delectable scents to her nose, stretched as far as the eye could see. Over there was the shimmering image of a stream. She could barely hear its happy burbling. And to her right, a large house, surrounded by a white picket fence. Huge oak trees provided shade on a warm summer day, and from one of those oak trees dangled a swing. A porch hosted two rocking chairs and a small table, upon which there was pitcher of what Janeway was willing to bet was icy cold lemonade.

"I've been here," she whispered, but the same heavy sensation that had slowed her true memories to a crawl now clogged her brain. She couldn't recall it. "Think, Kathryn, think!" she told herself in a harsh whisper. It wasn't a real place, she knew that much, but it was real, in its own strange way.

A sudden image of a little girl and a white rabbit appeared in her mind. This whole thing reminded her of the famous Lewis Carroll children's story, and she was most definitely cast in the role of Alice. Where, then, was the white rabbit, the one who had lured her here with the . . .

The gateway. She remembered now, remembered it all. The gateway was the rabbit hole into this strange, bizarre world, where the most dignified captain in the fleet had made a clumsy pass at her, where she was reduced to being a terrified cadet or elevated to the equally false rank of a hometown hero. The gateway had been real, and whoever was casting these illusions was real. No white rabbit, but a trickster par excellence.

She could identify the place now, though she did not recognize it per se. She was inside the very heart of the Q Continuum.

The door opened and closed with a bang. A little boy rushed out. He was towheaded and tanned, wearing a straw hat, shirt and shorts, suspenders, and nothing on his feet. For all the world, he looked like the classic image of Tom Sawyer. He uttered a delighted, incoherent cry when he saw her, and ran toward her. It was such a happy, living sound that it startled Janeway.

Barkley wriggled furiously in her arms. She struggled to hold on to him, but he leaped down and ran across the green grass to leap into the arms of a small boy. Both fell to the ground, joy writ plain in every movement, every laugh, every wriggle.

She had finally found Fluffy's master.

"The boy has formed such odd attachments to mortal creatures," came a voice right beside her that Janeway knew all too well. "Can't imagine where he gets it."

Janeway turned around with deliberate slowness to regard the grinning figure of Q.

Chapter 2

He was clad, as usual, in his appropriated Starfleet uniform. She was happy that Barkley had found his home and his master, who had obviously missed him terribly. She was much less than happy to see Q again. Even as she regarded him, struggling to keep her emotions down, anger roiled to the forefront.

"I might have known you would have something to do with this," she snapped. "It's got your stink all over it. I should have figured it out when Will Riker had nothing but good things to say about you."

He lifted his hands in mock horror. "Kathryn! You wound me to the quick. Such undeserved slurs!"

"Undeserved?" Janeway let her outrage come unchecked. She strode toward Q and shoved her face up to his. "Those gateways had to be your doing. It's just the sort of thing you'd get your sick amusement from—opening doors here and there, letting innocent people wander through and get lost. Let me count up all the deaths you're responsible for. There's the Ammunii ship—two hundred and ten lives. The Kuluuk, whom you didn't kill outright but who would most certainly be alive in their own space. That's four hundred and fifty-seven. There are the all the V'enah and Todanians who—"

"I repeat," Q said mildly, "you've got it all wrong. As you humans usually do. Calm down, dear Kathy, and have a spot of tea."

Janeway found herself sunk deep in the cushions of a flowery chair which had lace doilies on the arms and over the back. She struggled to extricate herself, realizing as she did so that she was clad in a full-length, constricting dress. It was a yellowish paisley pattern, and she strongly suspected that the thing restricting her breathing was a whale-bone corset.

On a lovely oak table in front of her was a delicious-looking spread of finger sandwiches and pastries.

Q, dressed in what Janeway guessed to be formal Edwardian, poured. "Would you like cream or sugar with your Earl Grey?" Suddenly he snapped his fingers. "Whoops, that's dear old Jean-Luc. You like coffee, don't you?"

And so quickly it was dizzying, Janeway was in a cozy nook at a coffee bar of the late twentieth century. She was now sitting on a wooden stool in front of a small, battered table. Soft jazz played in the background and in front of her was a large cup of coffee as black as night and smelling as rich as heaven.

She wanted to toss the steaming contents onto Q's smirking face, but restrained herself.

"All right," she said with an effort. "I think I know what happened, what you did, but you're telling me I'm wrong. So explain to me what really happened. I'm listening."

Q, dressed in black denim pants and a black turtleneck sweater, and sporting an earring in his left ear, took a sip of his own coffee. "Ah, delicious. I can see why you like it so much. Well, it's a very long story."

"My attention span is not," Janeway warned.

He pursed his lips, made a *tsk-tsk* sound, and then sighed. "What do you want to hear about first?"

"The gateways."

"Very well." Suddenly they were in a child's nursery. To her consternation, Janeway found herself to be a small child, wearing a frilly pinafore that horrified her. Her mind was the same, but trapped in a six-year-old's body. Q loomed over her, an enormous book in his hands. Its cover was of tooled leather and bore the title *The History of This Universe.*

Despite herself, Janeway would have given a lot to have been able to get her hands on that book.

"Once upon a time," said Q in a singsong voice, "there was a wonderful, remarkable, intelligent, benevolent, superior, humorous, witty, handsome—"

"Q," said Janeway, her high-pitched six-year-old's voice nonetheless managing to fully convey the depth of her impatience.

Q sighed. "Now, now, little Kathy, mustn't interrupt your bedtime story or you'll not get the answers you want." He glared at her over the enormous book propped up in his lap. Angrily, Janeway folded her small arms over her chest and sank back into the nursery chair. Q was a nearly omnipotent being. If he didn't want to tell her something, he wouldn't. In a very real sense, she was entirely at his mercy. She'd have to let this "story" unfold the way he wanted it to.

"Much better." A plate full of chocolate-chip cookies and a large glass of milk materialized on the table beside Janeway's chair. She didn't touch either.

"As I was saying," said Q, "once upon a time there was a race known as the Q Continuum. Now, of course, being such omnipotent and benevolent beings, they turned their attention some five hundred thousand years ago toward assisting other races in attaining culture and technology."

"You're lying again. That's a direct violation of what you've told us before," said Janeway. "It was my understanding that in the case of Amanda Rogers, for example, she had to either join the Continuum or forsake her powers."

"That's quite true. You may have a cookie."

One appeared in her hand. Irritated, Janeway tossed it back onto the plate. Warm chocolate clung to her fingers.

"However," Q continued, "that was a few short, human years ago. And the reason we have adopted this new, improved policy toward inferior species was because things had gone wrong earlier. You're vaguely able to grasp the wisdom of such strategies yourselves, you Federation types, with your own Prime Directive."

Janeway nodded. She was starting to get some answers, and she felt herself calming a little. She wiped her chocolate-stained fingers on the pinafore.

"So, there was a very pleasant and promising race called the Iconians."

"Iconians! The gateways . . . of course," breathed Janeway. It all made sense now. She had thought the strange portals had looked familiar, but she hadn't been thinking in terms of ancient, vanished technology. Therefore, she hadn't made the connection.

Q sighed heavily. "Kathy, do you want to hear the story or just go right to bed without any supper?"

"Q, please. A favor." The sound of a child's voice issuing from her own lips was driving her crazy. "Restore me to my adult image. Your talking down to me this way doesn't help my listening skills any."

"All you needed to do was ask," he said, maddeningly. In a heartbeat, they were on the porch Janeway had glimpsed earlier, both in the surprisingly comfortable rocking chairs. Between them was a small wicker table bearing, as Janeway had guessed, a pitcher of lemonade and two glasses with ice and slices of lemon. Moisture condensed on the metal pitcher and slipped silently down the side.

"No stories. No teasing." Suddenly Q was wearing a trench coat and a fedora. "Just the facts, ma'am." Just as suddenly, he was in his Starfleet uniform.

On the lawn in front of them, the little boy—Q's child, her godson—romped with Barkley/Fluffy. She wanted to hear about him too, but she needed to learn about the Iconian gateways first.

"The facts are these, and they're very simple. We liked the Iconians. We wanted to help them."

"We, or you?"

"Oh, I can't shoulder all the blame for this one," said Q. "There were others involved. We gave them technology, and they used it for benevolent purposes. Everything was working according to plan. Then, somebody got mad at them." He sighed. "A feeling I know all too well."

"So, in the end, their own technology—the technology you gave them—was their destruction," said Janeway.

"Well," and he squirmed a little in his rocking chair, "kind of. I'm not supposed to tell you everything."

"Well, for Heaven's sake, please at least tell me *something!*"

Q hesitated, choosing his words with care. "The technology that enabled them to become the fabled 'Demons of Air and Darkness' was what caused other civilizations who didn't understand their technology to become afraid of them. And that led to the downfall of their civilization."

Janeway wondered what the difference was between "destruction" and "downfall of their civilization." Then she inhaled swiftly: Q was hinting that the Iconians hadn't become extinct. That was a choice tidbit of information, but she kept silent about it.

Instead, she asked, "Then why did you give them something so powerful?" In over two hundred thousand years, no known civilization had come close to re-creating the transportation system of the Iconians. She'd reviewed the information Picard had provided, as all Starfleet captains had soon after the incident. What was it Captain Donald Varley had said, on those poignant records? Something about being a Neanderthal looking at a tricorder?

"It wasn't." Q sipped his lemonade and watched his son with affection.

"Excuse me?"

"It wasn't that tremendous a piece of technology." He shrugged. "Kathryn, I continue to manifest myself and the Continuum in ways that you can readily comprehend. You keep forgetting that. You think that this"—he waved an elegant hand down his torso—"is the real Q. That this happy, tranquil scene in front of you is the real Continuum. It's but an illusion. Remember, Kathy, my little q was able to pull planets out of their orbits when he was but a baby."

He cocked a meaningful eyebrow in the direction of his playful son. Janeway felt suddenly chilled, as if a dark cloud had passed over the sun.

"Do you mean to tell me," she said, slowly, "that all the Q Continuum gave the Iconians was the most casual piece of technology?"

"Bravo!" Q clapped his hands enthusiastically. Janeway was suddenly dressed in a black robe and wore a mortarboard on her head. The tassel flipped from one side to another as if by unseen hands. "You graduate at the top of your class!"

At once, the outfit was gone and Q had sobered slightly. "I wouldn't even go so far as to call it technology, really," he continued. "That's too grandiose a term. You've got no children of your own—not that you didn't have the chance, you know—but perhaps you are familiar with some archaic toys with which children of yesteryear used to play."

Janeway, who in truth had not had much contact with children in her career-oriented life, tried to think. Mobiles. Rattles. Tops. What other old-fashioned toys had yet survived as nostalgia pieces for infants? Kites. No, that was for older children. Blocks.

"Precisely," said Q. He had, of course, read her thoughts. "When a child plays with blocks," and he waved his hand to create a few, "he learns how to spell."

The blocks moved, turned, and spelled out the word "cat."

"Oops. Sorry. I meant," and suddenly the word "dog" was spelled out in large carved letters. "That's your favorite animal, isn't it?"

Janeway felt almost ill with the revelation. Q was right. By appearing to her as a human, and taking her places like dusty way stations and antebellum mansions, he had undercut the sheer wonder that she would of necessity feel toward beings so much more advanced. The thought that the fantastic gateways of the fabled Iconians, so magnificent and still so incomprehensible and awe-inspiring, were little more than child's toys to the Q was both frightening and humbling.

"q," called Q. The boy looked up. "Come here for a moment." Obediently the boy ran toward the porch, Fluffy/Barkley at his heels. "Show your aunt Kathy your block trick."

Little q made a face. "Aw, come on, Dad, that's baby stuff."

"I know, I know. But it wasn't such baby stuff a while ago, was it?"

The boy hung his head. "No," he admitted. Janeway was alert. What had happened?

"Now, show her your block trick, that's a good q."

The boy plopped down on the slatted white boards of the porch. Rolling his eyes, he assembled the blocks—there were seven of them now, Janeway noticed—to form a single word:

GATEWAY.

The hairs at the back of her neck prickled. Right in front of her, an Iconian gateway sprang up. She recognized its beveled interior, like the edge of a mirror, and saw in front of her not blackness, but the bridge of her own ship. Chakotay was seated in her chair, leaning forward, hands clasped. He looked worried and anxious. This was another reason she had not immediately recognized the gateway on the planet to be of Iconian design, when Fluffy/Barkley had first ambled into her life. An Iconian gateway, at least as far as she understood, showed what was on the other side, as it did now with this view of *Voyager*'s bridge. The gateway on the planet which opened into the Q Continuum had, both times, revealed nothing. Q had not wanted her to know what she'd be stepping into.

Typical.

"Now put the toys away," Q instructed. Little q disassembled the blocks and the gateway disappeared. He looked up questioningly at his father, who nodded. The child grinned and bounded back down the steps, to return to playing with his canine friend.

"I'm not sure I understand," said Janeway, forcing herself to sound calm and in control when she felt anything but. "Your son created these gateways?"

"Only the one. As he told you himself, it's baby stuff. He's moved on to other things now." Q beamed. "Bright little fellow."

"But the Iconian gateways existed hundreds of thousands of years ago. The technology to operate them has vanished."

"Very, very few things truly vanish, Kathy," said Q, and for once she could tell he was being quite serious. "More often, they're simply lost or forgotten. Sometimes, others come along and find them."

"So who activated the gateways?"

He rolled his eyes. "Must you know everything? You're worse than q. Why this, why what, where's my pet, who activated all the gateways. A little mystery is good for the soul. Besides, I'm not the only one who has the answer to that. The next time you chat with your little Starfleet friends, you might ask *them*." He waggled his eyebrows in a meaningful fashion.

Janeway smiled. "All right. I will. They probably will actually answer any questions I might have."

Q clutched melodramatically at his chest. "You wound me, madam. I thought I did answer most of your questions. All the ones I'm allowed to, anyway."

"I have more."

He sighed. "But of course you do."

Janeway didn't speak at once. She watched the young q child romping happily with the brief-lived creature on the lawn, and felt a pang.

"Fluffy won't live very long," she said softly. "Your son is going to get quite the lesson in loss, Q."

"I know, believe me." He looked suddenly haunted. "You've no conception of how often it's happened to me." He turned and beamed at her, chasing away the shadows that had lurked in his eyes. "And yet, I continue to care for you silly mortals."

"What happened with the one gateway? The one you said little q made?"

"Oh, that. Well, he was playing with his blocks, as I said. He'd already outgrown them, but he still liked traveling places and hasn't quite mastered *this* yet." Q swooped his hands in a flourish. Janeway braced herself for whatever might happen, but nothing did. Apparently, Q was just doing a "for instance." "So he and Fluffy, as you call him—"

"We also call him Barkley."

Q stared. "As in that oaf Reginald Barclay?"

Janeway nodded, feeling a smile curve her lips.

"Now *that,*" said Q, "is truly painful. As I was saying, he and Fluffy would go off exploring together. Once, Fluffy ran through a gateway and wouldn't come home. Little q kept looking for him, but his skills aren't yet mature. He's not allowed to leave the Continuum unsupervised yet, so he asked me to find his pet. I told him that since he was the one who carelessly misplaced Fluffy, he was the one who had to find Fluffy. It was time for him to learn responsibility."

"Why Q," said Janeway, only partially teasing, "I'm so proud of you."

Q beamed. "So am I. Little q left the gateway open in case Fluffy wanted to come home. Of course, Fluffy was in no real danger. His natural life is short enough as it is. I watched over him, making sure he was all right." He looked at Janeway out of the corner of his eye and an impish grin started to curve his full lips. "I knew he was in very good hands."

"You keep tempting me with puppies," said Janeway. "This time it worked. I'll miss him."

A thought occurred to her. "You said that neither you nor your son was responsible for all the Iconian gateways opening. But it wouldn't make sense that so many of them would open in the same area."

Now Q did look uncomfortable. Alert, Janeway fixed him with her gaze.

"Well," said Q, squirming a little, "I may have slightly . . . modified . . . where they opened, yes."

"To what end?"

"For their own good." He looked at her. "Who better to help lost little lambs than someone who's been lost herself for a while?"

She softened, and felt sorrow wash over her at the loss of life and, in the end, the loss of hope with the vanished gateways. "I think your trust was misplaced."

"Oh, I don't." He nodded toward the lawn. "Look how well Fluffy came through the ordeal. And think about the Iudka and the Nenlar. They might have destroyed one another, and instead—oh, wait. You don't know about that yet."

"The Nenlar? They weren't killed?" Janeway sat up straight in her chair, hope flooding through her.

Q waved a hand. "All in good time, be patient, Kathy. And the V'enah and the Todanians. It took an extreme situation in order to force Arkathi to show his true colors, and for that feisty Marisha to get herself together enough to throw off the shackles of slavery. Do you think that would have happened if they hadn't been separated from their homeworld? Not a chance! Not to mention the Ones Who Will Not Be Named." He sniffed a little. "Pompous term. *I* know their name. They've been around for quite some time and I have never seem them interact so deeply with another species. It was quite touching to see, really."

Janeway didn't respond. All she could think of were the failures. They were so tragic, they loomed large in her imagination. Especially the thought of the Kuluuk, knowing the last emotion they experienced was fear caused by someone they ought to have been able to trust.

"You did more good than harm, Kathy," said Q in a surprisingly gentle voice. "As you always do. And you took very good care of my son's beloved pet." He was suddenly serious. "I'd like to do something to thank you for that. Name your favor."

Janeway didn't have to think twice. "Send the others home," she said. "They've only been away a brief while. They've been through so much; they deserve to get home to their loved ones as quickly as possible."

"Well, that's easy enough for me to do," said Q. He leaned over toward her and said in a conspiratorial tone of voice, "But can't I tempt their team leader into the same journey?"

Smiling, Janeway leaned over her own chair arm in return until their faces were almost touching.

"We've been down this road before," she said. "I'll take no favors from you, Q. Who knows what strings they'll have attached to them?"

Q looked offended, but she pressed on quickly. "We've come so far, we mortals. On just our own courage and ingenuity and good, old-fashioned hope. You yourself know that we're in contact with Starfleet, and that doesn't look like that's going to stop. I want us to get home on our own, and I think we're going to do it. Don't take that victory from us, Q. Not when we've worked so hard, come so far."

Q said nothing.

"Besides," she added, looking at him intently, "I've got a feeling that we were meant to be here, somehow. That this was the journey my crew and I were supposed to be on, even though we didn't know it. Look at how many people we have helped, the good we have done. You yourself steered little lost lambs to us for help and guidance. Don't you, who know so much, agree that *Voyager* has a purpose being here in the Delta Quadrant all these years?"

"Ah, ah," remonstrated Q with a twinkle in his eye. "That would be telling."

Janeway's smile broadened. She had her answer.

Suddenly little q was standing beside her. He cradled Fluffy/Barkley in his arms. "I have something for you. Your ball rolled into our yard."

Suddenly Janeway was holding the small probe she had tossed through the gateway, what seemed like an eternity ago. She couldn't help but smile as she turned the small orb over in her hands.

"Thank you for finding my dog for me, Aunt Kathy, and for bringing him safely home."

The last four words made her eyes sting. Gently, Janeway reached out and patted Barkley/Fluffy's furry head for the last time.

"You're welcome. He's a good dog. And I know he missed you, q."

She took a long, searching look at her godson. Considering who his parents were, he had an interesting lack of arrogance about him. The boy, if such he could truly be called, had an open, sweet face. The smile was genuine, and the love in his eyes for the innocent, mortal creature was palpable.

She gazed a final time at her surroundings. Q had brought her to a dusty, stagnant way station, and a war-torn battlefield. She liked this view of the Continuum, a nurturing place with images of serenity and comfort, much better. If this was the direction in which the Q were truly headed, then there might be a whole new age of enlightenment for the galaxy.

"The galaxy? Pshaw," said Q, reading her thoughts again. "Try the universe. Or three or four of them." But his arrogant boast was tempered by a look of real affection in his bright, sparkling brown eyes. "Farewell, my wild, sweet Kathy. We'll meet again."

Janeway found herself standing outside the gateway, once again on the tranquil, uninhabited class-M planet. Even as she turned to see if she could glimpse the Continuum through the open door, it disappeared.

"Captain? Were you unsuccessful?" Tuvok's voice had more than a touch of concern in it.

She took a deep breath and mentally returned to the here and now. "On the contrary, Tuvok. Janeway to Chakotay."

"Captain?" Chakotay's voice sounded puzzled. "What happened? Were you somehow unable to get through the gateway?"

"I've come and gone," she replied.

"But you just . . . never mind. So, what was on the other side?"

Janeway debated telling him, then decided to keep this trip to the Continuum to herself. It really didn't involve the rest of the crew, and sometimes, silence was the best option.

"Fluffy's home." She gave Tuvok a mysterious smile. "Tuvok and I are ready to beam up, Commander. And I have some good news. I think the other ships in the caravan are going home."

Chapter 3

For a maddening second, Janeway wondered if she really had beamed back aboard her own vessel, or if Q was still playing tricks. She dismissed the thought, smiled briefly at Ensign Campbell, and headed straight for the bridge. She felt an odd sense of urgency. Now that she knew positive action was indeed to be taken—provided Q held to his end of the bargain—she was impatient to proceed.

Chakotay looked up when she entered, and she could tell that he was burning with curiosity. He'd just have to deal with it.

"Harry, open a channel."

"Ready, Captain."

Settling into her chair, Janeway couldn't keep the pleasure out of her voice as she spoke. "This is Captain Kathryn Janeway. All of us were prepared to stay here and make this place our new home. But I am very pleased to report that this is now not the only choice I can offer you. Although all the gateways through which you traversed have now closed, if all goes according to plan, every one of you now has the option of returning home."

Chakotay stared at her, and in the depths of his dark eyes, she saw the question: *Us, too?*

Smiling sadly, she shook her head and continued, absorbing the disappointment as yet another burden that she had to bear in order to do what she knew, deep in her bones, to be the truly right thing.

"How that will be accomplished is . . ."

Her voice trailed off. Her eyes widened as there on the screen, a huge, blazing ball of fire manifested in all its crimson and orange glory. She closed her eyes, then opened him. How Q loved the melodramatic flair. As she watched, the ball seemed to explode. Bright light assaulted her eyes for a moment. When she could see again, there was not one ball of fire, but several—one for each lost ship, save her own. The balls meandered off, each to take its position in front of the different ships.

Trying to keep from laughing, Janeway said, "These . . . balls of flames will guide you home. You may trust them."

"Captain, we're being hailed," said Kim. "It's Ellia."

"Put her on."

Ellia looked annoyed. "Captain, it's all very well and good for you to tell us that these fiery balls are going to take us home, but how can we be—" She was looking at her controls as she spoke and froze.

"Ellia?" For a long moment, the alien captain did not respond. When she did, it was with a smile.

"Well," she said, "you amaze me. The, er, ball seems to have just downloaded information into our computers that, shall we say, gives me reason to believe that whoever is behind it will indeed take us home. I don't know what you did, but I thank you. Farewell." Then she was gone.

"Another hail, Captain."

"On screen."

The image of Sook filled the viewscreen. He looked calmer and a good deal happier than when she had last seen him, when he had just managed to take control of the *Relka* and Sinimar Arkathi had escaped to who knew where. "Captain Janeway. It's good to see you again."

"And you, Sook. Should I address you as Commander now?" Janeway asked.

Sook fidgeted. "I suppose so, since I *am* now the commander. Thank you for your help, both with Arkathi and now somehow managing to find us a way home. I don't know how, but we've just received information that—"

"Makes you trust the fiery ball," smiled Janeway. "You're welcome. What have you done with the V'enah we returned to you? It was our understanding that you would welcome them."

Young Sook was positively grinning now. From offscreen, Janeway heard a familiar voice answer in his stead.

"So he has, Captain."

Sook widened the image and Janeway now saw that Marisha was seated beside him. The former slave's injuries had been completely healed. She now wore a formfitting jumpsuit that was similar in style to that worn by the *Voyager* crew, but was silver and gold in color. She looked relaxed, calm, in control. When her eyes met Janeway's, Marisha smiled widely. She and Sook exchanged an amused glance.

"Hello, Captain Janeway."

"Marisha. I see you're a man of your word, Commander Sook. Am I to understand that Marisha is now your second-in-command?"

"She is," said Sook. "I could think of no better way to show that I am determined to facilitate equality among both races. She has a lot of learning to do, but as you know, she's more than capable."

Janeway turned her attention to Marisha. "How are your crewmates doing?"

"We are all doing well, thank you." Marisha hesitated. "We are so grateful for all you have done for us—for all of us, Todanians and V'enah alike. All suffered under Arkathi, and now, we are all free. I am so pleased that you have been able to find the others a way home."

"The others? You're not going?"

Marisha shook her close-cropped head. "No."

Slightly worried, Janeway asked, "Is this your decision alone?"

"I know what you are thinking, and no, this is something that we all agreed on."

"You have seen perhaps the worst of our people in Arkathi," said Sook. "But that does not mean that he was the only one of his kind. Back in our home sector, it would be impossible for V'enah and Todanians to interact as we are doing here, on the *Relka*. We are a small number, Captain. Here, we can act as individuals. But millions of Todanians still own millions of V'enah, and we cannot liberate them on our own."

Disappointment knifed through Janeway. She had hoped that the reconciled, integrated crew of the *Relka* could take their lesson back to their worlds.

"But Sook, that's how it always starts," she said softly. "One person with a vision."

Marisha glanced down for a moment. When she looked up again, tears sparkled in her purple eyes.

"You speak truth, Captain Janeway. But what I am about to say is true, too. We have fought our battles, we V'enah and Todanians. We have made peace amongst ourselves. We do not wish to lose that precious beginning, have it trod underneath the careless, brutal feet of those who would espouse the way things have always been. Rest assured, Captain, if I and Sook can come to the conclusion that we have reached, others will, too. For now, though, I am weary of fighting. I want to explore this thing called freedom, to walk on soft . . . grass?"

She turned to Sook, seeking confirmation of the word. He nodded, smiling.

"To walk on soft grass, and see the open sky. I want that for everyone here, and if we settle on this planet, we can have that. We can form a new society, one in which the old designations have no meaning. We will not be V'enah or Todanians first of all—we will simply be people. And . . . we will not be alone."

To Janeway's utter amazement, her bridge was visited a second time by Leader. She felt its thoughts in her head again, and knew that the rest of her bridge crew did as well.

Captain. We will also decline your gracious offer of a way home. This voyage has been a remarkable one for myself and my crew. We have been moved by what we have witnessed here. We have found, some of us to our utmost surprise, that we enjoy interacting with other species. At least on a limited basis. We have a great deal to offer these people, and they have chosen to accept our help.

"What happens when you decide you need a break from them?" asked Chakotay.

Leader turned to "address" him. *It is a large sector, and we have the technology to retreat when we need to. We will have the ability to leave and return as we see fit. But we are committed to being there for the settlers to assist them, when they ask for it.*

Janeway could hardly believe what she was hearing. "One thing I had hoped for when we started on this strange journey was that feuding species would put aside their differences and learn to work together. I could not have imagined such a harmonious outcome. In the words of the sailors of old on my planet, I wish you godspeed."

And to you, Captain. I am sorry that you won't be returning home yourself.

Janeway wondered how Leader could have known that, then relaxed. It was hard to keep anything from a telepath. More than likely, Leader also knew about Q, and was choosing to respect her silence.

"We'll get home, one day," she reassured it.

He nodded, bowed, and then his image slowly faded.

"Captain," said Marisha, "there is one to whom I would like to say a personal good-bye, if I may."

Janeway knew who that someone was. "Of course. You may transport over here at once."

Unexpectedly, Marisha shook her head. "No. Thank you. I would simply like to speak to her."

"Harry, route Marisha to Astrometrics." She turned to face the screen. "Best of luck with this brave new world you're creating, Marisha. No one deserves peace more than you and your crew."

"Thank you, Captain."

"Hello, Seven."

The unexpected voice startled Seven. She turned to see Marisha on the small viewscreen. She didn't know what to say.

"Marisha," she replied at length.

"I've just finished talking with your captain." Marisha told Seven of the decision to stay on the planet. Seven agreed with the logic of the decision, but was surprised to hear that the Ones Who Will Not Be Named had also offered to stay and assist them. When Marisha had finished, she hesitated. "Seven, I wanted to thank you."

Seven frowned. "I did very little."

"That's not true. It was one thing to hear whispers of an uprising, a promise of freedom, from me. The V'enah were used to that. It was quite another thing for them to meet a member of another species who agreed with me. Who could see clearly the injustice being done, without having her vision being clouded."

Seven thought about it. "I do see your point. I am gratified that I was able to be of assistance. Was there anything else you wanted?"

Even as she spoke the words, hearing them cold, crisp, and precise in her own ears, she wished she dared speak what she really felt. She wanted to thank Marisha too, for the gift the V'enah woman had given her. It had felt good to be passionate about something, to want to fight for a cause that was so obviously the right one. The sensation Seven felt inside was an exquisite, heady one. She understood now why revolutionaries were so often willing to give their lives for what they believed in. Somehow, the cost seemed infinitesimal compared to what was at stake.

She was glad Marisha had not had to perform such drastic action, however. She longed to say how much Marisha had meant to her, even though they had known one another for such a brief time. Her mind went back to the first time they had met, when Marisha had tossed aside the posture of a submissive slave like an old coat, lifting her head and meeting Seven's gaze with a fire Seven had never before encountered but to which she responded immediately. Something had ripped through Seven at that moment, and she would never be the same. Seven of Nine felt again that sensation of righteous anger sweeping through her like a tide, tempered now by the knowledge that that goal, that dream of freedom, had been achieved.

How quickly Marisha had learned. She was intelligent and compassionate. She and the enlightened Sook would make a fine leader of this blended group of adventurers.

Marisha searched her gaze, seemed about to speak, then merely shook her head.

"No, I suppose there isn't. Good-bye, Seven." She extended a slender hand to terminate the conversation.

"Wait," Seven said, urgency flooding her voice. Marisha glanced up sharply. "Marisha . . . it is not logical, but it is true . . . I feel a connection with you."

Her face softened. "I feel it too, Seven. As if we were somehow kin, though that cannot be possible."

"There is a kinship that transcends blood," said Seven, knowing deep in her heart that the words were true. "We have that kinship. The common bond of an unjust imprisonment and a painful liberation."

"I wish you could come with us," Marisha blurted. For the briefest instant, Seven considered it. She knew Janeway would let her go, if Seven truly felt this was where she wanted to be. But she could not leave *Voyager.* She belonged here now. It was home.

"I cannot," she said, regretfully. "Nor can you come with us."

Sadly, Marisha shook her dark head. "We need to plant our feet somewhere solid. Most of the V'enah have never seen the sky, or walked on soil. Including me. I want that, Seven. I can't tell you how much."

"You don't have to," said Seven. She could see it in the other woman's eyes. "I wish you good luck," she said more formally, standing straight. Withdrawing the connection.

"Thank you. And you as well. I hope you find your home soon, as we have found ours. Good-bye, Seven. Sister."

Then Seven was looking at a blank screen. She was glad that Marisha had terminated the conversation, because she did not want the other woman to see the tears that suddenly, unexpectedly, welled in Seven of Nine's blue eyes.

Chapter 4

Most of the other ships had long gone, but a few wished to make formal good-byes. The Lamorians in particular had a long, drawn-out ceremony involving Commander Chakotay. He asked for, and was granted, permission to retire to his quarters to complete the farewell ritual. Janeway had no desire to have her bridge viewscreen taken up for what could conceivably be hours while the Lamorians dotted every I and crossed every T.

While she waited for him to return, she received a transmission from Kelmar. Kim put it onscreen.

"It's good to see you, Kelmar. I'm pleased your ship survived the last battle against Arkathi."

"I understand he was never captured or killed," said Kelmar. "A pity. He was against you from the beginning, Captain. We were alert to his treacherous nature early on, when he contacted me and tried to play the two of us against one another."

This revelation disturbed Janeway. "I wish you had told me earlier, Kelmar. The Kuluuk might not have had to die."

Kelmar did not seem disturbed by her comment. "You were aware of his nature even without my alerting you to it, Captain. Nothing I could have said would have accomplished anything to help the unfortunate Kuluuk. A man is not a criminal until he has committed a crime. And you must remember, we were not too certain of you early on in our travels, either. You had befriended the Nenlar, who had cause to hate us."

He was smiling, as if he was pleased about something. Janeway hoped she didn't know what it was. "I hope you are not taking pleasure in their deaths," she said.

Kelmar laughed aloud. "Hardly," he said, "as they are not dead." He motioned, and both Ara and Torar came into Janeway's vision.

She gaped. "You're alive! Thank goodness! What happened?"

"Commander Kelmar transported us aboard the *Nivvika* in the very nick of time, putting his own ship at risk," said Torar. "A truly noble gesture, considering that he knew who we were all along."

Janeway's confusion must have shown on her face, for the Nenlar and Kelmar all suddenly laughed. "Remember I told you that there were terrorists among the Nenlar?" said Kelmar. "Ara and Torar are close to the top of that list."

"What?" exclaimed Janeway. "You two are terrorists?"

"Were," said Ara. "Never again. And with any luck, soon there will be no such thing as Nenlar terrorists."

"We are going to return to Nenlar space," said Kelmar. "There's a chance it might be dangerous, but when you have two of the highest-ranking members of the Nenlar terrorist groups vouching for you, you feel a bit safer."

Genuinely shocked, Janeway stared at Ara and Torar. "What happened to your Nenlar timidity?"

"It is still there," Ara reassured her. "We have to battle with it every day."

"I never imagined you two would be the terrorists Kelmar spoke of," said Janeway.

"If we and Kelmar can return to Nenlar space together," said Torar, "we can perhaps teach the rest of my people that there is nothing to fear anymore from the Iudka. I know it is difficult for you to comprehend, Captain, but we do not enjoy terrorist activities. It goes against everything in Nenlar nature. We did it only because we truly believed that we had no alternative. I know the key people in the organization well, and if they can be convinced that there is nothing to hate about the Iudka, we will all be only too happy to turn our attention to peaceful, less frightening pursuits."

Janeway shook her head. It was almost inconceivable to her, but she had served in Starfleet long enough to know that not every species—in fact, very few—thought about and reacted to things the way humans did. She wanted to believe Ara and Torar, but they had lied to her, and the Iudka, already.

"Kelmar, I feel compelled to point out that you are one ship, heading into Nenlar space. You'll be quite vulnerable. And while I would love to trust Ara and Torar, they have misrepresented themselves before."

"Although Kelmar knew who we were, it was we who chose to reveal our identities first. We did not need to reveal ourselves at all, Captain," Torar pointed out. "Nor did the Iudka need to risk themselves to come to our aid. The fact that they placed hundreds of Iudka lives in jeopardy in order to save two Nenlar lives was not lost upon us. It will not be lost upon my people, either. We fought to prevent wrongs. We will not continue to harm people who have expressed such a willingness to befriend us."

"The past is the past." Janeway was aware that she was gaping at Kelmar. He threw back his head and laughed heartily. "Oh, Captain, hearts will not be changed overnight. I know that. And I'm certain that even Torar and Ara will clash with us from time to time. But that is so insignificant, compared with the riches peace has to offer. I'm willing to risk it. Thank you, Captain. We wish you the best of luck on your own journey home."

The *Nivvika* terminated the signal, and Janeway watched the huge Iudka vessel follow the receding ball of fire.

Only one ship now remained. "Hail them," she told Kim.

The ugly, mottled visage of the Hirogen Alpha filled the screen. Janeway took a deep breath, determined to try one last time.

"Alpha, I would like to take this opportunity to once again urge you to utilize our holographic technology. I know you understand the benefits, and—"

"Yes," said the Alpha, completely unexpectedly. "If you will transport it over, we will welcome it."

Janeway and Chakotay exchanged pleased glances. "Kim, get on it.

Alpha, within a few moments you'll be in receipt of the technology. May I ask why this sudden change of heart?"

"It was pathetically easy for prey to frame us," grumbled the Alpha. "Our reputation may strike fear into the hearts of prey, but it also a liability. I had not realized we were so . . . predictable. Had it not been for your ability to look more deeply into the situation, I am certain that we would have been killed. I have no wish to die for something I did not do, Captain. Perhaps if we learn to use this holographic technology for our hunts, we will not be so easy a target for others' hatred."

She could see it materialize in the far corner of the viewscreen. The Alpha glanced back, then returned his attention to Janeway.

"The transport of your holographic technology was successful," he said. "We thank you for it."

"I hope it will prove useful, and that you have many fine hunts with it," said Janeway.

The Alpha inclined his head. "As I said, we also owe you thanks for coming to our defense when the rest of the caravan would have enjoyed opening fire upon us."

"We believe in serving justice and in clearing the innocent," said Janeway. "I'm only sorry that Sinimar Arkathi escaped without having to account for his actions."

The Alpha shrugged. "It is of no importance to us. We will soon be in our own space. Again, thank you."

Janeway settled into her chair and watched the Hirogen ship disappear as it leaped into warp. The turbolift door hissed open and Chakotay entered.

"The Lamorians are gone," he said.

"You sound tired," she observed.

He smiled slightly. "I am. I enjoy ceremony as much as the next person, but even I would go insane if I had to live in that culture. How did the rest of our farewells go?"

"Fine, I hope. I'd like to believe that the Nenlar and the Iudka are truly about to launch a new era of peace."

"They all seemed like decent people. Let's think positively."

She nodded. "Bridge to engineering. Status?"

"Everything's back to normal, Captain. Once the gateways had stopped draining our power, it's as if it had never happened. We're ready to head back into No Man's Land."

Janeway sighed. Their troubles were far from over. They were back where they had started, back to navigating, alone, a treacherous part of space in which—

"Astrometrics to bridge." Seven's voice broke Janeway's dark musings.

"Go ahead, Seven. What's the next challenge? Asteroid belt? Black hole?"

"That's why I'm contacting you," said Seven, and there was puzzlement—and irritation at that puzzlement—in her voice. "There are no more challenges."

Janeway sat upright. "Explain."

"The route which we charted several days ago is now completely clear. It is normal space ahead for as far as our sensors can determine. We could proceed safely at warp eight, according to my calculations."

"I don't understand," said Janeway. "I saw what you showed us. Four asteroid belts, as I recall. Singularities, red giants, gravity waves . . ."

"Captain," and now there was irritation in that smooth voice, "I know precisely what you saw, because I charted it. I was not incorrect. My readings were completely accurate. However, I repeat: None of the obstacles we had anticipated traversing is present. Nothing."

"Some stellar phenomena are mobile," said Chakotay, his voice hesitant in the shocked silence that followed Seven's report.

"Not red giants. Not singularities," said Janeway. And then she understood.

Q.

She wouldn't let him send them home, but he obviously had wanted to find some way of thanking her for returning his child's adored pet. So, if he could not finish this strange odyssey for them, he had at least cleared their path. It would certainly be a safer voyage now, and a shorter one. Silently, she thanked him.

And in her head, she heard an answering: *You're most welcome, Kathy.*

"Captain?" Chakotay was looking at her, concerned.

She smiled then, an easy, relaxed, heartfelt smile such as she had not indulged in since they had learned about No Man's Land.

"I say, let's not look a gift horse in the mouth," said Janeway. "Mr. Paris, plot us a new course with Seven's updated data. Straight as the crow flies. Let's shave a little time off this journey, shall we?"

Paris, too, looked at her with a confused expression in his blue eyes. Then he shrugged, grinned, and said, "Looks like we got a break for once," then turned back to the conn.

"Something happened," stated Chakotay. He leaned in toward her. "Didn't it?"

Grinning, she, too, leaned in to whisper conspiratorially, "Yes. Something did."

Then, taking a playful enjoyment in Chakotay's confusion, she reclined in her chair. She was going to enjoy the next several days, which promised to be uneventful.

Q? she thought.

Yes, Kathy?

You really ought to put a collar on that animal.

The Alpha stood in front of the viewscreen, his eyes on the peculiar fiery ball that Captain Janeway had told them would guide them home. Thus far, he had no reason to question her or the orb itself, which had told them things that had convinced him that it was to be trusted. Shortly after they had parted company with the human captain, they and their vessel had undergone a strange shimmering sensation, during which light-years had been traversed. According to their databanks, they were well on course for home and should arrive within a few hours.

It had been a bizarre encounter, with its share of difficult moments. Yet, as always, the Hirogen had emerged with honor and victory. They had kept their word to the prey, and while he had no problem acknowledging the role Janeway and her vessel had played in showing the Hirogen innocence, the outcome had never been in any real doubt as far as the Alpha was concerned.

Who in their right minds would have believed for a moment that the noble and proud Hirogen, master hunters, would stoop to slaughtering prey that collapsed and died of fright? The very concept was ludicrous. And even if the prey had decided otherwise, more of them would have died than Hirogen, if had come down to it.

Fortunately, it had not. The Alpha loved his life as much as any living creature, and while it would have been no shame to lose it in pursuit of prey, there was nothing to be gained in throwing it away either.

His gaze flickered from the stars to the piece of equipment Janeway had given him. He had let her think that she had convinced him of the rightness of this path, the path of nonkilling killing. It was simply easier, and the more she believed that she had tamed the Hirogen, the less carefully she would look at them when they left. So he had accepted the holographic technology she offered, had nodded at her smile of pleasure. And then he had had it beamed aboard and placed down without a second thought.

He would not use it to create substitute prey. No one in his crew could use it for that pathetic purpose. They would examine it, and might find other uses for it. He mused for a moment, realizing that this would be a superior way to set up an ambush for living prey. Perhaps Janeway had indeed given them something to add to the thrill of the hunt, though not in the least the way she had expected.

The Alpha turned completely around and gazed at the prize, the prize that had been snatched from space in that brief moment when all eyes had been on the rainbow-hued gateways, and none on a tiny escaping vessel.

Sinimar Arkathi hung from chains fastened about his wrists and ankles. He had put up quite a fight when they had beamed him aboard, attacking two fully armed Hirogen and fleeing through the ship for an astonishing twenty minutes before the Alpha himself had corralled him and defeated him with his bare hands. He was greatly pleased.

But now Arkathi was quiet, except for the occasional moan. The Gamma Hirogen stood stiffly at attention, awaiting his Alpha's orders. The Alpha strode up to the prisoner, grabbed the ugly head in one big hand, and turned Arkathi's face to his.

"You were worthy prey," he stated. "You contrived a scheme that was nothing short of brilliant to ensure that the Hirogen would be blamed instead of you. With a single plot, you exonerated yourself, and diverted suspicion to an enemy you knew was a true threat. If you had picked a species other than the gutless Kuluuk, you might have gotten away with your scheme. But even the foolish prey know of the mighty Hirogen, know that we would never stoop to such pathetic prey. The relic of a Kuluuk would be nothing to us."

At first, Arkathi's eyes seemed dead, empty, without focus. The Alpha tasted disappointment. He had hoped that this prey would delight him to the very end. But as the Alpha spoke, Arkathi came back to life. Understanding stirred in those eyes, and then, most satisfactorily, fear.

He nodded in approval, and continued. "You erred, and that was your downfall. You underestimated us. I dare say that you are not underestimating us at the moment."

Arkathi shook his head wildly. "Please," he began, "you may have the rest of the crew. But let me go."

The Alpha stared, then broke into loud laughter. "And amusing, too. Ah, Arkathi. It has been a glorious hunt. And the sweet irony is that what we will do with you would be considered a justice by the other prey. What a tale we will have to tell when we encounter other Hirogen. And you will be the evidence that the tale is true."

He glanced over at the waiting, eager Beta, and nodded.

Arkathi began to scream.

STAR TREK®
NEW FRONTIER
DEATH AFTER LIFE
Peter David

Mackenzie Calhoun, captain of the *Excalibur,* was so cold that it took his body long minutes to realize that he was once again in warmth.

It didn't happen immediately, or all at once. Instead it occurred in stages. First his fingers and toes, frozen nearly to frostbite stage, began to flex. Then his lungs, which had been so chilled that Calhoun had practically forgotten what it was like to breathe without a thousand needles jabbing in his chest, began to expand to their normal size. There was pain at first when they did, but that started to subside. He gave out a series of violent coughs that racked his body, and it was only then that his brain processed the information that the rest of his body was providing him.

He was so dazed, so confounded, that he had to make the effort to reorder events in his mind so that he could recall how he'd come to this pass.

The cold . . . the cold was so overwhelming that, for what seemed an endless period of time, he couldn't think of anything beyond that. There had been cold, and blistering winds that would have flayed the skin from his body if he'd been out there much longer. Cold, and bodies . . . two bodies . . .

Yes. The Iconians. A male, and a female, both named Smyt. Both dead. Lying there, faceup in the snow, mere feet away from the great gateway. And words . . . words etched in the snow by the male, just before he died, carved in the snow with a hand so frozen and useless that it was not much more than an iced club of meat. The words had been: *Giant Lied.* What the hell did that mean? What giant? What had he lied about? Why had the male Iconian felt so strongly about this that he had used his final moments of life to report this transgression? The Iconians . . . *grozit,* they had . . . they had caused trouble . . . so much trouble, for two races . . . for himself . . . for Shelby . . .

Shelby . . .

Calhoun lay there, flat on his back, arms and legs splayed, trying to put together the pieces of his body and the pieces of his life, the ground hard and gritty beneath him, the heat of an unknown sun pounding down upon him, his extremities starting to tingle with the resurgence of blood circulating to them. And that was when he remembered Shelby.

Elizabeth Paula Shelby, captain of the good ship *Trident,* who had been swept away along with him to the frozen world that had—for a time, at least—promised to be their final resting place. She had been there . . . with another man. Yes, yes, it was starting to come back to him. A man named Ebozay, leader of a people called . . . called . . . what? The . . .

"Markanians." The word was barely a whisper between cracked and bleeding lips, and the voice was hardly recognizable as his own. Indeed, he almost thought it was someone else for a moment before he realized with vague dismay that, yes, it was he who had spoken.

Yes, that was right. Ebozay of the Markanians. He had wound up on the wasted, frozen world along with Shelby. Then they had fallen into a crevasse, and Shelby survived, but Ebozay didn't. Simple as that.

"Shelby" was the next word Calhoun managed to get out, obviously one that was nearer and dearer to his heart than "Markanians" had been. He said it again, a bit louder this time, and had no idea whether anyone was going to respond. It was at that point that he realized he was blind.

No . . . no, not blind. But his eyes were closed, and absurd as it sounded, he didn't have the strength to open them. He was trembling, his body seizing up, and he coughed once more. Shelby . . . Shelby had been unconscious in his arms. He had cradled her, like a groom delicately transporting his bride over the threshold on their wedding night, but there had been nothing remotely romantic about it. She had been unconscious, freezing in his arms, injured from her fall and the frostbite, and he had held her as if he could will his own body heat into her in order to save her.

It hadn't worked. Naturally it hadn't worked; it was a ridiculous notion. And yet that was all he could think of to do, as exposed and relatively naked to the elements as they were, with the snow and wind pounding at them as if angry that they had the temerity not to roll over and die instantly upon being faced with their predicament.

Calhoun had spat out curse after curse, cried out against the unfairness of their circumstances, had simply refused to believe that it was going to end there, on some nameless ice world who-knew-where. Certainly after everything they'd been through, that couldn't be anything approaching an equitable finale for their lives.

"It's . . . not fair," Calhoun grunted.

And a voice from nearby, rough and hard and disinterested in hearing any sort of griping of any sort, said, "Life isn't fair. Deal with it."

It had been so long since he had heard that voice that, at first, he didn't recognize it, except in the way that one does when one thinks, *Damn, that voice is familiar, I should really know it.* And then it came to him, roared toward him with the ferocity of a star exploding in fiery nova.

"Father . . . ?" he whispered, and that was it, the shock was too much, because Mackenzie Calhoun realized that he was dead, that was all, just dead, because his murdered father was speaking to him, and he'd never really made it through the planet of ice at all. It had all been some sort of cruel joke, and at that moment, he and Elizabeth were lying on the planet's surface becoming crusted over with sleet and snow. And at that dismal image, that final miserable end that had been inflicted upon them . . . the mighty, fighting heart of Mackenzie Calhoun gave out. It wasn't for himself so much; Calhoun had no fear of death. In many respects, he couldn't quite believe that he'd lived as long as he had. No, the despair that broke him was the thought that he had let down Shelby. That he had carried his wife in his arms, whispered to her frozen ear that he would make things better, that he would save them somehow, and he'd failed. He'd let *her* down.

Even as he was half sitting up, the physical and mental stress all caught up with him at once, and Calhoun fell back without ever having opened his eyes. He struck his head hard on the barren and crusty ground beneath him, but never felt it.

And so died Mackenzie Calhoun, without ever having a chance to see the sun set.

Mackenzie Calhoun, captain of the *Excalibur,* was so cold that it took his body long minutes to realize that he was once again in warmth.

It didn't happen immediately, or all at once. Instead it occurred in stages. First his fingers and toes, frozen nearly to frostbite stage, began to flex. Then his lungs, which had been so chilled that Calhoun had practically forgotten what it was like to breathe without a thousand needles jabbing in his chest, began to expand to their normal size. There was pain at first when they did, but that began to subside. He gave out a series of violent coughs that racked his body, and it was only then that his brain processed the information that the rest of his body was providing him.

He was so dazed, so confounded, that he had to make the effort to reorder events in his mind so that he could recall how he'd come to this pass.

The cold . . . the cold was so overwhelming that, for what seemed an endless period of time, he couldn't think of anything beyond that. There had been cold, and blistering winds that would have flayed the skin from his body if he'd been out there much longer. Cold, and bodies . . . two bodies . . .

Calhoun lay there, flat on his back, arms and legs splayed, trying to put together the pieces of his body and the pieces of his life, the ground hard and gritty beneath him, the heat of an unknown sun pounding down upon him, his extremities starting to tingle with the resurgence of blood circulating to them. And that was when he remembered Shelby.

"Eppy . . ." he whispered, his concern for her pushing away anything else that could possibly be going through his mind. "Eppy," he said, revolted by how weak and whispery his voice sounded.

It was at that point that he realized he was blind.

No . . . no, not blind. But his eyes were closed, and absurd as it sounded, he didn't have the strength to open them. He was trembling, his body seizing up, and he coughed once more. For a moment he wanted to surrender to despair, to dwell upon how unfair all of this was. But then he thought, *Unfair? Unfair? And who ever claimed life was fair in the first place? Certainly not Calhoun. Certainly not his father, the man from whom he'd learned so much. The man who had died, broken in body but not in spirit by soldiers representing an oppressive race whom young Calhoun had eventually driven off his world. If he were here right now,* Calhoun realized, *he'd be telling his son to stop lying about and dwelling upon his unfair lot in life. He was still alive, after all, and that was all that was important. Now get up.* The voice of his own, which so echoed that of his father, chided him yet again, and said even more sternly, *Get up! Your wife needs you. On your feet, damn you, if you be a man . . .*

Why was he thinking about his father? It had been years since he had dwelt on him . . . so long, in fact, that he would have thought he'd forgotten the very sound of the man's voice. But for some reason, there it was, clear as anything in his head, as if he'd heard it just yesterday.

Oddest feeling of deja vu . . . no . . . more than that . . . as if he'd already experienced all of it during some sort of . . . of odd dream . . .

The air of his surroundings was warm in his chest as he drew in great lungfuls of it. It was the breath of life; he'd never been so fundamentally grateful for the simple act of breathing. Slowly he sat up, his back stiff, the circulation only now hesitantly returning to his feet, his arms. He let out a low groan, felt the dampness of his clothes sticking to him as the ice and snow that had coated them melted. It was a most uncomfortable sensation.

He opened his eyes and immediately squinted against the brightness of the sun. He put up an arm and winced at the motion, feeling a stiffness in the joint that made him wonder whether he'd injured the arm in its socket. But his only vocal acknowledgment of the pain was a low, annoyed growl, even as he continued to shield his eyes against the sun. There was more pain, racing down his back, and in his elbows and knees, but he was beginning not to mind it so much. It was, after all, a reminder that he was alive.

"Eppy," he said again, and there she was, miraculously, sitting up a few feet away from him on the parched ground. She looked as utterly disheveled as he imagined he did, with her uniform just as wet, and her strawberry blond hair hanging down in sodden ringlets. But the way she was looking at him, with those eyes that seemed to own his entire soul, spoke of both gratitude and appreciation of the purely miraculous, because obviously she had never expected to see him again. She had probably never looked quite as awful in her entire life, and she had never looked quite as good to Calhoun as she did at that moment. When she smiled at him, it lit up her entire face.

"Hey, Mac," she got out, and her voice sounded as cracked and strained as did his. But none of that mattered, none of it at all . . .

Because he wasn't looking at her. He was looking through her, around her. For all the attention he was paying her, she might as well not have been there at all. Apparently she was aware of it, for her face fell and her lips thinned as she reflexively shoved her hair out of her face. "Mac," she said, making no effort to keep the annoyed disapproval out of her voice and failing spectacularly. "Mac . . . I'm right here."

Calhoun still wasn't listening. Instead he was getting to his feet, and astoundingly all the pain, all the hurt, all the stress that his body had been through was instantly forgotten. His legs were strong and firm again, blood pumping through them as if they were the legs of a twenty-year-old. And although there was a look of utter incredulity upon his face, there was also calm certainty, as if he was convinced that what he was looking upon couldn't possibly be there . . . but if it was, it wasn't going to daunt him. As if, upon seeing this, he could handle pretty much anything.

"Mac," she said again, but this time her tone of voice had changed, for clearly she was aware that not only was it odd that they were alive, but odder still that her environment had changed so radically. It only made sense, Calhoun realized; she had not, after all, been conscious when they went through the gateway. The last thing she had known was that they were upon a nameless ice world with death imminent. "Mac . . . Mac, what's wrong? Where are we?" She glanced over her shoulder and an instant later she was squinting as well. "God, it's bright here!"

"And dry," he said.

"Where . . . are we?" she asked in wonderment. She had staggered to her feet, and was pulling on the bottom of her uniform shirt, wringing it out as best she could. Enough water to boil up a nice cup of tea poured out of the cloth as she twisted it. "It . . . seems familiar . . . but I . . . I'm not sure . . ."

"You've been here . . . but you haven't been here. Neither have I."

"What . . . ?"

In the near distance, Calhoun studied the castle-like structures that dotted the horizon. The towers were tall, powerfully built, gleaming defiantly in the scorching sun . . . so strong, so new, that Calhoun didn't know whether to laugh or cry. They were not freestanding; instead they had been carved right out of cliffs of solid rock. Calhoun had looked upon similar structures in his youth, but they had always been silent and empty . . . a mute testimony to more ancient times when such fortresses provided great measures of security. Back before invaders from another world had shown up with mighty weapons that were capable of reducing such places to shattered shadows of their former selves. Never had Calhoun looked upon such a fortress— "keeps," they were called—in such pristine condition. Not only that, but even at this distance he could see people moving through it, walking the parapets, going from one carved entrance to the next with confidence and casual athleticism. It was like watching history come to life. Along the bottom ridge of the fortress wall was an array of tents, private accommodations for some of the privileged higher-ups.

It took him a moment to realize that Shelby was speaking to him, and he focused his attention on her with effort. "What did you say, Eppy . . . ?"

"Mac . . . where are we?" she asked with genuine concern. He saw how she was looking at him, as if worried that he'd somehow taken leave of his senses . . . or, at the very least, lost track of his priorities.

"Xenex." He couldn't quite believe it until he actually said it. It was as if the spoken name of the place lent it reality that it didn't have moments before.

"Xenex," she repeated tonelessly. "Your homeworld. Xenex."

He nodded. "I . . . think so, yes."

"How the hell did we get to Xenex?"

"A gateway," he said. "There was a huge one on the ice world . . . much bigger than either of those transportable devices that the Iconians had. It was activated, and I took us through there to here . . ."

" 'Here' being Xenex." She adopted a professional, clinical attitude, sizing up the sky, the sun. "It . . . could be," she said slowly. "I was only there the one time, but—"

"It is, Eppy, trust me. I was there a hell of a lot longer than one time," Calhoun told her. He stayed rooted to the spot, unwilling to move, worried in some absurd fashion that if he did, what he was seeing would simply vanish like a passing soap bubble. His nostrils flared slightly, and he frowned. He looked for some hint of smoke or damage or signs of battle from the Keep, but there was nothing, which certainly seemed at odds with what his other senses were telling him.

He was so focused on his environment that he started slightly when Shelby stepped right in front of him. "Mac," she said firmly, "what's happening? I know you. I know your body language better than I do my own. You're tense . . ."

"We just stepped through a gateway onto Xenex, Eppy. Isn't that enough reason for tension?"

It was a sign of how dire their situation was that Shelby didn't tell him to dispense with the annoying nickname of "Eppy" that he favored. "There's even more going on here than that," she said. "It's as if you're in full battle mode. Like you're detecting an immediate threat. What's going on? I have a right to know, a right to be as prepared as you."

"You couldn't possibly be," he said, and then instantly regretted the harshness of his phrasing.

Shelby, however, did not appear to take offense. Instead she simply inclined her head slightly, and said, "If you mean I can't be the fighter you are, considering your background, fine, point taken. But my mind's as sharp as yours, Mac, and information will help me as much as it will you."

He drew in a deep breath of air to confirm that which he'd already surmised. "There's been fighting," he said.

"How do you know? I don't see any sign of it."

"Nor do I," he admitted. "But . . . I can smell it."

"What do you smell?"

His instinct was to protect her from the situation, but it was an instinct that he had to override. He knew she deserved better than to be coddled and sheltered, and besides, if he was right, she was going to find out sooner or later anyway. "Blood. There's blood in the air. Blood and death."

"Really? What does that smell like?"

He was annoyed by the flippancy in her voice. "It smells like chicken. What do you *think* it smells like?"

"I don't know, Mac!" she said with a frustrated wave of her arms. "I never noticed blood having a particular scent, and death is more concept to me than something definable by one's nose."

He took a step toward her, looking down at her, and he felt a looming darkness behind his eyes. "That, Eppy, is because you've never been up to your elbows in it."

"Screw you, Calhoun," she shot back. She faced him, her hands on her hips. "Maybe I wasn't a teenage warlord, hacking my way through corpses stacked five feet high, but I had a starship and crew dying around me when I fought the Borg, so don't tell me what I know and don't know, all right?"

"Fair enough," he said mildly. "In that case, the smell in the air should be slightly familiar to you."

She took a deep breath, then admitted slowly, "It is. Slightly."

"Come on."

"Where?"

He pointed to the Keep. "There."

"Why there?"

Shrugging, Calhoun asked, "Do you have a better idea?"

"Good point," she said.

They started walking. Somewhere along the way, Calhoun reached over and took Shelby's hand. It felt warm and comforting, and not only that, but he couldn't believe how quickly and thoroughly he'd recovered from near death. All the discomfort was forgotten, the paralysis gone from his feet and fingers. Even more remarkable was Shelby's recovery. It had seemed to Calhoun that she'd been perhaps a few heartbeats away from death, and yet now here she was, as hale and hearty as he was, walking at a brisk distance-eating stride that easily matched his.

They crossed the plain, approaching the mountainous area where the Keep was ensconced. Little clouds of dust were kicked up under their feet, and the dirt crunched beneath their boot soles. "The sun's setting," he said abruptly.

She blinked, apparently surprised by the gravity of his pronouncement. "So? Suns do that. At least once a day, as I recall."

But Calhoun shook his head, racking his brain, trying to remember. "There's . . . more to it, though. I . . . remember the sun starting to set . . . I think . . . didn't see it through, though. And . . . I know I didn't I see it rise . . . so how . . . ?"

"I don't know, Mac. I don't know why a gateway would drop us on Xenex, I don't know why I'm feeling so completely recovered in such a short period of time . . ."

So she had *noticed . . .*

". . . but what I do know," and she squeezed his hand, "is that I'm with you. And that's the most important thing. Together we can handle just about anything."

He smiled at that. The vote of confidence seemed ever-so-slightly naïve on her part, but he certainly wasn't going to say that. Instead he appreciated the sentiment for what it was.

Calhoun was about to reply to her when a sudden explosion tore the air.

It froze Shelby and Calhoun in their tracks and they looked ahead to the Keep, eyes wide, as one of the lower sections suddenly erupted in flames. People were running, screaming, shouting defiance. Another section of the Keep exploded, and people fell off the parapets, arms pinwheeling in futility as if they were hoping they could grab handholds from the very air.

"Come on!" shouted Calhoun, yanking on Shelby's hand.

She stayed where she was, looking at him incredulously. "You want to head *toward that?!*" she demanded. "You're crazy!"

"We have to!" he told her.

"Forget it!" she said. "We're not budging from—!"

Calhoun heard it, smelled it before he actually saw it: a giant, flaming mass of burning slag, descending from overhead, a misfire from a catapult that was falling well short of its target—namely the Keep. It was, however, descending right toward the two Starfleet officers, and it was too large, nowhere to run, and even as Calhoun yanked on Shelby's arm to try and get clear of it, he knew in his heart that it was too late.

The slag struck them, crushing their bodies and obliterating them, leaving no trace that they had ever been there.

And so died Mackenzie Calhoun and Elizabeth Shelby, without ever having a chance to see the sun set.

". . . but what I do know," and she squeezed his hand, "is that I'm with you. And that's the most important thing. Together we can handle just about anything."

He smiled at that. The vote of confidence seemed ever-so-slightly naïve on her part, but he certainly wasn't going to say that. Instead he appreciated the sentiment for what it was.

Calhoun was about to reply to her when a sudden explosion tore the air.

It froze Shelby and Calhoun in their tracks and they looked ahead to the Keep, eyes wide, as one of the lower sections suddenly erupted in flame. People were running, screaming, shouting defiance. Another section of the Keep exploded, and people fell off the parapets, arms pinwheeling in futility as if they were hoping they could grab handholds from the very air.

"Come on!" shouted Calhoun, yanking on Shelby's hand.

She stayed where she was, looking at him incredulously. "You want to head *toward that?!*" she demanded. "You're crazy!"

"We have to!" he told her.

Shelby knew beyond any question that it was madness. Despite the fact that Calhoun insisted this was Xenex, there was still some vague doubt in her mind. But if there was one thing she wasn't doubting, it was that running toward some major battle was the height of folly. Far better to turn around and put as much distance between themselves and it as possible.

But even as that thought went through her mind, something told her that it was the wrong move. That they were in an insane situation, and it would be far better to surrender to that insanity and just . . . just go along with it, even though it didn't seem to make much sense.

"All right, fine!" she said, and allowed Calhoun to haul her forward.

Abruptly the air behind them was superheated, and seconds later Shelby was knocked off her feet by the impact of some sort of flaming mass of . . . she had no idea what. All she did know was that it had crashed to the ground right where they'd been standing.

Her blood thudded in her temples as she realized just how close a call that had been, but Calhoun gave her no time to dwell on it. "Let's go!" he said, yanking on her arm once more, and Shelby had no choice but to follow.

Death. Death in the air. Yes, she could smell it now, just as Calhoun had been saying yesterday—

"Yesterday?" The word hung in her mind even as it tumbled out of her mouth for no reason she could determine.

Calhoun glanced at her, clearly not understanding what she was referring to. "What about it?"

"Nothing. Nothing." She didn't fully comprehend herself what had prompted her to say that, and she certainly didn't have the time to dwell upon it. "That was . . . that was just a close call, that's all."

"I was thinking the same thing," he said dryly. "Come on."

They pounded across the plains, and Shelby was amazed at how easily she was keeping up with Calhoun. She didn't think he was running particularly slowly, but nevertheless she was pacing him with no difficulty. He wasn't even pulling on her arm anymore since she was able to maintain an equal speed with him. Calhoun obviously was becoming aware of it as he cast an appraising glance in her direction, even as they kept moving.

"Why are we running . . . toward the site . . . of the battle?" she shouted over the sounds of explosions as her arms pumped furiously.

"Because it's better than being out in the open! And the Keep is returning fire! See?"

And he was right. From the upper reaches, a catapult-like device had appeared, and they were dispatching giant flaming wads of whatever at their still-unseen aggressors. Men and women were crawling along the upper reaches of the Keep like so many spiders, and what had at first seemed like disordered panic to Shelby now came across as a clearly organized response to the assault.

There were outcroppings of rock ringing the outer edge of the Keep, only a few feet high. "These aren't enough to keep anyone out!" Shelby said.

"It's enough to prevent wheeled war vehicles from drawing too close," Calhoun responded, even as he clambered up the ridge. Shelby immediately followed suit. "That's why it was so useful in the old days. In the new days, when we were attacked by flying ships and such, well . . ." He let his voice trail off.

"You sound . . . almost nostalgic . . . for ground combat," she grunted as she hauled herself over, scraping herself rather thoroughly as she did so.

"When a man's trying to kill you, you should be able to look him in the eye."

"How sweet."

They tumbled up and over, Shelby throwing her arms over her head to shield it on the roll down. She bounded to her feet, feeling more invigorated, more alive than she'd ever been. It was as if the danger that surrounded her had flipped some sort of switch within her brain, making her savor all the more every breath she took in the face of danger.

"Come—!" Calhoun started to say, but with a sharp gesture she silenced him and snapped, "If you say 'Come on' to me one more time, I break your neck."

He laughed at that, but it seemed to her a laugh of sheer joy, as if he was thrilled to be sharing this . . . this demented escapade with her. She had no real idea what the hell was going on, or whether they were really in Xenex's past somehow, or any of it. But the one thing she did know, beyond any doubt, was that she was absolutely loving every minute of it. Was this what it was like, she wondered, to see the world through the eyes of Mackenzie Calhoun? To savor danger, to thrive on personal risk? It frightened her a little, but only a little. The rest of it made her nearly giddy over the jeopardy.

They ran toward the Keep, and although a couple of the flaming masses of whatever-the-hell-they-were landed near them, nothing came as close as that earlier one had. They were drawing within close range of the defenders in the upper reaches of the Keep, and the defenders were pointing at them now, shouting to one another. For an instant Shelby was extremely concerned. What if these people took Calhoun to be an enemy and opened fire on him?

And Calhoun was slowing down, looking at the defenders in wonderment. "Mac . . . Mac, what is it?" Shelby asked, shaking his arm when she got no immediate response. "Mac . . . ?"

"It . . . can't be . . . " he breathed.

"Mac . . . ?"

Suddenly there was a howl of fury behind them, a hundred voices shouting as one, and Shelby spun just in time to see a horde of Xenexians pouring over the ridge that they had just climbed over. They were armed to the teeth, swords in their hands, rage in their eyes, charging full-bore toward the Keep. Their armor was of the most primitive sort, brown and black leathers that would turn away only the most glancing of blows. But they were heavily muscled, with bristling beards and wild purple eyes like Mac's. There were women as well, appearing no less vicious than the men, although their hair was shorn near to baldness. Their collective goal was clear: to assail the Keep. The defenders of the Keep responded in kind, cascading down the wall toward their attackers.

Xenexians . . . both sides . . . thought Shelby in confusion, remembering that Calhoun had once told her that—although certainly there had been disagreements, disputes, fragmentations (usually along family lines)—throughout the course of his world, there had never been any sort of civil war among his people. But what else could one possibly call this? No quarter being asked, none given, as two sides fueled by murderous rage pounded toward one another.

"Mac! We've gotta get out of here!" shouted Shelby, but even as she said it she realized there was nowhere to go. Furthermore, she doubted at that moment that Calhoun had even heard her. The two sides were converging, with Shelby and Calhoun right in the middle, and there was no escape.

Calhoun didn't even try.

Instead, with a roar as loud and primal as anything torn from the throats of the attackers, Calhoun charged the men coming in behind them. As Shelby watched, stunned, Calhoun dropped to his hands and knees at the last second, and one of the foremost attackers slammed into him, upending, feet flying high over his head. He hit the ground directly in front of Calhoun, and with a roar Calhoun was upon him. Calhoun grabbed his head with both hands, twisted once, and snapped his neck.

My God . . . so easily . . .

For years, Shelby had always known that deep inside—perhaps not so deep at that—Calhoun was a warrior born, a savage, cloaked in the appearance of a civilized man. She had convinced herself that, over the years, Calhoun had become more comfortable with that civility. She now realized, though, that it had been the thinnest of veneers, for he had tossed it aside in a heartbeat. Moreover, when he had done so, she was sure that it had been with a sense of relief on his part. *My God . . . he reverted so, so easily . . .*

Calhoun was not taking the time to dwell upon matters of civilized and uncivilized behavior. *"Behind me!"* he screamed at Shelby, and this time there was no hesitation as she darted behind. He had already grabbed up the sword of his fallen opponent, and howling a battle cry in a voice barely recognizable as his, Calhoun fought back. There was no artistry to his tactics, no style, no elegant form as one would see in fencing. This was nothing short of mere butchery as Calhoun hacked and slashed like a bladed windmill.

Everything seemed to be moving around her in a hazy, dreamlike manner. In moments Calhoun was covered in blood, as was she. Their clothes were soaked through with it, and she thought at first that it belonged solely to other people, but then she saw cuts and slashes piling up on Calhoun. There were too many swords, too many men, and however many he managed to hack away from him, more came. She wanted to scream *Enough! Enough!* But none would have heard her, or cared.

At the last second, she saw that someone had worked his way behind Calhoun, and was coming at them. She lashed out with a side kick, and felt the satisfying crunch of bone and ligaments as the kick connected perfectly with his knee. He went down, writhing, clutching at his leg, and Shelby tried to pick up his sword, but it might as well have weighed half a ton. She couldn't budge it. Instead she settled for snatching a dagger off his belt, wielding it as best she could, slashing away as others came near. But they were laughing at her derisively, sneering at the dagger, almost daring her to come at them.

Then she heard a scream, and the tip of a blade brushed against her back, causing her to jump away. That was when she realized, with a deep horror, that the blade had actually come right through Calhoun's body, driven through from the other side.

She whirled just as Calhoun fell against her, coughing up blood. "Eppy," he managed to croak out as she sank to her knees, cradling him.

She saw the massive redness spreading across his chest, and she knew that he was dying even as she said, "It's all right . . . you'll be okay . . . you're going to be fine . . ." He looked up at her and it was hard to tell whether he was annoyed at her pathetic attempts to lie, or amused because she was so wretchedly bad at it.

Then she felt a pinch at her back, a pain, and suddenly it felt worse, and that was when she saw a blade protruding from between her breasts. *Just missed the heart . . . that was lucky,* she thought, amazingly lucid even as her upper body jerked when the blade was yanked clear. She felt her lungs start to fill with fluid, felt the world blurring around her, and—although she was sure she was imagining it—heard the sounds of battle receding. For some reason she thought about when she was seven and rode a pony for the first time. Then she'd had ice cream until she'd gotten sick. That was a good day. A lot better than this one.

She wasn't imagining it. The fighting had stopped. Instead everyone seemed to be grouped around, staring at the two of them with interest, as if surprised to see them. Calhoun was returning the stare, and his mouth moved for some moments before he finally managed to get out the strangest words: "You're all dead . . ."

At first she thought he meant it literally. That, even in his dying moments, Calhoun was threatening them with a fearful vengeance that he would take upon them. Then he coughed, and said again, "You're all dead . . . how can you be here . . . when you're all dead . . . ?" and that was certainly enough to confuse the hell out of her.

Then the crowd of warriors seemed to separate, making way for someone. He was a burly man, with a strong chin evident even though he had a beard, and wild black hair tinged with gray. Aside from some glistening metal armbands, he was naked from the waist up, his torso rippling with power, but scars, also. Deep, livid, angry scars that looked as if they'd just been made yesterday, but not by swords, no. They were too blunt, too rounded. Whip marks, perhaps, or some kind of rod . . .

Her chest was on fire, and she realized with a distant sort of interest that the pain had been increasing for some time. They were all staring down at her impassively now, and as her lifeblood mingled with that of Calhoun, she managed to say, "You . . . you murdering bastards . . . why . . . why . . . ?"

The burly man, the one she took to be their leader, chuckled at her pain, which angered her all the more. He sounded condescending until he spoke, at which point he sounded . . . familiar.

"He knows why," he growled, pointing a sword at Calhoun. "Don't you, son?"

Calhoun, his face horribly sallow and pasty, managed a nod.

But Shelby didn't understand at all. All she knew at that moment was that her one wish was not to die in ignorance.

"Welcome," said Calhoun's father, "to Kaz'hera."

Shelby didn't get her wish.

The last thing she saw, just before she died, was the sun setting. It was the most beautiful thing she'd ever seen, and she hoped that Calhoun, at least, had had a chance to see it as well.

Calhoun awoke to sunlight on his face. It wasn't direct sunlight; rather, it was filtered through the cloth of a tent. Calhoun wondered where in the world a tent had come from, and then he remembered that there had been tents lining the bottom of the Keep. The ground was bumpy beneath him, although he was lying on some rough-hewn blankets which provided at least some measure of cushion. Nearby outside, he heard swords clanging, and for a moment he thought that there was another battle in the offing. But then he realized that it was just two people, and there was a distinct absence of shouting or panicked running about. So it was probably some sort of training session or private lesson.

The tent flaps were pushed aside, allowing more sunlight to flood in, and Calhoun blinked against it. His father's frame filled the door.

"It's a fine, Xenexian sun. Never used to bother you. Have you gone soft?" he asked, his voice slightly challenging.

Calhoun didn't respond at first. Instead he stood slowly, unsteady on his legs, but determined not to fall over. Even though the evidence of his own eyes was right before him, he still couldn't help but ask, in a tone of utter disbelief, "Father . . . ?"

Gr'zy of Calhoun, father of M'k'n'zy of Calhoun, sized up his son and did not seem to be especially approving of what he saw. "Look at you," he said in annoyance, stepping forward and gripping Calhoun by the chin, turning his face from side to side. "You call this a beard?"

"I . . . I haven't been growing it for that long, sir," Calhoun managed to say.

"Well . . . it will have to do, I suppose. And your muscles!" As if sizing up an unworthy slab of meat, Gr'zy squeezed Calhoun's biceps and shook his head. "Nothing to them! By this age, they should be hard as rock by now! Too busy surrounding yourself with weapons and security men to stay as fit as you should be! Well? What do you have to say for yourself!" he fairly thundered.

"I . . . I'm sorry, sir," said Calhoun.

"Sorry! You're sorry! Well . . ." and then Gr'zy's face broke in a wide smile. "It will have to do, then! Hah!" And he smacked Calhoun on the back so hard that Calhoun was almost positive Gr'zy had broken his back.

Calhoun had always wondered, in the back of his mind, whether in the intervening years since his father had died—beaten to death by Danteri soldiers—Calhoun had somehow built his father up in his recollections. He remembered Gr'zy as being big, powerful, indomitable. It was a pleasure to see that his recollections had not been misleading. That Gr'zy was everything Calhoun recalled him to be.

"You lasted long enough to see a sunset!" Gr'zy told him approvingly, taking a step back. His voice was so boisterous as to be deafening, and his breath smelled like burnt animal flesh, since Gr'zy usually preferred his meat thoroughly charred. "That's good! That's good! And that, as you know, entitles you to an eternity of sunrises!"

"Father, I . . . " Suddenly overwhelmed by emotion, Calhoun took a step toward Gr'zy, his arms wide. But immediately his father re-treated, his face darkening. "Father, what . . . ?"

"Are you insane?" his father demanded.

"What? I don't . . ."

"Look at you," and this time there was no jest or gentle jibe in his father's voice. "About to embrace me? *Me?* Has this Federation of yours made you softer than I thought?"

For a moment, Calhoun felt anger bubbling within him, but he sup-pressed it. "No, sir," he said firmly.

The clanging of swords outside was getting faster and faster. Gr'zy ignored it. "Good. Because this is Kaz'hera, my son. Such . . . delicate emotions are inappropriate here. Softness of body and spirit are not re-warded, as you well know. For that matter," and he took a step toward Calhoun, his voice low and confidential, "I am concerned about the fe-male you came with."

"Shelby?"

"If that is her name, aye. The simple fact is that she may not fit in here, M'k'n'zy. She may not fit in here at all."

"I . . . I don't understand. She's a warrior at heart, Father . . . you just have to see that—"

Suddenly from outside, Calhoun heard metal slide against metal, and an abrupt female shriek which Calhoun recognized instantly. "Eppy!" he shouted, and immediately pushed past his father.

The blinding brilliance of the sun didn't bother him. Instead he skidded to a halt and focused, to his horror, on the body of Elizabeth Shelby. She was lying flat, her arms and legs flopping about like a stringless puppet, her head to the side with a face of permanent sur-prise etched into it. There was a sword lying near her, having just slipped out of her lifeless hand. Standing over her was a burly master-at-arms, gripping a sword still dripping with blood. He was looking down at Shelby with mild frustration and, even as her blood pooled around her, turned to Calhoun and said—with amused annoyance in his voice—"Slow learner, but she'll get the hang of it."

Calhoun did not hesitate. He strode quickly across the ground to Shelby. He gave her no outward sign of affection, did not kneel over her, shut her sightless eyes, cry out, beat his chest, rend his garment, or in any other way, mourn her. Instead he simply picked up her fallen sword, turned it around, and ran himself through with it.

"You lasted long enough to see a sunset!" Gr'zy told him approvingly, taking a step back. His voice was so boisterous as to be deafening, and his breath smelled like burnt animal flesh, since Gr'zy usually preferred his meat thoroughly charred. "That's good! That's good! And that, as you know, entitles you to an eternity of sunrises!"

"Father, I . . ." Suddenly overwhelmed by emotion, Calhoun took a step toward Gr'zy, his arms wide. But immediately his father retreated, his face darkening. "Father, what . . . ?"

"Are you insane?" his father demanded.

"What? I don't . . ."

"Look at you," and this time there was no jest or gentle jibe in his father's voice. "About to embrace me? *Me?* Has this Federation of yours made you softer than I thought?"

For a moment, Calhoun felt anger bubbling within him, but he suppressed it. "No, sir," he said firmly.

The clanging of swords outside was getting faster and faster. Gr'zy ignored it. For some reason, though, it caught Calhoun's attention. He wasn't sure why, but he was quite positive that it was . . . important somehow. "Good," said Gr'zy. "Because this is Kaz'hera, my son. Such . . . delicate emotions are inappropriate here. Softness of body and spirit are not rewarded, as you well know. For that matter," and he took a step toward Calhoun, his voice low and confidential, "I am concerned about the female you came with."

"Shelby?" He hadn't been thinking about Shelby for the past moments, but now that her name was mentioned, it hit him with such force that he wondered why she wasn't uppermost in his mind.

"If that is her name, aye. The simple fact is that she may not fit in here, M'k'n'zy. She may not fit in here at all."

"I . . . I don't understand. She—"

All at once Calhoun stopped talking. And he wasn't sure why, but he suddenly knew, beyond any question, as sure as he had ever known anything, that Shelby was in mortal danger. With a cry of warning—although he didn't know what he was warning against—Calhoun charged toward the tent flap just as a high-pitched scream came from outside the tent.

Calhoun dashed outside . . . and skidded to a halt.

Shelby was standing there with a bloody sword clenched in her hands and a look of pure fury on her face. She was breathing hard, and was covered with sweat. Facing her was the master-at-arms, minus one of those arms. It was lying on the ground next to him, the hand still clutching its sword, and blood was pouring from the ruined arm.

"Then again," said Calhoun's father appraisingly, "perhaps she'll fit right in."

Shelby's wolfish grin of pleasure lasted for as long as it took to fully register upon her what had just happened. Then, slowly, her eyes widened as she focused upon the master-at-arms. He had dropped to his knees and was rather comically, and absurdly, trying to reattach his fallen arm by shoving it against the shoulder from which it had been severed. He was having about as much success with the endeavor as one would expect. The only thing he was managing to accomplish was to amuse the other Xenexians who were pointing and laughing at his hapless antics. Shelby gasped, unsure of what to say or do, at which point Calhoun walked to her quickly and pulled her away. The laughter of the Xenexians followed them as Calhoun distanced himself from them. Within moments they had left the encampment behind.

Shelby's face was turning the color of paste, and her eyes were wide with confusion and horror. "Mac . . . Mac, what's happening, what's . . ."

"We're in Kaz'hera," he told her matter-of-factly.

"Of *course!*" she said as if that explained everything. "We're in Kaz'hera! I mean, up until now, I was confused because I was operating under the mistaken belief that we were in Tuscaloosa, but it turns out we're in Kaz'hera—!"

"Eppy . . ."

She whirled and gripped him by the shoulders with such force that he was sure he was going to have a permanent imprint of her fingernails in his flesh. *"Where the hell is Kaz'hera!"*

"Eppy . . ." he started again.

"Why did I wake up in some *tent,* only to have some bruiser drag me out into the morning air and start giving me *sword lessons?!* And why, when I chopped his arm off like it was a piece of *goddamn mutton,* was I *happy about it?!?"* She was trembling with agitation. "Where . . . what is . . . how . . ."

"Are you going to let me tell you?"

"No!" she said, trembling, and then she put her hands to her face, breathing in deeply to steady herself. "Okay . . . go . . . tell. Now. Hurry. Before I crack up."

"All right." He let out a slow breath, tried to figure out the best way to explain what was essentially inexplicable. "Does the name 'Valhalla' mean anything to you?"

"Uhm . . ." She ran her fingers through her hair. "It's, uh . . . a starship. Excelsior-class. Named after a famous American Revolution battle centuries ago, I think . . ."

"What? What're you . . . ? *No!"* he moaned. "Eppy, that's the *Valley Forge,* for crying out loud. I'm talking about Valhalla, the literary reference . . ."

"Dammit, Mac, I'm a captain, not a librarian! How am I supposed to . . . wait . . . wait . . ." She frowned, racking her brain. "It's, uhm . . . that place. Norse mythology . . ."

"Right . . ."

She was flipping her hand around as if trying to swat an annoying insect. "Where the warrior women lived . . . the Valkyries . . . and they'd come and bring fallen warriors to this place, this hall of dead heroes, and that was Valhalla . . ."

"Exactly, yes. Well, the, uhm," he cleared his throat, "the interesting thing about myths, Eppy, is how entirely different civilizations, even worlds, have different versions of the same thing. Flood myths, for instance, are prevalent in many—"

She looked around at the forbidding landscape, cutting him off before he could continue. "Are you telling me we're in the Xenexian version of Valhalla?"

"More or less, yes."

She took that in for a moment, and then threw her arms wide as if blocking a football pass and cried out, *"Are you insane?!"*

"I don't *think* so," he said, trying to sound reasonable.

"Mac, the gateways take people through space and, occasionally, time! They don't transport you to mythical places! Places like . . ."

"Tuscaloosa?" he suggested.

She moaned. "No, that's a real place," she said, sagging back against a boulder.

"Really? Where?"

"Arizona, or maybe Alabama . . . some damned state. I don't remember."

"The point is, Eppy, that this place is Kaz'hera. The big guy who came out of the tent I was in . . . that's my father."

She was silent for a moment when he told her that. Then, very softly, she said, "Mac . . . I know your losing your father at a young age was traumatic for you . . . but . . ."

"But what? What are you implying? That I'm imagining it? I'm having a dream, and you're in it with me?"

"Believe it or not, Mac," she said, folding her arms, "I find that easier to believe than what you're suggesting."

"Eppy . . . Kaz'hera is where Xenexian heroes, cut down in battle, go to die. When you first arrive," he said, as if reciting a beloved bedtime story, "you have to survive to see your first sunset in Kaz'hera. If you don't, you keep going back to the point where you left off. And once you've done that, you awaken every morning to a day of warfare and battle. And it doesn't matter if you get hurt, or if you die, because come the sunset, the day ends and the next morning you wake up and it's a new day. And the only thing you remember from the day before is anything that you've learned that's of immediate use. Otherwise you continually, blissfully spend every day for the rest of eternity engaged in pleasant and endless mayhem."

"I see. I see." She smiled in a way that looked, to Calhoun, like it was just shy of patronizing. "And why—just out of curiosity—did all those men attack you? I mean, you were their warlord once upon a time, right? Of at least some of them, I mean. And you obtained freedom for their world. So one would think they'd have some loyalty to you."

"Taking a guess," he said ruefully, scratching his chin, "they're probably carrying grudges. I mean, yes, I led Xenex to freedom, ultimately. But I also led a lot of men to their deaths. They may take pride in the manner of their death, but no one is going to be enthused about the actuality of dying. After all, that means they didn't get to enjoy the fruits of their labor. I recognized a good number of the men there, in that crowd. They looked angry with me. So I suppose they took the opportunity to avenge themselves on me. But I doubt they'll carry grudges. Carrying a grudge for eternity is simply too much work."

Having said that, he waited for her reaction, and found it to be exactly what he suspected it was going to be: an amused shaking of her head. She was dismissing it out of hand. He supposed he couldn't entirely blame her. "Mac, it's ridiculous. We can't be someplace that's *not real.*"

"I agree with you. Which leads us to one conclusion . . ."

She stared at him, the amused smile slowly vanishing from her face. "You're saying that this . . . this . . ."

"Kaz'hera."

"This Kaz'hera . . . that it's real."

"As real as Tuscaloosa."

"And . . . we're dead, is what you're saying."

"I'm not sure about that one," he admitted. "I mean, it's possible that we simply froze to death . . . but if that's the case, then I'm not sure why you'd be here, since you're not Xenexian. So far more likely that we came through the gateway—"

"Straight to the eternal playground of your youth. And what's next, Mac? Hmmm?" She put her hands on her hips and gave him a defiant look. "Maybe we'll find our way back to the gateway, jump through, and find ourselves in heaven, face-to-face with God."

"Is that what this is about, Eppy?" he demanded. "You have trouble believing in higher powers, and as a consequence, all this is too much for you to cope with?"

"I cope with being your wife, Calhoun. That's enough coping for one lifetime."

He stepped in close to her and said tightly, "How about an eternity of lifetimes, Eppy? Because that's what we've got here. And you can spend eternity arguing about it, and refusing to accept what's right before you . . . or you can start taking things on faith."

And he stomped away, so incensed over Shelby's refusal to accept what he was telling her that he didn't notice the freshly dug ambush pit until it was a millisecond too late. As he plunged, with the jagged, sharpened stones rushing to meet him, he cursed Eppy with his dying breath and wondered how many times he'd made *that* curse . . .

"Is that what this is about, Eppy?" he demanded. "You have trouble believing in higher powers, and as a consequence, all this is too much for you to cope with?"

"I cope with being your wife, Calhoun. That's enough coping for one lifetime."

He stepped in close to her and said tightly, "How about an eternity of lifetimes, Eppy? Because that's what we've got here. And you can spend eternity arguing about it, and refusing to accept what's right before you . . . or you can start taking things on faith."

He started to stomp away, and at that moment, Shelby felt a sudden warning in her head. She had no idea why, no clue as to what could or would happen, but it was enough to make her cry out, as if his life depended on it, "Mac!"

He stopped, but remained with his back to her. She walked quickly to him, boots crunching against the dry ground, and she wondered if it ever rained in paradise. Taking him by the elbow, she turned him around to face her. "What's going on here, Mac?"

"What do you mean, 'What's going on here'?" he said, looking and sounding defensive. "I've already explained the—"

"No," she shook her head. "I mean what's going on here, with you. I've never seen you like this."

He looked at her uncomprehendingly. "I don't know what you mean—"

"Yes, you do, Mac." She took a deep breath. "Actually . . . I don't think you have to tell me. I think I know what's going through your mind."

"Do you?"

In the distance she saw the Xenexians going through training maneuvers. For all she knew, another wave of opponents—she couldn't call them "enemies," really—would come charging from across the way at any time. And why not? That's what it was all about, after all, wasn't it? Endless strife? Endless battle? She let out the breath she'd taken and told him, "I think you want to stay."

"That's ridiculous."

"No. No, it's not. I think it's damned attractive to you. No rules, because they don't matter. What you do by the book one day, you throw out the next day, and none of it makes any difference for as long as the sun rises and sets. But this place, Mac . . . this place . . . it can't be. There's nothing that says the gateways can actually take us to . . . to otherworldly spheres. We're having a . . . a mutual delusion or something, trapped in some sort of other-dimensional limbo perhaps. It's a spacial equivalent of a holodeck. There have been cases, documented cases, of sections of space where the mind makes reality out of fantasy . . ."

"Why are you doing this?" he demanded, and she saw that he was getting angry, really angry. "Why is it so damned impossible for you to believe? I've been hearing stories of Kaz'hera, believed in it, since as . . . as early as I can remember . . ."

"And I heard about the Hundred Acre Woods, Mac, but I'm not going in search of Winnie-the-Pooh. This, all of this . . . it's not real. It's what we said before, a sort of . . . of mutual delusion. But it's not real . . ."

"It's as real as we want it to be," said Calhoun forcefully. Then his eyes widened as he realized, "Xyon . . ."

"Your son? What about him?"

"I . . . I thought he was dead. But I haven't seen Xyon here. Maybe . . . maybe he's alive. Maybe . . ."

She took him by the shoulders and said firmly, "Mac . . . we have to leave."

He looked at her defiantly. "If this is being formed by our mutual delusion, why is it only someplace that I'm familiar with?" he demanded. "Why aren't we in whatever you picture as heaven?"

And with all the sincerity that she was capable of mustering, she said, "Because I believe in you more than I believe in anything in this world . . . or the next. But now," and her voice dropped to barely a whisper, filled with urgency and pleading, "you've got to believe in me . . . or, at the very least, believe me when I tell you that I'm leaving here. This place isn't for me. It's not for you, either. You've grown beyond this. You know that in your heart."

"Grown beyond it? What are you talking about?"

"Mac . . . think. Think about where we just came from, how we got here." He was looking at her blankly, and she thought, *Oh, my God, he really doesn't remember . . . he's got amnesia or something. It's this place, it's done it to him.* Speaking faster, she said, "Two races, the Aerons and the Markanians, who were engaged in a centuries-long battle. Battling over their own version of paradise, a planet called Sinqay, and their battle of mutual extermination was aided by two Iconians, each with their own gateway devices. We all wound up on Sinqay, only to discover the planet was a desolate wasteland thanks to generations of fighting that had gone on previously . . ."

"Yes," Calhoun said briskly, "and then both Smyts turned on their gateways, and it created some sort of force whirlpool that sucked us into the ice planet, where that gigantic gateway was waiting for us, and why are you telling me all this when I already know it?"

"Oh." She felt a bit stupid for a moment. "I . . . I thought you'd, uhm . . . forgotten."

"How could I forget?" he asked, as if she'd lost her mind. "It didn't happen last century."

"You're missing the point, Mac!"

"Well, what the hell was the point?!"

"The point is that you can't stay here!"

"Because you say it's not real, and so I'd be wasting my time," he said, and there was such bitterness and anger in his voice that she was taken aback by it. "Because it's something that *you* can't believe in, and therefore there's something wrong with me for contemplating— even for a moment—embracing it. Because you have trouble believing in anything greater than yourself, and since that's the case, you'd deny me the opportunity as well."

She stepped away from him and, because she couldn't look him in the eye, looked around at the vast plain instead. Rocks and craggy areas nearby them, and the endless vista of . . . of nothingness. In the distance she could hear the shouts and laughter of the Xenexians in the Keep, and even as far away as she was, she was able to pick up words here and there, all of them in anticipation of the next battle, and the one after that, and the one after that. Xenexian paradise.

Death without permanence, the thrill of battle without the threat of long-term damage.

"Maybe you're right," she said softly. "Maybe . . . I'm afraid to believe in the reality of this place . . . because then it implies that other things . . . things I'm not . . . comfortable with . . . might also be real . . ."

He looked at her with confusion. "Why . . . 'not comfortable'?"

"Because, Mac," sighed Shelby, "things like heaven . . . or angels . . . or God . . . these are things that are, by definition, unknowable. I don't . . . *accept* . . . the concept of 'unknowable.' Anything that is . . . I should be able to explore. To touch. To face. It's right in the Starfleet credo, Mac. If it exists . . . I want to be able to boldly go there, even if no one has before. I don't want anyone, or anything, putting up signs and saying, 'This far and no further.' If mankind can't discover it, learn from it . . . what's the point of it?"

To her surprise, he laughed gently at that. "Humanity is a very egocentric species," he observed.

"Well, I guess we haven't come all that far from a time when we believed the sun orbited us." She'd been leaning against another rock, and she pushed off it and stood in front of Calhoun, taking one hand in each of hers. Not for the first time, she noticed how rough his hands were, and the corded strength in each of his fingers. "Mac . . . what I was saying before about the Aerons and Markanians . . . I was trying to make you realize that endless fighting is a useless way to spend one's life. It doesn't matter whether you're Markanian or Xenexian. Even if this is all real . . . even if we're in Xenexian Valhalla . . . *you deserve better than this.* Useless remains useless, and it's a tremendous waste of the man you've become and the man you could be! Okay? Do you get that now, Mac? Do you get what I'm saying?" His face was inscrutable. She could get no read off him at all, and she knew it was time to draw the line. "Tell me now, because whether you get it or not, I'm leaving."

"Leaving? Leaving for what?" he asked skeptically. "Even if we manage to retrace our steps, even if we find the gateway . . . all it'll do is put us right back out onto the ice world."

"Maybe we'll be rescued."

"Not a lot of time to be rescued in, Eppy. More likely we'll die."

"Well then," she shrugged, "maybe I'll get to explore the whole heaven thing after all."

For a long, long moment he was silent, and in that moment, she was absolutely positive that she had lost him. That she was going to wander around, on her own, trying to find—perhaps unto eternity—the gateway. Hell, the damned thing probably wouldn't even be open.

He wasn't moving. Well . . . that was that.

She stood on her toes, kissed him lightly on the cheek, and she wasn't sure what prompted her to say it, but she whispered, "Godspeed" into his ear. Then she turned and started to walk away, and found—to her surprise—that she was praying for Mac to come with her.

From behind her, he called, "You're asking me to give up everything I believe in, in order to be with you. And if we go back and we die together . . . I'd likely wind up back here, and you would be . . . wherever . . ."

She stopped, turned and smiled. "I guess that's what 'till death do us part' is all about, isn't it, Mac?"

They faced each other then, a seeming gulf between them, and she wondered whether they'd ever faced each other like this before. Whether they were, in fact, replaying a moment over and over and over again, coming this far together and no further.

Calhoun let out a heavy sigh, then, and it seemed to Shelby at that moment that a very, very small part of him died just a little bit when he did so.

" 'Till death do us part,' " he agreed, and walked toward her. And with a cry of joy that was slightly choked, Shelby ran to him and threw herself into his arms, holding him so tightly that she found it hard to believe, at that moment, that there had ever been a time when they weren't embracing one another.

That was when, from behind them, a gruff voice growled, "Is this what you've come to, then?"

They turned and Gr'zy was standing there, the mustache under his nose bristling, his purple eyes dark and furious as the sea. His hand was twitching near the great sword that hung from his hip, but he did not draw it. "Is this what you've come to?" his father said again. "A chance to be with me . . . to be with your own kind . . . and you throw it all away to run off with . . ." He could barely get the word out. *". . . her?* You would place love above the glory of battle? Have you no priorities?"

"I have mine, you have yours," said Calhoun. Shelby had no idea what that pronouncement was costing him, but he said it with conviction and certainty. His mind was made up, and for that she felt abundant relief, because there was nothing in the universe more stubborn, more determined, and more implacable than a Mackenzie Calhoun with his mind made up.

"You're no son of mine," said his father angrily, turning away.

"No son of yours?" Calhoun repeated the phrase with obvious incredulity. But when he spoke, it was not in a pleading or whining tone, the voice of a child imploring a parent for approval. It was the voice of a man who knew his mind, knew in his heart that he was right, and was setting the record straight for someone too dense to see it. "Everything I did, I did in your memory. Every Danteri bastard I cut down with my sword, I did so avenging your death. I freed a planet on your behalf and if that isn't good enough to earn your approval in the afterlife, then to hell with you."

Gr'zy took a step toward him, drawing a hand back as if ready to belt his son across the face. Calhoun made no move to stop it; merely stood there, his chin upturned, as if expecting it. Gr'zy froze like that for a long moment, and then turned without another word and strode away.

A feather-light hand on his arm, Shelby whispered, "Mac . . . are you okay?"

He looked at her and, for just a moment, there was infinite pain in his eyes, and then—just like that—it was gone, masked. "I'm fine," he said. "Let's get out of here."

They moved quickly across the plains, no words exchanged between them. Calhoun led the way, scanning the ground, looking for signs of where they'd been, tracking, using his expertise, missing nothing. "This way," he said firmly. "I'm reasonably certain that if we follow this path, tracking these clods of dirt, and the chipped-away bits of . . ."

"Or we could just head for the gateway," she said, her eyes wide, clearly unable to believe her luck as she pointed ahead of them. And there, sure enough, was a glowing in the air. It was a distance away, but it was unmistakable: the gateway.

Suddenly the ground below them began to rumble, and for a moment they both thought that the gateway was about to explode. But then they realized what it was: an army in pursuit. They looked behind themselves to see a horde of angry warriors coming after them, shouting Calhoun's name, shouting fury that he was expressing such disdain for their paradise that he was actually daring to try and leave it.

And the gateway . . . the gateway was fading. Whether they'd come through an hour or an age ago, it was impossible to tell, but whatever it was, it was running out. The gateway was about to cycle shut, and they'd be trapped in Kaz'hera forever.

"Run!" shouted Calhoun, and they tried, but within moments they were overrun, and even though they fought back, they were cut to pieces, and the ground ran red with their blood.

Suddenly the ground below them began to rumble, and for a moment they both thought that the gateway was about to explode. But then they realized what it was: an army in pursuit. They looked behind themselves to see a horde of angry warriors coming after them, shouting Calhoun's name, shouting fury that he was expressing such disdain for their paradise that he was actually daring to try and leave it.

And the gateway . . . the gateway was fading. Whether they'd come through an hour or an age ago, it was impossible to tell, but whatever it was, it was running out. The gateway was about to cycle shut, and they'd be trapped in Kaz'hera forever.

"Run!" shouted Calhoun, and they tried, but within moments they were overrun, and Calhoun tried to fight a delaying action while Shelby ran, but they were cut to pieces, and the ground ran red with their blood.

Suddenly the ground below them began to rumble, and for a moment they both thought that the gateway was about to explode. But then they realized what it was: an army in pursuit. They looked behind themselves to see a horde of angry warriors coming after them, shouting Calhoun's name, shouting fury that he was expressing such disdain for their paradise that he was actually daring to try and leave it.

And the gateway . . . the gateway was fading. Whether they'd come through an hour or an age ago, it was impossible to tell, but whatever it was, it was running out. The gateway was about to cycle shut, and they'd be trapped in Kaz'hera forever.

"Run!" shouted Calhoun, and they tried, but within moments they were overrun, and although Calhoun marveled at Shelby's display of sword prowess, they were cut to pieces, and the ground ran red with their blood.

Suddenly the ground below them began to rumble, and for a moment they both thought that the gateway was about to explode. But then they realized what it was: an army in pursuit. They looked behind themselves to see a horde of angry warriors coming after them, shouting Calhoun's name, shouting fury that he was expressing such disdain for their paradise that he was actually daring to try and leave it.

And the gateway . . . the gateway was fading. Whether they'd come through an hour or an age ago, it was impossible to tell, but whatever it was, it was running out. The gateway was about to cycle shut, and they'd be trapped in Kaz'hera forever.

"Run!" shouted Calhoun, and they tried, but within moments they were surrounded, and that was when a roar like a shattering planet filled the air, and there was a clang of swords, and Calhoun could actually hear bodies being sliced apart.

Unstoppable, Gr'zy cut a path to Calhoun and Shelby, and the others fell back, confused and angry and regrouping, their hesitation lasting only moments. But it was moments enough for a ragged Calhoun to look up at the dark face of his father and say, "I thought you said I wasn't a son of yours."

Gr'zy grumbled, "Yes, well . . . I realized that sometimes you're more your mother's son. And I loved her dearly. But she was no warrior. I miss her terribly . . . as much as I'll miss you. Go."

"Father, I—!"

"Go, damn you!" he shouted, and shoved Calhoun as hard as he could. Shelby caught him and they ran, and it was an incredible thing to see. The warriors tried to get past Gr'zy, tried to pursue his son, and it should have been impossible to hold them back, as impossible as a single sand bag keeping back the ocean tide. But Gr'zy was everywhere, as was his sword, and no man passed as Calhoun and Shelby sprinted

the remaining distance. Calhoun gripped Shelby's hand as tightly as he could, and together they leaped through the gateway. And the last thing he heard his father cry out was, *"This has been a good day!"*

And the sun set on Kaz'hera.

Just as before, the transition was instantaneous, except this time it was far more brutal. One moment they were bathed in warmth, and the next the wind and ice were hammering them with the force of a thousand nails.

Calhoun went down, Shelby tumbling on top of him. Almost instantly he was losing feeling in his face, in his hands and feet, and even taking a single breath was agony for him. He clutched Shelby to him, and when he looked at her his heart sank in dismay. While in Kaz'hera, she had healed. But here, back in this marvelous "real world" to which she'd been so anxious to return, she was as banged up and bruised as before they'd gone through the gateway.

There was no place to run to, no place for them to take shelter. Calhoun thought it was a miracle that their hearts hadn't simply stopped from the shock of going from one extreme to another, but then he thought better of it. After all, what kind of miracle was it when all it did was spare them a quick death in exchange for a slower and more agonizing one?

Then he looked down at Shelby, who was gazing up at him, unable to move, barely able to speak, and he understood. It was a miracle because it was giving them a few last moments together, and any time that they were together was miraculous.

As the wind screamed above them, trying to drown out anything they might have said to one another, Calhoun leaned in close to her, put his lips right up against her ears. "Till death do us part," whispered Calhoun. She nodded mutely, and then they kissed passionately, holding each other close, icing over, the gateway silent behind them . . .

And then there was a roar near them, and in his near-death delirium, Calhoun wondered whether Valkyries were descending from Valhalla. They were, after all, freezing to death, and that was certainly evocative of the icy climes that the Norsemen hailed from . . .

He managed to barely roll over just then, and saw with distant astonishment that a long-range shuttlecraft was approaching.

What do Valkyries need with a shuttlecraft? Calhoun wondered, right before he passed out.

When Shelby opened her eyes, she saw Calhoun smiling down at her, felt the distinctly unglacial warmth around her, and for just a moment she thought, *You bastard . . . you brought us back through the gateway . . . we're back in your idea of paradise . . . here we go again . . .*

And then a familiar voice, brisk with efficiency, said, "Step aside, please, Captain." Calhoun did so, and then Dr. Selar was standing over her, guiding a medical tricorder along her and nodding approvingly. "Full circulation has been restored. However, I would advise that you not—"

Shelby immediately sat up. An instant later the world spun around her and she flopped back. The only thing that prevented her from cracking her head badly was Calhoun's arm catching her as she fell.

"—sit up too quickly," the Vulcan doctor finished acidly.

It was at that point that Shelby realized they were in a shuttlecraft. She looked up at Calhoun in confusion, her face a question.

Easily reading her mind, Calhoun took her hand and said, "Back on Sinqay, our respective science officers managed to re-create the energy field that hauled us through to the ice world. Once they did that, they sent a shuttlecraft through after us."

"But . . . but how will we . . . get back from here? Back through the energy field?"

"No." It was Dr. Selar who spoke up. "We tried. But the field is rather unique in that it appears to be only one way."

"Then . . . how—?"

"No need to worry," Calhoun assured her. "McHenry's helming the shuttlecraft. He has us pegged as three days out of Thallonian space."

That was immediately enough to assuage Shelby's worries. Mark McHenry may have struck her as one of the odder crewmen on the *Excalibur,* but if there was one thing that was certain, it was that his ability to know where he was anywhere in the galaxy was unerring, even uncanny. If he said it was going to take them three days to get back home from wherever the ice world had been, then that was quite simply that.

"You were very fortunate," said Selar.

"You mean that you showed up when you did?" asked Calhoun.

"That too. But I was referring to the fact that I am your doctor." And with that, she headed toward the front of the craft, leaving Shelby and Calhoun alone in the rear section.

She squeezed his hand tightly. "Any regrets?" whispered Shelby.

He smiled and said, "I'll tell you after I'm dead."

And for a moment, just a brief moment . . . she thought that she saw pain and a longing for something he now knew he could never have, or never be happy with. But then, just like that, it was gone once more.

THE OTHER SIDE

Robert Greenberger

Prologue

Deanna Troi, carefully cupping her mug of hot chocolate, curled her feet underneath her legs and stared at the viewscreen in the captain's quarters. She disliked the decor and would have preferred to let the *Marco Polo*'s real captain keep his space, but he was far from his starship and she was in temporary command. She had grown accustomed to making snap decisions and thought she was doing an adequate job, especially when her Sabre-class vessel had been bombarded by enemy fire.

The counselor-turned-commander had grown fond of her adopted crew and thought they performed well, especially since, like her, they had been thrown together with little warning. She missed the ones that had been dispatched for what Will Riker called "extended baby-sitting," but they were doing their duty. As she was doing her own.

What Deanna truly came to discover about command, though, was that when being the one in charge, you quite often had to wait for the crew to perform their tasks before you could issue your next orders. And the waiting was more dangerous than Romulan disruptor fire.

"Any change, Will?" she asked the image on the viewscreen.

Riker, looking like he had not slept in a day, shook his head. He was speaking from his personal quarters on the *Enterprise,* just a few hundred kilometers away but seeming like he was in another quadrant.

"Nothing at all," he replied. *"The captain's been gone for six hours now without a word."*

She sipped at her chocolate, hoping its magical restorative powers would keep her alert for the next shift, which began in less than fifteen minutes. "And Doral?"

"Still sitting in his guest quarters, looking at images of his remaining ships. When power failed on one, we had to help evacuate the crew to other ships nearby. They're down to forty-eight and it's getting a little cramped for them."

"The odds improve, don't they?"

"Our sixteen against their forty-eight is still three-to-one odds. Wouldn't expect that to stay the same the way things are going." Riker seemed to be busying himself onscreen but she couldn't figure out what it was.

Finally she asked, "What *are* you doing, Will?"

"Oh, just working on a new recipe," he admitted with a grin.

"Well," she said with a warm smile, "practice makes perfect."

Just talking to him made her feel better and kept the harsh reality of their situation just a little further away. "What's to become of the Petraw?" she asked, turning back to the immediate problem.

"Their drive to expand their reach means getting them home during their lifetime is impossible," he replied. *"Doral can't even say for certain if the Petraw Empire even exists anymore. They remain close to the galactic center, way beyond any portion of space any of us have ever explored. Desan told me there's been no evidence of the Petraw in their Empire."*

"Has the *Glory* restored power yet?" The Romulan warbird had been seriously injured when they first found the Petraw ships.

Riker shook his head again, an uncertain expression on his face. *"She won't admit to it, but Data thinks he pierced their shielding enough to determine the quantum-singularity drive has been ruptured beyond repair. I've got him working on emergency evacuation plans since I doubt they would all fit on the* Jarok.*"*

"Captain Brisbayne tells me much the same about *Mercury*. He's taking it very hard, losing his first command," Troi added. "I think he hoped to retire without ever losing a ship or getting in a serious firefight."

"Given the Borg and the Dominion War, he's a rarity among

Starfleet captains," Riker said. *"Geordi's dispatched his alpha team to help with repairs so we've got hope."*

Troi sipped in a silence for a moment, wondering what progress was being made by their own captain, who stepped through the Iconian gateway found aboard Doral's lead Petraw vessel. Six hours with no knowing what he found on the other side. His orders had been strict: no one was to follow him through.

Chapter 1

Picard emerged from the gateway into a forest that sang with birdcalls and swarmed with large insects. A short distance from his position, he saw the building first glimpsed from the engineering deck of the lead Petraw vessel. It was a gleaming domed building and now before him, he saw red and orange filigree at the dome's base and watched it snake up toward the top. The oval dome itself was a cobalt blue, shining wetly in what he presumed to be the late-afternoon sun.

Sweat had already begun to trickle down his neck and he realized how warm it was, too warm to be pleasant and humid enough to indicate it had recently rained. Picard considered himself fortunate he missed the shower as he opened his tricorder. With some alarm, the captain found the instrument dead. His right hand reached for his phaser and saw that it, too, registered no power. This was not the first time he had arrived to find technology dampened, but he had hoped to be better prepared for what was to come.

With greater caution, Picard began walking around the dome, looking for sentries or even an accessway. There was little doubt he needed to get inside and speak with the people—the ones he hoped were the one true Iconian people. No one had seen them in over two hundred millennia and no pictures of them were found on any of the worlds that had direct links to the Iconian culture. It was one of the more intriguing mysteries about them.

His boots beat down wild flowers, thick ropy grass strands, and even fallen twigs. The rain helped moisten everything so it kept his movements quiet. To his practiced eye, Picard noted that everything outside the domed structure was left to its natural state. The air seemed pure so the dome gave off no harmful emissions. It also made no sound; there was not even a hint of a power current.

After twenty minutes, Picard estimated he had managed his way around a third of the dome. Nothing had changed although the sun had dried out more of the surroundings and wild animal calls could be heard. He guessed they had come out from their hiding spots. The captain wished it would be cooler since the sun was that much lower, but it was not to be.

"Captain Picard?"

He whirled about, instinctively reaching for the useless weapon, surprised someone managed to get this close to him. The captain looked up, for the figure measured at least seven and a half feet tall. She was a willowy figure, not much in the way of musculature, but it was a decidedly female form. Bipedal, she seemed to be not that different from the many humanoid variations he had encountered over his journeys. She wore a dark maroon dress that reached the tops of her covered feet, and the material was embroidered with filigree similar to the dome. There was a jeweled headpiece atop her long, red hair, which extended far down her back. He could not guess her age but the smooth face implied youth. She also had a scarlet tattoo of some design, from cheekbone to jawbone, on the right side only.

"I am Jean-Luc Picard," he finally replied.

"Welcome to our world," she said. Her voice was soft and gentle although it also sounded slightly distracted. She remained still as Picard studied her without trying to seem rude about it.

"Do you know why I have come?"

"Of course, we have been studying your activity." She didn't seem interested in saying more and also seemed content with remaining in place, hands clasped before her.

"Can you help me?"

Sunlight caught her dark eyes and made them twinkle a bit, which added merriment to the emotionless expression. Without answering, she turned and raised her left arm, revealing a plate of metal covering the forearm. It must have sent a signal, since a panel set within the base of the structure opened, one he would never have found given its engineering. The space within was well lit but the captain could not discern what was inside. The woman turned and began walking with a steady gait and he presumed he was to follow. Once Picard began moving, he noted that she made less sound than he did and that he could see her small footprints faintly amid the flora and fauna.

The moment Picard passed the threshold, the door began to seal itself and he caught the modulated, cooler air, for which he was thankful. She did not pause and continued down the corridor, which was devoid of decoration and was mostly silver and metallic. Again, he heard no noise and without markings, was fairly convinced he would be lost once he got deeper within the complex.

They walked on in silence for several minutes and Picard kept his counsel, studying her movements, caught up in the thrill of the moment. After all, he had studied the Iconians for many years, was considered Starfleet's expert on the long-gone race, and here was a chance to see them in all their glory. At least he hoped it was glory, since that would mean their culture was preserved, which in turn might let him solve the problem back home.

She finally turned left, going down a similar corridor, but after less than a minute extended her left arm once more and a door opened. Everything seemed well maintained given the utter silence of the mechanics.

The room he found himself in was immense, with a gigantic viewscreen directly before him. On the screen was the gateway found on Doral's flagship; he could see a Klingon sentry keeping guard. No one else was in sight. To his right was a bank of color-coded computer controls that seemed similar to the ones he found on Iconia some years earlier. To his left were long benches, and seated on them were five others, two more women and three men, all in similar maroon clothing. The cuts were different, as were the jeweled headpieces that all five wore atop their heads. Each also had tattoos of similar design, but theirs were purple, to her red.

"Captain Picard, you have arrived here when we sought to stay apart from galactic society," a woman on the bench said. Her voice was deeper than her colleague's, he noted.

"If you are truly the Iconians, then you know it is your technology we seek to control, to stop what others have begun," Picard explained.

"It has not been in use in a very long time," one of the men said.

"Impressive, is it not?" the woman beside him asked.

The first woman turned to him, her eyes showing concern. "What has gone wrong? The gateways function."

Picard cleared his throat and succinctly explained how the Petraw found the technology and sought to sell it to further their personal goal of extending their empire. They knew enough to turn on the entire network but not how to shut it down or even program direction. As a result, the unchecked access had resulted in widespread trouble, even loss of life.

"You have a bright people," the woman said. "We have studied you since the first gateway was activated in many hundreds of years. Your response has been, in the past, to blow up our technology."

The captain inwardly winced at the realization. The first gateway that had been discovered, on a Kalandan outpost a century ago, was destroyed by Spock on the *Enterprise*. The gateways found on Iconia, Alexandra's Planet, and Vandros IV had all been destroyed as well, by Picard, Elias Vaughn, and Benjamin Sisko, respectively. He could see their point.

"If you have studied us," he replied, "then you know such destruction is a last choice. We would much rather simply turn them off, preserving your legacy."

"Yes, we have seen that," one of the men said. He couldn't tell which since they seemed remarkably similar in appearance. At best, the cut of clothing was the only major difference he could tell. Men and women alike kept their hair long, tied neatly behind their heads.

"When the first gateway was used by these Petraw," the woman closest to Picard said, "it activated an alarm here. We had no idea what it meant—it has been so long since the last such alert—but we finally figured out that it meant our equipment was in use. Our leader at the time had to consult the computer records to find out what the alarm signified and what we were to do."

"We were formed," the final man on the bench said. He stood and gestured to the six Iconians in the room. "We are the Sentries, gathered when our equipment is in use. Our laws say we are to monitor the use, record the species that employ the gateways, and watch."

"Watch for what?" Picard asked.

"Watch for incursion," the man replied. "We left your space to be on our own, to pursue new interests and not to be bothered."

Picard frowned at the answer. The Iconians built their empire, invented technology far beyond their peers, and just walked away from it all? What could they be building now?

"The use of the entire network was something none of us had witnessed before," a woman said. "We were intrigued to see what would happen, all you people flitting here and there like insects drawn to nectar."

"Ships, peoples, things, it all moved back and forth with no one harnessing the equipment to its fullest potential," the woman beside her said.

"You've just watched people steal, people die?" Picard was incredulous and found an anger building within him he wanted to avoid. The last thing he wanted was to be mad at the people he had longed to meet.

"Our laws say we are to watch, remain vigilant in case we were threatened," a man said. "We obey our laws here."

Picard approached them and no one moved. He glanced at the viewscreen and saw nothing had changed there either.

"I am sworn to protect *my* people and I need your help to do that. I need to know how to shut down the entire network."

The five seated Iconians looked from one to another, either silently communing or totally lost. Picard prayed it wasn't the latter. He noted they looked to the woman to his right, who shifted her feet.

"The laws are vague about helping other species," she admitted.

"Are you six speaking for your people?" the captain demanded.

"We have very little need for governance," she said. "As it is, there have been gaps in the information flow. I think we can help you. While I should not speak for the others, I have personally been intrigued by how you and your ships help more than hurt."

The others remained silent and still, not agreeing or disagreeing with the opinion. Picard had expected something different from these people and wanted to keep his disappointment private.

"If I shut down the gateways, won't that enable you to return to your . . . studies?"

"Yes it would," one man said, almost with glee.

"Then help me, please," he said.

The woman walked over to the console of controls, flipped four cobalt-blue buttons, and waited. Information streamed across a panel and she read for a moment, activated a control, and read some more. She seemed to be seeking information and while she did so, everyone, even Picard, remained quiet. There was an aloofness to these people that disturbed him. He was certain these six had never spoken to an off-worlder and his presence probably made them nervous or annoyed. He could not be sure at all.

"The computer records show we do not have the control mechanism here," she said matter-of-factly.

Picard was stunned but kept his silence. He wanted to force her to speak, to provide more information. After several tense moments, she began again.

"It seems our ancestors left the controlling device on the last world we visited before settling here. I wonder why." She paused, thoughtful, then continued. "The records refer to a Master Resonator, but I can access no details. We can send you to that world to seek the device."

Now she fell silent and the captain absorbed the disheartening news. He had come a great way to seek these people and they seemed far from enlightened, far from human in their interactions. Maybe they were closer to the title "demons of air and darkness" than he ever wanted to admit.

"Do the records say what I am to do with the device?"

She shook her head, but one of the other women spoke up. "The gateways are attuned to one another, so I have believed that the Resonator can be inserted into any control panel and close down the entire system."

Picard nodded at the logic behind having an emergency cutoff switch; the principle made sense. "And once I find the Master Resonator, how do I return to my ship?"

"Through a gateway, of course," said the standing woman. It seemed such a simple answer, really, and her look betrayed her surprise at the question. Picard once more felt anger at the situation.

"Why did you leave our region?"

The woman looked at Picard blankly and she turned to the others. A man stood, the one with the largest tattoo on his face. He spoke up to cover the distance. "Our presence threatened to tamper with the natural order on too many worlds. Such changes were not always welcome ones, as I understand it. A change of heart, a change of government . . . something made our people stop and reconsider our presence. As a result, we migrated across space, until we reached here. Since then, we have abandoned contact with other people, concentrating on studying realms our gateways could not reach."

In his mind's eye, Picard recalled the devastation he found on Iconia, and Data's analysis that the planet had been attacked. He wondered if these descendants knew of the attack and might actually not have had a choice but to leave. The notion of other realms also caught his attention. Could they have meant time and space—piercing the dimensions and centuries? The mind boggled at the notion of such power—especially in the hands of a people that did not display any moral compass.

"We are merely sentries, Captain Picard," the woman said. "We watch and protect our people. You have a charter that obligates you to protect others. I find that admirable and will help you find the item you need. But after that, we will once again merely watch."

The man spoke up again. "If you can, Captain, please do not destroy the remaining gateways. Our history has shown that our people have changed their minds now and then. I would hate to deprive us of the option of coming home."

Picard looked at them and realized that they were out of their element. Nothing prepared them for first contact, nothing taught them what to do on the day another race stepped foot on their planet. However great the Iconians were two hundred thousand years in the past, these people were far removed from them. Whatever realities they studied kept them from the one they lived in and they were clueless how to act.

His anger dissipated and all he felt was pity.

"I cannot waste time," Picard said. "If I am to seek this Master Resonator, then send me."

One of the other men rose and walked to the console. He labored over the controls, constantly consulting the screen, as if he were being fed directions. They seemed not to know their own equipment and tools, Picard noted.

Minutes ticked by and everyone remained in now uncomfortable silence. Finally, the man seemed done and turned back to the group. "I have found the world. Captain, I am not sure I speak for all, but for myself, I wish you luck. I, too, do not want to see these gateways destroyed. It might be nice to visit newfound . . . friends."

At least one of the others seemed embarrassed by the sentiment and one remained stonily silent, but the others nodded in agreement.

A gateway formed in the room, with no apparent generating device. Merely a rip in reality, large enough for one man to enter—just like the gateway on Iconia that Picard had used a decade earlier. There was one location in sight: a lush, green world, not dissimilar to the one they stood on.

Picard nodded toward the Iconians, not sure of what to say. Of all the meetings he dreamed about, this was not among them. The thrill of meeting these idols was muted by the reality and it was a disappointment. And a lesson to be learned about idol worship.

Without a backward glance, Picard once more stepped into the gateway.

Chapter 2

"Message from Admiral Ross," Data said.

"On screen."

"Commander Riker, have we heard from the captain?" Clearly Ross was anxious for some good news.

"Not at all, sir." Riker wished for word from his friend, too, but at least was closer to the action. He could busy himself with monitoring forty-eight potentially lethal ships and maintaining a fragile alliance where the now long-gone Gorn had already betrayed them once.

"Damn" was all the admiral would say. After all, he remained on Earth and could merely absorb reports from the fleet, most of which were of a catastrophic nature. All in all, Riker was glad to be on the *Enterprise*.

"How go things back home," Riker asked, knowing full well that it would not be pleasant.

"We've achieved a holding action, which is better than being deluged," Ross admitted. While not quite a victory, it was the first positive news in too many hours. *"We have some news from Deep Space 9. The Orions are officially out of the bidding, at least, and they managed to successfully evacuate Europa Nova. Unfortunately, it looks like Colonel Kira may have been lost."*

Riker winced. He had only met the Bajoran woman a few times, but

233

he'd been impressed with what he saw. The commander also knew that Ross had great respect for her.

"We're still waiting for word from the Excalibur *and the* Trident, *but I can't get them to tell me everything."*

"Captain Calhoun is known for his unorthodox methods," Riker said dryly.

"That's just it. I'm beginning to think that neither Calhoun nor Shelby are aboard their respective ships, but I can't get them to tell me where they are."

A moment was all it took for the realization to hit the first officer. "You think they entered a gateway and are lost, don't you?"

Ross's silence confirmed the worst for Riker. Before either could speak, Lieutenant Vale interrupted. "There's a message from Desan coming in on the other channel."

"Back to your duty, Commander," Ross said, and the screen blinked once and his hangdog look was replaced by the more attractive visage of the Romulan commander.

"How can I help you, Commander?" Riker asked, leaning back in the command chair. It would never be comfortable, he realized. Not with his friend missing in action.

"Why are we rigging a simultaneous connection among all the Petraw vessels?"

Riker blinked. She looked unhappy about the matter and he matched her mood. It wasn't something he had assigned.

"News to me," Riker began, when he heard the turbolift doors slide open. Before he could turn around, the heavy footsteps were a clear signal.

"Are we not to be consulted?" thundered Captain Grekor, leader of the Klingon delegation.

"Listen to me, both of you, I didn't order anything of the sort and we're going to take a moment and figure this out. Commander, tell me what you know."

"We received a Starfleet communiqué informing us to participate in rigging all forty-eight ships with a single link, to remain on an open channel. The message gave us an hour to comply."

Riker nodded and looked at the very unhappy Grekor, who nodded in agreement with the message. His stance showed he was pretty angry, feet firmly planted deep into the bridge's carpet, arms crossed before his chest, which rose and fell quickly.

"Lieutenant, did we issue such a order?"

Vale scanned one end of the tactical station to the other before responding. Of course, she found nothing.

"Raise Captain Brisbayne, please," Riker said, trying to sound polite, but betraying the anger in his tone.

Carter Brisbayne, captain of the wounded starship *Mercury,* appeared on the screen after a matter of moments. He seemed restless, like everyone else, and he had every right to be. On approaching the Petraw ships, they took heavy fire and were left limping in space, possibly irreparable.

"Did you issue an order, Captain?"

He stiffened at Riker's tone, and directed himself at the camera. *"God damn right I did, Commander,"* he replied.

"Captain Picard left me in command of this group, Captain, and with all due respect, I ask that you honor those wishes."

"You can have this 'fleet,' but we are not going to get caught with our pants down."

Riker shifted in the chair, as it seemed to get more uncomfortable by the minute. "Explain."

"By maintaining an open link, we can avoid sabotage and surprise," the older captain said. *"If just one thing goes amiss on one ship, we all know immediately—or if one ship cuts the signal, we can spot the problem. I'm not one for waiting."*

Riker stroked his stubbly chin and saw that the explanation, while sensible, did not mollify the Klingon. He couldn't easily let Brisbayne off the hook.

"Everyone is here voluntarily, Captain," Riker said evenly. "We do not hand out orders while at yellow alert. If you want to make further useful suggestions, we must all be consulted. Riker out."

The first officer rose to address Grekor, who remained immobile. It was a good sign that he came alone; there would be no "honor" to defend before his own crew. Riker had the advantage but didn't feel the need to press it.

"He acted on his own authority, but the thinking is sound. I suggest we complete the task, backing up the crew we have on the Petraw ships. Such a breach of protocol won't happen again, Captain. You have my word on it."

The rotund Klingon nodded and finally moved, turning to head back to the lift. "I will hold you to it, Commander."

"As will I," Desan added, cutting the signal.

Once the Klingon left the bridge, Riker settled down once more and felt a fresh ache in his shoulders.

The good news was there was no dampening field on the verdant planet. The bad news was nothing technological was showing up on the screen. Picard completed several full-circle turns before shutting down the tricorder and pocketing it.

There were plenty of life signs. The planet was teeming with humanoid life, birds, animals, and insects. No electronic signals were detected, no radio communications, nothing to imply anything more than primitive development. As a result, Picard was faced with the full impact of noninterference directives. He had to somehow find the device, which failed to register in the vicinity of the gateway, and do so in a manner that prevented the culture he was to find from being altered.

He believed in the Prime Directive, absolutely. It was just coming into play at a damned inconvenient time.

Picard exhaled for a moment, clearing his mind and preparing to plot a course of action. As he inhaled, and concentrated, he detected the faint aroma of cooking meat. First, it told him there were intelligent people nearby, which was a start. Second, it provided a direction. Finally, it triggered a rumble in his stomach, reminding him that he needed to find food for himself or he would jeopardize the mission by starving to death. He set out from the cluster of trees he had been standing in, which provided comfortable shade. Like the new Iconian homeworld, this planet promised plenty of sunshine and warmth, perhaps too warm for his full uniform. He unzipped the jacket to let the cooler air caress his body.

A well-worn path from the trees indicated that people used this area. It made sense that there would be an encampment of some sort nearby. He noted that the planet must have had lighter gravity than

Earth, as each step seemed to carry him farther than expected. Noting the size and shape of the trees and plants, he was proven correct, mentally filing the information away.

His trail led him to the forest's edge, which opened up to a small village. There were thatched homes, made from sturdy thin wood. Each structure seemed tall and wide, probably two stories, and they were clustered in a traditional block pattern, with all paths leading to a central square. He concluded that there was no chance of finding the Resonator without dealing with some of the planet's inhabitants, so he had to start somewhere.

And the cooking food smelled so good.

Before entering the village, Picard stopped to study the people, withdrawing the tricorder once more to take comparative readings. Like the Iconians, they were tall, thin folk. Their skin was copper-colored, darkened by the sun. Each wore what appeared to be cured animal skins for clothing and all carried walking sticks topped with ornate carvings. Around their waists were thick, wide belts that seemed to have pockets bulging with . . . well, he could not tell from the distance. The men seemed to all sport shaggy beards while every woman he spotted had hair pulled back in a ponytail. The sheer uniformity of their appearance was remarkable to the captain.

The tricorder also told him one important detail: the food being cooked was safe for a human to eat.

One of the men caught a glimpse of Picard and shouted out a cry of some sort. Seven other men rushed to his side and they looked at Picard, alone and feeling naked on the path. He hoped the Universal Translator would unlock their language quickly, but of course it needed a sample to work with. Wisely, he chose to stand his ground rather than appear threatening to the men. The last thing he wanted was to be clubbed to death by a mob.

With long strides, the men hurried toward the captain, who remained in place, knowing full well that he was likely to be poked and prodded, tested before anyone let down their guard. He could smell the men before they arrived, dirty and smoky, but that made sense given their apparent lifestyle. None made threatening moves, which pleased him. As they got closer, they began spreading out, and within moments the eight men who stared with wide-eyed wonder circled Picard.

The one who'd spotted him nodded to the others and they all reached to a pocket in the rear of their belts. All removed what was remarkably a weapon of sophisticated design. Picard could see the refined metal in their hands, recognizing the pistol design despite the men holding the weapons at right angles to the proper manner. It seemed more ceremonial than anything else, but not taking chances, Picard raised his hands to shoulder height. To his surprise, the men imitated the move.

Picard next lowered his arms and once again, men imitated the move. Before he could try something else, the men once more held out the weapons at the silly angle. Picard slowly reached for his phaser and, adjusting it to imitate their handling of the pistols, held out the phaser, turning in a slow circle so all the men could see the action. They made comprehending noises but it didn't sound like language. He thought back on his training and spoke out. His first word was "hello." They all stared at him.

After a moment, the men tried to repeat the word and failed miserably. Once again, Picard said "hello" and they tried to repeat the sound, improving on the second chance. They began to look expectantly at the captain, who was hoping they would say something to him next. Instead, the silence grew, so he tried again. Holstering the phaser, Picard pointed to himself and said his last name.

The men pointed to themselves and repeated the word. They seemed remarkably pleased with their progress.

One man, though, turned to another and said something that was clearly in a language. Picard made minute steps toward them, hoping it didn't appear as a threat. Instead, he was trying to make certain the translator picked up the words to begin processing. Another two began to whisper and before long, everyone was whispering, so all the captain heard was gibberish.

Finally, one of the men said loudly, "Hello!" The captain looked directly at him and smiled. The others took turns calling out the name and he responded to each in kind. It might not have been translating according to the manual, but they were making progress.

The circle broke and the leader gestured toward the village, shouting his name while one of the others bellowed back, "Hello!" The nine moved toward the buildings as more curious men and women filled the center, where the meat had continued to cook. Along the way, Picard tried to catch snippets of conversation back and forth and hoped the translations would start soon. Very soon.

On his way toward the center, he took time to notice the decorations on the buildings and he came to realize each home had some piece of sophisticated technology as a door hanging, more decorative than anything else. Clearly, there had been a superior civilization on this planet, but something had happened, and, darkly, he fretted over the Iconians' role in the planet's past.

Children stood before their parents and looked in amazement at Picard, who was shorter and stockier than these people. Some gestured to one another and patted their heads, clearly remarking on his bald scalp compared with their thick manes. The men and women commingled, sharing comments and unashamedly staring at the newcomer.

". . . smarhsgehb . . . funny-looking . . ."

Finally, the translator began working and he smirked at the timing involved. People looked up in amazement as they heard the electronic device at work.

"Greetings," the captain said, a smile on his face. He tried to look as friendly as possible. "I am Picard and I have come from a long way away."

The man he presumed to be the village leader came toward him, a huge grin on his face. "Picard! We welcome you!"

"It has taken me a little time to learn your language, but I am now able to speak with you all," the captain explained.

"Excellent. I am Hamish, elder of the village."

"I have come from far away seeking a special item. A very old item."

Hamish, definitely among the older ones in the village as witnessed by the almost white hair, looked thoughtful. He reached once more behind his back and withdrew the weapon. "Something like this perhaps?"

Picard shook his head. "No, Hamish. I cannot tell you what it is, but I do know it is a singular item while it seems all your men have that."

He shook his head and laughed, a deep-throated laugh, which was pleasing to the ear. "No worry, Picard. We all have these because they were given to us by our fathers. It is our symbol of welcome and while yours is different, it clearly is similar. I see yours looks newer and cleaner. We have lost count of the generations these have remained in the village."

"Why do you seek this object?" asked a woman from his right side.

"I have many people in trouble at home, and ones wiser than I tell me it will help." Not at all a lie and boiled down enough to be clear to these pleasant folk.

"Wiser than you?" This from a young girl, behind Hamish.

"My daughter Hemma," he said by way of introduction.

"Yes, Hemma," Picard replied. "I knew no other way to help my people than to ask for the help of those who built the item I seek. It is the way of my people, to ask for help when we must. We in turn offer help to those who ask."

"Picard, are you from the west?"

The captain stared at the old man. Truthfully, his path led west, but he was not of the west and he couldn't begin to imagine what the question implied. His answer could turn them against him if his words were chosen poorly.

"My travels have taken me in all directions," he answered a moment later.

Hamish laughed once more and stepped closer to Picard, who noticed the stench of dried sweat. "As I expected. Young Gods on their ordeal must have traveled the world to gain their *granita*." Picard couldn't even begin to imagine what a *granita* implied but being called a young god set off internal warning bells. He'd been mistaken for a god once before by a low-tech culture, and it was not an experience he was eager to relive—for his sake, or for the sake of these good people.

Several other old men approached Hamish and they clustered, whispering back and forth. Picard took the opportunity to study more of the village and its inhabitants. Everyone seemed healthy, well fed, and protected. However they developed, he knew his presence must not change that status quo. He seemed not to frighten the children, which pleased him. While he might be uncomfortable around them, he never wanted to chase them away. Many stayed close to adults, family members most likely, and just studied him, as he studied them. A few smiled, while most kept their opinions to themselves.

"Picard," Hamish called, regaining the captain's attention. "If you seek things closer to our ceremonial welcome tools, then we think you must travel to the City. It is but three days' walk from here, and must be part of your path. It is filled with many unknown things and it may hold your heart's desire."

Poetic, he mused, but accurate. There was nothing he wanted more than to find the Resonator and return to the *Enterprise*. He sniffed and then realized there was one more thing he desired: dinner.

"Very well," he said. "I shall start at sunrise if you would be so kind as to provide me with directions."

Hamish smiled and began walking toward the fire. The other men followed and slowly the other members of the village began to head for the center. Most talked and laughed among themselves, and Picard seemed uncertain of what he might have missed.

"Come, Picard," he called as he stopped before the huge pit, where some animal roasted on a spit. "Even gods must eat, eh? You'll eat and sleep and eat once more, then begin the final part of your journey."

With that, the elder turned to the fire, grabbed a long metallic item, and poked roughly at the meat. It hissed as juices dribbled from the scored carcass into the flames. Children had gathered up plates that seemed formed from clay, along with short, wide cups. They walked past the fire and to long tables, setting places as they passed. A few sang a song he was too far away to translate but he found the melody pleasing.

Three men hefted the meat off the fire and carried it to a small hut, where the meat was swiftly carved and placed on a large earthen slab, the color of rust. They, too, joked among themselves, ignoring Picard, who just watched.

Finally, a girl left her mother's side and walked over to the captain and looked up at him. He estimated her age to be five or six, but she was already tall compared with human children. Her hair was past her shoulders but nowhere near as long as the mature women in the group. Unlike the women, her belt was not stuffed with tools but with a round plastic item and some bright stones. With a hand gesture, she indicated he was to follow her and happily he did. There was no awe in her, as if young gods visited the villages regularly. He wouldn't ask her, not before they ate, and he wasn't sure if he should. This might be one of those times ignorance was bliss and there was less likelihood of crossing the Prime Directive.

She led him to the smallest of the tables, where the older women already sat. He was placed between two whose hair had long since stopped shining in the sun but showed age. They seemed pleased to have him with them, so he smiled and nodded to them all.

"Picard is it?" the woman to his right asked.

"Yes," he answered.

"From the west are you?"

"And other places."

"Been to the depths? To the stars?" She laughed at her joke, seemingly not to believe he was anything more than a funny-looking native. The other women laughed at the jest and he took it in stride.

Finally, adolescents brought platters of meat and broth to each table. They remained to serve those seated and then took their own places. Picard noticed that none began eating. All looking toward Hamish to speak.

"Our food gives us life, your sun gives us warmth. For this we are thankful. And we thank you, too, for sending one of your children among us. We will be a better people for his presence."

Everyone bowed low, their heads carefully touching the rims of their plates, so Picard imitated the gesture. Within seconds, the sounds of eating, drinking, and laughter filled the air. They seemed a happy, stable people, one the captain would have found fascinating to study, but while they laughed, more people, closer to home, suffered.

The meat was soft and tender, and was well marinated in some sweet native spices. Picard ate his fill and drank the local wine, which struck him as flat and without much bouquet. He was impressed by their overall politeness as no one, not even the children, pestered him with questions. Instead, he heard hunting stories, local gossip, and gained an impression that between here and the City there were farms and smaller enclaves of people. He was pleased that the path sounded clear so he could try and cut the march from three days to two. At least, he mused as he finished his drink, the Iconians sent him to the right continent.

After the meal, those who served went from table to table and collected the remains. Picard nodded in approval to see how neat and orderly they were, not letting much go to waste. Women and men gathered their children and started herding them back to the huts for bedtime. The older ones went toward the fire and sat there in companionable silence, enjoying the warmth. One took out an item from her belt and began fiddling with it while another reworked a piece of wood with a stone carving knife. Hamish waved Picard over and he was more than happy to join the group.

"What have you seen, on your travels?" an old man asked. He barely had any hair left and his scalp was sunburnt a deep red.

"Much the same as you, I would imagine," Picard said in a friendly tone. "I have traveled on the seas and watched great storms. I have walked in the woods and across a desert, seeing the remains. I have slept at night under the same stars as you, and have dreamed what might be out there." All true, he reminded himself.

"Are there many like you?" the woman who fiddled with a metal item asked.

"Here? No, I don't think so."

He stared at the item in her vein-popped hands, as she turned it over and over again. Something about it seemed familiar and, instinctively, he knew it was out of context. Letting his mind drift a bit, he pictured it in his head.

"That is a tool, is it not?"

"I don't know," she said seriously. "I've had it four or five seasons now—found it while doing the summer planting."

"May I?" The woman handed over the item without hesitation, clearly curious to see what the newcomer might do with it.

It was denser and heavier metal than Picard imagined. The item was smooth to the touch, oblong with an indented opening at one end. He saw a small seam and recognized it could be twisted and he gave it a tug. At first, it resisted his touch and then it began to move. He unscrewed the item into two distinct pieces and saw that within one end was an apparatus that could fold out. Slowly, he brought it into the light and studied its composition.

"I believe this is a garden tool," Picard proclaimed. "Once opened, you pull out this part and it helps dig deep holes for the seeds. Capped together, it can be a digging implement as well." It was not too dissimilar from tools he knew were of Iconian-derived manufacture on Iccobar, and, of everyone involved in this mission, he might have been the only one to recognize it.

This delighted the woman and confirmed for Picard that the Iconians had indeed used this world for a time before departing. Had they been hunted down from Iconia to here? More mysteries to ponder, and he was beginning to believe he'd never know the answers. Thankfully this was a fairly benign discovery, not one to totally alter the culture. After all, they seemed to lack the ability to manipulate metal ore.

"The Young God knows much," Hamish said in admiration.

His being a god to them, though, *that* could pose problems.

La Forge looked at the tricorder and showed it to Kliv, the engineer who appreciated the intricacies of the Petraw hodge-podge technology as much as he did. The Klingon nodded once and then stared deep into the open panel of the gateway device.

"There's nothing left to do," he said in a matter-of-fact tone.

"No doubt about it," La Forge agreed. He snapped the device closed and tapped his communicator. "La Forge to Riker. Sir, there's nothing left to do. We've rerouted everything possible, but there's no way to stop this ship from being destroyed."

Once the gateways throughout the galaxy were turned on, each used their sophisticated programming to stay powered up—even at the expense of all nearby sources of power. In this case, it meant the lead Petraw ship was a ticking time bomb and the best efforts of the two engineers could not defuse it.

"The Ambassador is about done with the evacuation onto the other Petraw ships," Riker reported. *"You and the security team will be the final ones to come back."*

Geordi was already moving, leaving the massive engineering deck, heading for the bridge in the ship's center. Kliv remained at his side, a tight bond having been quickly formed between the men. One would not leave without the other and neither would leave the ship until the remaining vessels were safe. Their fast walk became a trot until the two were racing from deck to deck, making sure there would be sufficient time remaining to do their duty.

Boots echoed on the metal deck plating as heavy feet moved with increasing speed. Neither said a word as they wended their way to the ship's nerve center. Once they entered the now-vacant space, each took one of the low-slung stations and began entering coordinates. They called forth details to each other in a rapid staccato, making sure all the redundancies were in synch. A star chart on Kliv's station showed the vessel moving away from the pack, heading away at an accelerating speed.

"We'll never make warp the way this thing is sucking the energy reserves," Geordi said.

"Then today might be a good day to die, after all," Kliv replied, stabbing blunt fingers at a side control panel.

"Not yet," his partner replied. "The engine integrity fields will collapse in about four minutes. Maybe we'll be far enough away."

Kliv shook his head.

Before he could say anything else, La Forge snapped his fingers and summoned his commander once more. "Beam us back, and at the same time, have Kerim push us farther away with concentrated tractor bursts. Every inch will be useful."

"Acknowledged. Stand by to beam up."

Once back aboard the *Enterprise,* the two once more raced for a bridge, this time to watch the fruits of their labors. Out of breath and perspiring, La Forge couldn't help but notice that his partner seemed utterly fit and not even breathing hard. He vowed to start Dr. Crusher's exercise regimen, ignored for two months now, tomorrow.

"Nice work, gentlemen," Riker said from the center seat. Data flashed them a thumbs-up gesture that made Kliv blink in confusion. Chuckling, La Forge showed his friend the engineering station and they monitored the death throes of the Petraw engine core.

Within seconds, the ship began to buckle then flare and a moment later, nothing remained on the viewscreen.

"Shock waves in five . . . four . . . three . . . two . . . one," Data announced.

The mighty starship bucked once, then twice, then settled down without incident. La Forge rolled out the chair at the aft station and sat, letting out a breath he never knew he was holding. Kliv stood impassively by his side.

Perim turned to Riker, who was still tightly gripping the arms of the command chair, and asked, "How will the captain return now?"

He had no answer for her, and it was a question he avoided asking himself. With the gateway destroyed he couldn't even send a search party after Picard, in direct defiance of his orders no less. Wherever his friend was, he hoped he was safe and would return soon.

It was considerably more comfortable when Picard woke the following morning. The sun was rising in the sky and he could tell the villagers had been moving about for a little while now. People were already eating, children were chasing a wooden hoop, and something that seemed more pet dog than wild beast was snuffling around the waste pit.

Hamish was tending the fire, which never seemed to die out, when Picard approached. He had already been offered some food and drink so felt refreshed. He liked these people and could only wish them well. Still, he felt the press of time, and needed to be on his way.

"I need a direction so my journey can continue," Picard said.

"You really cannot linger any longer?"

"Would that time permitted me, but without this object, people will continue to die."

Hamish looked at him with a grave expression on his face. It seemed to just be dawning on him the importance of the task. "This item you seek—it has that much power?"

"It is a key to something that will give me the power to save lives."

"The remainder of this world is very different from our village, is it not?"

"I have not seen it all, but can tell you that it is very lively and I would like to keep it that way."

"You will make a great God," Hamish said with finality.

Picard winced but shook his head slightly. "I am trying to be a good man, first."

An hour later, he was on a worn path leading away from the village, heading in a southeastern direction. Hamish had insisted on giving him two skins of water and some dried meats tied in a large leaf for safekeeping. He tried to extract a promise of a return visit from Picard, but the captain dodged it while trying to remain respectful.

He truly enjoyed their company and had wanted to spend more time, but like the Petraw, he was forced to keep moving. Now, he was walking in and out of shade, as he skirted the edge of a forest. The trees grew quite tall, with thin but sturdy sand-colored trunks. As the village was near water, Picard could hear a stream or river to his right, assuming most of the people lived near whatever natural sources they could find. The smaller trees that seemed to be closer to the water were short and more like overeager bushes, but they burst with orange and beige fruits.

It was quiet and Picard was alone with his thoughts. How different this world was from the harsh remains of Iconia, he considered. Knowing they spent time here would force him to reconsider their path across the galaxy, and he was mentally ordering information for the eventual paper that he would write. This pleasant world was well on its way to full recovery from whatever the Iconians had left behind, and he would have to stop and take some tricorder readings to help determine the age of these artifacts. If the City was what he imagined to be their largest remains, he would have plenty of samples to work from.

He was also pleased to note that the lighter gravity gave an extra bounce to his step and he was making rather good time. The sun was not too hot compared with yesterday, and Picard hoped he would see the City before nightfall and reach it by sundown tomorrow. Hamish and the villagers didn't measure distance in miles or kilometers. They apparently had little dealing with those beyond the village so they never quite developed a precise measurement for such distances.

Within time, Picard noticed tracks in the path, parallel ruts that indicated some form of wheeled vehicle had been by, recently enough for the tracks not to have been washed away by the previous day's rain. He saw no such thing at the village so presumed it to be from a neighboring enclave. This led him to conjecture about differing developmental paths for humanoids in the same general vicinity. It was certainly true for tribes found in Africa or the South American rain forest, the captain knew. As a result, he felt a need to stay more alert . . . just in case.

Sure enough, after less than an hour, he heard sounds. The noise was not that of wheels in mud, but of concerned voices. There was definitely a problem, so he quickened his pace and hurried forward. Within a few minutes, the road rounded a bend and he saw the remains of a wagon teetering over a huge rock and pinning a man underneath. The wide, low platform, filled with bales of something akin to hay, seemed stable, but the axle for the rear wheels had splintered over the rocky path. The man was conscious and moaning, clearly in pain. Watching in fear were women and children, dressed differently from people in the village Picard had visited. These had on lighter-colored clothing that seemed actually spun from natural materials as opposed to the skins the villagers wore. Physically they were the same, even down to the long hair.

Picard saw they were paralyzed to the point of inaction, so he stepped forward and approached the wagon. "Don't be scared, help has arrived," he said.

The woman behind him had stopped wailing and stared at him. He heard a whisper or two but it had grown fairly silent except for the trapped man's moans.

It was clear that the lighter gravity would allow Picard a physical advantage, so all he needed to do was lift up an edge of the wagon so the man could be freed. He took several deep breaths, focusing his energies. Then, placing his back to the wagon, he firmly gripped the corner, planted his feet far apart, and began exerting his strength.

As expected, the wagon full of hay made the effort tough, but his muscles responded and he strained. Not a young man anymore, Picard prided himself in staying physically fit and knew he was up to the challenge. He gritted his teeth and continued to apply pressure, finally feeling the wagon rise.

"Quickly, come clear him away!" Picard ordered, not wanting to shift his focus.

The women hesitated, but three of the children, most seeming around ten years old, rushed forward and tugged at the man's exposed leg. He grunted louder than Picard, making for an odd duet. Finally, Picard could tell he'd have to let go in a matter of moments, as the children continued to slowly drag the man away.

Finally, the man was clear and Picard let the heavy wood slip from his fingers. It shattered some more as it resettled itself against the rocks but he doubted anyone would care. Wiping the sweat from his brow, Picard saw that the man was having his leg tended to by one woman while another was giving him water.

He took a drink himself and then slowly walked over to check on the injured person.

"You saved him, thank you, Young God!"

"Yes, thank you, Young God."

Picard was feeling particularly uncomfortable for being repeatedly singled out and called a god. It made sense that there would be mores and beliefs carried from village to village but he was nothing like a god.

"Will he be all right?"

"I think so," the woman responded.

"Good, then I will be on my way." Picard turned toward the path, hoping to make a fast escape from these emotionally distraught people.

"Why leave us so quickly, Young God?" The speaker was a young girl, one of the children who helped him.

"I must go to the City," he replied.

"Stay so we can thank you properly," she said.

"I wish I could, but I must hurry."

"The sun is going down, you won't make it there today," she argued. "At least let us feed you supper."

Picard glanced at the sky and noticed it growing deeper in color, and that it was beginning to cool. He had hoped to glimpse the City today but it seemed not to be. There was safety in numbers, he knew, and the man might need attention.

It seemed decided for him so he smiled at her and accepted the invitation.

Within an hour, the area was transformed into a small campsite with vegetables being grilled on a small fire. Lean-tos were established by the forest's edge, and the boy had brought back water from the nearby stream. The man, who was named Yanooth, had slept on and off as he recovered from the shock. The leg was badly broken and the women successfully placed it in a neatly made splint.

Picard's offers of help were refused, so he sat back and spoke quietly with the children. They told him of their village, which was beyond the City, and how they loved traveling. Their innocence and resourcefulness charmed him.

One young boy seemed quite taken with Picard's actions but didn't act like he was a god, which he found refreshing. Instead, the boy asked questions about lifting the wagon, how his muscles felt, how he could manage to do such feats for himself. His named was Chanik, and he wedged himself between one of the women and Picard when they sat to eat the vegetable stew.

"I've been to the City once," he proudly announced.

"Really?" asked Picard. "Tell me about it."

"Well, it's like no place you've ever seen," he said between mouthfuls of food. "Tall huts, mostly broken, with weird-looking vines connecting some of them together. It's as big as this forest, maybe bigger, and the animals all avoid it so it's a good place to hide."

Picard processed the information, trying to imagine the place, and wondered how much of it still functioned given how long-lived the Iconian technology was. "I'll find out for myself soon, won't I?"

"And I'm going to show you!"

Picard was alarmed by the pronouncement. He had already learned that Chanik had attached himself to this traveling party, and was from one of the villages nearby. The last thing he needed was to be responsible for someone's life while he was rushing to save countless others.

"I can't do that," he declared. "I must move quickly and I won't be able to properly look after you."

Chanik put down his wooden bowl, wiped his mouth with the back of his left hand, and grinned. "I'll be looking after you, Young God Picard. After all, I know how to get in there and you don't."

The captain, recognizing a universal tone in his young voice, sat quietly, suspecting he was going to have company, like it or not. He resolved to make the best of the situation, since the youth's experience just might allow him to move through the City quicker.

The notion though, kept him awake as he lay on a bed of fern leaves, trying to sleep.

Chapter 3

The morning sun had Picard awake before the others. He could feel the excitement building in his chest as he checked to make sure his equipment was still where he had secured it the night before. The captain had decided to use the phaser and tricorder as little as possible, refusing to raise the notion that a god, young or otherwise, might need such devices.

He checked the campfire and saw there were still embers he could coax back to cooking heat and proceeded to busy himself with preparing the breakfast. It was the least he could do, he decided, since the others had been good enough to feed him the previous night. With a glance, he saw Chanik rolling over, still asleep. The youth was full of possibilities, the captain recognized, but also full of risk, and he still disliked the notion that he would be joining him. The captain shoved the thought from his mind and continued to build the fire and then find the remains of dinner to reheat into breakfast. There were some fruit trees nearby, so he went over and carefully judged which were the ripest. The branches grew tall, the fruit yellow and fat, and the captain had to reach quite a bit to snag the ones ready to eat. He grabbed enough, hoping to have extra to bring along with him since he doubted there'd be much in the way of food once they entered the City.

He heard the stirrings of his companions and was pleased since it meant they could eat and he could be on his way that much sooner. His goal was to reach the City quickly and then use the tricorder to track

252

the Master Resonator. With it, he hoped to return to the portal he had emerged from—or find another functioning gateway in the city. Geordi La Forge had shown him how they focused the portal's reach, so he had high hopes of finding his way directly back to the *Enterprise.*

"Young God Picard, today's our day for adventure!" Chanik ran across the encampment and held out his hands to help hold the fruit. He must have just woken up but was already at full speed. Picard smiled at this, and appreciated having the extra arms to hold the fruit, which had a fuzzy outerskin, but felt firm and ripe in his hands.

"We'll eat some and travel with the rest," Picard said by way of explanation.

Chanik nodded eagerly, impressed with the bounty.

The breakfast went by without incident, and within the hour Picard and Chanik were ready to depart. Yanooth was in good spirits, despite his leg injury, which pleased the captain. He figured the traveling party would be in good shape for the remainder of their journey back to their home village. The grateful man insisted Picard take a leather satchel, and needing something with which to carry supplies, the captain graciously accepted. Limiting his contact with all, after this, was his best course of action, although he suspected shaking Chanik loose would be a problem later on.

"How far to the City?"

Chanik took his first steps on the trail, a small backpack filled with water, fruit, and whatever personal belongings he had tucked in. His smile was bright, despite the dingy teeth, and he pointed up the trail and declared, "We could see it just after midday."

"Excellent, then let's begin," Picard said.

But the boy was already walking briskly ahead of him; the journey was under way. With a smile, Picard picked up his pace and followed along.

The trail continued to skirt the forest, but within two hours, it had thinned and ended, opening up to wide fields that seemed full of grains, growing tall in the sun. The area seemed lush and golden, thanks to the water nearby. He tried to spot animals grazing but saw little beyond native birds that were too high up to study.

Chanik was just as comfortable chatting as he was with silence, which only pleased the captain. Were the boy overly inquisitive, he knew, it would only make him defensive, spoiling the hike. They did chat briefly, talking about other places Chanik had been, comparing them with the forests they left behind. The boy seemed to prefer open space to the closed-in feel given by the trees, but he also admitted to minimal experience in forests, since there were not many where he grew up.

As they walked, Picard began to note uniformity to the fields, row upon row of similar grains followed by sections with tidy rows of other plants. Farming principles seem to be fairly universal, he thought. From what he could judge, the society he had encountered had come a far way from the high-tech civilization it had once been, but they had learned to work with nature rather than let it overwhelm them. Had the Iconians abandoned this world two hundred millennia ago, and the Cities all fell to ruin, he estimated the number of centuries before nature thoroughly reclaimed the space. While the technology might have survived the passage of time, nature would find its way to reassert itself. The people might have had a difficult adjustment, but he doubted he would ever learn. He had seen no books yet, just simple people living a peaceful existence. The remains of the Iconian culture obviously had been the foundation for modern mythology, but that was only natural.

"Someone is doing an excellent job maintaining these lands," Picard noted.

Chanik looked out to see what the captain was talking about. He clearly hadn't made a point of observing the farmland and was looking at it appraisingly. "How can you tell?"

"The farmers are rotating their crops in the field, keeping everything in neat rows," Picard said. He gestured and added, "The uniform height of the grains shows they must have been planted at roughly the same time, so they run a well-organized operation."

The boy nodded, clearly never having considered anything like farming. He was probably more a hunter and gatherer, considering there were no parents to teach him. Picard smiled at the boy with regret crossing his features. Every boy deserved a parent to teach him about the world, he knew. And for a moment, he considered his nephew, now dead, and all the opportunities that were not to be. Forcing the notion from his mind, Picard continued on.

By the noon hour, Picard could see a man at work near the edge of the trail. He was wearing a one-piece outfit, dyed a deep blue, a floppy hat providing shade. The farmer was checking some of his crops, dark fingers weighing a stalk in his hand.

"Fair weather," the man said as the duo approached.

"Fair weather," Picard repeated, figuring it was a safe reply. "I have been admiring your fields. You do excellent work."

The farmer looked directly at Picard, recognizing his somewhat different appearance. He said nothing for a bit and finally nodded in acknowledgment.

"Been dry," he said.

"I can still hear the river so water must be plentiful."

"Maybe. Can only carry so much of it."

"I see your point. Is it a problem?"

"Heat's making the stalks short, will have to harvest them sooner than I'd like."

"Has it been dry here long?"

"Long enough," came the reply. "Not from around here, are you?"

Chanik finally chirped up. "This Young God is Picard and I'm taking him to the City."

At the words "Young God," the farmer once more stared at Picard. The words meant something to him and there was a moment of suspicion. He must have decided the captain wasn't a threat and just went back to looking at his grain.

"Do you grow much else?"

"Got my house by the water, grow me some berries, make a little wine."

"I see. How do you make the wine?"

The man looked at Picard once more, a look of surprise on his face. The expression read as if everyone knew how to make wine, why would a Young God be asking?

"Soak the berries for a day or two, mash them in a bag . . . you know, the usual way."

Picard nodded but asked, "Hot or cold?"

"The wine? Neither, serve it natural."

"No, the soaking. Do you use hot water or cold?"

"Just pull water from the river, fill up the basins and dump in the berries."

"I see. I think you might find the wine more flavorful if you use hot water for the soaking. Do you add anything to the berries?"

"Nope, just let 'em ferment."

"How long before you serve it?"

"From soakin' to servin', must be a few months." The farmer was looking less suspicious, caught up in the discussion of tradecraft.

"What do they ferment in?"

"Earthenware jars—keep 'em in a shed back of the house."

"There's plenty of wood nearby—if you make barrels, I think you will find they age better. And I'd let them sit longer before serving, maybe up to a year." He wasn't sure how long they measured their time, but given the day-night cycle he'd witnessed, it wasn't too far from Earth norms.

"That a fact?"

Chanik stayed silent, watching in fascination as Picard continued to question the methods and suggested alternatives. The farmer didn't dispute the comments, nor was he agreeing with them, just nodding occasionally.

Picard reached into his bag and pulled out one of the yellow fruits, which Chanik had called a *quint.* "For variety, you might want to try adding some fruit juice. Something like this might be good, or mix some other fruits. I would, though, only add about two fistfuls of juice to a barrel as high as your knee."

"Fruit in my wine? What for?"

"Good as your berries are, wouldn't you want some wines that are sweeter or tarter throughout the day or year?"

"Maybe. Never thought about it."

"I grew up learning the craft," Picard said, his mind's eye picturing the Picard family vineyards and the years he spent helping his father.

"That a fact."

"That it is," Picard replied. "I'd really like to stay and show you, but Chanik is right: We're going to the City and I am pressed for time."

The farmer chuckled at the word "pressed" since it was a winemaking term. He nodded in acknowledgment. "Well, I wish you luck. Might try some of your ideas."

"I think you'll find yourself the envy of the area," Picard said with good humor.

"Going with just the *quints?*"

Picard nodded, not really giving his food supplies much thought.

"My house is just a little bit up the road; let me give you a few other things. Way to thank you for the advice."

"That would be most gracious of you," Picard said.

"Never hurts to thank a Young God," the farmer said, tossing the grain on the ground and starting to walk. "Might be some rain in it."

Picard did not reply, inwardly sighing at the notion of his "godhood."

Some twenty minutes later, the captain and the boy had some dried meats, additional fruits, and a small skin full of the farmer's wine. The farmer hadn't said much else, and Picard did not see any telltale signs of a wife or children in the small three-room house. He recognized it as a rather solitary experience, making him feel more than a little sad for the man.

Chanik was thrilled with the additional supplies and was chattering on about how this would make their stay in the City nicer. He admitted there might be some wild berries or fruits in the City, but mostly weeds covered the streets.

"You seem to know so much," Chanik said.

"I have been well taught, and in my years, I have experienced quite a bit," Picard replied with a smile.

"Who taught you?"

"My parents, teachers, things I learn by observing. You seem to know much for one so young."

Chanik looked up in eager anticipation. "Do I?"

Picard realized that much of what he learned was through life experience. He doubted that anyone spent that much time showing Chanik how to accomplish much. That spoke of a certain intelligence, which would benefit the boy over the years ahead. Still, Chanik had to survive to grow and for that he needed something more than a nomad's life. Even one life can alter a society's direction, Picard knew, but he had to skirt the Prime Directive since he required Chanik's experience with the City.

The captain himself didn't mind the delay too much but was now trying to make up for time. After another hour or so, Chanik excitedly pointed out the first glimpse of the City's silhouette. Sure enough, spires and skyscraping buildings were topping the horizon. The captain estimated the City to be perhaps half a kilometer in width and another hour or two away. He withdrew the tricorder and scanned ahead, receiving no sign of active power sources. His estimates seemed to be right on the mark so there'd be several hours for him to search the City before dark.

He frowned, though, when his device also showed two figures some meters ahead, hiding behind some of the taller bushes. Even here, he mused, highwaymen existed to prey on the innocent.

"My sister would be considered quite the catch, Ambassador."

"No doubt," Worf replied. He had allowed Captain Grekor to come to the newly dubbed lead Petraw ship to conduct further studies of their navigational systems. Any race that traveled farther and farther away from home had to have sophisticated tools at its disposal.

On the other hand, it also invited more discussions from the overweight, overbearing warrior, seeking some way to restore glory to the fallen House of Krad. Worf was interested in many things but finding a replacement mate for his late wife Jadzia Dax was at the bottom of such a list. He suffered the comments in silence, totally ignoring the beseeching looks Grekor shot his way.

"You will find their star charts of the Beta Quadrant to be very thorough," Worf offered, hoping it would be a sufficient distraction.

"Already copy them to the *Enterprise,* did you? Share them with the others?"

"We felt it fair to share our findings with the entire allied fleet," the ambassador said stiffly.

"Feh. More Ferengi to worry about."

"You will find, Captain, that the Ferengi have done a remarkable job opening up previously untouchable regions. They are a resource to use as much as they are an irritant."

"Spoken like a true ambassador."

In truth it was spoken by someone who had hoped that praising the Ferengi would make him seem a less viable mate for the captain's sister, but Worf simply grunted in reply.

Grekor attached his recording device to the navigational computers and instructed the frightened Petraw to begin downloading. It seemed the very presence of Klingons was more troubling to the aliens than that of the humans or Romulans. Worf found it an odd fact, but accepted it.

He walked away from the self-satisfied captain and looked at the largest viewscreen. He saw several Petraw ships nearby, and recognized the Deltan and Carreon ships farther away. They hung in space without moving, stars not even twinkling much in the background. Almost like a still photograph, he mused. Bright light suddenly filled the screen, enough to make Worf cover his eyes, and he heard chattering from the Petraw surrounding the bridge.

"Which one?" demanded the Klingon captain.

A moment later, the screen cleared, and Worf, who had been studying the image, recognized that it was a Deltan ship that had exploded.

Grimly, he began speculating as to the culprit.

Picard did not say anything to Chanik as they approached the ambush. He listened for some sound as a giveaway, hoping he would not need to use the phaser. It was two against one, odds he thought he could manage.

Finally, the men calmly stepped from behind the bushes and blocked the path. They were thin of body and hair, wide-eyed. The taller of the two held a thick branch as a club.

"We'll lighten your load, thank you very much."

"I can share if you're hungry," Picard offered, trying to appear unthreatening.

"What are you?"

"He's a Young God!" Chanik declared.

"Not very likely," the tall one said. "No such thing as Gods."

"He's right here! How can you say that?"

"Quiet, Chanik. I can share the food, even the water, but you will not leave me with nothing."

The two stepped forward, club raised. "I think we will."

"Oh yes, we will."

They took another step forward, clearly ready to cause harm in exchange for the food. Picard had tensed himself, and had considered his surroundings. He also recognized his advantage given the planet's lighter gravity. He quickly dropped his satchel, just as the tall man began to swing the branch. Picard crouched briefly, then jumped into the air, cleanly rising above the moving branch.

Landing, he ran forward, outstretched arms before him, battering the two men. The one with the branch was caught off-balance because of the swing's momentum. The other spun to his side, hands balling into fists.

Picard stepped to his left, and with his boot cracked the branch into uselessness. His raised his right arm, blocking a swing from the other one. Just as quickly, he let go with two quick punches to the man's midsection, knocking him backward. The tall one righted himself and rushed Picard, who merely sidestepped, letting the man move past him. As the attacker got close, Picard grabbed an arm and swung him about, directly into the other man. Both tumbled to the ground and Picard loomed over them.

"I think we're done, don't you agree?"

They looked at him with newfound respect . . . and fear.

"I thought we could settle this nicely, with you sharing in my food. But clearly, you need a lesson."

"Don't kill us!" the shorter one yelled.

"Kill you? Not at all. Teach you, yes. An hour or so back this way, you will find a farm. The man who tends it works by himself and could benefit from help. In exchange for work, he might feed you, and you will benefit from learning how to work for yourself."

The men exchanged surprised glances.

"I offer you no guarantees," Picard said, dusting himself off. He spotted Chanik standing nearby, a mix of emotions crossing his face. The boy seemed more surprised than anything.

"Thank you, Young God!" they both said, stepping over each other's words. They got up, and walking clearly around Picard, began on the path as recommended.

Once they were out of sight, Picard took a drink of water and tossed the skin to the boy. He once more began his journey.

"Why didn't you kill them?"

"They were hungry, Chanik. Not evil. Even a world as lush as this seems to be filled with those less fortunate. They also seemed to need a trade, so I suggested one. I think this could work out well for one and all."

"What trade should I perform?"

Picard thought about it a moment and looked down at the eager boy. "I don't assign professions, Chanik. You will find your own path and I trust you will do it with integrity."

"Spoken like a true God!" Chanik exclaimed.

Picard winced, sighed, and continued walking toward the City.

Chapter 4

The red alert klaxon woke Riker out of a not-very-sound sleep. He had managed very little uninterrupted rest since he and the *Enterprise* were first dispatched to end the quarrel between them and the Carreon.

Still, years of training led Riker to be fully awake as the klaxon sounded.

"Bridge, report!"

"Data here," the android replied. *"One of the Deltan ships exploded."*

"What? How!"

"Sensor readings are still coming in. It seems to be totally destroyed with all hands."

"Was it Captain Oliv's?"

"No, sir."

"Get him on the com. I'll be on the bridge in a minute."

It was more like eight minutes later, but Riker was back in uniform, settling into the captain's chair. Data had wisely instructed a yeoman to have a cup of coffee ready for the acting captain. There was bustling activity around the large space but he noted the absence of his closest comrades. La Forge was still working to salvage the *Mercury,* Troi remained in command of the *Marco Polo,* and Picard was . . . somewhere. That continued to trouble him with each passing hour.

As he took a sip from the steaming cup, Riker watched Captain Oliv appear on the screen. He was clearly agitated, which was natural.

"Captain Riker, what will you do about this?"

"I just arrived on the bridge. What happened, Captain?"

"One of our ships exploded!"

Riker turned to Data, who walked his way and elaborated. "Sensors show there was a failure of the magnetic seals around their warp core. The overload was instantaneous."

"Was this a natural accident?"

"Insufficient detail is known, sir. We are still studying the results."

"Send the sensor logs to Geordi for a look. Captain," Riker said, addressing the viewscreen, "we'll get to the bottom of this. You have my sympathies for your loss."

"Sympathies do nothing to bring them back. What you can provide me with is justice."

"Just as soon as we figure out if anyone was behind it. *Enterprise* out." As the screen returned to the image of space, he addressed the second officer. "Data, I'll want to address the fleet in a moment. Given what we know, any speculation on someone behind this?"

The android resumed his seat and shook his head. "I have too little to go on to offer a valid opinion."

"Damn. I knew it had been too quiet."

What amazed Picard the most was the utter silence as they got closer to the City, to the point where it was almost as silent as it had been on the planet where he'd met with the Sentries. Chanik was right that animals avoided the place. His earlier estimates were off; it had to be easily closer to a kilometer in width, with the tallest buildings at least that in height. The metal constructs seemed dull in the sun, mostly copper and greens. In terms of architectural style, he was still too far away to tell if it matched what he had seen of the Iconians.

At least one building had crumbled, either from age or attack. The City itself was ringed with smaller buildings that grew in size the closer to the center they were. He did notice that all the structures were rounded, the style seeming to prefer curves to edges. Birds swooped between the buildings, their long tails whipping back and forth. But on land, he spotted nothing.

"We're making good time, Chanik," Picard said happily. He was looking forward to once more exploring and learning. Pleasant as the countryside was, it did little for his spirit.

They continued to walk, speaking very little as if respectful for the silence surrounding the dead City. After a time, they heard sounds. Picard immediately recognized them as voices, angry ones at that. He looked down at Chanik, who shrugged.

"The nearest village has to be at least a day's walk to the east," he said. "Just the remains of very old buildings here."

Picard thought about it, unsure of what they would find. Very old could mean old to the villagers or old to a youth or could be Iconian remains.

When he heard the baby's cry, he decided it was time for action. Breaking into a sprint, the captain soon left Chanik behind, his every step carrying him farther than he was used to. In less than a minute, he spotted a cluster of people, forming a loose circle. Outside the circle was the infant, crying pitifully, naked and unattended.

It turned out that very old was accurate, since the crumbling structures were made from fabricated materials, leading the captain to suspect they were Iconian in nature. He counted four such structures and heaps of rubble that might have meant there had been more at one time. Perhaps related to the City or some independent dwellings. He would speculate on that later.

The general vicinity was devoid of overgrowth, leading Picard to believe the nearby villagers used the area. Paths were clearly marked, heading toward the forest behind him and, ahead, toward the City. The purpose eluded him.

Picard slowed and tried to make out what was being shouted. He couldn't tell but suspected the baby might have something to do with it.

As he approached, people noticed him coming, and once again he was treated differently because of his unusual appearance. Gradually, the circle broke open and the captain could see a woman, her rough-spun clothes in tatters, lying on the ground. Standing over her, yelling epithets without stop, was an older man. He had a gray beard, wore some sort of skull cap, and had his fists raised in anger.

A murmur replaced the shouting as one after another, people began speculating as to the arrival of the strange man. Picard looked among them and saw that each was holding something hard and metallic, fairly uniform among them. This was not spontaneous, he realized, but deliberate. He could feel anger growing in his heart.

"What is going on?" Picard managed to keep his voice neutral, recognizing the need to respect local laws and customs.

"You're not from around here," a man said, a little fear in his voice.

"No, I come from a far land. But why is this baby being ignored?" Its cries were the only sound now.

"The baby is a sin," shouted the graybeard. "What should have been mine is not!" He was holding the largest item of the group, oval in shape at one end, and spiky at the other.

"And you know this how?" Picard figured that by asking questions and talking he could get them to calm down, maybe see reason. If he had to let their brand of justice be carried out, he would.

"I can count! I was not home the eight turns ago when this would have started."

Picard looked down at the woman, who was quietly sniffling into her one intact sleeve. She seemed absolutely distraught, emotionally caught up in the moment, and seemed oblivious of the conversation going around her.

"And you will do what?"

The man looked at Picard as if he, too, were a newborn. "I brought her here for the testing. She will live or die. If she survives, then her innocence is clear and she can bring the baby home."

"And if she dies?"

"She deserved it."

Picard disliked this notion of justice and felt he needed to act. But his respect for the Prime Directive made him proceed cautiously.

"Has she spoken for herself?"

"Haven't asked!" He adjusted his grip on the item, making certain the pointed end was aimed at the woman. The others similarly played with their items, all of which looked like smaller versions of the weapon. Picard couldn't begin to imagine what they were holding, but knew it was totally alien to them and dated hundreds of thousands of years before. The woman looked up and whimpered once. No one else said a word.

Picard reacted with instinct, not thought, and rushed the man, knocking into him. The weapon's weight in his hands forced him to tumble backward to the ground. Now it was Picard who loomed over the man.

"Where's the justice in using something so sharp? You want the truth? Ask her! If she betrayed you, then let justice be done. But if she has been honest, your 'test' would surely take her away from you and the child. You're letting anger cloud your judgment."

He then turned to the rest, who just watched in silence. Picard also spotted Chanik finally coming into view. It just dawned on him how much ground he must have covered but was thankful for the advantage.

"And you," he said in a cold tone. "You would let this man exercise faulty judgment? First and foremost, this woman should have a say in defending her honor. Second, if your custom is for the stoning to happen, then she needs a fair chance to survive. What he was using would have killed and there's no justice in that!"

With that, Picard walked over to the infant, whose cries had grown intermittent. He scooped it up and instantly the baby grew silent. Gently, he checked for bruises, saw none, and walked back to the woman. She was sitting up now, and gingerly, he handed over the child. "Tell the truth" was all he said to her.

"What are you?" one of the women asked.

"Just a traveler and I am on my way," Picard said. He shot a glance at Chanik, giving him a warning look that said *speak nothing of godhood.* The boy nodded once, clearly struggling with himself not to speak. Picard appreciated the boy's enthusiasm but had had enough chatter about deities for the day.

People spoke up, asking questions of the stranger in their midst, but Picard ignored it all. He did not want to get further involved in their lives, disgusted as he was with their notions of justice.

"She might have deserved something," Chanik opined as they moved away.

"Yes, a fair hearing. Chanik, the accused must have a chance to speak in their defense. The accusation itself is not enough to prove guilt or innocence."

"Really?"

"People can make accusations to cause trouble, put others in danger. Where I come from, we have a very complicated set of laws so the innocent are protected and the guilty are found out with facts, not guesses."

"Wow, that's very involved. How do you keep all those things straight?"

"Protecting our laws is a trade given much importance in my land."

"All those laws and rules and things could make my head hurt," Chanik said.

"Or give you a reason to live," Picard said. "Still, you're too young to worry about a trade. Besides, first we must complete this adventure."

The City was close now and all he wanted to do was arrive and begin his hunt.

La Forge strode from the turbolift directly to the ready room, where Riker waited. The acting captain was studying reports with a small stack of padds littering Picard's desk. The engineer knew Riker was normally a most effective first officer, but the current situation kept him from being at his best.

"Welcome back," Riker said with a tired grin.

"Wish I had better news, but I think the *Mercury*'s scrap."

Riker looked up at that, placing the padd on the tallest stack. "Captain Brisbayne must be pretty mad."

"Stoic is the word you're looking for," La Forge said, as he took a seat. He saw that everything else in the room was its normal neat perfection. "Brisbayne cursed the fates a lot but is now prepping the crew and their gear. We'll have to make room for them."

"Captain Troi can only take so many, and we can handle the rest. I'll have the quartermaster work on details." Riker looked directly at La Forge, hardness replacing exhaustion in his expression. "Did you study the sensor readings?"

"Data's right about the magnetic seals failing," La Forge began. "But it seems they all went at once, not in any sort of cascade as would be normal. The details are scant, but it's the best I can determine."

"So it was sabotage."

"Yup."

"Can we guess as to who?"

La Forge settled back a moment, deciding whether or not to voice his concerns. He decided better get it said now than later. "It can't be the Petraw, we have them locked down. I think we need to look at the Carreon."

Riker nodded, silently agreeing with the assessment. "Landik Mel Rosa fought well, even lost a ship. I'm surprised he'd do anything right now."

"But we don't know him, and don't really know the people."

"True. Okay, let's say it's the Carreon. How could they accomplish this?"

"I would think someone beamed aboard their ship and set up an explosive," La Forge said.

"Check the logs and look for any trace of transporter activity near those ships," Riker ordered. "Let's get our facts in order before talking to Mel Rosa or Oliv."

La Forge nodded, stood and left the room, thanking the powers that be that he was not the one left in charge of the fleet.

"How do we enter the City? Are there defenses of some sort?"

Now it was Picard's turn to ask a lot of questions of his companion. Chanik tried to answer at almost as rapid a clip. The captain had learned already that the City had no electronic defenses—at least none he could detect. If anything, the place was laid open for all to enter. Nature, though, saw to it the City was well guarded. Weeds, plants, even the occasional tree had taken root from the outskirts of the City, choking the streets. Thick ivy-like vines practically enveloped the smaller buildings circling the city so the closer Picard and Chanik got, the less city-like the place looked.

"Do people live nearby?"

"Just the village where those people came from," Chanik replied, sucking on the water skin. "Might be others on the other side of the City, but I've never been."

Picard looked at the vegetation and then at the sun in the sky. He estimated they had four hours of good daylight left, although that might be severely diminished once they entered the City itself. With his superior strength, the captain thought, he might be able scale some of the ivy-covered buildings, but the youth certainly would be left behind.

"Have you a way in that you've used before?"

"Of course," Chanik replied. "Follow me."

The youth led the captain to the left of the trail and entered a wild, untamed section filled with tall bushes. They had walked in silence for fifteen minutes or so when Chanik raised a hand to signal they slow down. He started looking around one structure that seemed gift-wrapped with the green and gold ivy. Rejecting it, the boy moved far-ther to his left, passing one structure after another. Finally, he ran toward the next one, which seemed indistinguishable to Picard from the preceding ones.

"This is it! I cut my way through here the last time I came to the City." Sure enough, Picard could see some of the thick ivy cut away, revealing hand- and footholds that allowed one to reach a second-story window. The window itself was cleared of growth and whatever used to seal it was missing.

The two slowly climbed up, with the captain noting the strength of the ivy, how it was as tough as some rope he was familiar with. He was also pleased with how easily Chanik kept up—he might have been young, but he seemed surefooted and experienced.

Within minutes, the two made it through the window opening and stood in a small room. The door had been ripped from its housing, ex-posing some of the wall. It seemed made of a plastic material while the door was something heavier. The contents of the room were shat-tered, splintered plastic, metal, and other materials, so the captain could not begin to guess what purpose it served. Wires hung from openings in the ceiling and Picard could only imagine whether this was the result of an attack or curious natives centuries after the Iconians left. Withdrawing his tricorder, Picard took readings and pic-tures, deciding he could study them at another time.

"What is that? You keep pulling it out."

"I call this a tricorder and it lets me take recordings or pictures, among other things. It's a very powerful and useful tool to help me explore."

Chanik was clearly befuddled by the response but merely shrugged and walked to the doorway leading to the rest of the building.

Picard followed, trying to imagine how he would ever find the device in a city this size.

Chapter 5

"You know, Will, something like this was bound to happen."

"What, lose a ship to sabotage?" Riker stared at the image of Deanna Troi while seated at the ready room desk, an unfinished plate of pasta to the side, the stack of padds just a little larger. It had been an hour since the explosion and he was no closer to understanding who caused the destruction of a starship. He had security check on Doral, the Petraw leader, but he remained in his quarters, on board, silent.

"There are dozens of ships, with many layers of enmity between some of these races. With the Gorn gone, it didn't lessen the danger any."

"Thanks a lot. What am I supposed to tell Captain Oliv? What if one of Desan's people did it?"

"Don't make rash accusations. With all the sensors working in this area, someone else may have picked up something."

Riker's eyes snapped wide. "I'm too tired to do this job," he muttered.

"What have you thought of, imzadi?"

"Hold on, I'll patch you in," Riker said, tapping a control on the desktop. "Riker to Taleen."

"Go ahead, Commander."

"Can you check your translocator logs, going back an hour or so?" the commander asked.

"For the entire region?" Taleen's brown eyes narrowed and she frowned. *"You suspect the Deltan ship was sabotaged, don't you?"*

"I'm afraid I do."

"I'll check and be back to you in a few minutes."

Picard and Chanik walked carefully, stepping around vines, roots that broke through streets, and the remains of a civilization that once ruled the world. They had poked their way into various buildings, walked up staircases, crossed bridges that linked buildings, and were generally frustrated by their slow pace.

Now they were well into the City, so the buildings were taller, obliterating the sunlight. Night was falling even more quickly here. With what light remained, Picard recognized he would have to stop the hunt and prepare a campground for them. He sent Chanik to find enough wood for a fire while he prepared some lean-tos for shelter. Their dinner would be some of the cured meat from the farmer and Picard would indulge in some of the wine but would sip carefully. Even though there was no hint of animal life, that didn't mean predators did not exist in the ruins.

"How do we know where to look?"

"That, Chanik, is an excellent question," Picard replied, as he watched the boy build an expert campfire. It seemed the youth possessed some skill at survival and was more than happy to contribute to the expedition. The question was on his mind long before the boy asked. Aimless wandering would mean the Resonator might be days away from discovery. He doubted the Alpha Quadrant would wait for days. As it was, he feared the days here already meant suns had gone nova. The worst part was, he had no way of knowing.

The pair ate in silence as Picard let his mind sort through possible ways to find the Resonator. It couldn't be too large but had to fit the equipment, he suspected. But that could mean something as small as a data chip or as large as his fist. And where would a tool like that be maintained? With no power emanations, he couldn't begin to suspect which building might have housed the gateway . . . or were there multiple gateways in something this large?

Chanik kept silent, working on the tough strips of meat. His only comment had been about it being so bland compared with what he was used to.

Picard withdrew the tricorder from his pocket and studied reports from previous gateway encounters. He was looking for some kind of clue. Maybe something in the placement of the device, or the architecture or ornamentation . . . He struggled with the small screen, enhancing every image until his eyes hurt with the strain. Giving up for the night, he pocketed the device and finished a piece of fruit.

"I like the stars," Chanik said idly.

"Me too," Picard agreed.

"I like that they're there when I go to sleep. I think about what they are, what's between them, and if anyone lives up there."

"People have wondered that since the beginning of time, I think," Picard said warmly.

They sat in companionable silence for a little while and Chanik scanned the skies with concentration. "Picard, look to the left. See those four stars going up and down in a straight line? It's like a staff."

"Yes, it might be. We call clusters of stars that make a picture constellations."

Chanik tried out the word and smiled. "Who's holding the staff?"

Picard scanned the night sky and tried to connect random stars to complete the picture but finally shook his head. "I'm not sure."

"So it's not your home? I thought Young Gods came from the sky."

"Just a story," Picard said, wary of any answer. "People make up stories when they're not sure of the truth. Sometimes it gives them comfort."

"Like my sky pictures?"

"Exactly. You should try to sleep now. I need to push on early tomorrow."

Once again, he had an uneasy night's sleep, worried about time lost, worried about natural predators, worried about the world Chanik would grow up in.

Dawn's light woke Picard and he marveled at the beauty of unfettered nature replacing what had been a superior technology. He felt rested although his mind immediately turned to the problem at hand. He had to find the Master Resonator today and return home.

Chanik was still asleep and their fire had died out, but there was little chill in the air.

Picard took a sip from a water skin and noted the intricate swirling pattern that had been etched onto one side. Staring at it, he let his mind wander for a moment, and he thought about the odd-pointed end of the device nearly used on the accused woman the day before. Its oval nature was similar to the pattern on the skin and it occurred to Picard that the domed structure on the new Iconian world was more oval than circular. Could the oval shape be significant?

If so, then what?

Picard concentrated on the shape of architecture on Iccobar and Dewan, two of the other worlds that traced their lineage to the Iconians. Sure enough, ovals played a part of the overall design, but how could he use the knowledge to find the device?

He once more turned on the tricorder and studied the interior design of the Iconian building where he first encountered a gateway. The room was more rectangular than oval so that did not help, but he read over the description of the control pattern of the machinery itself that Data had provided. He wished he had an actual image of the room, but Picard himself had ordered the tricorder that had recorded the room destroyed both to avoid the sabotage of the Iconians' invasive computer probe and to keep the information out of Romulan hands.

The layout of the controls offered no clue but he read over the description again. There was something he was missing and it nagged at him.

He switched the controls to the exterior of the domed home to the Iconians. There, the captain studied the colors and shapes, but merely glanced at the filigree work. That is, until his mind wandered for a second and his eyes lost their sharp focus and suddenly, all he saw were the spikes at different points to the design. Picard hastily reran the analysis and quickly grabbed a stick and sketched on the ground. He copied the points only of the oval sphere's profile. With a smile, he noted that it was an exact match on the reverse profile.

He drew grid lines in the dirt, seeing how the points matched and there was the missing pattern. Quickly, Picard sketched further, completing the oval from a bird's-eye view, repeating the grid lines and spikes. A picture emerged, the points leading the eye to a specific section of the grid, which could be the location of the City's gateway. From memory, Picard estimated where he and Chanik entered the City and their approximate location. With a silent curse, he realized they were far from the building but at least had an idea of direction. Using the tricorder, he scanned the image and would use it as a crude map.

While he wanted to let the boy sleep more, he felt an urgent need to get moving. Gently, he woke Chanik and gave him fruit for breakfast. Within twenty minutes, they were moving again, this time in a direction that Picard hoped would bring a resolution to the problem.

"There were multiple moves between Petraw ships," Taleen reported to Riker. *"Just as Doral moved among many ships to elude you, a single transport crossed a dozen ships before stopping at the Deltan vessel. And from there, crossed seven more ships to return."*

"Which one?" Riker demanded, angry at being duped.

"It's one of the older vessels," she said, tapping at an image screen behind her, identifying a single vessel in the bottom right portion of the screen.

"Data, who do we have watching that ship?"

The android turned and replied, "Subcommander Rivel of the *Glory.*"

"Riker to *Chargh.*"

"Grekor here."

"Captain, can you maneuver toward the vessel identified on our screens?"

"Can't I just blow them up and solve the problem?"

Riker shook his head in frustration, because he felt the temptation as well.

"Sorry, I don't think that's wise at this time. I do intend to do something about this. After all, I promised Captain Oliv."

"Very well. Chargh out."

"Thank you, Taleen. I owe you one. Riker out."

Riker stood and walked over to Data's station, standing to the android's side. He was tired and annoyed and worried. If one saboteur could get out and cause such damage, could more? How was he to protect the entire fleet? He doubted the ships could generate enough of a dampening field to stop the entire Petraw fleet. As it was, he had people stationed on every ship, so bringing them back to their home ships would be problematic. And how much longer should he wait for Picard to return before acting on his own?

"You are preoccupied."

"Very much so, Data," Riker admitted. "The captain was not specific about his return and how long I need to wait. I can't endanger all the ships. I want you and Geordi to theorize a way to stop these transports from happening again."

"Understood, sir. I will be in engineering if you need me."

"Good. Lieutenant Vale, take a detachment to the saboteur's current ship and let's get ahold of him . . . or them. Meantime, I need to have a word with Commander Desan about her staff's efficiency."

"How did you figure out a direction?"

Chanik had asked variations of this question since they headed out and each time, Picard tried to explain without giving away too much information. The boy was inquisitive and bright, so he couldn't say too much.

"It's like the stars we saw last night. If you let your mind wander, you find patterns in the shapes. I did that with things I have seen in my journeys and suddenly I saw a pattern that I took to form a map. I could be right or I could be wasting precious time."

Chanik grinned at the captain as he struggled to keep up with the older man's long strides. "You'll be right. You were right every time we had to choose yesterday. You taught the farmer, stopped the highwaymen, saved the baby. Young Gods know how to do things better than people."

"I *am* people, Chanik. Call me Picard or Young God, I still breathe and eat and walk like you do," Picard said. He knew he was skirting theological issues and wanted to keep the boy focused on the walk. He quickened his pace and forced the boy to trot to catch up, stopping the questioning for now.

They had been moving from street to street for three hours now with just one break. The boy was resilient and his endurance was a marvel. Together, they cut through overgrown passageways and hefted fallen branches from trees that had taken up residence in plazas. Using the sun as a guide, Picard continued to refine his estimates of where they were headed, correcting their path time and again.

With luck, they would reach the building in question just after lunch. That would provide him with plenty of daylight to thoroughly search the area to find if his guess was correct. If it wasn't, then he could easily have passed it earlier and would never know.

"We must hurry," Picard said over his shoulder. "I think we're on the right path and I'm eager to see if I'm right."

"I'm right behind you," he said, puffing just a little.

He was wrong. They arrived at the targeted building much after lunch and he saw the sun was already starting toward the horizon. With the taller buildings surrounding them, it would be dark within a few hours.

Compared with the rest of the City, the building was nondescript. If it truly housed a gateway, one could not tell by design or ornamentation. The outside was reds and oranges with two windows missing. It stretched maybe ten stories tall, dwarfed by some of the surrounding structures. If there was anything to differentiate it from the other structures, it was the how wide the street grew around it. Picard speculated that might have to do with the volume of people arriving to access the gateway. He admitted that might be stretching the facts to make his point, but it was all he had to go on.

"Should we go in?" Chanik asked.

"Oh, of course," Picard said, realizing just then how he had stared at the building for a while. He certainly didn't feel nervous about it, but he had proceeded cautiously around it. Perhaps he was trying to avoid disappointment or apprehension about what he might find within.

The entranceway was rusted in spots and Picard had to grip the door with both hands, gaining a hold between door and frame. He gave it a test pull and felt how tight it was. Planting his feet firmly on the ground, he tensed his muscles and pulled against the door. He maintained the pressure for longer than he was used to, letting the lighter gravity once more help him.

Finally, after a minute of exertion, the door began to give. Picard stopped, catching his breath and looking at his sore fingers. Once more, he gripped the door and gave it one hard pull, feeling the muscular strain down his legs. And once more, the door gave in to his exertions and swung open. The captain nearly lost his footing as the door was freed but Chanik steadied him. He grinned at the boy and stepped inside the building.

The first floor was filled with pillars supporting the entire building, but also had a series of rooms that seemed uniform in size and shape. Some had desks, others tall cabinets made from something akin to marble. Whatever papers might have been were long gone, and weeds crept through the open windows and spilled out across the floors. Mold and mildew were also in evidence, producing an unpleasant, but by now familiar odor. Chanik wrinkled his nose in disgust.

Unlike most buildings, though, this had a very wide staircase, spiraling down below ground level. It had polished wooden railings that time had done little to. The stair coverings were eaten through and some weeds had snaked down ahead of them. It was also dark since the natural light could not penetrate far. Picard would need something and returned to the main level and looked about.

"Chanik, we need to build torches so we can explore below. Most other buildings do not seem to have basements, but this one does. I believe our goal is down there. Can you find two very sturdy, heavy wood poles, branches, or sticks?"

"Sure can," the boy said. Despite being tired from all the walking, he fairly sprinted from the building out to the streets in search of supplies. Picard had already decided he was correct and was willing to use his phaser to ignite the torches rather than the more laborious natural method of starting a fire.

It took him a few minutes, but Chanik came back, dragging two branches. One was longer than he was tall, and Picard sighed since he would have to reduce it in size. The other was more manageable but the captain was convinced he would be better with two light sources—just in case.

Within five minutes, the torches were cut to size and ignited. The boy marveled at the phaser's effective use, which sadly served to reinforce the notion of Picard being a god. To the captain, it was mild contamination since Chanik could tell what he saw and not be believed. And when he grew up and tried to replicate the tools he had witnessed, he would discover no way to refine the metal or create the duotronic circuits required. Not ideal, but it would pass Starfleet scrutiny. It certainly was better than the legendary story of an officer who left a communicator behind on a world and helped change an entire society.

Once more they descended the stairs, and with the improved light, Picard saw that the basement extended some thirty meters down. A gateway would be very well protected so deep, he mused.

As they reached bottom, he saw illustrations of landscapes that were unfamiliar. They certainly did not match anything he had seen on this world. The artwork had been inlaid along the walls, part of the construction. There were snowscapes, oceans, mountain views, and cities. None looked familiar and the city's buildings were a far cry from the architecture above. Colored circles in the walls seemed to form directional patterns, most leading to his left.

They moved slowly, listening and hearing nothing. The pictures stopped after a bit and instead, tablets with alien script appeared. Picard took out the tricorder and recorded them for later analysis although he suspected there would be matches for other cultures. Turquoise, violet, olive, and cinnamon-colored circles all converged down one hallway so Picard chose to follow them. He was rewarded with the hall opening up to a large chamber.

In the center was a familiar control panel, one he first saw on a world countless light-years away.

This was the gateway control room.

It seemed large enough to open quite a number of gateways and it suddenly occurred to Picard that the pictures outside were recommended locales. The Iconians had stayed here long enough to send their people on vacations, forcing him to revise his notion that they were chased here by whatever race firebombed their homeworld. Still, everything was open to interpretation and he realized now was not the time for it.

"What does that do, Picard?"

"When it worked, Chanik, it could help people find their way to other locations. It's very old equipment and I doubt it functions anymore." In reality, he knew it would have to work to send him home and there was little doubt that the equipment still functioned. Compared with the gateway on Iconia, this was a much newer model, so if the original worked, so too would this one.

Picard studied the chamber carefully, looking for some place the Master Resonator might be housed. The walls seemed smooth and there were no other halls leading to the space. With the torch held high, Picard checked every inch of the walls, taking his time to watch shadows play against joints where floor and ceiling met wall.

He then meticulously studied the console itself, but found no hidden panels or hatches. It grew frustrating, as Picard knew he had found his goal but the ultimate object eluded his grasp.

Chanik, growing bored standing in the same space, had been wandering in and out of the chamber, using the hallway as a place to run. At one point, Picard watched him with a sad smile. So full of energy and eager to help, but everything was beyond his grasp. However, Picard watched a little more and saw something catch the youth's eye. Chanik walked along the hallway with his torch and looked closely at a section, just before the hall opened into the chamber. He placed his tiny hand on a section of wall and pushed, revealing a doorway mostly hidden in the shadows.

Picard quickly stepped over to him, and together, their torches dancing together above them, they peered into the newly discovered room. The air was stale and musty to Picard but that wasn't important. What was vital, though, was the rack set against the far wall. On it was the Master Resonator—he was sure of it.

What confused him at first, though, was that there were fourteen of them, identical to one another in size and shape. The Resonator was larger than Picard's fists together, but flat and copper-colored. On top were four keys: two amber, one brown, and one a deeper shade of brown. He stepped toward them and touched one, feeling the cool metal. Picking it up, he found that it felt light, and as he turned it over, saw indentations that at first puzzled him.

"Is this it?"

"I think so, Chanik. I just didn't expect to find so many."

"Maybe they were being careful in case one broke."

"Maybe," Picard agreed halfheartedly, but he doubted it. To date, he had never encountered spare parts of any sort. The Iconians, it seemed, built things to last. Which meant all fourteen Resonators were meant to be used.

"*Merde,*" he muttered to himself.

* * *

Christine Vale had seen plenty of action since joining the *Enterprise* nearly a year earlier. There had been other planets, other ships to help, and plenty of time to train her team to perform at peak efficiency. Being anything but the image of the typical security chief, she felt driven to make certain she earned the respect of those around her.

And she loved her work.

As she materialized aboard the Petraw ship, she used two quick hand signals that sent her three other crewmen into quick defensive positions. All had phasers in hand; one also had a phaser rifle strapped to his broad back. The corridor was close enough to the weapons room that it took little time to fan out and cover the door and entry points along the corridor. While its being empty helped, they still moved quietly and quickly, because she knew that fortunes could change with a single heartbeat.

To her right, Choloh, a hulking Tellarite, checked his tricorder and nodded. The armory was indeed occupied and the single digit held in the air told her it was just the one.

Well, she considered, checking the phaser setting, if you had to hide anywhere, an armory made an awful lot of sense.

Choloh adjusted his settings and pocketed the device, flexing his thick fingers around the phaser, nodding. The others also trained their attention on the single door that separated them from their target.

Vale stepped forward and rapped her knuckles on the door.

"Go away! I'm armed." The voice was expectedly agitated and she was prepared for him to act irrationally given the desperate situation he was in.

"No kidding," she replied. "Be awfully silly of you to sit in an armory and not test the merchandise. We can go about this a few ways, but me, I always go for the nice and easy ones. How about you?"

"What are you talking about?" The voice fairly screamed at her through the metallic door.

Vale stepped to her right, projecting her voice straight at the door. "We could storm the room, have lots of weapons discharge at once, and potentially blow a hole through the hull. You could come out firing and we, clearly outnumbering you, shoot you down. You could toss out the weapon and make a run for it, but that just means we get to pick for who chases and tackles you. Or . . ."

"Or, you could talk me to death!"

Vale frowned at that. "Hadn't thought about that one. Maybe next time. Right now, we need to bring you to Commander Riker and I'm running out of patience. Decide."

The silence lasted only four seconds, but seemed far longer to Vale, who licked her lips once, tightening her grip on the phaser. She strained her ears to hear what he might be doing but the door muffled it.

"I'll come out," the voice said, so softly that Vale wasn't sure of the words at first.

"Unlock the door, open it with your weapon on the ground, hands up on your head." With hand signals, she had her people move into position, flanking the door. Crouching, she was poised to roll out of the way of weapons fire or scurry into the armory. By staying low, she hoped to be clear of whatever he might desperately try to use against her.

As the door slid open, however, there was little to fear. The Petraw that came out was young and in his natural appearance. There was a scared look to the eyes and the security chief noted the trembling hands against the scalp. With her right hand, she gestured for him to step forward out of the lethal room and he did, with hesitating steps. He was scared and she would have to act accordingly, since that meant he might panic or do something irrational. Vale nodded and Choloh stepped forward with restraints, which firmly affixed the Petraw's hands behind his back, and to a belt. There was no resistance, and finally Vale let out a breath and lowered the weapon.

"I will be damn well heard, Riker," bellowed Brisbayne.

"Captain, this is not open to discussion," Riker said, trying to contain himself. The argument stopped being interesting when the *Mercury*'s captain began repeating himself, as if that would change the nature of the problem.

"Picard has been gone days, you've let the Petraw blow one of us up, I must insist on taking command of the mission."

Riker shook his head sadly, recognizing the mixture of bluster and frustration. Brisbayne was no doubt a fine officer, but his record did not indicate that he was at all equipped for commanding something of this nature.

"Sir, with all due respect," Riker continued, "were I willing to turn command over to someone, I would sooner give it to Desan or Grekor. You have shown a disrespect for the chain of command, while they both have the kind of strategic thinking this requires." He leaned into the camera, his face set in a stern expression. "But I have no intention of stepping down. Captain Picard will be given a little more time and then I will make a decision. I think we're done now." With a finger gesture learned from Picard, he signaled to Data to cut the communication.

"Commander, how much longer will you give Captain Picard?" Data inquired.

Riker settled back in the command chair, not at all comfortable. "Just a little bit more. Without him and the solution, we might have to destroy all the gateways."

"That would be a loss to the quadrant," Data said.

"I see you have not lost your sense of understatement."

Riker considered the chronometer and mentally decided on six more hours. Long enough to show Brisbayne who was in command, but short enough so he could act before too many more lives might be lost. From reports he read a little while earlier, two planets were already critically crippled by the Iconian technology adapting native energy to keep the gateways powered. A small war had broken out in an unaligned star system and raids by Cardassian pirates were reported along the Klingon border. It was painful to read, but Starfleet Command remained convinced that this delegation could solve the problem and he did not want to disappoint.

"Riker to La Forge."

"Go ahead, Commander."

"Just in case I need a Plan B, please begin estimating the minimal amount of explosive power required to take out each gateway." He could hear the whistle as La Forge processed the command.

"We've seen different sizes, so it'll take me a little time."

"You have four hours. Out."

As he had spoken with Geordi, Vale appeared on the bridge, bringing with her the Petraw saboteur. She smiled in triumph but had a fellow officer take charge of the prisoner, and she returned to her post, a finger trailing along the top displaying pride in ownership.

"Trouble?"

"Not at all, sir," she said.

Riker stood and moved closer to the prisoner, noting the panicked look in his eyes.

"We've ceased the hostilities with your people and are working to bring about an end to this madness. What makes you think you can ruin that with blowing up a ship?"

"To be free of you, to get back to our journey," the Petraw said.

"Do you have any idea the number of lives you've taken?" Riker was trying to modulate his voice, contain his anger, but it was a struggle.

"We do what we must to fulfill our goal," came the reply, and it sounded rote, as if it was something the Petraw were taught in school or church.

"And now you must pay. I'll wait for the captain to return to determine what that is. Have him taken to the brig and keep him away from Doral." Riker turned his back to the alien and resumed his place in the center seat. As he adjusted his position, he eyed his usual spot and wondered when things would return to normal.

"What do they do?"

Picard walked back to the console, hefting one of the Resonators, holding it above the control panels. He realized this would be tricky, explaining things to Chanik, but the boy deserved an answer.

"I believe this will give me control over the mechanism, something I lacked back home."

"Does this mean your quest for *granita* is over? You can return home now?"

"I hope so, Chanik," the captain said.

Gently, Picard lowered the device, trying to fit it over several of the control keys. After two failed attempts, the device fit snugly atop a cluster of amber and blue keys to the console's right. Moments after he placed it, the entire Resonator began to glow, adding significant light to the space. Other keys lit up and a thrum of power started up which startled the boy, who backed away several feet. The power sounded constant to Picard, impressed once more with how well the Iconians built things to last. He idly thought of how they compared with the poor Petraw, who had patchwork ships to show for their legacy.

After half a minute or so, a small ball of light began to form above the Resonator and one of the amber keys began to blink. The light grew in size and began to alter shape, forming a sphere that swelled to engulf the top of the control panel. Within the sphere, smaller swirls began forming, and Picard realized that it resembled nothing more than a model of the Big Bang theory. As the seconds passed, the stars began twinkling and the image altered slowly as galaxies formed and moved off camera, as it were. Picard felt Chanik at his side, the image too fascinating to ignore.

"Those are the stars, aren't they?"

"I believe so," Picard said softly.

"Why are we seeing so many?"

"I don't know. It may be trying to show us where the people who built this might have gone."

"Gone?"

"Hush," Picard said as the image changed and the Milky Way was clearly in his sight. The familiar spiral shape filled the light bubble and then, one at a time, purple lights began to show themselves in a concentration that Picard recognized as the Alpha Quadrant.

In all, there were thirteen purple lights.

Picard stared at the representation and concentrated. The amber light continued to blink, so Picard tentatively reached out, thinking he needed to activate the switch. His fingers brushed the blinking light but a sharp sound was his only reward.

"It didn't like you touching it," Chanik said, clearly stating the obvious.

Picard frowned and considered the likely options. After a minute or more, he realized he had no choice. He needed to return with the thirteen keys, then get them to the highlighted gateways. He suspected all thirteen consoles would have blinking lights and that none would do anything useful unless they were all touched at once. Fourteen pieces to a single key and somehow the Iconians didn't know that.

Somehow, this lack of precision comforted Picard. Even they were not perfect.

Reaching into his pocket, he withdrew the tricorder and recorded the light patterns and the purple markers. The *Enterprise* computers would be able to match this map against their own star charts and, adjusting for the time difference since these maps were first recorded, figure out where the keys needed to go.

Spinning on his heel, Picard strode to the antechamber, Chanik on his heels. "What's going on?" he kept asking. The captain ignored him at first, emptying his small bag of dried meat and other odds and ends. He then began filling it with the thirteen Resonators. There was little question in his mind that somehow all fourteen signals would synchronize and somehow they would gain control of the devices once that occurred. What troubled him, though, was the fourteenth key. Someone would need to activate it from this planet.

His first thought was sending the keys through a gateway and including an instruction to Riker and the others. It felt wrong—he needed to be there, be home when this happened. If the Resonators simply shut off the gateway, he would be trapped on this world. While it was a pretty place, he had no interest in remaining a Young God for the remainder of his life.

The next idea also had its concerns. Chanik would have to get involved but that raised concerns over tampering with a culture. On the one hand, the Iconians left these people to fend with their remains, and on the other, what harm could there be in asking a boy to press a button?

"Chanik, I must ask a favor of you."

"Of course, Picard," the boy said, eyes bright with excitement.

"I need to return to my people with these," he said, shaking the bulging bag slightly. "All of them must be fit onto similar machines and then all of us must press the blinking button. I think we need to do it at once."

"How will I know?"

Picard frowned at the basic question. He didn't have a definite answer and suspected he would not be able to speak with the boy.

"I'm not sure, to be honest. I think the machine will do something to indicate it is ready for you to do your part."

Chanik smiled and nodded a few times. "It will be safe, right? Then I will have helped a Young God!"

The captain broke into a happy grin. "Yes, it will be quite a story for your friends. But once this is done, I suspect the machine will go dark and you should keep its existence to yourself. It will be our secret." He returned to the console and studied it. His right hand began flipping switches, as he recalled doing on Doral's battered ship. There was a subtle shift in power and then a gateway sprang to life near the far wall. Chanik began to walk toward it but Picard called him back.

"But what is it?"

"It's called a gateway," Picard said as he concentrated on trying to recall the coordinate controls. He tapped a few, corrected a mistake, and continued. As happened on the ship, the gateway began spinning, showing different locales.

Each adjustment refined at least one of the destinations. Quickly, Picard spied a familiar waterfall on Risa, then a sand-swept city that he suspected was Nimbus III. He continued to fiddle with the controls, hoping he could at least find a starship's bridge. A part of his mind suspected that thoughts did have some influence over the location definition. What was it he was telling Riker the other day? About a book where the lost man only wanted to go home. Picard thought about the *Enterprise*-E bridge as he continued to work on the controls.

The next image was not one for young eyes and Picard was pleased to see it replaced by a huge vessel, the likes of which he had never imagined. It was gone in a flash, the gateway next showing a satellite hurtling through space, a message of welcome from one race to its galactic neighbors.

There! He spotted La Forge walking across the rear of the bridge. The next two images were of planets he vaguely recognized but he paid them scant attention as he adjusted the controls. The *Enterprise* finally remained constant and Picard counted off time between rotations so he could step through correctly.

It was time.

Turning, he saw Chanik watch the gateway intently, occasionally looking at the galactic image still floating quietly over the console. He liked the boy and appreciated his company and his savvy under less than ideal situations.

"They dress like you; is that where the Young Gods live?"

"They are my companions and we try and do the right thing, much like you," Picard said. Then he crouched lower to bring his face close to the now-sad boy.

"I have no doubt that you will grow into a fine young man," the captain told him. "This world has much to offer someone like you. However, it is time I go home myself. I need to step through the gateway and leave you to wait for the right moment to act. I can't tell you how long it will be. Definitely more than a day."

"That's okay, Picard. I'll be fine. You've shown me so much and I can think about it. I'll be ready. You can count on me."

Picard reached out and gently stroked his cheek. "Thank you."

With that, he straightened his uniform and strode toward the gateway, counting off as it rotated. As the time approached, he bent his knees slightly and at the right moment, leapt into the gateway.

Chapter 6

Geordi La Forge was crossing the bridge, a padd in his hand, and Riker knew it was coming time to make a decision. He didn't want to make it, didn't necessarily feel as if he was the right officer to decide the fate of the Iconian legacy. It was, after all, his captain's fascination for all these years. No, it didn't feel right at all to be the one to decide to destroy the gateways. The specter of guilt was already hanging over his head.

"We can do it, but we still don't know where they all are," La Forge said, handing the padd to the commander.

"Data, how is Captain Solok doing with the mapping mission?"

"Our latest information shows that a preliminary map is due to be delivered to Admiral Ross in fifteen and one quarter hours."

Somehow, an android and a Vulcan would be comfortable with such precision. To Riker, fifteen hours from now would suffice. By then, the decision would have been made and it would be out of Riker's hands. What remained to be decided, though, was what to do with the Petraw. They had remained silent since the sabotage effort so the jamming signal was doing its job, but they couldn't maintain that in perpetuity.

Riker stood with the padd and studied the engineer's recommendations as he strolled toward the ready room. He would contact the other captains from there and announce the decision. The commander was so absorbed with the information he did not notice the crewman coming his way and they collided. Both men tumbled to the deck.

Once on the carpeted floor, Riker looked up and saw Picard's face. "Sir!"

"At ease, Will," Picard said with a smile. Both men scrambled to their feet and were the center of attention as everyone else on the bridge stood and came close to their commanding officer.

"Is everything all right? Did you find the answer?"

"I believe so," Picard said, patting the bag that remained at his side.

Quickly, Riker updated the captain on what had transpired, and in turn Picard explained his planet-jumping and search for the Resonators. He handed the tricorder to Data and asked him to begin the required analysis.

"We can swap details later," Picard said. "Let me notify the others that I am back and that we will need to act shortly. And then, I think, I need a shower and hot meal."

Riker broke into a grin. "I think I can watch things a little while longer."

"Very well." The captain began toward his ready room, paused, then turned around. "It's good to see you again, Number One. I've missed the ship."

Riker nodded, still smiling, and once more settled into the command chair. It didn't feel so uncomfortable for a change.

A few hours later, a refreshed Picard sat at the conference table with Riker, La Forge, Crusher, and Data. He had asked Captain Troi to patch in from her post on the *Marco Polo* to get her input. The others would be notified after the briefing. Data was standing by the monitor screen that showed a stellar map with the thirteen purple sites still highlighted.

"The pattern of dispersal does not, as yet, make sense," the android began. "All are located on planets and fortunately, all thirteen planets still exist. All are within Klingon, Romulan, Ferengi, or Federation space, aside from two that are within the former Thallonian Empire in Sector 221G."

"Data," Picard said, "does overlaying this pattern with the pattern of migration from Iconia tell us anything?"

"No immediate pattern is discernible. However, I will give the matter further study."

Picard frowned briefly but nodded. "How do we get the thirteen Resonators into position?"

"I have endeavored to work out a travel plan. It will require relaying the Resonators to fast ships from here. My initial plan indicates it will take some twenty-eight point five hours if every ship makes its scheduled rendezvous. This will require the *Enterprise, Marco Polo, Chargh,* and *Jerok* to leave the area, spreading the Resonators to others."

Nodding, Picard said, "Obviously, we should use the *Excalibur* and the *Trident* for the two Thallonian gateways."

"Captain," Riker said hesitatingly, "Admiral Ross suspects both Captains Calhoun and Shelby entered a gateway."

"I see," the captain said slowly. Then he smiled. "I am not at all surprised, Number One. No doubt he'll have his own story to tell and it's one I'm looking forward to."

Riker let out an exasperated sigh and said, "I'll talk to Mueller and Burgoyne and make a plan." He shook his head, clearly thinking about the crew of the ill-fated starships.

Data went on, detailing how the ships should move out with recommended warp speeds and courses. Working at his superhuman speed, he managed to work out thirteen different itineraries that would cover a vast swatch of the galaxy in the minimum amount of time. Picard was impressed all over again with how smoothly his crew functioned.

"Captain," Troi said from the adjacent viewscreen. *"What about the Petraw?"*

"I have not come up with a satisfying answer as yet," Picard admitted. "As we leave, I will need the *Qob* and *Glory* to take charge."

"With their attempt at sabotage, they cannot be trusted to remain complacent with fewer ships present," Data said.

"I recommend we disable as many of the ships as possible," La Forge suggested.

"I'm not sure I see a better solution," Picard said slowly, not happy with the notion. "Prepare your plans, Geordi. Will, contact the vessels we'll be meeting with. Deanna, relay word to the other captains in the area. Let's try and leave within the hour. Dimissed."

Quickly and efficiently, the crew stood and went about their business and Picard was left alone in the observation lounge. While it felt good to be home, he disliked waiting more than a day to conclude the business at hand. And he kept thinking back to the world and little Chanik, faithfully waiting for the signal that would help protect a galaxy from chaos.

As expected, the Romulan commander was the first to be in touch with the captain. She seemed cool and collected despite her ship being anything but battle-ready.

Picard was now in his ready room, having caught himself up on status reports from his ship and around the fleet. He looked at the screen on his desk and acknowledged the darkly attractive woman.

"If you leave, it will only embolden the Petraw to try and conduct more sabotage."

"Have you a suggestion?"

"Destroy a handful of random ships, disable more, and even the odds."

"How Klingon of you," Picard noted, satisfied at the scowl marring her pleasant features. "I have my chief engineer preparing plans to disable the entire Petraw fleet as opposed to destroying anyone. This way, when we're done, we can decide what to do with them."

"You don't have a plan? I am most surprised."

"Honestly, Desan, I have been more than a bit busy."

"Just what did you find on the other side?" She leaned toward the screen, intense curiosity replacing the scowl.

"The Resonators were found on the last Iconian stronghold in the Alpha Quadrant, a world reduced to much more primitive standards. But, they're developing nicely, and one in particular helped me find them. It was quite an enlightening experience. When I return, if time permits, we can talk some more of it. But for now, I want you to know that I am placing my faith in the accords between our people and my personal trust in you to maintain the peace."

Desan seemed surprised by the vote of confidence and her expression betrayed her, pleasing the captain. She would make a questionable poker player, he considered. She merely nodded at the words and clicked off the communication.

Before he could pick up the next padd on the tall stack to his right, the screen beeped once and he saw that it was the *Kreechta* captain calling. This might be a problem or, more likely, a diverting conversation.

"How can I help you DaiMon Bractor?"

"I want you to know I appreciate your faith."

This surprised Picard, who rested his chin on his fist and considered the situation. The Ferengi had a reputation for underhandedness overall. His own dealings had proven they could be spiteful and capable of killing.

"To be honest with you, DaiMon," Picard said, a smile on his face, "trust has to be earned and you have earned it."

Bractor bowed in appreciation. *"There can be profit in many forms, I'm told. I consider this an investment against the future."*

"The results should bring us closer together," Picard said hopefully.

"Thank you," the toothy captain said in all sincerity. *"Will you bring Doral along with you to keep him from influencing the others?"*

"I hadn't considered him," the captain admitted. In fact, he hadn't even asked after the dejected Petraw leader. "But what you say makes sense, so yes, he will accompany us."

"And should you find something of value when you put all the Resonators in place . . ."

"As promised, if there's something to share, it will be shared with all. You need not fear being cheated."

"All hands have returned," Jessie Davison told Captain Troi.

She smiled and turned to face the screen before her. Already, the hulking *Jerok* was moving off, heading out at sublight speed and clearing distance until it could go into warp. The *Enterprise* was to move off next and then it would be their turn. The flight plan had already been entered, thanks to Data's inhuman speed. Mia Chan, her conn officer, grumbled good-naturedly about having nothing to do during the flight. Troi reassured her that they had stops to make along the way and her skills would be required.

The turbolift doors snapped open, admitting a trio onto the bridge. Johnny Rosario, the tactical officer, strode out first, looking a bit tired after his "baby-sitting" duties on one of the Petraw ships. No sooner did he enter the bridge than Chan jumped from her seat and ran to him.

She gave him a fierce bear hug that startled him and he wasn't sure where to place his hands. A look of panic was in his eyes when it became clear everyone was watching. After a few moments, when it became apparent Chan wasn't letting go, he tentatively placed his arms around her and returned the unbridled affection.

"I think I have feelings for you," she said giddily.

"I see, I see," he said slowly. The others around the bridge chuckled at that understatement.

"Affectionate crew," rumbled a voice from behind the couple. Troi knew it in an instant and stood at attention.

"Welcome aboard, Ambassador," she said, a wide grin showing her pleasure. She and Worf had been lovers once but now they were friends and she was genuinely glad to see him. Despite the length of the mission, not once did they have a chance to speak.

When the others realized the Klingon was in their midst, most returned their attention to padds or consoles. The couple blocking his entrance to the bridge started disentangling themselves, making excuses and apologies but accomplishing it with little grace.

"I try to run a comfortable ship," Troi said, finally walking around her embarrassed officers and giving Worf a much briefer hug of her own. Worf, like Rosario, was at first discomfited with the display, but gave her the briefest of hugs in return.

"The Resonators are still in the transporter room," he said, returning to business.

"*Enterprise* is beginning to move out," Science Officer Kal Sur Hol said. The look of distaste on his face made Troi want to laugh. The Tiburonian seemed disdainful of anything not by the book, and interpersonal relationships seemed a bit beyond him. She had hoped to work on him, but hadn't come close.

"Do you think Geordi's plan will work?"

"As I understand it," Worf said, "he is using the escape patterns already programmed by the Petraw ships and is sending along polaron bursts to prevent them from beaming or using their engines. The Nyrians were most helpful in setting this up."

"Seems we made new friends," Troi said.

"They still want to return home," the ambassador noted.

"With luck, the captain will get them on their way. Okay, time to go to work." She shifted in her seat, leaning slightly forward.

"Helm, prepare to execute. Engineering, when we go to warp, we need to maintain maximum speed so keep an eye on the readings. Everyone, stand by to move out," Troi commanded. The staff snapped to work, a chorus of "aye's" filling the air. Worf stood by her side and seemed impassive.

Within a minute, they were clear to leave and the *Marco Polo* executed a clean arc, angling itself in a direction that would bring them to the first of two rendezvous locations. At sublight, they would need several minutes before they could enter warp space and the time was filled with status reports, relay checks, and the quiet hustle of any starship in Starfleet.

"Ready for warp," Chan announced, her hand tugging at her ear, her only display of nervousness.

"Warp seven, engage," Troi said.

The ship surged forward and the screen showed the shift into warp space and then another round of status checks filtered the air. Finally, the Klingon leaned down and whispered, so only Troi could hear, "You command them well. I am impressed."

Rather than say anything, she leaned up, kissed him on the cheek and laughed as his eyes went wide. Davison, to her right, chuckled, and Worf left the bridge, his speed making the ambassadorial robes flutter.

"Time to rendezvous with the *Trident* and *Excalibur,*" Riker asked.

"Fourteen minutes," Data responded.

The *Enterprise* had been cruising along at warp nine with no incidents. They had left the Petraw ships behind them ten hours earlier, allowing the crew to return to their normal routines. Which meant a rested Riker was in command and Picard was off-duty. People had time to eat or sleep, La Forge was able to run required diagnostics to prepare a maintenance schedule for their next stop at a starbase, and things were feeling normal for the moment.

Against all that, though, was the specter of chaos represented by the still-functioning gateways. Wars had broken out, natural disasters were occurring more frequently as the ancient technology began to harm the worlds it had once serviced. If Picard was right, the fourteen Resonators would either automatically close down the gateways, or at the least, give him control over them for the first time. If the latter, it represented awesome power and crushing responsibility. Starfleet, though, trusted him to make the right decision, since he had not once let them down.

Riker also took time to quickly review what he knew of the ships he was meeting. The *Excalibur* he had very briefly taken command of a few months back was gone, destroyed thanks to a madman. The ship on its way was a rechristened Galaxy-class vessel that Mackenzie Calhoun took command of in the wake of his return from the "dead." Picard was there for the christening, and had regaled his crew with the story of how he was ready to make Elizabeth Shelby the captain just as Calhoun turned up. He wound up with the ship; Picard wound up performing the wedding ceremony between the two. Shelby got command of the *Trident,* an Ambassador-class vessel.

Shelby irritated the first officer, mostly because of her strident attitude, but deep down he suspected they were more alike than not and that was where the problem lay. A key difference between them was her ambition, and he presumed she should be somewhat mellowed now that she had both Calhoun and a ship of her own.

Still, the reports from Starfleet were disturbing, since they indicated that both ships were involved in trying to settle a gateway-inspired war between the Aerons and the Markanians. Somehow, this led both Captains Shelby and Calhoun to enter a gateway and were now presumed missing. If they were not recovered, it would be a tremendous loss.

"Trident *to* Enteprise."

Riker looked up and saw an attractive woman with dark blond hair tied in a knot at the top of her head, cobalt-blue eyes, and an intriguing scar on her left cheek. This was Kat Mueller, who had been the night-shift commander on the previous *Excalibur.* "Riker here."

"Commander Mueller, in temporary command of the Trident.*"*

"So I understand. Sorry to hear about Captain Shelby. She was a fine officer."

"I would disagree," Mueller said, a hint of humor in her eye.

"I'm sorry?"

"She is a fine officer and will be rejoining us just as soon as we complete this assignment."

Riker smiled at that and added, "Well, that's good news. Calhoun as well?"

"The man cheats death more often than anyone in the Fleet." Riker was growing to like this woman by the moment. He hadn't gotten to know her very well during his brief tenure on the *Excalibur.*

"I'll take that as a yes. We won't have a lot of time so we're hoping to beam the Resonator en route."

"Beam a single object as we pass one another at high warp? That's imaginative."

"Born out of desperation, I admit," he said.

"Very well, we trust you will get it right the first time."

"Well, there's no time for a second attempt if we're to repeat this with *Excalibur.*"

As expected, the highly trained staff of the *Enterprise* managed the feat with minimal fuss and the two ships sped off toward different stars. Less than thirty minutes later, the *Excalibur* came within range. This time, Riker was exchanging pleasantries with Burgoyne 172, the ship's newly minted first officer.

"We'll be transporting the Resonator in about a minute," Riker told the Hermat. He remembered Burgoyne to be a complex but companionable person, and suspected s/he would make a fine first officer.

"Don't you find this a tad convenient?"

"In what way?"

"Needing both of our ships and you being the only ship to bring us the Resonators?"

"I'm sorry, Burgoyne, I don't follow you. There was no other ship with the power to make the contact while we had our own objective. Did you want some other ship?"

"No, just odd us crossing over like this," Burgoyne said archly.

Riker shook his head in confusion and let the subject drop. Instead, he monitored the two ships' trajectory and saw the five-second window that would enable the transport to occur. A signal came from the transporter chief that the *Enterprise* was now down to carrying just one Resonator. Nodding in agreement, he turned to Data and had the ship adjust course to their final destination.

Troi and Worf had just finished a meal in her temporary quarters, two old friends catching up their lives and friends. It was quite pleasant for her to share her happiness with the Klingon and she saw that the melancholy he normally wore as a cloak was just a bit lighter. Time was finally beginning to heal the wound caused by Jadzia Dax's death. She saw he was not at all ready to find another partner, but at least was comfortable back among his people.

"I think being an ambassador agrees with you," she said, placing the dishes in the replicator bay for recycling.

"It has its challenges . . . and rewards," Worf agreed.

"When this is over, what's next?"

"Back to Qo'noS, and moving on to the next assignment."

"Do you think our politics have been permanently altered by these events?"

"No," Worf said after a moment. He took the glasses from the table and brought them to her. "This is like any disruptive event we've encountered such as viruses or the Borg. We adapt and grow and learn from it."

"Captain to the bridge," rang out the intercom.

"Troi here. What is it, Commander?"

Davison replied, *"We have the* Defiant *on our sensors. Contact in five minutes."*

Troi concentrated a moment, recalling the specific instructions for this phase of the mission. "Slow to sublight, I'll be right there." Together, they left the cabin and quickly found their way to the bridge, where everyone snapped to attention. Clearly the presence of the hulking Klingon ambassador made everyone act by the book. This inwardly made her chuckle but kept her expression all business. Taking her seat, she checked a status chart, then activated the communications system.

"Marco Polo to *Defiant."*

"Vaughn, here." Elias Vaughn, just over one hundred years of age, appeared on the screen. He still had his full beard, his hair all gray, but

she saw that he seemed as relaxed as he was when they had last seen each other on the *Enterprise* a month earlier. Clearly, his decision to take a post at Deep Space 9 was the right choice, despite Starfleet's reservations.

"Always a pleasure to see you, Commander."

"Imagine my surprise to find you with your own command," Vaughn said, humor filling his voice. *"I see it agrees with you. Ian would be proud. And greetings to you, Ambassador Worf."*

"Commander," Worf said in return. Troi suspected that Worf had not seen Vaughn since they had met at Betazed during the war. Then, Vaughn was a floating tactical operative without a specific ship assignment. Now he was first officer on DS9 and also had Worf's old job of commanding the *Defiant*.

They shared a laugh and then it was all business as Troi gave a series of commands that led to the Resonator and Ambassador Worf being beamed to the *Defiant*. That ship's designation took it close to the Klingon border and should any problems flare up, it made the most sense for the ambassador to be present. The *Chargh*, already deep within the Empire, would collect Worf later on and bring him back to the Klingon homeworld. She gave him another long hug as he left the bridge and then returned to her center seat.

"I don't know much about Commander Vaughn," Davison said. "What's he like?"

Troi smiled. She'd known Vaughn since she was a child—the "Ian" he had referred to was Troi's father. Enigmatically, she said, "He's an interesting fellow."

The planet was barren and desolate, so small and unimportant the stellar cartographers never bothered to give it a name. It was catalogued as PI-3–3 over a hundred years earlier and Starfleet's records indicated that no one had ever been there. Far from the trading lanes, it was strategically unimportant, and barely Class M, so not worth the effort to colonize.

Picard stared at the viewscreen and was unimpressed. Yet, down below was a gateway, the farthest from the Petraw fleet and their ultimate goal. Data was already conducting a survey to make certain nothing threatening awaited them. La Forge was busy studying output from the gateway and Vale was already arming a detachment for the away team.

"It is devoid of life-forms," Data reported. "Plenty of flora but I cannot find even a bird or a fish."

"The gateway is functioning like all the others, but seems to have huge energy reserves," La Forge added.

"Sounds fairly safe," Picard said, looking over at his first officer. They shared a familiar look, the one that told Riker that his captain was going to the planet and there would be no discussion over the matter. After all, Picard went in search of the Resonators, had met the Iconians, and deserved to be involved in this, the final act.

"Captain, I think you should not go down alone," Vale said.

"I agree," the captain said. "Just because we don't detect life doesn't mean there's nothing threatening. Geordi, come with me as well, in case there's something unusual with the technology."

"Just come back this time," Riker said.

"I wouldn't have it any other way," Picard said with a smile. With that, he stood and strode off the bridge, heading straight down to the planet.

The *Excalibur* was bucking as the edge of an ion storm threatened their schedule. Burgoyne was gripping on to hir command chair as crew scurried back and forth. They detected the problem minutes earlier as the night crew struggled to avoid contact with the disruptive energy. S/he was awoken from a sound sleep by the alarm klaxon. Quickly, leaving Selar to check on Xyon, their infant son, s/he headed straight to the bridge.

"Helm is sluggish," reported Keefer, a beefy crewman who seemed to dwarf the console. He stabbed at controls but Burgoyne felt the ship continue to buck.

Burgoyne had no problem with crew of lesser experience handling things under normal conditions, but this was far from normal—even for the *Excalibur.* "Burogyne to senior staff," s/he barked. "All hands to the bridge."

In less than two minutes, Robin and Morgan Lefler and Soleta arrived on the bridge. The Vulcan went straight to the science station and began checking readings on the storm. Robin went to ops and performed similar checks, looking to her side to watch Keefer struggle with the helm. To her surprise, Morgan, her stately mother, strode over to the younger man and leaned over his right shoulder.

"You need to ignore the sensor readings and use more manual control to steer clear of a storm like this," Morgan advised.

"Morgan, relieve Mr. Keefer, please," Burgoyne said. "No offense, Ensign, but we have little time for lessons."

As the woman slid into the chair, Robin exclaimed, "What do you think you're doing?"

"Steering the ship," Morgan replied, her hands dancing across the controls. She paused briefly to intertwine her fingers, loosening them up as if she were going to play the piano. Then she expertly began easing the starship from the edge of the storm without losing speed.

Robin spun in her chair, looking at the first officer. "How can you do that?"

"Simple," Burgoyne replied. "If Captain Calhoun trusted her skill at science, then I can trust her at the helm. Sounds like she knows what she's doing. Look, we've stopped being shaken like a bad drink."

"But, but," Robin stammered, looking at her mother, who acted unperturbed by both the storm outside the vessel and inside the bridge.

"We've lost about five minutes from our schedule," Morgan reported without turning around. She seemed totally absorbed by the board below her fingers.

"I can fix that," Burgoyne replied. "Bridge to engineering. Time to heat up the engines. Give us warp nine point eight until I say otherwise."

And the ship surged forward, heading to a world that once proudly flew the flag of the Thallonian Empire.

"Helm, status," Vaughn said.

Ensign Prynn Tenmei said, "On course, ETA seventeen minutes."

For Vaughn, all seemed to be performing according to plan. Europa Nova had been successfully evacuated, Ro's covert mission to Farius Prime had been successful, and Dax had just called in reporting that Kira was not dead as previously reported, and had returned safely to the station. He looked forward to discussing her odyssey when he returned. But for now, they had to arrive at Dinasia and find the gateway. He intended to go down with Ensign Thirishar ch'Thane, leaving Lieutenant Nog in charge. Normally, he would be wary of leaving so inexperienced an officer in charge of the *Defiant* without backup. But the ship's previous commander, Worf, was on board, even if he wasn't strictly speaking Starfleet anymore, in case things got out of hand. Besides, Vaughn admired Nog's style.

"Ensign ch'Thane," Vaughn said, "you and I'll beam down with the Resonator. If I encounter any problems, you can help me with the equipment."

Shar looked mildly apprehensive. "My technical skills are not the best, sir. Perhaps Lieutenant Nog—"

Vaughn knew that the young Andorian had a reputation as being something of a klutz with equipment—he was a science officer, more comfortable with theory than practice—but Vaughn also knew that he wouldn't get any better without experience. "I have faith in you, Ensign. Mr. Nog, you have the conn in my absence."

Nog, Vaughn noticed, gave Shar a look of encouragement.

Minutes later, the ship achieved orbit and Shar quickly found the operating gateway on a remote island. It was devoid of Dinasian life-forms and Vaughn suspected they shunned it given the planet's Iconian roots. Whatever the reason, it meant they could move freely, which gave him confidence.

Within minutes, he and Shar materialized on the island, the tangy smell of the sea greeting them immediately. Wind blew water onto the rocks, causing high surf, trees swaying with the force. It was small, with no other island in sight, totally isolated. An odd place for a gateway, Vaughn mused, but who knew what the topography had been like two hundred millennia ago?

Shar spotted the cave entrance first and led the duo toward the island's one and only hill. The entrance was wide but low, forcing them to crouch to get inside. It was damp within, with lichen growing thick on the walls. About ten feet inside the cave stood the active gateway, the control mechanism to the left, closer to the men. Cautious, Vaughn withdrew his tricorder and took readings, noting it was functioning as expected. No surprises as yet.

Within the aperture, the rotating images were of three different interior destinations, none of which looked vaguely familiar to Vaughn. He glanced over at Shar, who shook his head.

The commander was holding the Resonator and recognized there was no reason not to place the device atop the control panel. The tricorder chronometer said he was running about ten minutes early from Data's elaborate plan. Still, he had no way to communicate with the thirteen other people doing the exact same task. As a result, he had to have faith and act.

The Resonator fit snugly atop the controls, as Picard had described. And just as expected, the machine acted accordingly, and the light show began. . . .

. . . a map of the universe began to appear before Captain Grekor, who stood alone on a desert planet that had been conquered by Kahless's son in one of the earliest additions to the Empire. The lights shifted and the images coalesced . . .

. . . and the Milky Way appeared to Subcommander Torath. Standing deep within a cave on a planet considered remote by the Romulan Star Empire, she was just following directions with no clarification from the Praetor's staff. Torath shielded her eyes from the brightness for a moment and then studied her universe as a single entity, no imaginary lines dividing it into quadrants, no lines marking territory, just a swirl of stars thickly clustered here and there . . .

. . . purple lights began to appear, one after another, dotting all over the galaxy, and Soleta nodded in appreciation for the precision. She knew little of the Iconians, but understood them to be a technologically proficient people and this device, hidden deep within a mountain range, proved the assumption correct. She matched the purple images against her tricorder reading, arched an eyebrow, and saw that her planet was the ninth to be lit. She idly wondered if there was significance to the pattern. . . .

. . . Bractor fingered the Resonator as it quietly hummed and continued to show highlights of key gateway locations. He wondered what would become of the items when the mission was complete and who might be interested in bidding to own one. Good as he was captaining a ship, the financial reforms on his homeworld required him to change his retirement strategy and he needed one major windfall. This could be what he needed. . . .

. . . Solok contemplated a people that could design such a device. With the *T'Kumbra* crisscrossing the Alpha Quadrant, they had mapped only a small portion of the gateway connections and there was an elegance to the patterns. His crew had contemplated the possibilities during their off-duty shifts and it led to much discussion, which pleased the captain. It was a fruitless task, but a vital one to help shed light on the work. But here, as he stood before the gateway on Titan, Jupiter's largest moon, he felt as if he was participating in something in concert with the rest of the quadrant and that brought a satisfaction he rarely felt as a captain. . . .

. . . the captain thought, *Damn you, Conklin.* He was running late and was certain the entire galaxy was waiting for him. But it couldn't be helped: the *Magellan* had blown out one dilithium-crystal relay, which resulted in cascading problems that not even his entire engineering team could solve in under an hour. Then he had pushed the engines past the redline to make the schedule, which would mean a week at the nearest starbase, but it would be worth it. He rushed into the chamber, past four cloaked monks, and snapped his Resonator into place and was stopped in place by the light show that immediately began. . . .

. . . Command had its privileges, Captain Klag thought, as he watched the gateway on Ufandi III, a home to pirates and black-marketers. When the *I.K.S. Gorkon* arrived, he laughed mirthlessly as two scores of one-man craft broke orbit and scattered in all directions. Having a reputation to be feared could come in handy now and then—this was exactly one of those moments. When Worf had asked for his help, he was only too glad to once more provide a service to the ambassador and his people. He had bloodied his *bat'leth* in maintaining order along the border and was ready to do something of consequence. . . .

* * *

. . . Kila Vet, Trill captain of the *Repulse,* watched frost form on his environmental suit while a meter before him, the console seemed thoroughly unaffected by Tethys III's hydrogen-helium atmosphere. It functioned normally, as did the gateway just beyond the control panel. He watched in fascination as he saw a Romulan bridge, a smoldering volcano, and a trading outpost he did not recognize. The thirteen purple lights finished forming and the amber button continued to blink. He figured that meant all the pieces were not yet in position . . .

. . . Every first officer he'd had, from Will Riker to the late Dina Voyskunsky to his current one, Mikhail Buonfiglio, would never have wanted him to beam down. But Robert DeSoto managed to convince Commander Bounfiglio to let him go down alone. There was nothing dangerous about the gateway on Gault. It was a Federation world, offering no threat to anyone, and the planetary defenses kept the curious at a distance. He'd seen a lot in his decades of service, but nothing of this nature, which went to show that being a Starfleet captain was never going to be boring. He and Picard, who was countless light-years away, had discussed the matter at the Captain's Table once. Picard explained how he learned never to give up the center seat, and they were words DeSoto took to heart. With a steady hand, he placed the Resonator atop the control panels and felt it glide into place. With a slight change in tenor, the lights changed on the board. . . .

. . . Kat Mueller was startled to see the amber light stop blinking, sure that meant the final Resonator was in place. She could only stand and wait—either for an order from Picard, or for an instruction from the Iconian device itself. Telling herself she could be patient, she watched the board and the holographic representation of the universe. She studied the console, checked a cracked fingernail, adjusted a stray hair from her usually perfect style, rechecked the console, checked in with the *Trident,* bit her lip, and did everything possible to avoid tapping her foot. Nothing seemed to change until . . .

. . . the purple lights on the graphic shaded to a deep royal color and Deanna Troi's eyes grew wide. The graphic began displaying alien typography that was characters, symbols, and some odd blend of the two. All the lights blinked in unison once, twice, and then stayed lit. She couldn't tell what it meant but figured the machinery was performing as programmed. She would remain patient. If this mission taught her anything, it was learning to wait with grace. . . .

. . . All Picard could think about was his friend Donald Varley. Had his colleague not discovered the Iconian homeworld, they would not have had the past decade to learn more about the legendary people. It cost Varley his life and that of his crew aboard the *Yamato,* but it gave them an advantage when it came to dealing with the Petraw. Had they shown up posing as Iconians without that knowledge, many would have been susceptible to the pitch. Now he stood on this dead world, watching the console go through the motions, and continued to wait for a sign that he needed to act.

The light show changed once more as one after another, the alien words faded from view one site at a time. When the graphic cleared, the purple lights began to wink off, again one at a time. It seemed that the graphic was deconstructing itself. Perhaps it meant the link was being broken—that the gateway network was shutting down.

Picard's eyebrows rose in surprise as the lights shifted, pulsating a bit, and then a face greeted him. He did not recognize the human features, but it structurally matched the Iconians he had met, what, days ago? It was a placid, female countenance and seemed to be waiting, much like Picard and the other members of the unusual coalition.

It spoke, but in a language Picard had never heard before. After a sentence, it seemed to wait for a reply. Then it tried again, this time with another language. Again the silent wait and again another language. Picard let out a breath, hoping it would reach a language he knew. Wisely, he held out his tricorder and recorded the exchange, hoping it would help linguists at Starfleet Command. Minutes slipped by and he tried to retain his good humor but it was growing first frustrating, then irritating that he could recognize not a single syllable. The computer interface seemed not to share his feeling and for a moment, he considered asking Data to join him. Before he could act on the notion, he recognized a word.

It was Vulcan.

The Vulcan people dated back further than humans, but not the two hundred thousand years that would make them contemporaries of the Iconians. Then, a distant lesson came to mind. It was speculated that the Vulcan people might have ancestors dating back to the war-torn planet that existed some five hundred thousand years gone by. By the Iconians' time, the language would have been refined but still, too much time would have gone by for him to recognize the words.

"May I help you, Captain Picard?"

Startled, the captain looked at the interface and saw its expression had not changed. The words were in French, his native tongue.

"Yes, you may," he said in the same language. "How do I disengage the gateways?"

"Our controls work both verbally and manually. If you wish to address the controls, give straightforward commands."

Clearing his throat, Picard swallowed and then said, "Please shut down the gateway network."

"Configuring the relays."

There was a long pause but Picard could hear the mechanism at work and noticed he was holding his breath in anticipation.

"Networks closed down, relays disconnected. Do you require anything further?"

Could it be that simple? Picard stared at the system and saw that it seemed no different from before. "Computer, could the system have been deactivated by any of the fourteen stations?"

"No," it replied. *"The Master Resonator works off the biosignature of the one to make first contact. That would be you, Captain Picard."*

"Has no one else used these controls?" Wait, it knew his name. Again, the level of sophisticated technology gave him pause.

"The Master Resonator is our emergency shutdown system and has not been required before now."

"Can the network be used anymore?"

"Yes. You would have to give me a restart instruction."

"How does the system shut down otherwise?"

"I cannot answer that."

"Why not?"

"I do not have that information."

Picard stared at the system with more than a little disbelief. He literally had the power over the gateways in his hands and no one else in the galaxy could take control. All it would take was for him to remove his unit and lock it away, and the gateways would no longer pose a threat. And only he knew this fact.

This was power he had promised to share, but he could not. He would be hunted for his DNA to restart the system, or be kidnapped in an attempt to gain control. Such information couldn't even go into the restricted files of Starfleet for fear that the insidious Section 31 would gain the knowledge. No, he would have to keep this to himself and take it to his grave. And what then? Would his death prevent the gateways from ever being used again? The thought was staggering.

No, he could not believe that. Just as the computer did not know its full capabilities and the current Iconians knew little of their heritage, Picard had to believe that there was a way to properly use the system. He would hold on to that belief, since the alternative made him shiver.

Could he control one unit at a time, directing the device from a remote location? Picard queried the computer, which answered in the affirmative. He considered that for a moment and then a thought occurred to him. Quickly, he tapped his communicator and had Riker patch him through to the Nyrian ship.

"Sure thing," Riker responded. *"Did you succeed?"*

"I believe so, Number One. Please have Data check all frequencies and see what he can learn." He waited patiently as the link to the distant starship was made.

"What's wrong, Captain?"

"Nothing, Taleen. However, I have gained control of the gateways and have shut them down. I can activate one, though, and send you close to home. We don't have the coordinates and will have to guess, which means you may wind up as lost as poor *Voyager.* Or you may stay here and join us. You must make the choice; I cannot do it for you."

"Captain Janeway has shown me great courage," Taleen told him. *"Send us home. But first, thank you for your help and kindness."*

Picard checked their best-guess coordinates, already researched by Ensign Paisner in stellar cartography thanks to Riker's diligence. He gave the verbal directions to the computer and the interface acknowledged.

"Gateway activated." And once more Picard waited for things to happen parsecs and parsecs away.

After some minutes, Riker contacted the captain and informed him that the long-range sensors at Starbase 134 showed the Nyrian ship had vanished. Mission accomplished.

"Computer, shut down the gateway and then close down," Picard instructed.

"As you wish," it said, and a moment later the image vanished. The computer whirled to a close and the lights went dim.

It was over. The galaxy could go about its business without threat of further interference.

Oddly, it felt disquieting, but Picard would adjust and learn to keep such secrets deep in his mind. He signaled his ship and was transported home.

The glowing face spoke in gibberish, but Chanik could tell it was speaking to someone, Young God Picard he assumed. There were pauses, then it spoke, then it stopped. Sounds indicated the system was changing and Chanik thought it might be dying. It took Young God Picard away and he was told this was a good thing but he missed the man.

The lessons he learned from Picard had filled his mind in all the hours he waited for the machine to perform its magic. Things were not always what they appeared and justice could take many forms. The lessons were good ones and maybe, when he was a little older, he could teach them to others. Teaching sounded like a good thing to do, he considered, chewing on the last strip of meat. But first, there was more for him to learn. Perhaps he would return to the farm they had passed together. Maybe the farmer took in the thieves and maybe there was room for him, too. He could work for food, learn to plant or make wine. And then he could watch and see if Picard's instructions would be followed.

A plan set, he turned to walk out of the cavern, ready to leave the City behind him and start something new.

Chapter 7

Doral had not left the guest cabin once. He had learned to manipulate the ship's computer and seemed to be accessing a wide variety of files, none of which posed a threat to the ship or crew. Christine Vale assured Picard that no sabotage was possible from the Petraw leader.

The *Enterprise* was en route back to the Petraw fleet. As soon as the captain returned to the bridge, contact with Starfleet was established and it was clear that the computer had followed its programming. Admiral Ross reported that all indications were that the gateways had stopped functioning, which meant more than a handful of planets were spared further damage. The cleanup work would take months, complicating the Dominion War rebuilding, but that was a task for the Starfleet Corps of Engineers. Ross complained that they never seemed to be moving forward, always rebuilding or recovering from some problem. His tone sounded upbeat, though, and Picard accepted the heartfelt thanks with a tight smile.

Now he stood before the Petraw's cabin, making up his mind. Bractor was right: he had not really considered the beaten explorer's fate. His hands tugged his uniform straight and he then pressed the door chime.

Within moments, he stood before Doral, who seemed slighter, less haughty than when they first met some days before. He had been viewing a recording about the horsehead nebula, a half-drunk cup by his elbow. If he were fully human, Picard would suspect he had slept little, his eyes looking more haunted than alert.

"It's over; we shut down the gateways," Picard said.

"I see."

"Your ploy caused immense loss of life and great destruction," the captain continued. "We estimate that relocating the lost will take some months. We have diplomats rebuilding peace accords and our work will allow us to remember the Petraw for quite some time."

"And what will become of my people?"

Picard looked at the defeated man and fought the feeling of pity that was welling within him. He would not allow it. "Your people subscribe to a different moral code. I was distressed to see that one felt strongly enough to take action which cost more lives. I am not certain what should be done, to be honest. What you did, you did from some biological imperative, but I cannot forget that there were alternatives to the approach you took.

"I could leave you to the mercy of a coalition court, but that would detain you when that is clearly not of use to anyone."

"No, I suppose not." The words were flat, the tone devoid of emotion.

"I will bring you and your acolyte back to your ship but will suggest to the others that we pool our resources and come up with a purpose for your people."

Doral looked up with a questioning expression, the first sign of life since the captain had entered.

"You are explorers by nature and there is much of the galaxy left to visit. Many of us used tricorders to study the mechanism that activates the gateways. I believe Mr. Data can collect and analyze the information and provide you with a course that will allow you to fulfill your imperative while keeping you from interacting with any of the races you tried to dupe."

"We're banished?"

"No," Picard said carefully. "The universe is teeming with life and we're letting you go out and find them before any of us get the chance. Turn it to your advantage and open your minds to the possibilities."

Doral nodded, taking in the words, obviously surprised that the course of action did not involve trial or death.

Picard figured there would be time enough to talk further so left him alone to his thoughts. Instead, he needed a long rest.

"It's certainly been interesting," Davison told Troi with a grin.

"When dealing with the *Enterprise,* there is no other way," Deanna replied. They were standing in the captain's quarters and Troi was done packing her bag. Her home ship had returned to the alliance an hour earlier and it was time to report. The mighty starship would tow the *Mercury* home with the *Marco Polo* flying escort and Brisbayne coming over in temporary command. Already, the *Glory* was limping into a point position, preparing to lead the Petraw fleet in its new direction. The *Qob* was arcing around, ready to head back to the Klingon Empire, the other ships positioning themselves accordingly.

"What should I do with this?"

Troi looked at the item and smiled wickedly. "Ask the chief to have it beamed directly to my quarters. I'll need it soon."

The two shared a humorous look and then proceeded to the bridge. Troi had grown fond of the crew and wished she had more time to work with them. They'd always be her first crew and that made them memorable. She still wasn't sure if she wanted command for herself. After all, she hoped to spend the rest of her life with a man born to sit in the center seat. Working alongside him seemed good enough, either as counselor, first officer, lover—or wife.

"Captain on the bridge," Hol called as the doors snapped open.

That, she would miss.

"I just wanted to thank you all, for the hard work," she said by the door. The crew had turned and given her rapt attention. All taut at their posts, the *Enterprise* fittingly on the viewscreen. "Starfleet Command will read our reports and I suspect you will all find yourselves with satisfactory assignments in the months to come."

"But our assignments have been changed, our ships have moved on," the Tiburonian science officer said, his voice bordering on a whine.

Troi grinned at him and answered, "Actually, with everyone mobilized to handle the gateways, Command clearly has to rethink deployments. You're to follow us back to Earth and we'll see what happens."

Mia Chan rose, her eyes dividing time between Troi and Rosario.

313

The counselor recognized that the pair was ready to begin a relationship and she wished them well. She knew how tough it would be for any couple to establish a strong bond while serving on the same ship, especially one this small, but it was possible.

"You were so great to work with," Chan gushed.

"We all worked well together," Troi said calmly. "There's still more to be done. We won't leave until the Petraw ships are on their way, just in case."

"Shall I keep a weapons lock on the lead ship?" Rosario asked.

"No," Troi countered. "We still have the dampening field in effect. In fact, we need to lower it in order to get me back to the *Enterprise.*"

She stood another moment, uncertain if there was more to say. Once more, she beamed a smile at her crew and turned, counseling herself to keep her emotions in check. Without a look back, she put a reassuring hand on Davison's forearm and entered the turbolift.

Picard walked the bridge, checking station by station, ready to bring this entire matter to a close. Geordi La Forge was leaning over the engineering station, one of the aft duty posts on the vast bridge. He had been monitoring the polaron bursts that put the Petraw in check and so far everything ran with textbook efficiency.

"Ready to drop the field," he reported. Picard saw the screens and returned to his place in the command seat.

The captain turned to Riker, his face a mask of determination. Riker acknowledged the look and kept his counsel. Finally, Picard said, "I'd sooner sail through an ion storm than have to go through those kinds of negotiations again. While I had Admiral Ross's support, the Federation Council was dubious. Even after I got them to see my point, our representative races had their own notions of justice. Having turned off the gateways gave me more than a little additional clout, which carried the day."

"Not a perfect plan is it?" Riker asked.

The captain shook his head slowly before replying. "We've certainly been tidier in our affairs," he admitted. "But under the circumstances, it's the best solution."

Picard and Riker shared a quick glance as the captain settled in and Riker spoke out, "Do it, Geordi."

The readings were clear, space was returning to normal, and the engineer looked over his right shoulder and announced that space was safe for transporters once more. He remained studying the readouts, just in case a Petraw chose to commit a violent act.

"Riker to transporter room, ready to bring Captain Troi aboard."

Picard leaned back, feeling relaxed for the first time in a week. "I look forward to having the family back home."

"Sooner or later, we're going to have to leave the nest," Riker said. "The days of letting a captain keep his crew together for decades are pretty much over."

"Trying to tell me something, Number One?"

"Not at all," Riker said, the usual twinkle in his eye. "Just making an observation."

"Perhaps I need to find you a ship after all," the captain said, coming as close to light banter as he dared on a topic that he disliked thinking about. Of course his crew would get promoted and move on. Some, like Tasha Yar, died in the line of duty, but others, like O'Brien and Worf, had moved on, pursuing their own destinies. Even Data had been placed on detached assignment here and there.

He would just have to cherish whatever time he had left with these special people.

"Counselor Troi is back aboard," the transporter chief reported.

"Excellent," Picard told him. "Lieutenant Vale, please have our Petraw guests brought to the transporter room. I will meet them there."

"Very good, sir," she replied, and entered the commands.

Picard left Riker on the bridge and took a lift below. By the time he arrived, Doral stood a forlorn figure on the platform. The younger saboteur stood sullenly in the rear. Two security officers remained off to the side, at full alert, and the transporter chief kept his hands on the controls.

"It's time," Picard said.

"I know," Doral replied.

"Mr. Data has already sent the coordinates to your entire fleet. He even took the liberty of organizing flight patterns that would provide maximum safety to the older vessels. You should be in excellent shape for the new adventure."

Doral looked at him blankly.

"This region of space has been through a tremendous ordeal over the last few years," Picard noted, his tone hard, without its soft, cultured tones. "One race after another has had to beat back the encroachment of the Borg, followed immediately by a quadrant-wide war initiated by people from the far side of the Milky Way. Between the two, we've lost too many innocents, too many dedicated officers and ships. But we're still here.

"Do you know why, Doral? Because, when we had to, we put aside the little differences between our peoples, trusted one another to go into battle side-by-side. And we persevered. We stopped the invasion and preserved myriad ways of life. Because . . . it was the right thing to do.

"And when the Petraw came skulking into our space and preyed upon our trust, set one against another in a petty bidding competition, we once again managed to stand up to the threat . . . together. I find these moments invigorating because it means we are beginning to respect one another a little more every day.

"Know this, should you find your way here again, you will be greeted with less than open arms. If necessary, we shall draft even more races together to help keep the peace."

Picard took a deep breath, let it out slowly and watched Doral's still somewhat bewildered expression. There was a modicum of comprehension under the furrowed brow but not enough to satisfy him. It was time to bring this to an end.

"Consider this the beginning of the next step in Petraw history," the captain said to him. His expression turned hard. "You cannot return here—you will likely not be welcome by some of the neighboring governments. Seek your destiny and forget about your homeworld. Be realistic and look forward, not behind. There is so much to discover and experience, you can make your own history. But do so honestly and with integrity."

The Petraw leader just looked at him, the expression indicating surprise and bewilderment.

"We're sending you back to your ship. Please be out of this area within the hour." Picard looked over his shoulder to the chief. "Energize."

It took seconds for Doral to vanish from the *Enterprise,* and Picard realized he still felt mixed emotions, but mostly disappointment at what their desperation had brought to so many worlds. He might never know the death toll. The Federation could not administer proper justice and having them voluntarily leave this portion of the quadrant made the most sense. After all, the Klingons, the Romulans, and even the Carreon might demand Petraw deaths as payment for loss of sovereign lives. Already, he had heard rumblings that this might damage politics for a time.

Still, it needed to be done this way. He could not condone the Petraw's actions, nor could he be a party to their deaths. It would be an empty payment that benefited no one.

As he cleared his mind of such thoughts, he took a moment to enjoy the notion that everyone had returned to his ship hale and hearty. It was time for his loved ones to be together in safety. "Mr. Riker," the captain said as he entered the turbolift, "I'm on my way up. Why don't you take a moment and welcome the counselor back?"

"Aye, aye, sir," Riker answered, the humor filling his voice.

Riker couldn't wait to see his *imzadi.* Even though they had been separated by space, she had remained available to help him through the tough moments during the mission. He couldn't imagine life without her and he intended to do whatever it would take to make sure she remained a part of it.

Standing before her cabin door, he pressed the announcement key and heard the soft chime beyond the door. Within seconds, the door opened and a hard object was jabbed into his chest, his hands reflexively reaching out to grab it.

"What . . . oh . . . are you . . . ?"

"Mad at your lack of confidence in me?" Troi answered from within the cabin. Riker remained frozen in place, uncertain about her feelings right then and there. "Annoyed at being embarrassed by having this presented before my first command? Amused at your little joke? What do you think?"

Riker was left speechless.

"You're a commander," she said, stepping closer. "Make a command decision. Say something."

Still holding the crash helmet he had given Troi as a gag going-away present, Riker felt a mixture of amusement, abashment, and confusion. Remembering lessons from their years together, he answered from his heart. "I missed you."

Her hands reached over the threshold, grabbing fistfuls of duty jacket, and yanked him right into the cabin. That's when he noticed she was wearing the diaphanous pale lavender item that left one shoulder bare and little to the imagination.

"Better put that helmet on," she said, letting go of the uniform as the door closed. "You're going to need it."

Picard sat in his ready room, looking at the tricorder images taken on the world on which he had found Chanik and the Master Resonators. He'd miss the youth and knew he had the power to go back and visit but also recognized that he would never do so. The captain could never imagine an instance when circumstances would force him to use the gateways. It was power he would hide, a secret he would no doubt take to his deathbed.

Instead, he would prepare a report to Starfleet Command, complete with recommendations for reparations and commendations for selected staff, starting with Troi. The Petraw ships had started forming as Data directed and they would be gone shortly. Once they were off long-range sensors, he could return to Earth and accept his next assignment. As with most his missions, whatever they gave him, it would never quite turn out as the mission specs spelled out.

And he wouldn't have it any other way.

THE POCKET BOOKS
STAR TREK TIMELINE

David Bowling, Johan Ciamaglia,
Ryan J. Cornelius,
James R. McCain, Alex Rosenzweig,
Paul T. Semones, and Corey W. Tacker

with
David Henderson and Lee Jamilkowski

The Pocket Books *Star Trek* Novel Timeline

Created by The Timeliners: David Bowling, Johan Ciamaglia, Ryan J. Cornelius, James R. McCain, Alex Rosenzweig, Paul T. Semones, and Corey W. Tacker.

With collaboration by David Henderson from *http://www.psiphi.org/* and Lee Jamilkowski.

And special thanks to Jason Barney, Keith R.A. DeCandido, James E. Goeders, Robert Greenberger, Bob Manojlovich, and John J. Ordover.

This is a complete timeline to the Pocket Books *Star Trek* novels, short stories, Simon & Schuster Audio original audiobooks, eBooks, novelizations, and Minstrel Books young adult books published through December 2001. Any yet-to-be-published books listed are tentatively placed, based on descriptions from authors and editors. The actual placement of these books may change in the next version of this work. Some books or stories have been moved as "further evidence" was uncovered. When known, dates are given in both Earth calendar dates and *Star Trek* stardates. When placing items in the Timeline, the Timeliners sometimes had to correct inconsistent stardates so that continuity among the *Star Trek* television episodes and books would remain as correct as possible.

Please note that dates marked with a bullet (•) represent portions of a story that take place at times other than the time of the central portion of the story.

LEGEND:
Trek Series
CHA—*Star Trek: Challenger*
DS9—*Star Trek: Deep Space Nine*
NF—*Star Trek: New Frontier*
SCE—*Star Trek: Starfleet Corps of Engineers*
TNG—*Star Trek: The Next Generation*
TAS—*Star Trek*: The Animated Series

TOS—*Star Trek*: The Original Series
VGR—*Star Trek: Voyager*

Other Abbreviations
EL—*Enterprise Logs* anthology
SNW—*Strange New Worlds* anthology
TLOD—*The Lives of Dax* anthology
YA—Young adult book

c. 1600
"If I Lose Thee . . ." (TOS short story, SNW III)
• 2269 — [Framing story] Set at some point after "The City on the Edge of Forever" (TOS)
1776
"Veil at Valcour" (EL short story)
Historians' Note: Story is set on October 11, 1776.
1864
"A Q to Swear By" (TNG short story, SNW III)
• 2370 — Set after "Parallels" (TNG) but before "All Good Things . . ." (TNG)
1930
"Triptych" (TOS short story, SNW II)
• 2267 — [Framing story] Set during "The City on the Edge of Forever" (TOS)
1938
"Captain Proton and the Orb of Bajor" (DS9 short story, SNW IV)
Historians' Note: This story is a Captain Proton radio drama script written by Benny Russell and incorporating elements of Deep Space Nine. *It was broadcast on October 28, 1938.*
1940
"The Adventures of Captain Proton, Chapter 1: The Space Vortex of Doom" (VGR short story, *Amazing Stories* #598)
Captain Proton: Defender of the Earth **(VGR)**
1942
"World of Strangers" (EL short story)
Historians' Note: Story is set on October 26, 1942.
1953
"Isolation Ward 4" (DS9 short story, SNW IV)
Historians' Note: This story is told as Dr. Wykoff's notes about Benny Russell, dated from December 14, 1953, to April 2, 1954.
• April 4, 1968—[Final entry]

1969
"The Aliens Are Coming!" (TOS short story, SNW III)
1974
The Eugenics Wars: The Rise and Fall of Khan Noonien Singh
(hardcover duology)
- 1984–1986— Khan as a teenager
- 1996 — Khan as an adult
- Late 2269 — Framing story Stardate 7004.1
1991
"The Man Who Sold the Sky" (Short story, SNW)
1998
"Research" (DS9 short story, SNW II)
1999
Spock vs. Q: Armageddon Tonight **(TOS/TNG audio)**
Spock vs. Q: The Sequel **(TOS/TNG audio)**
2063
"A Private Victory" (TNG short story, SNW III)
Second Contact **(TNG/X-Men comic)**
Historians' Note: Story is set immediately after the 2063 portion of Star
Trek: First Contact.
- 1996 — Set in an alternate version of Earth
- 2050 — Set in an alternate version of Earth
- 2367 — Set during the Battle of Wolf 359
"Almost . . . But Not Quite" (VGR short story, SNW II)
Historians' Note: Story is set shortly after the 2063 portion of Star Trek:
First Contact.
- 1996 — Major part of the story takes place at this time
2065
Federation **(TOS/TNG hardcover)**
- 2062 — Cochrane demonstrates warp capability to Brack
- 2063 — Cochrane breaks the light barrier with the *Phoenix*
Timeliners' Note 1: From Star Trek: First Contact, *not mentioned in this*
book.
- 2064 — Cochrane leaves for Alpha Centauri on the *Bonaventure*
Timeliners' Note 2: We assume the Phoenix *(seen in* Star Trek: First
Contact*) was an experimental ship designed to demonstrate manned warp*
capability and the Bonaventure, *mentioned in this book, was a ship de-*
signed for interstellar travel.
- 2065 — [Part One, Chapters 1 and 2] Cochrane returns from his first
interstellar trip to Alpha Centauri; shortly after his return, Cochrane again
leaves Earth for Alpha Centauri to flee Thorsen

Timeliners' Note 3: The March 2061 date contradicts the Star Trek Chronology *and has been adjusted to March 2065.*
- 2078 — Cochrane backstory
- 2117 — Cochrane backstory
- 2267 — [Kirk portion] Stardate 3849.8 to 3858.7, immediately follows "Journey to Babel" (TOS)
- 2271 — Kirk visits Cochrane monument on Titan
- 2293 — [Prologue, Epilogue] Stardate 9910.1, Kirk visits Guardian of Forever

Timeliners' Note 4: The 2295 date contradicts the Star Trek Chronology *and has been adjusted to 2293.*
- 2366 — [Picard portion] Stardate 43920.6 to 43924.1, immediately after "Sarek" (TNG)
- 2371 — Picard and Riker visit the Cochrane monument, a few weeks after the 24th century events of *Star Trek Generations.*
- And Beyond . . . — [Epilogue] New stardate 2143.21.3, a ship called *Enterprise* about to begin a voyage where no one has gone before . . .

2075
"First Steps" (TLOD short story)
2159
"Dead Man's Hand" (TLOD short story)
Historians' Note: Story is set during the third year of the Romulan Wars.
2161
***Starfleet: Year One* (serial novel)**
2245
"Old Souls" (TLOD short story)
2246
"Though Hell Should Bar the Way" (EL short story)
Historians' Note: Story is set on October 10, 2246, and occurs simultaneously with the Tarsus IV incident.
2248
***Starfleet Academy: Crisis on Vulcan* (TOS-YA #1)**
Historians' Note: Story is set before Spock joins Starfleet Academy in 2249.
2250
***Starfleet Academy: Aftershock* (TOS-YA #2)**
Historians' Note: Story is set soon before Starfleet Academy's winter break in Kirk's freshman year, 2250.

2251

***Starfleet Academy: Cadet Kirk* (TOS-YA #3)**

Historians' Note: Spock mentions meeting Pike a "few years ago," which occurred in Starfleet Academy: Crisis on Vulcan *(TOS-YA #1).*

2252

***Vulcan's Glory* (TOS #44)**

2254

(TOS) "The Cage"

"Conflicting Natures" (EL short story)

Historians' Note: Story is set nine years after the launch of the Enterprise.

***The Captain's Table #6: Where Sea Meets Sky* (TOS)**

• 2266 — [Framing story] Stardate 1626.8, shortly before Pike's crippling accident

2265

Enterprise*: The First Adventure* (TOS giant)

"Sins of the Mother" (TLOD short story)

• 2280 — [Framing story] Audrid's letter, describing the events of the story

• Kirk's first five-year mission begins.

(TOS) "Where No Man Has Gone Before" — Stardate 1312.4 to 1313.8

***My Brother's Keeper* (TOS trilogy: Republic (#85), Constitution (#86), Enterprise (#87))** — Stardate 1313.8

• 2251 — *Republic* backstory

• 2259 — *Constitution* backstory

• 2264 — *Enterprise* backstory

2266

(TOS) "Corbomite Maneuver" — Stardate 1512.2

(TOS) "Mudd's Women" — Stardate 1329.8

(TOS) "The Enemy Within" — Stardate 1672.1

(TOS) "The Man Trap" — Stardate 1513.1

(TOS) "The Naked Time" — Stardate 1704.2

(TOS) "Charlie X" — Stardate 1533.6 to 1535.8

(TOS) "Balance of Terror" — Stardate 1709.2

***Shadow Lord* (TOS #22)** — Stardate 1831.5

(TOS) "What Are Little Girls Made Of?" — Stardate 2714.4

(TOS) "Dagger of the Mind" — Stardate 2715.1

(TOS) "Miri" — Stardate 2713.5

(TOS) "The Conscience of the King" — Stardate 2817.7

"A Private Anecdote" (TOS short story, SNW) — Stardate 2822.5

• 2255 — [Pike backstory]

2267

(TOS) "The Galileo Seven" — Stardate 2821.5

(TOS) "Court Martial" — Stardate 2947.3

(TOS) "The Menagerie" — Stardate 3012.4

(TOS) "Shore Leave" — Stardate 3025.3

Heart of the Sun **(TOS #83)**

Historians' Note: Story is set not long after "Court Martial" (TOS).

(TOS) "The Squire of Gothos" — Stardate 2124.5

(TOS) "Arena" — Stardate 3045.6

(TOS) "The Alternative Factor" — Stardate 3087.6 to 3088.7

(TOS) "Tomorrow Is Yesterday" — Stardate 3113.2

Web of the Romulans **(TOS #10)** — Stardate 3125.3 to 3130.4

Historians' Note: Story is set shortly after "Tomorrow Is Yesterday" (TOS).

Timeliners' Note: A footnote that refers to "All Our Yesterdays" (TOS) contradicts the computer malfunction subplot of the story.

(TOS) "Return of the Archons" — Stardate 3156.2 to 3158.7

"The Avenger" (EL short story)

(TOS) "A Taste of Armageddon" — Stardate 3192.1 to 3193.0

(TOS) "Space Seed" — Stardate 3141.9 to 3143.3

The Joy Machine **(TOS #80)**

(TOS) "This Side of Paradise" — Stardate 3417.3 to 3417.7

(TOS) "The Devil in the Dark" — Stardate 3196.1

(TOS) "Errand of Mercy" — Stardate 3198.4 to 3201.7

(TOS) "The City on the Edge of Forever"

Final Frontier **(TOS Giant)**

Historians' Note: Framing story takes place immediately after "City on the Edge or Forever" (TOS).

• 2245 — [Captain April backstory] Takes place before the *Starship Enterprise*'s first five-year mission

(TOS) "Operation—Annihilate!" — Stardate 3287.2 to 3289.8

Ishmael **(TOS #23)**

Historians' Note: Framing story takes place after "The City on the Edge of Forever" (TOS).

• 1867 — Spock time travels back to Earth to this date

(TOS) "Catspaw" — Stardate 3018.2

(TOS) "Metamorphosis" — Stardate 3219.4 to 3220.3

(TOS) "Friday's Child" — Stardate 3497.2

Invasion! #1: First Strike **(TOS #79)**

Historians' Note: Story is set immediately after "Friday's Child" (TOS).

(TOS) "Who Mourns for Adonais?" — Stardate 3468.1

(TOS) "Amok Time" — Stardate 3372.1 to 3372.7

(TOS) "The Doomsday Machine"

(TOS) "Wolf in the Fold" — Stardate 3614.9

***Across the Universe* (TOS #88)**

(TOS) "The Changeling" — Stardate 3451.9

(TOS) "The Apple" — Stardate 3715.0 to 3715.3

(TOS) "Mirror, Mirror"

(TOS) "The Deadly Years" — Stardate 3478.2 to 3479.4

***Faces of Fire* (TOS #58)** — Stardate 3998.6

Historians' Note: Story is set about halfway through Kirk's first five-year mission.

(TOS) "I, Mudd" — Stardate 4513.3

(TOS) "The Trouble with Tribbles" — Stardate 4523.3 to 4525.6

"Missed" (TOS short story, SNW IV)

Historians' Note: Story takes place immediately after "The Trouble with Tribbles" (TOS).

(TOS) "Bread and Circuses" — Stardate 4040.7

***Mission to Horatius* (The first *Star Trek* novel)** — Stardate 3475.3

Historians' Note: Story is set after "The Trouble with Tribbles" (TOS).

***Twilight's End* (TOS #77)**

Historians' Note: Story is set after "A Taste of Armageddon" (TOS).

(TOS) "Journey to Babel" — Stardate 3842.3

***The Vulcan Academy Murders* (TOS #20)**

***The IDIC Epidemic* (TOS #38)**

Historians' Note: Story is set after The Vulcan Academy Murders.

(TOS) "A Private Little War" — Stardate 4211.4

2268

***The Disinherited* (TOS #59)**

Historians' Note: Story is set just before "The Gamesters of Triskelion" (TOS).

(TOS) "The Gamesters of Triskelion" — Stardate 3211.7

(TOS) "Obsession" — Stardate 3619.2

***Day of Honor* #4: *Treaty's Law* (TOS)** — Stardate 3629

Historians' Note: Story is set after "Errand of Mercy" (TOS).

Timeliners' Note: Stardate for the story is from Day of Honor #2: Armageddon Sky.

• 2288 — [Framing story] Set 20 years after the main events of the novel

***The Rings of Tautee* (TOS #78)** — Stardate 3871.6

(TOS) "The Immunity Syndrome" — Stardate 4307.1

(TOS) "A Piece of the Action"

(TOS) "By Any Other Name" — Stardate 4657.5

The Klingon Gambit **(TOS #3)** — Stardate 4720.1 to 4744.8

Mutiny on the **Enterprise (TOS #12)** — Stardate 4769.1 to 5012.5

Historians' Note: Story is set immediately after The Klingon Gambit.

(TOS) "Return to Tomorrow" — Stardate 4768.3

(TOS) "Patterns of Force"

Uhura's Song **(TOS #21)** — Stardate 2950.3 to 2962.3

Historians' Note: Story is set after "A Private Little War" (TOS).

• 235 B.C. — [Flashback, pages 177–179]

(TOS) "The Ultimate Computer" — Stardate 4729.4

(TOS) "The Omega Glory"

(TOS) "Assignment: Earth"

(TOS) "Spectre of the Gun" — Stardate 4385.3

(TOS) "Elaan of Troyius" — Stardate 4372.5

(TOS) "The Paradise Syndrome" — Stardate 4842.6

Double, Double **(TOS #45)** — Stardate 4925.2

(TOS) "The *Enterprise* Incident" — Stardate 5027.3

(TOS) "And the Children Shall Lead" — Stardate 5029.5

The Abode of Life **(TOS #6)** — Stardate 5064.4 to 5099.5

Timeliners' Note: Inconsistent crew continuity with both Yeoman Rand and Dr. M'Benga aboard.

Dreams of the Raven **(TOS #34)** — Stardate 5302.1 to 5321.12

Timeliners' Note: Using McCoy's age for chronology is problematic, so the stardate was used.

(TOS) "Spock's Brain" — Stardate 5431.4

How Much for Just the Planet? **(TOS #36)**

Historians' Note: Story is set after "Omega Glory" (TOS).

(TOS) "Is There in Truth No Beauty?" — Stardate 5630.7

Ghost Walker **(TOS #53)**

Historians' Note: Story is set during fourth year of Kirk's first five-year mission.

(TOS) "The Empath" — Stardate 5121.5

Legacy **(TOS #56)** — Stardate 5258.7

• 2254 — [Pike backstory]

(TOS) "The Tholian Web" — Stardate 5693.2

The Starship Trap **(TOS #64)**

Historians' Note: Story is set after "The Immunity Syndrome" (TOS).

Windows on a Lost World **(TOS #65)** — Stardate 5419.4

Section 31: Cloak (TOS)

Timeliners' Note: Story is set several months after "The Enterprise *Incident" (TOS) and shortly before "for the World is Hollow . . ." (TOS).*

(TOS) "For the World Is Hollow and I Have Touched the Sky" — Stardate 5476.3

The Badlands (Book 1, TOS story) — Stardate 5650.1

Historians' Note: Story is set several months after "The Enterprise *Incident" (TOS).*

(TOS) "Day of the Dove"

(TOS) "Plato's Stepchildren" — Stardate 5784.2

First Frontier (TOS #75)

Historians' Note: Story is set after "The Omega Glory" (TOS).

• 64,018,143 B.C. — The *Enterprise* time-travels to Earth of the past

(TOS) "Wink of an Eye" — Stardate 5710.5

(TOS) "That Which Survives"

Gateways #1: One Small Step (TOS)

Timeliners' Note: Story is set immediately after "That Which Survives." (TOS).

Mudd In Your Eye (TOS #81)

Historians' Note: Story is set after "I, Mudd" (TOS).

(TOS) "Let That Be Your Last Battlefield" — Stardate 5730.2

(TOS) "Whom Gods Destroy" — Stardate 5718.3

Sanctuary (TOS #61)

Historians' Note: Story is set after "Let That Be Your Last Battlefield" (TOS).

(TOS) "The Mark of Gideon" — Stardate 5423.4

2269

(TOS) "The Lights of Zetar" — Stardate 5725.3

(TOS) "The Cloud Minders" — Stardate 5818.4

(TOS) "The Way to Eden" — Stardate 5832.3

"The Quick and the Dead" (TOS short story, SNW II)

(TOS) "Requiem for Methuselah" — Stardate 5843.7

(TOS) "The Savage Curtain" — Stardate 5906.4

"First Star I See" (TOS short story, SNW IV)

(TOS) "All Our Yesterdays" — Stardate 5943.7

(TOS) "Turnabout Intruder" — Stardate 5928.5

Assignment: Eternity (TOS #84) — Stardate 6021.4 to 6021.6

Historians' Note: Story is set one week after "Turnabout Intruder" (TOS).

• 1969 — [Chapters 1 and 22] July 19 and 20

• 2293 — [Framing story] During the end of *Star Trek VI: The Undiscovered Country*

Yesterday's Son (**TOS #11**) — Stardate 6324.09 to 6381.7

• 2703 B.C. (approx.) — Time travel to the past

Killing Time (**TOS #24**)

Historians' Note: Story is set after "The Enterprise *Incident" (TOS).*

The Three-Minute Universe (**TOS #41**)

Historians' Note: Story is set after "Plato's Stepchildren" (TOS).

Memory Prime (**TOS #42**)

Historians' Note: Story is set after "The Lights of Zetar" (TOS).

Renegade (**TOS #55**)

Historians' Note: Story is set two years after "A Private Little War" (TOS).

From the Depths (**TOS #66**)

Prime Directive (**TOS giant**) — Stardate 4842.6 to 6987.31

Timeliners' Note: Prime Directive *makes a convenient transition point between the live-action episodes (TOS) and the animated episodes (TAS).*

From the Star Trek Chronology *editors' note (page 78): "Although this chronology does not use material from the animated* Star Trek *series, Dorothy Fontana suggests that she would place those stories after the end of the third season, but prior to the end of the five-year mission."*

(TAS) "Beyond the Farthest Star" — Stardate 5221.3

(TAS) "Yesteryear" — Stardate 5373.4

(TAS) "One of Our Planets Is Missing" — Stardate 5371.3

(TAS) "The Lorelei Signal" — Stardate 5483.7

(TAS) "More Tribbles, More Troubles" — Stardate 5392.4

(TAS) "The Survivor" — Stardate 5143.3

(TAS) "The Infinite Vulcan" — Stardate 5554.4

(TAS) "The Magicks of Megas-Tu" — Stardate 1254.4

(TAS) "Once Upon a Planet" — Stardate 5591.2

(TAS) "Mudd's Passion" — Stardate 4978.5

(TAS) "The Terratin Incident" — Stardate 5577.3

(TAS) "The Time Trap" — Stardate 5267.2

(TAS) "The Ambergris Element" — Stardate 5499.9

(TAS) "The Slaver Weapon" — Stardate 4187.3

(TAS) "The Eye of the Beholder" — Stardate 5501.2

(TAS) "The Jihad" — Stardate 5683.1

(TAS) "The Pirates of Orion" — Stardate 6334.1

(TAS) "Bem" — Stardate 7403.6

(TAS) "The Practical Joker" — Stardate 3183.3

(TAS) "Albatross" — Stardate 5275.6

(TAS) "How Sharper Than a Serpent's Tooth" — Stardate 6063.4

(TAS) "The Counter-Clock Incident" — Stardate 6770.3

***The Trellisane Confrontation* (TOS #14)** — Stardate 7521.6 to 7532.8

***Corona* (TOS #15)** — Stardate 4380.4 to 4997.5

Historians' Note: Story is set years after "Devil in the Dark" (TOS).

***The Final Reflection* (TOS #16)** — Stardate 8405.15

Historians' Note: Framing story is set after "Day of the Dove" (TOS).

• 2230 — [Part One]

• 2238 — [Part Two]

• 2244 — [Part Three]

***Tears of the Singers* (TOS #19)** — Stardate 3126.7 to 3127.1

Historians' Note: Story takes place after "Day of the Dove" (TOS) and "Time Trap" (TAS).

***Pawns and Symbols* (TOS #26)** — Stardate 5960.2 to 6100.0

Historians' Note: Story is set after "Day of the Dove" (TOS) and "More Troubles, More Tribbles" (TAS).

"The Girl Who Controlled Gene Kelly's Feet" (TOS short story, SNW)

Historians' Note: Story is set after "Once Upon a Planet" (TAS).

***The Cry of the Onlies* (TOS #46)** — Stardate 6118.2 to 6119.2

***The Great Starship Race* (TOS #67)** — Stardate 3223.1

Historians' Note: Story is set after "A Taste of Armageddon" (TOS).

***The Patrian Transgression* (TOS #69)** — Stardate 6769.4

2270

***Crossroad* (TOS #71)** — Stardate 6251.1

***The Wounded Sky* (TOS #13)** — Stardate 9250.0

***Rihannsu #1: My Enemy, My Ally* (TOS #18)**

***Mindshadow* (TOS #27)** — Stardate 7003.4 to 7008.4

***Crisis on Centaurus* (TOS #28)** — Stardate 7513.2 to 7521.6

***Demons* (TOS #30)**

Historians' Note: Story is set after Mindshadow.

• 2229 — [Pages 22–26] Sarek and Amanda's courtship

***Chain of Attack* (TOS #32)**

***Bloodthirst* (TOS #37)**

Historians' Note: Story is set after Demons.

***The Final Nexus* (TOS #43)**

Historians' Note: Story is set after Chain of Attack.

***Doctor's Orders* (TOS #50)**

Historians' Note: Story is set after The Wounded Sky.

***The Entropy Effect* (TOS #2)**

• 2250 — [Flashback, pages 42–45]

Black Fire **(TOS #8)** — Stardate 6101.1 to 6205.7

Dreadnought! **(TOS #29)** — Stardate 7881.2 to 8180.2

Battlestations! **(TOS #31)** — Stardate 3301.1 to 4720.2

• 2267 — [Pages 97–118] Piper is a Starfleet Academy senior

• Kirk's first five-year mission ends and the Starship *Enterprise* returns to spacedock (*Star Trek Chronology*).

Timeliners' Note: The placement of this event is drawn from "Q2" (VGR). We assume that this event occurred roughly in mid-2270.

"A Little More Action" (TOS short story, SNW IV)

Historians' Note: Story takes place on the last night before Spock leaves Earth to return to Vulcan.

2271

The Lost Years **(TOS hardcover)**

Historians' Note: The bulk of The Lost Years *takes place in early 2271.*

Timeliners' Note: Page 53 establishes Spock as 41, and sets a 2271 year for the book.

• A.D. 30 (Vulcan Old Date 140005) — [Prologue] Set during Surak's life

• 2270 — [Chapters 1 and 2] Stardate 6987.31, six months prior to the bulk of the book

Traitor Winds **(TOS #70)**

Timeliners' Note: Story is set "shortly after the end of the Enterprise*'s five-year mission, immediately following the events chronicled in* The Lost Years*." This occurs after Spock decides to pursue Kohlinar, contradicting the December 2269 date on page 1.*

2272

A Flag Full of Stars **(TOS #54)**

Timeliners' Note: Story spans from July 4 to July 20 and is set "shortly before the events chronicled in Star Trek: The Motion Picture*." Since dates placing this novel during the Apollo 11 tricentennial contradict the* Star Trek Chronology*, we assumed the story to be centered around the tricentennial of the Apollo space program (1969–1972) instead.*

• 2246 — [Pages 111–118] Young Kirk and Kodos on Tarsus

Recovery **(TOS #73)**

Historians' Note: Story is set weeks before Star Trek: The Motion Picture.

Timeliners' Note: Several references to Kirk having been Chief of Operations for approximately a year suggest a late 2272 time period for this novel, some 4 months after A Flag Full of Stars *(TOS #54).*

2273

"Night Whispers" (EL short story)

Historians' Note: Story is set immediately before Star Trek: The Motion Picture.

Star Trek: The Motion Picture **(TOS movie novelization)** — Stardate 7412.3 to 7414.1

Timeliners' Note: Page 21 of the novelization establishes that Spock has been pursuing the Kolinahr disciplines for 2.8 years. This establishes the event in mid-2273.

Spock's World **(TOS hardcover)** — Stardate 7412.1 to 7468.5

• *c.* 5–2 Billion B.C. — [Vulcan One] Birth of the planet Vulcan

• *c.* 500,000 B.C. — [Vulcan Two] Appearance of early Vulcan hominids

• *c.* 10,000 B.C. — [Vulcan Three] Early Vulcan tribal cultures

• *c.* 3000 B.C. — [Vulcan Four] Ancient Vulcan civilization

• *c.* 300 B.C. — [Vulcan Five] Early Vulcan space travel

• 79 B.C. to A.D. 60 — [Vulcan Six] The life of Surak

• 2191 to 2230 — [Vulcan Seven] Sarek of Vulcan

The **Kobayashi Maru (TOS #47)**

Historians' Note: Story is set shortly after Star Trek: The Motion Picture.

• 2244 — [Scott backstory]

• 2254 — [Kirk backstory]

• 2259 — [Sulu backstory]

• 2267 — [Chekov backstory]

Home Is the Hunter **(TOS #52)**

Historians' Note: Story is set shortly after Star Trek: The Motion Picture.

• 1600 — [Sulu backstory]

• 1746 — [Scott backstory]

• 1942 — [Chekov backstory]

Enemy Unseen **(TOS #51)** — Stardate 8036.2

Historians' Note: Story is set shortly after Star Trek: The Motion Picture.

2274

The Prometheus Design **(TOS #5)**

Triangle **(TOS #9)**

Historians' Note: Story is set seven years after "Amok Time" (TOS).

New Earth #1: Wagon Train to the Stars **(TOS #89)**

Historians' Note: Story spans several months. October 31, 2272, has been adjusted to 2274.

• 2274 — [Pages 69–85] Set three months earlier

2275

New Earth #2: Belle Terre **(TOS #90)**

New Earth #3: Rough Trails **(TOS #91)**

Historians' Note: Story is set six months after New Earth #2: Belle Terre.

New Earth #4: The Flaming Arrow **(TOS #92)**

New Earth #5: Thin Air **(TOS #93)**

New Earth #6: Challenger **(TOS #94)**

The Better Man **(TOS #72)** — Stardate 7591.4 to 7598.5

• 2236 — [Pages 7–11] McCoy at age 9

• 2244 — [Pages 12–15] McCoy at age 17

• 2254 — [Pages 30–33, 35–37, 66–68, 129–130, 150–157] After McCoy graduates from medical school

• 2270 — [Pages 62–63] Toward the end of Kirk's first five-year mission

Gateways #2: Chainmail **(CHA)**

2276

The Covenant of the Crown **(TOS #4)** — Stardate 7815.3

• 2258 — [Pages 23–29] Kirk is a lieutenant commander, therefore set 18 years before the rest of the story. This allows him to be a lieutenant during the events on the *Farragut* as established in "Obsession" (TOS), and then be promoted after that.

Timetrap **(TOS #40)**

Rihannsu #2: The Romulan Way **(TOS #35)**

Historians' Note: This story takes place eight years after "The Ultimate Computer" (TOS).

• A.D. 30 — Rejecting Surak's reforms, S'task and 80,000 followers leave Vulcan in search of a new world

• *c.* A.D. 500 — The Travelers make planetfall on the twin worlds of ch'Rihan and ch'Havran

Rihannsu #3: Swordhunt **(TOS #95)**

Rihannsu #4: Honor Blade **(TOS #96)**

Timeliners' Note: Page 90 of Swordhunt *establishes these two books as beginning approximately a month and a half after* The Romulan Way *(TOS #35).*

2277

Ice Trap **(TOS #60)**

Death Count **(TOS #62)**

Shell Game **(TOS #63)**

Firestorm **(TOS #68)**

Timeliners' Note: Uniform references contradict other references to the story taking place five years after "Elaan of Troyius" (TOS). However, following the latter references would cause further inconsistencies.

2278

***Rules of Engagement* (TOS #48)** — Stardate 7818.1

*Timeliners' Note 1: The 2213.5 stardate given in the book is too low since it would put the story during Kirk's first five-year mission. We took the liberty to adjust it to fit a post-*Star Trek: The Motion Picture *time-frame.*

Timeliners' Note 2: Page 244 suggests this novel takes place about "a dozen years" after Kirk's encounter with the Organians.

"The Name of the Cat" (TOS short story, SNW IV)

• 2371 — between "All Good Things . . ." and *Star Trek Generations*

***Deep Domain* (TOS #33)** — Stardate 7823.6 to 7835.8

Historians' Note: Story is set at the end of Kirk's second five-year mission.

"Family Matters" (TOS short story, SNW III)

• Kirk's second five-year mission ends and the Starship *Enterprise* returns to spacedock.

2281

***The Pandora Principle* (TOS #49)**

Historians' Note: Story is set after Saavik enters the Academy.

*Timeliners' Note 1: Page 9 establishes that the Vulcans' journey to Hellguard is only months after *Star Trek: The Motion Picture.

• 2274 — Spock rescues Saavik from Hellguard

• 2274 to 2275 — Spock takes a one-year leave to train Saavik

Timeliners' Note 2: Spock's leave would conflict with a number of other novels. Reconciling this is left to the reader.

***Dwellers in the Crucible* (TOS #25)**

Historians' Note: Story is set after Saavik enters the Academy.

2283

***Time For Yesterday* (TOS #39)**

Historians' Note: Story is set 14.5 years after "All Our Yesterdays" (TOS).

• 2683 B.C. (approx.) — Time travel to the past

"Just Another Training Cruise" (EL short story)

Historians' Note: Story is set in Saavik's second year at the Academy.

2284

***Strangers from the Sky* (TOS giant)** — Stardate 8083.6 to 8097.4 [Book 1]

• 2045 — [Book 2]

• 2265 — Stardate 1305.4, before "Where No Man Has Gone Before" (TOS)

2285

"Infinity" (TLOD short story)

Historians' Note: Story is set before Star Trek II: The Wrath of Khan.

***Star Trek II: The Wrath of Khan* (TOS movie novelization)** — Stardate 8130.3 to 8141.6

"Prodigal Father" (TOS short story, SNW IV)

Historians' Note: Story is set during the final battle in Star Trek II: The Wrath of Khan.

***Star Trek III: The Search for Spock* (TOS movie novelization)** — Stardate 8201.3

"Countdown" (TOS short story, SNW IV)

Historians' Note: Story is set during Star Trek III: The Search for Spock.

"Allegro Ouroboros in D Minor" (TLOD short story)

2286

***Star Trek IV: The Voyage Home* (TOS movie novelization)** — Stardate 8390.0

• 1986 — Kirk and crew travel back in time

"The Last Tribble" (TOS short story, SNW)

2287

"Scotty's Song" (TOS short story, SNW IV)

Historians' Note: Story is set one week prior to Star Trek V: The Final Frontier.

***Star Trek V: The Final Frontier* (TOS movie novelization)** — Stardate 8454.1

• 2229 — [Prologue] Sybok is five years old

• 2230 — [Flashback] Spock is born

• 2253 — [Flashback] McCoy's father dies

In the Name of Honor (TOS #97) — Stardate 8461.7

• 2267 — [Flashback, Chapter 5] Stardate 4524.2

• 2279 — [Chapter 1 and 2] Stardate 7952.4

Probe (TOS hardcover) — Stardate 8475.3 to 8501.2

The Rift (TOS #57) [Second Contact]

• 2254 — [First Contact, Pike backstory]

2288

Starfleet Academy (TOS computer game novelization)

Historians' Note: Story is set two years before Captain Hikaru Sulu takes command of the Excelsior *in 2290.*

2290

The Captain's Table #1: War Dragons **(TOS)**

• 2265 — [Kirk backstory] Stardate 1298.9, shortly after "Where No Man Has Gone Before" (TOS)

• 2293 — [Framing story] Takes place between *Star Trek VI: The Undiscovered Country* and *Star Trek Generations.*

2291

"*jubHa'* " (short story, SNW III)

Timeliners' Note: This story is written entirely in the Klingon language. Placement of this story was based on a comment from the author, Dr. Lawrence M. Schoen.

Cacophony **(TOS audio)** — Stardate 8764.3 to 8774.8

Envoy **(TOS audio)** — Stardate 9029.1 to 9029.4

2293

Star Trek VI: The Undiscovered Country **(TOS movie novelization)** — Stardate 9521.6 to 9529.1

Timeliners' Note: The story ends with the Enterprise *heading home for decommission.*

Shadows on the Sun **(TOS hardcover)** — Stardate 9582.1 to 9587.2 [Book One]

Timeliners' Note: The story begins with the Enterprise *heading home and ends with the* Enterprise *heading home.*

• 2254 — [Book Two, McCoy backstory]

Best Destiny **(TOS hardcover)**

Timeliners' Note: The story begins with the Enterprise *almost home but ends with the* Enterprise *gaining a reprieve from retirement. This would have to be after* Shadows on the Sun *and would explain why the* Enterprise *is still active for* Sarek *and* Mind Meld.

• 2249 — [Captain April backstory]

Sarek **(TOS hardcover)** — Stardate 9544.6

Historians' Note: Story is set after the reprieve in Best Destiny.

• 2229, June 14 — [Pages 60–62] Sarek and Amanda's courtship

• 2229, September 16 — [Pages 155–159] Sarek and Amanda marry

• 2230, November 12 — [Pages 200–202] Spock born

Timeliners' Note: The book says 2231, contradicting the Star Trek Chronology.

• 2237, December 7 — [Pages 211–215] Young Spock runs away, based on "Yesteryear" (TAS) events

• 2249 — [Pages 258–264] Spock chooses Starfleet and alienates Sarek

• 2285, March 14 — [Pages 373–375] Sarek and Amanda wonder what happened to Spock's katra, probably set right before *Star Trek III: The Search for Spock*

Mind Meld (TOS #82)

Historians' Note: Story is set after the reprieve in Best Destiny.

• 2314 — [Chapter 16]

The Ashes of Eden (TOS hardcover)

Historians' Note: Story is set after the Enterprise-*A has been decommissioned.*

The Fearful Summons (TOS #74) — Stardate 9621.8 to 9625.10

Timeliners' Note 1: The story has a retired Kirk and no Enterprise.

Timeliners' Note 2: The Spring 2294 date contradicts the Star Trek Chronology.

"The Lights in the Sky" (TOS short story, SNW)

Historians' Note: Story is set just before the TOS-era portion of Star Trek Generations.

"One of Forty-Seven" (TNG short story, SNW III)

"The First Law of Metaphysics" (TOS short story, SNW II)

Historians' Note: Story is set the same day Kirk "dies."

Star Trek Generations (TNG movie novelization) — Stardate 9715.5 *[See main entry in 2371]*

Timeliners' Note: Some authors place this portion of the movie later in 2294 or 2295.

2294

The Captain's Daughter (TOS #76)

• 2271 — [Section Two: First Date] References on pages 53 and 148 establish this placement

• 2278 — [Chapters 15–17] Around the time of the *Bozeman*'s launch

• 2284 — [Chapters 18 and 19]

• 2285 — [Chapters 20 and 21] Set immediately after *Star Trek III: The Search for Spock* and during *Star Trek IV: The Voyage Home*

2296

Vulcan's Forge (TOS hardcover) — Stardate 9814.3 to 9835.7

Timeliners' Note: The "about a year after Kirk's disappearance" references are inaccurate.

• 2247 — [Spock backstory]

"Shakedown" (EL short story)

Historians' Note: Story is set after The Captain's Daughter.

2301

"The Hero of My Own Life" (TOS short story, SNW II)

Timeliners' Note: If we suppose Gillian Taylor was the same age as actress Catherine Hicks in Star Trek IV: The Voyage Home, *she was 35 when*

*she arrived in the 23rd century with Kirk and crew. In this story, she is in
her fifties; hence this story's placement in 2301.*

2314

Transformations **(TOS audio)** — Stardate 11611.8 to 11618.2

• 2294 — [Sulu backstory] Stardate 9619.9 to 9622.4

2322

Starfleet Academy: Starfall **(TNG-YA #8)**

*Historians' Note: Story spans the period from the fall of 2322 to the fall
of 2323.*

2323

Starfleet Academy: Nova Command **(TNG-YA #9)**

*Historians' Note: Story starts at the beginning of Picard's freshman year
at Starfleet Academy.*

2332

"Hour of Fire" (EL short story)

2333

The **Valiant (TNG hardcover)** [Book 2]

• 2069, December 30 — [Book 1] The original *Valiant*

Timeliners' Note: The December 30, 2069, date contradicts the Star Trek
Chronology, *which places the destruction of the* Valiant *the same year that
it leaves on its mission in 2065. The author has placed the destruction in
2069 to allow time for the starship to reach the edge of the galaxy.*

• 2070 — [Book 3] Survivors of the *S.S. Valiant* find a planet that will
support them

2334

"Together Again, for the First Time" (TNG short story, SNW)

2341

Starfleet Academy: Mystery of the Missing Crew **(TNG-YA #6)**

*Historians' Note: Story is set in the Earth year 2341, when Data entered
Starfleet Academy.*

• 2338 — [Prologue]

Starfleet Academy: Secret of the Lizard People **(TNG-YA #7)**

*Historians' Note: Data has been a cadet at Starfleet Academy for three
weeks at the beginning of this story.*

Starfleet Academy: Deceptions **(TNG-YA #14)**

*Historians' Note: Data has been a cadet at Starfleet Academy for three
months at the beginning of this story.*

2342

Starfleet Academy: Loyalties **(TNG-YA #10)**

*Historians' Note: Story is set during Beverly Crusher's (née Howard)
first year at Starfleet Academy Medical School.*

2344
Vulcan's Heart **(TOS hardcover)**
• 2329 — [Flashback] Stardate 21096.3
2347
"A Ribbon for Rosie" (VGR short story, SNW II)
Historians' Note: Story is set 27 years before Seven of Nine's arrival on
Voyager *in "Scorpion, Part II" (VGR).*
"Flash Point" (TNG short story, SNW IV)
Historians' Note: The "flashback" parts of the story take place when Ro
Laren is 7 years old.
• 2364 — Ro on Garon II
• 2367 — Ro in the Jaros II prison
2350
Double Helix #6: The First Virtue **(TNG #56)**
2353
"The Music Between the Notes" (TLOD short story)
Starfleet Academy: Lifeline **(VGR-YA #1)**
Historians' Note: Story is set as Janeway begins at Starfleet Academy in
2353, according to the "Starfleet Timeline" in this book.
Starfleet Academy: Capture the Flag **(TNG-YA #4)**
Historians' Note: La Forge has been a cadet at Starfleet Academy for
three weeks at the beginning of this story.
Starfleet Academy: The Chance Factor **(VGR-YA #2)**
Historians' Note: Conversation in this story indicates it takes place in
the same year as Starfleet Academy: Lifeline.
Starfleet Academy: Quarantine **(VGR-YA #3)**
Historians' Note: La Forge is mentioned as being a first-year cadet in
this story.
Starfleet Academy: Atlantis Station **(TNG-YA #5)**
Historians' Note: La Forge is a first-year cadet at Starfleet Academy in
this story.
Starfleet Academy: Crossfire **(TNG-YA #11)**
Historians' Note: La Forge and Riker are first-year cadets at Starfleet
Academy *in this story.*
2354
Starfleet Academy: The Haunted Starship **(TNG-YA #13)**
Historians' Note: Story is set during the spring semester of La Forge's
first year at Starfleet Academy.
Starfleet Academy: Breakaway **(TNG-YA #12)**
Historians' Note: Story is set during Troi's first year at Starfleet
Academy *in 2354, according to the "Starfleet Timeline" in this book.*

2357

***Starfleet Academy: Worf's First Adventure* (TNG-YA #1)**
***Starfleet Academy: Line of Fire* (TNG-YA #2)**
***Starfleet Academy: Survival* (TNG-YA #3)**
Historians' Note: These three stories are set during Worf's first year at Starfleet Academy.

2364

***Encounter at Farpoint* (TNG episode novelization)** — Stardate 41150.7 to 41254.7

(TNG) "The Naked Now" — Stardate 41209.2 to 41209.3

***Double Helix #1: Infection* (TNG #51)** — Stardate 41211

• 2364 — [Prologue] Set approximately two weeks prior to the main events of the story

(TNG) "Code of Honor" — Stardate 41235.25 to 41235.32

(TNG) "Haven" — Stardate 41294.5 to 41294.6

(TNG) "Where No One Has Gone Before" — Stardate 41263.1 to 41263.4

***Ghost Ship* (TNG #1)**

• 1995 — [Russian aircraft carrier backstory]

(TNG) "The Last Outpost" — Stardate 41368.4 to 41368.5

***The Peacekeepers* (TNG #2)**

(TNG) "Lonely Among Us" — Stardate 41249.3 to 41249.4

(TNG) "Justice" — Stardate 41255.6 to 41255.9

(TNG) "The Battle" — Stardate 41723.9

(TNG) "Hide And Q" — Stardate 41590.5 to 41591.4

(TNG) "Too Short a Season" — Stardate 41309.5

(TNG) "The Big Goodbye" — Stardate 41997.7

(TNG) "Datalore" — Stardate 41242.4 to 41292.5

(TNG) "Angel One" — Stardate 41636.9

(TNG) "11001001" — Stardate 41365.9

(TNG) "Home Soil" — Stardate 41463.9 to 41484.8

(TNG) "When the Bough Breaks" — Stardate 41509.1 to 41512.4

(TNG) "Coming of Age" — Stardate 41416.2

(TNG) "Heart of Glory" — Stardate 41503.7

***The Children of Hamlin* (TNG #3)**

(TNG) "The Arsenal of Freedom" — Stardate 41798.2

***Survivors* (TNG #4)**

• 2352 — [Chapter 1] Tasha is 15, leaves Turkana IV

• 2357 — [Chapter 3] Tasha in her later years at Starfleet Academy

• 2359 — [Chapter 5] Tasha is almost 23

• 2364 — [Chapter 12] Set immediately after "Skin of Evil" (TNG)

(TNG) "Symbiosis"
(TNG) "Skin of Evil" — Stardate 41601.3 to 41602.1
***The Captain's Honor* (TNG #8)** — Stardate 41800.9
Historians' Note: Story is set shortly after "Skin of Evil" (TNG).
(TNG) "We'll Always Have Paris" — Stardate 41697.9
(TNG) "Conspiracy" — Stardate 41775.5 to 41780.2
(TNG) "The Neutral Zone" — Stardate 41986.0
2365
(TNG) "The Child" — Stardate 42073.1
***Strike Zone* (TNG #5)**
(TNG) "Where Silence Has Lease" — Stardate 42193.6 to 42194.7
(TNG) "Elementary, Dear Data" — Stardate 42286.3
(TNG) "The Outrageous Okona" — Stardate 42402.7
***Power Hungry* (TNG #6)** — Stardate 42422.5
(TNG) "The Schizoid Man" — Stardate 42437.5 to 42507.8
(TNG) "Loud as a Whisper" — Stardate 42477.2 to 42479.3
(TNG) "Unnatural Selection" — Stardate 42494.8
(TNG) "A Matter of Honor" — Stardate 42506.5
(TNG) "The Measure of a Man" — Stardate 42523.7
***Metamorphosis* (TNG giant)** — Stardate 42528.6
(TNG) "The Dauphin" — Stardate 42568.8
***Masks* (TNG #7)**
(TNG) "Contagion" — Stardate 42609.1
(TNG) "The Royale" — Stardate 42625.4
(TNG) "Time Squared" — Stardate 42679.2
(TNG) "The Icarus Factor" — Stardate 42686.4
(TNG) "Pen Pals" — Stardate 42695.3 to 42741.3
(TNG) "Q Who" — Stardate 42761.3 to 42761.9
(TNG) "Samaritan Snare" — Stardate 42779.1 to 42779.5
(TNG) "Up the Long Ladder" — Stardate 42823.2 to 42827.3
(TNG) "Manhunt" — Stardate 42859.2
(TNG) "The Emissary" — Stardate 42901.3
***A Call to Darkness* (TNG #9)** — Stardate 42908.6
(TNG) "Peak Performance" — Stardate 42923.4
(TNG) "Shades of Gray" — Stardate 42976.1
2366
***Double Helix #2: Vectors* (TNG #52)**
Timeliners' Note: Dr. Pulaski is leaving the Enterprise *and Dr. Crusher is returning.*
***A Rock and a Hard Place* (TNG #10)**
(TNG) "Evolution" — Stardate 43125.8

(TNG) "The Ensigns of Command"
***Gulliver's Fugitives* (TNG #11)**
(TNG) "The Survivors" — Stardate 43142.4 to 43153.7
(TNG) "Who Watches the Watchers" — Stardate 43173.5 to 43174.2
***Doomsday World* (TNG #12)** — Stardate 43197.5
(TNG) "The Bonding" — Stardate 43198.7
(TNG) "Booby Trap" — Stardate 43205.6
(TNG) "The Enemy" — Stardate 43349.2
(TNG) "The Price" — Stardate 43385.6
(TNG) "The Vengeance Factor" — Stardate 43421.9
***Exiles* (TNG #14)** — Stardate 43429.1
(TNG) "The Defector" — Stardate 43462.5 to 43465.2
(TNG) "The Hunted" — Stardate 43489.2
(TNG) "The High Ground" — Stardate 43510.7
(TNG) "Déjà Q" — Stardate 43539.1
(TNG) "A Matter of Perspective" — Stardate 43610.4 to 43611.6
(TNG) "Yesterday's *Enterprise*" — Stardate 43625.2
"The Fourth Toast" (TNG short story, SNW III)
• 2344 — [Backstory]
***Q-in-Law* (TNG #18)**
(TNG) "The Offspring" — Stardate 43657.0
***Fortune's Light* (TNG #15)**
(TNG) "Sins of the Father" — Stardate 43685.2 to 43689.0
(TNG) "Allegiance" — Stardate 43714.1
***The Eyes of the Beholders* (TNG #13)**
(TNG) "Captain's Holiday" — Stardate 43745.2
***Boogeymen* (TNG #17)** — Stardate 43747.3
(TNG) "Tin Man" — Stardate 43779.3
(TNG) "Hollow Pursuits" — Stardate 43807.4 to 43808.2
(TNG) "The Most Toys" — Stardate 43872.2
(TNG) "Sarek" — Stardate 43917.4 to 43920.7
(TNG) "Ménage à Troi" — Stardate 43930.7
**"What Went Through Data's Mind 0.68 Seconds Before the
Satellite Hit" (TNG short story, SNW)** — Stardate 43945.4
*Timeliners' Note: The 42945.4 stardate given in the book was adjusted to
fit a timeframe shortly after "Ménage à Troi" (TNG).*
***Contamination* (TNG #16)** — Stardate 43951.6
*Timeliners' Note: The 44261.6 stardate given in the book was adjusted to
fit a timeframe shortly after "Ménage à Troi" (TNG).*
(TNG) "Transfigurations" — Stardate 43957.2 to 43960.6
(TNG) "The Best of Both Worlds" — Stardate 43989.1 to 43993.5

2367
(TNG) "The Best of Both Worlds" Part II — Stardate 44001.4
"Civil Disobedience" (TNG short story, SNW)
(TNG) "Family" — Stardate 44012.3
Dark Mirror **(TNG hardcover)** — Stardate 44018.2
Timeliners' Note: The 44010.2 stardate given in the book was adjusted to fit a timeframe after "Family" (TNG).
(TNG) "Brothers" — Stardate 44085.7 to 44091.1
(TNG) "Suddenly Human" — Stardate 44143.7
Reunion **(TNG hardcover)**
(TNG) "Remember Me" — Stardate 44161.2 to 44162.8
Perchance to Dream **(TNG #19)** — Stardate 44195.7
Timeliners' Note: The 45195.7 stardate given in the book was adjusted to fit a timeframe before "Final Mission" (TNG).
(TNG) "Legacy" — Stardate 44215.2 to 44225.3
Spartacus **(TNG #20)**
(TNG) "Reunion" — Stardate 44246.3
(TNG) "Future Imperfect" — Stardate 44286.5
"See Spot Run" (TNG short story, SNW)
(TNG) "Final Mission" — Stardate 44307.3 to 44307.6
(TNG) "The Loss" — Stardate 44356.9
"Prodigal Son" (TNG short story, SNW IV)
Historians' Note: This story is concurrent with "The Loss" (TNG).
Vendetta **(TNG giant)**
• 2326 — [Picard backstory]
(TNG) "Data's Day" — Stardate 44390.1
"Tears for Eternity" (TOS short story, SNW IV)
Historians' Note: Story is set 100 years after the events of "The Devil in the Dark" (TOS).
• *c.* 52,267 — Set approximately 50 millennia after "The Devil in the Dark" (TOS).
"Of Cabbages and Kings" (TNG short story, SNW)
(TNG) "The Wounded" — Stardate 44429.6
(TNG) "Devil's Due" — Stardate 44474.5
(TNG) "Clues" — Stardate 44502.7
(TNG) "First Contact"
(TNG) "Galaxy's Child" — Stardate 44614.6
(TNG) "Night Terrors" — Stardate 44631.2 to 44642.1
Chains of Command **(TNG #21)**
(TNG) "Identity Crisis" — Stardate 44664.5 to 44668.1
(TNG) "The Nth Degree" — Stardate 44704.2 to 44705.3

(TNG) "Qpid" — Stardate 44741.9
The Forgotten War **(TNG #57)**
(TNG) "The Drumhead" — Stardate 44769.2
(TNG) "Half a Life" — Stardate 44805.3 to 44812.6
(TNG) "The Host" — Stardate 44821.3 to 44824.4
Imbalance **(TNG #22)** — Stardate 44839.2
(TNG) "The Mind's Eye" — Stardate 44885.5 to 44896.9
(TNG) "In Theory" — Stardate 44923.3 to 44935.6
(TNG) "Redemption" — Stardate 44995.3 to 44998.3
2368
(TNG) "Redemption, Part II" — Stardate 45020.4 to 45025.4
"Calculated Risk" (TNG short story, SNW II)
(TNG) "Darmok" — Stardate 45047.2 to 45048.8
(TNG) "Ensign Ro" — Stardate 45076.3 to 45077.8
The Badlands **(Book 1, TNG story)** — Stardate 45091.4
Historians' Note: Story is set immediately after "Ensign Ro" (TNG).
(TNG) "Silicon Avatar" — Stardate 45122.3 to 45129.2
(TNG) "Disaster" — Stardate 45156.1
War Drums **(TNG #23)**
(TNG) "The Game" — Stardate 45208.2 to 45212.1
Unification **(TNG episodes novelization)** — Stardate 45233.1 to
45245.8
Timeliners' Note: This book novelizes Parts I and II of the episode.
"Last Words" (TNG short story, *Amazing Stories* #593)
(TNG) "A Matter of Time" — Stardate 45349.1 to 45351.9
(TNG) "New Ground" — Stardate 45376.3
Sins of Commission **(TNG #29)**
Historians' Note: Story is set shortly after "New Ground" (TNG).
(TNG) "Hero Worship" — Stardate 45397.3
(TNG) "Violations" — Stardate 45429.3 to 45435.8
(TNG) "The Masterpiece Society" — Stardate 45470.1
(TNG) "Conundrum" — Stardate 45494.2
Imzadi **(TNG hardcover)**
• 2359 — Riker and Troi meet for the first time
• 2364 — Riker and Troi are reunited on the *Enterprise*
Timeliners' Note 1: The 42372.5 stardate given in the book is a mismatch
with the "Encounter at Farpoint" (TNG) stardate of 41150.7.
• 2408 — [Framing story] Set 42 years after "The Offspring" (TNG)
Timeliners' Note 2: The 2408 portion of the story must be regarded
as an alternate future which is divergent from the "mainstream" uni-
verse.

The Last Stand (**TNG #37**) — Stardate 45523.6

(TNG) "Power Play" — Stardate 45571.2 to 45572.1

(TNG) "Ethics" — Stardate 45587.3

(TNG) "The Outcast" — Stardate 45614.6 to 45620.4

Nightshade (**TNG #24**)

(TNG) "Cause and Effect" — Stardate 45652.1

(TNG) "The First Duty" — Stardate 45703.9

(TNG) "Cost of Living" — Stardate 45733.6

(TNG) "The Perfect Mate" — Stardate 45761.3 to 45766.1

Grounded (**TNG #25**) — Stardate 45823.4

Timeliners' Note: Alexander is mentioned, which sets the story after "New Ground" (TNG). The 45223.4 stardate given in the book was adjusted to fit the specified timeframe.

(TNG) "Imaginary Friend" — Stardate 45852.1

(TNG) "I, Borg" — Stardate 45854.2

The Devil's Heart (**TNG hardcover**) — Stardate 45873.3 to 45873.6

• *c.* 70 B.C. — [Picard's vision] The Ko N'ya stone is given to Surak

Timeliners' Note: This vision may be historically unreliable. There are contradictions with Spock's World *regarding Surak's parents.*

(TNG) "The Next Phase"

The Romulan Prize (**TNG #26**)

(TNG) "The Inner Light" — Stardate 45944.1

"The Promise" (TNG short story, SNW IV)

Historians' Note: Story is set within Picard's vision of life as Kamin in "The Inner Light" (TNG).

(TNG) "Time's Arrow" — Stardate 45959.1 to 45965.3

2369

(TNG) "Time's Arrow, Part II" — Stardate 46001.3

The Best and the Brightest (**TNG**) [Year One]

Historians' Note: The Year One part of the story is set just after "Time's Arrow, Part II" (TNG).

• 2370 — [Year Two] Just before "Journey's End" (TNG)

• 2371 — [Year Three] Just after "The Search" (DS9)

• 2371 — [Summer] Just after *Star Trek Generations*

• 2371 — [Year Four] Just after "The Die is Cast" (DS9)

(TNG) "Realm of Fear" — Stardate 46041.1 to 46043.6

(TNG) "Man of the People" — Stardate 46071.6 to 46075.1

Relics (**TNG episode novelization**) — Stardate 46125.3

• 2294 — [Scotty backstory]

(TNG) "Schisms" — Stardate 46154.2 to 46191.2

***Here There Be Dragons* (TNG #28)**
(TNG) "True Q" — Stardate 46192.3 to 46193.8
(TNG) "Rascals" — Stardate 46235.7 to 46236.3
(TNG) "A Fistful of Datas" — Stardate 46271.5 to 46278.3
"On the Scent of Trouble" (TNG short story, *Amazing Stories*
#593)
***A Fury Scorned* (TNG #43)** — Stardate 46300.6
(TNG) "The Quality of Life" — Stardate 46307.2 to 46317.8
(TNG) "Chain of Command, Part I" — Stardate 46357.4 to 46358.2
(TNG) "Chain of Command, Part II" — Stardate 46360.8
***Debtors' Planet* (TNG #30)**
Historians' Note: Story is set after "First Duty" (TNG).
***The Captain's Table #5: Once Burned* (NF)**
Historians' Note: Story spans about three months.
• 2348–2349 — [Pages 1–30] Calhoun is 14, spans about a year
• Mid-2374 — [Framing story] Soon after "Honor Among Thieves"
(DS9)
*Timeliners' note: The book says this portion of the story takes place
six years before the framing story, which would place it in 2368.
However, we placed it in 2369 after "Chain of Command" (TNG), when
Jellico was a captain, owing to the fact that Jellico is an admiral in this
story.*
***Emissary* (DS9 episode novelization)** — Stardate 46379.1 to
46393.1
• 2367 — [Sisko backstory] Stardate 44002.3
(DS9) "Past Prologue"
***Guises of the Mind* (TNG #27)** — Stardate 46401.9
*Timeliners' Note: The 45741.9 stardate given in the book was adjusted to
fit the post-"Emissary" (DS9) timeframe.*
• Late 2369 — [Epilogue] Set six months later than the main part of the
story
(DS9) "A Man Alone" — Stardate 46384.0 to 46421.5
***The Siege* (DS9 #2)**
*Timeliners' Note: The novel states that Keiko is a teacher, which would put
the story after "A Man Alone" (DS9). References to Molly's age are incor-
rect.*
(TNG) "Ship in a Bottle" — Stardate 46424.1
***Invasion! #2: The Soldiers of Fear* (TNG #41)**
(DS9) "Babel" — Stardate 46423.7 to 46425.8
(TNG) "Aquiel" — Stardate 46461.3
(DS9) "Captive Pursuit"

(TNG) "Face of the Enemy" — Stardate 46519.1

(DS9) "Q-Less" — Stardate 46531.2 to 46532.3

(TNG) "Tapestry"

(DS9) "Dax" — Stardate 46910.1

(TNG) "Birthright, Part I" — Stardate 46578.4

(DS9) "The Passenger"

(TNG) "Birthright, Part II" — Stardate 46579.2

***The Star Ghost* (DS9-YA #1)**

(DS9) "Move Along Home"

(DS9) "The Nagus"

(TNG) "Starship Mine" — Stardate 46682.4

***The Death of Princes* (TNG #44)**

Historians' Note: Story is set before "Timescape" (TNG).

(TNG) "Lessons" — Stardate 46693.1 to 46697.2

(DS9) "Vortex"

***Double Helix #3: Red Sector* (TNG #53)**

• 2353 — [Chapters 1–6] 15 years prior to the main body

• 2357 — [Chapters 7–10] 11 years prior to the main body

(TNG) "The Chase" — Stardate 46731.5 to 46735.2

***Bloodletter* (DS9 #3)**

Historians' Note: Story is set before the episode "Battle Lines" (DS9).

(DS9) "Battle Lines"

(TNG) "Frame of Mind" — Stardate 46778.1

***To Storm Heaven* (TNG #46)**

***Dark Passions* (all-series duology)** — Stardate 46722.4

Timeliners' Note: Story takes place over the course of several months in the Mirror Universe of "Mirror, Mirror" (TOS), and ends before "Crossover" (DS9).

(DS9) "The Storyteller" — Stardate 46729.1

(TNG) "Suspicions" — Stardate 46830.1 to 46831.2

(DS9) "Progress" — Stardate 46844.3

(TNG) "Rightful Heir" — Stardate 46852.2

***Warped* (DS9 hardcover)**

Historians' Note: Story is set after "Battle Lines" (DS9) and before "The Homecoming" (DS9).

(DS9) "If Wishes Were Horses" — Stardate 46853.2

***The Romulan Stratagem* (TNG #35)** — Stardate 46892.6

(TNG) "Second Chances" — Stardate 46915.2 to 46920.1

***Foreign Foes* (TNG #31)** — Stardate 46921.3

Timeliners' Note: The 47511.3 stardate given in the book was adjusted to fit a timeframe shortly after "Second Chances" (TNG).

(DS9) "The Forsaken" — Stardate 46925.1

Stowaways **(DS9-YA #2)**

(DS9) "Dramatis Personae" — Stardate 46922.3 to 46924.5

Requiem **(TNG #32)** — Stardate 46931.2

Timeliners' Note: The 47821.2 stardate given in the book was adjusted to fit a late 2369 timeframe prior to the departure of Ensign Ro.

• 2267 — Picard time travels to just two days before the events of "Arena" (TOS)

• 2345 — [Prologue] Stardate 16175.4

(TNG) "Timescape" — Stardate 46944.2 to 48945.3

(DS9) "Duet"

Descent **(TNG episodes novelization)** — Stardate 46982.1 to 46984.6

Timeliners' Note: This book novelizes Part I of the episode, which is set in late 2369, and Part II, which is set at the beginning of 2370.

• 2370 — [Part II] Stardate 47025.4

(DS9) "In the Hands of the Prophets"

2370

Warchild **(DS9 #7)**

Historians' Note: Story is set between the first and second seasons of Star Trek: Deep Space Nine.

Valhalla **(DS9 #10)**

Timeliners' Note 1: Most references in this book would place it between the first and second seasons of Star Trek: Deep Space Nine.

Timeliners' Note 2: A reference to the Defiant *on page 5 was accidentally added during editing, since the book was published after the* Defiant *was introduced at the beginning of the third season of Star Trek: Deep Space Nine.*

Betrayal **(DS9 #6)**

(TNG) "Liaisons"

(DS9) "The Homecoming"

(TNG) "Interface" — Stardate 47215.5

Blaze of Glory **(TNG #34)**

Historians' Note: Story is set before "Force of Nature" (TNG).

(DS9) "The Circle"

(TNG) "Gambit, Part I" — Stardate 47135.2

(DS9) "The Siege"

(TNG) "Gambit, Part II" — Stardate 47160.1 to 47169.2

(DS9) "Invasive Procedures" — Stardate 47182.1

Prisoners of Peace **(DS9-YA #3)**

(TNG) "Phantasms" — Stardate 47225.7

(DS9) "Cardassians" — Stardate 47177.2 to 47178.3

***The Big Game* (DS9 #4)**

Historians' Note: Page 148 describes the events of "A Matter of Time" (TNG) as occurring "a few years ago."

(TNG) "Dark Page" — Stardate 47254.1

(DS9) "Melora" — Stardate 47229.1

***Star Trek: Klingon* (TNG/DS9 game novelization)**

Historians' Note: Story is set one year before "Defiant" (DS9).

• 2368 — [Backstory] Takes place after "Redemption" (TNG)

(TNG) "Attached" — Stardate 47304.2

***Possession* (TNG #40)**

(DS9) "Rules of Acquisition"

***Fallen Heroes* (DS9 #5)** — Stardate 47237.8

(TNG) "Force of Nature" — Stardate 47310.2 to 47314.5

***Dyson Sphere* (TNG #50)** — Stardate 47321.6

(DS9) "Necessary Evil" — Stardate 47252.5 to 47284.1

***Infiltrator* (TNG #42)** — Stardate 47358.1

(TNG) "Inheritance" — Stardate 47410.2

(DS9) "Second Sight" — Stardate 47329.4

***Into the Nebula* (TNG #36)**

Historians' Note: Story is set after "Force of Nature" (TNG).

***The Pet* (DS9-YA #4)**

Historians' Note: Story is set during the first anniversary of the discovery of the Bajoran Wormhole on stardate 46379.1.

***Devil in the Sky* (DS9 #11)** — Stardate 47384.1

Timeliners' Note: A historian's note places this story in the second season of Star Trek: Deep Space Nine. *The 46384.1 stardate given in the book was adjusted to fit the specified timeframe.*

(TNG) "Parallels" — Stardate 47391.2

(DS9) "Sanctuary" — Stardate 47391.2

"Life Itself Is Reason Enough" (TNG short story, *Amazing Stories* #598)

(DS9) "Rivals"

***Arcade* (DS9-YA #5)**

Historians' Note: Story is set three years after the Borg attack at Wolf 359 in 2367.

(TNG) "The *Pegasus*" — Stardate 47457.1

(DS9) "The Alternate" — Stardate 47391.7

(TNG) "Homeward" — Stardate 47423.9 to 47427.2

***Q-Squared* (TNG hardcover)**

Historians' Note: Worf mentions he encountered a similar type of dis-

location before. Hence, the story is set sometime after "Parallels" (TNG).

• 2265 — [Gary Mitchell backstory] Set during "Where No Man Has Gone Before" (TOS)

(TNG) "Sub Rosa"

(DS9) "Armageddon Game" — Stardate 47529.4

(TNG) "Lower Decks" — Stardate 47566.7

***Field Trip* (DS9-YA #6)**

(DS9) "Whispers" — Stardate 47569.4 to 447581.2

(TNG) "Thine Own Self" — Stardate 47611.2

***Balance of Power* (TNG #33)**

Historians' Note: Story is set shortly after "Thine Own Self" (TNG).

(DS9) "Paradise" — Stardate 47573.1

***Gypsy World* (DS9-YA #7)**

Historians' Note: Story is set in the first or second season of Star Trek: Deep Space Nine.

(TNG) "Masks" — Stardate 47615.2 to 47618.4

(DS9) "Shadowplay" — Stardate 47603.3

***Dragon's Honor* (TNG #38)** — Stardate 47616.2

Timeliners' note: The 47146.2 stardate given in the book was adjusted to fit a timeframe shortly before "Eye of the Beholder" (TNG).

(TNG) "Eye of the Beholder" — Stardate 47622.1 to 47623.2

(DS9) "Playing God"

***Highest Score* (DS9-YA #8)**

(TNG) "Genesis" — Stardate 47653.2

(DS9) "Profit and Loss"

"Whatever You Do, Don't Read This Story" (TNG short story, SNW III)

(TNG) "Journey's End" — Stardate 47751.2 to 47755.3

(DS9) "Blood Oath"

"I Am Klingon" (TNG short story, SNW II)

(TNG) "Firstborn" — Stardate 47779.4

(DS9) "The Maquis, Part I"

(TNG) "Bloodlines" — Stardate 47829.1 to 47831.8

(DS9) "The Maquis, Part II"

***Cardassian Imps* (DS9-YA #9)**

(TNG) "Emergence" — Stardate 47869.2

(DS9) "The Wire"

***Antimatter* (DS9 #8)**

Historians' Note: Story is set late in the second season of Star Trek: Deep Space Nine *when the Runabout* Mekong *was in use by DS9 personnel.*

"The Naked Truth" (TNG short story, SNW)
(TNG) "Preemptive Strike" — Stardate 47941.7 to 47943.2
***Rogue Saucer* (TNG #39)**
Historians' Note: Story is set shortly after "Preemptive Strike"
(TNG).
(DS9) "Crossover" — Stardate 47879.2
***All Good Things . . .* (TNG episode novelization)** — Stardate
47988.1
  • 3.5 billion years ago — Q takes Picard to this time of human history
  • 2364 — [Anti-past] Stardate 41148 to 41153.7
  • 2395 — [Anti-future]
Timeliners' Note: The anti-time portions of the story must be regarded as
an alternate past and future which are divergent from the "mainstream"
universe.
(DS9) "The Collaborator"
***Space Camp* (DS9-YA #10)**
(DS9) "Tribunal" — Stardate 47944.2
(DS9) "The Jem'Hadar"
2371
"Doctors Three" (TOS short story, SNW II)
Timeliners' Note: Story is set prior to Voyager*'s launch.*
***Intellivore* (TNG #45)** — Stardate 48022.5
***The Search* (DS9 episodes novelization)** — Stardate 48212.4
Timeliners' Note: This book novelizes Parts I and II of the episode.
***Proud* Helios (DS9 #9)**
Timeliners' Note: Page 12 of this story mentions that the Defiant *is un-*
dergoing repairs, which would be consistent with the damage inflicted on
the Defiant *during "The Search" (DS9).*
***Day of Honor* #1: *Ancient Blood* (TNG)**
Timeliners' Note: Reference to Alexander as being 12 years old is incor-
rect.
(DS9) "The House of Quark"
***Double Helix* #4: *Quarantine* (TNG #54)**
Timeliners' Note: The Star Trek Chronology *mentions Tom Riker was*
on the Ghandi *for about a year before joining the Maquis. Two statements*
in this novel that indicate that he was on the Ghandi *for two years are in-*
correct.
***Crossover* (TNG hardcover)**
Historians' Note: Story is set during Picard's eighth year of command of
the Enterprise-D.
(DS9) "Equilibrium"

Kahless **(TNG hardcover)**
• A.D. 800 (approx.) — [Heroic Age]
The Captain's Table #2: Dujonian's Hoard **(TNG)**
• 2371 — [Framing story] Set a couple of months after the events of Picard's narrative
Timeliners' Note: Picard's gray uniform on the cover is not indicative of the uniform in use in the story.
"The Captain and the King" (EL short story)
(DS9) "The Abandoned"
"Flight 19" (TNG short story, SNW IV)
(DS9) "Second Skin"
Tooth and Claw **(TNG #60)**
(DS9) "Civil Defense"
(DS9) "Meridian" — Stardate 48423.2
Star Trek Generations **(TNG movie novelization)** — Stardate 48632.4 to 48650.1
Timeliners' Note 1: There is also a Young Adult novelization available.
• 2293 — [TOS-era portion] Stardate 9715.5
Timeliners' Note 2: Some authors place the TOS-era portion later in 2294 or in 2295, which contradicts the Star Trek Chronology.
"Reflections" (TOS short story, SNW) — Stardate 48649.7
"The Change of Seasons" (TNG short story, SNW III)
(DS9) *"Defiant"* — Stardate 48467.3
Triangle: Imzadi II **(TNG hardcover)**
Historians' Note: Story is set shortly after Star Trek Generations.
• 2374 — [Framing story] Set right after "Tears of the Prophets" (DS9)
(DS9) "Fascination"
The Laertian Gamble **(DS9 #12)**
Historians' Note: Keiko O'Brien is "on an all-too-brief hiatus from her botanical research on Bajor," so it is placed immediately after the episode "Fascination" (DS9).
(DS9) "Past Tense, Part I"
(DS9) "Past Tense, Part II" — Stardate 48481.2
The Return **(TOS/TNG hardcover)**
Historians' Note: Story is set a month after Star Trek Generations.
The Badlands **(Book 2, VGR story)** — Stardate 48305.8
Historians' Note: Story begins prior to "Caretaker" (VGR) and continues through the beginning of that episode.
Caretaker **(VGR episode novelization)** — Stardate 48315.6

***The Escape* (VGR #2)**
• 307,629 B.C. (approx.) — The unique time travel device in this novel also allows for a few other jumps in time, always in increments of 500,000 years.
(VGR) "Parallax" — Stardate 48439.7

***Ragnarok* (VGR #3)**
Historians' Note: The author, Nathan Archer, suggests this novel takes place during the first half of the first season of Star Trek: Voyager.

"The Ones Left Behind" (VGR short story, SNW III)
• 2371 — [April] Three weeks after "Caretaker" (VGR)
• 2372 — [January]
• 2373 — [February] Almost two years after "Caretaker" (VGR)
Timeliners' Note 1: A reference to the Dominion War is erroneous, as the Dominion War did not start until very late in 2373.
• 2374 — Immediately after "Message in a Bottle" (VGR)
Timeliners' Note 2: Erroneously referred to as June 2375.
• 2374 — Between "Who Mourns for Morn?" (DS9) and "Far Beyond the Stars" (DS9)
Timeliners' Note 3: Erroneously referred to as May 2375.
• 2374 — Between "Far Beyond the Stars" (DS9) and "Hunters" (VGR)
Timeliners' Note 4: Erroneously referred to as June 2375.
• 2374 — Stardate 51501.5, during "Hunters" (VGR)
(VGR) "Time and Again"

***Violations* (VGR #4)**
Historians' Note: References in this novel and its publication date suggest a Star Trek: Voyager *first season timeframe.*

"Unintived Admirals" (VGR short story, SNW IV)
• 2374 — Shortly after "Message in a Bottle" (VGR)
• 2376 — Between "Pathfinder" (VGR) and *Gateways #5: No Man's Land* (VGR)
(DS9) "Life Support" — Stardate 48498.4

***Incident at Arbuk* (VGR #5)** — Stardate 48531.6
Timeliners' Note: The book mentions a stardate of 48135.6, which we took the liberty to modify since the story is set after "Caretaker" (VGR).
(VGR) "Phage" — Stardate 48532.4
(DS9) "Heart of Stone" — Stardate 48521.5
(VGR) "The Cloud" — Stardate 48546.2
(DS9) "Destiny" — Stardate 48543.2
(VGR) "Eye of the Needle" — Stardate 48579.4

(DS9) "Prophet Motive"
(VGR) "Ex Post Facto"
(DS9) "Visionary"
(VGR) "Emanations" — Stardate 48623.5
(VGR) "Prime Factors" — Stardate 48642.5
(VGR) "State of Flux" — Stardate 48658.2
(DS9) "Distant Voices"
"Touched" (VGR short story, SNW II)
(DS9) "Through the Looking Glass"
(VGR) "Heroes and Demons" — Stardate 48693.2 to 48710.5
(DS9) "Improbable Cause"
(VGR) "Cathexis" — Stardate 48734.2 to 48735.9
(DS9) "The Die Is Cast"
(VGR) "Faces" — Stardate 48784.2
(DS9) "Explorers"
(VGR) "Jetrel" — Stardate 48832.1 to 48840.5
(DS9) "Family Business"
(VGR) "Learning Curve" — Stardate 48846.5 to 48859.3
(DS9) "Shakaar"
***The Murdered Sun* (VGR #6)** — Stardate 48897.1
Timeliners' Note: The 43897.1 stardate given in the book was adjusted to fit a Star Trek: Voyager *first season timeframe.*
(DS9) "Facets"
***The Long Night* (DS9 #14)**
• 1571 — [Prologue]
(DS9) "The Adversary" — Stardate 48959.1 to 48962.5
***Station Rage* (DS9 #13)**
Historians' Note: Story is set between "The Adversary" (DS9) and "The Way of the Warrior" (DS9).
(VGR) "Projections" — Stardate 48892.1
***Objective: Bajor* (DS9 #15)**
Historians' Note: Story is set between "The Adversary" (DS9) and "The Way of the Warrior" (DS9).
(VGR) "Elogium" — Stardate 48921.3
***Invasion!* #3: *Time's Enemy* (DS9 #16)**
Historians' Note: Story is set between "The Adversary" (DS9) and "The Way of the Warrior" (DS9).
(VGR) "Twisted"
***Invasion!* #4: *The Final Fury* (VGR #9)**
Historians' Note: Story is set roughly around the same time as Invasion! *#3:* Time's Enemy.

(VGR) "The 37's" — Stardate 48975.1
2372
Saratoga (DS9 #18)
Historians' Note: Story is set between the third and fourth seasons of Star Trek: Deep Space Nine.
(VGR) "Initiations" — Stardate 49005.3
***Wrath of the Prophets* (DS9 #20)**
Historians' Note: Story is set between "The Adversary" (DS9) and "The Way of the Warrior" (DS9).
(VGR) "Non Sequitur" — Stardate 49011
***The Way of The Warrior* (DS9 episode novelization)** — Stardate 49011.4
***Ghost of a Chance* (VGR #7)**
(DS9) "The Visitor"
(VGR) "Parturition" — Stardate 49068.5
***Cybersong* (VGR #8)**
(DS9) "Hippocratic Oath" — Stardate 49066.5
***Bless the Beasts* (VGR #10)**
(DS9) "Indiscretion"
***The Black Shore* (VGR #13)** — Stardate 49175.0
Timeliners' Note: 491750.0 was the original stardate for the book, which contained an extra "0" after the "5." We believe Captain Janeway added it for luck.
***The Tempest* (DS9 #19)**
Timeliners' Note: References to Molly's age are incorrect.
(DS9) "Rejoined" — Stardate 49195.5
(VGR) "Persistence of Vision"
(DS9) "Little Green Men"
(VGR) "Tattoo"
(DS9) "Starship Down"
***Mosaic* (VGR hardcover)**
Historians' Note: Framing story is set during the second season of Star Trek: Voyager.
- 2339 — [Janeway flashback, Chapter 2]
- 2344 — [Janeway flashback, Chapter 4]
- 2347 — [Janeway flashback, Chapter 6]
- 2349 — [Janeway flashback, Chapter 8]
- 2352 — [Janeway flashback, Chapters 10 and 12]
- 2353 — [Janeway flashback, Chapter 14]
- 2356 — [Janeway flashback, Chapter 14]
- 2357 — [Janeway flashback, Chapter 16]

• 2362 — [Janeway flashback, Chapter 18]
• 2363 — [Janeway flashback, Chapter 20]
• 2367 — [Janeway flashback, Chapter 22]
(VGR) "Cold Fire" — Stardate 49164.8
(DS9) "The Sword of Kahless"
(VGR) "Maneuvers" — Stardate 49208.5
(VGR) "Resistance"

Ship of the Line (TNG hardcover)

Timeliners' Note: Since the Enterprise-E *must have been launched after the events of "The Way of the Warrior" (DS9), some of the references in this book to Klingon/Federation/Cardassian relations are problematic. We suspect that a second major Klingon invasion of Cardassia space was in the works during the events of this book.*

• 2278 — [Pages 1–52] Story of the *Bozeman*
• 2368 — [Pages 52–73] Right after "Cause and Effect" (TNG)
• 2373 — [Chapter 26] During the beginning of *Star Trek: First Contact*
(DS9) "Our Man Bashir"
(DS9) "Homefront" — Stardate 49170.65
(DS9) "Paradise Lost"

"Reflections" (TLOD short story)

• 2352 — [Flashback] Jadzia, age 11
• 2367 — [Flashback] Just before Jadzia's joining with the Dax symbiont

Trapped in Time (DS9-YA #12)

Historians' Note: Story is set immediately after "Paradise Lost" (DS9).

Timeliners' Note 1: The historian's note placing this book in the first or second season of Star Trek: Deep Space Nine *is incorrect.*

Timeliners' Note 2: This story presents the first meeting between Sisko and the Temporal Investigators, Dulmer and Lucsly, even though they appear to never have met each other in "Trials and Tribble-ations" (DS9).

• June 1, 1944 — Jake, Nog, and O'Brien travel back in time

The Garden (VGR #11)

(VGR) "Prototype"
(VGR) "Alliances" — Stardate 49337.4
(DS9) "Crossfire"
(VGR) "Threshold" — Stardate 49373.4

Day of Honor #2: Armageddon Sky (DS9)

Historians' Note: Story is set three months after dissolution of Khitomer accords, right before Day of Honor #3: Her Klingon Soul.

Timeliners' Note: A stardate of 3962 is mentioned on page 214. We are unsure whether this is a colloquial shortening of a current stardate, or whether it a reference to the TOS-era stardate for Day of Honor #4: Treaty's Law.

Day of Honor #3: *Her Klingon Soul* (VGR) — Stardate 49588.4

(DS9) "Return to Grace"

(VGR) "Meld"

***The Heart of the Warrior* (DS9 #17)**

Historians' Note: Story is set in the fourth season of Star Trek: Deep Space Nine.

(DS9) "The Sons of Mogh" — Stardate 49556.2

(VGR) "Dreadnought" — Stardate 49447

(VGR) "Death Wish" — Stardate 49301.2

(DS9) "Bar Association"

***The 34th Rule* (DS9 #23)**

***Chrysalis* (VGR #12)**

(DS9) "Accession"

(VGR) "Lifesigns" — Stardate 49504.3

(VGR) "Investigations" — Stardate 49485.2

(VGR) "Deadlock" — Stardate 49548.7

(DS9) "Rules of Engagement" — Stardate 49648.0 to 49665.3

(VGR) "Innocence" — Stardate 49578.2

(DS9) "Hard Time"

(DS9) "Shattered Mirror"

***Trial By Error* (DS9 #21)**

Historians' Note: Story is set after "Bar Association" (DS9).

"The Bottom Line" (DS9 short story, SNW III)

Historians' Note: Story is set between "Little Green Men" (DS9) and "The Ascent" (DS9).

(DS9) "The Muse"

(VGR) "The Thaw"

(DS9) "For the Cause"

(VGR) "Tuvix" — Stardate 49655.2 to 49678.4

(VGR) "Resolutions" — Stardate 49690.1 to 49694.2

"Out of the Box, Thinking" (TNG short story, SNW III)

Historians' Note: Story is set "years after" "The Nth Degree" (TNG) in late 2367, and after the launch of Voyager *in early 2371.*

Section 31: *Rogue* (TNG) — Stardate 50368.0 to 50454.1

Historians' Note: Story is set six months prior to Star Trek: First Contact.

• Stardate 50907.2 to 50915.5—[Prologue, Epilogue] Shortly after *Star Trek: First Contact*

(DS9) "To the Death" — Stardate 49904.2

(DS9) "The Quickening"

Rebels (DS9 trilogy: *The Conquered* (#24), *The Courageous* (#25), *The Liberated* (#26)

• 2342 — [Flashback]

(DS9) "Body Parts"

***Vengeance* (DS9 #22)**

Historians' Note: Story is set after the episode "Body Parts" (DS9).

(DS9) "Broken Link" — Stardate 49962.4

(VGR) "Basics, Part I"

Note: The second edition of the *Star Trek Chronology* ends with 2372. Subsequent sequencing is based on air date until the *Star Trek Chronology* is updated again.

2373

(VGR) "Basics, Part II" — Stardate 50023.4

"Where I Fell Before My Enemy" (DS9 short story, SNW)

Historians' Note: Story is set after Worf joins the DS9 crew, but before the Dominion War.

***Flashback* (VGR episode novelization)** — Stardate 50126.4

• 2293 — [Tuvok backstory] Set during the events of *Star Trek VI: The Undiscovered Country*

(VGR) "The Chute" — Stardate 50156.2

(VGR) "The Swarm" — Stardate 50252.3

(DS9) "Apocalypse Rising"

(VGR) "False Profits" — Stardate 50074.3 to 50074.5

"Seeing Forever" (TNG short story, SNW IV)

(DS9) "The Ship" — Stardate 50049.3

(VGR) "Remember" — Stardate 50203.1 to 50211.4

"Life's Lessons" (DS9 short story, SNW)

(DS9) "Looking for *par'Mach* in All the Wrong Places"

(DS9) "Nor the Battle to the Strong"

(DS9) "The Assignment"

***Day of Honor: Honor Bound* (DS9-YA #11)**

Historians' Note: Story is set one year after Day of Honor #2: Armageddon Sky.

(VGR) "Sacred Ground" — Stardate 50063.2

***Trials and Tribble-ations* (DS9 episode novelization)**

• 2267 — Stardate 4523.7 during "The Trouble With Tribbles" (TOS)

(VGR) "Future's End"

(DS9) "Let He Who is Without Sin . . ."

(VGR) "Future's End, Part II" — Stardate 50312.5

"Ambassador at Large" (VGR short story, SNW)

Historians' Note: Dialogue on page 252 indicates that this takes place about two years after "Caretaker" (VGR).

Echoes (VGR #15)

Historians' Note: Story is set some time after "Deadlock" (VGR) but before Kes leaves the ship.

(DS9) "Things Past"

(VGR) "Warlord" — Stardate 50348.1

(DS9) "The Ascent"

(VGR) "The Q and the Grey" — Stardate 50384.2

***Star Trek: First Contact* (TNG movie novelization)** — Stardate 50893.5

Timeliners' Note: There is also a Young Adult novelization available.

• 2063 — [Backstory]

(VGR) "Macrocosm" — Stardate 50425.1

(DS9) "Rapture"

(DS9) "The Darkness and the Light" — Stardate 50416.2

(VGR) "Fair Trade"

"A Night at Sandrine's" (VGR short story, *Amazing Stories* #595) — Stardate 50446.2

Timeliners' Note: The 50396.2 stardate given in the story was adjusted to fit a timeframe shortly after "Fair Trade" (VGR).

(VGR) "Alter Ego" — Stardate 50460.3 to 50471.3

(DS9) "The Begotten"

***The Captain's Table #3: The Mist* (DS9)**

Historians' Note: Story is set after "The Ascent" (DS9) and before "For the Uniform" (DS9).

• 2374 — [Framing story]

Timeliners' Note: Reference to the Klingon invasion of Cardassia on page 12 is inconsistent with the rest of the main story.

(VGR) "Coda" — Stardate 50518.6

(DS9) "For the Uniform" — Stardate 50485.2 to 50488.2

(VGR) "Blood Fever" — Stardate 50537.2 to 50541.6

"The Second Star" (VGR short story, SNW III)

***The Badlands* (Book 2, DS9 story)** — Stardate 50502.4

Historians' Note: Story is set "just prior to the Dominion War," specifically, just before "In Purgatory's Shadow."

(DS9) "In Purgatory's Shadow"

(VGR) "Unity" — Stardate 50614.2 to 50622.5

(DS9) "By Inferno's Light" — Stardate 50564.2

"Gods, Fate, and Fractals" (TNG short story, SNW II) — Stardate 50564.2

• Limbo — [Dulmer and Lucsly's discussion]
(VGR) "The Darkling" — Stardate 50693.2
(DS9) "Doctor Bashir, I Presume"
***Avenger* (TNG hardcover)**
Historians' Note: Story is set two years after The Return.
• 2246 — [Flashback, Chapter 1] Young Kirk and Kodos on Tarsus, same time as *A Flag Full of Stars*
(VGR) "Rise"
"Monthuglu" (VGR short story, SNW) — Stardate 50714.2
(VGR) "Favorite Son" — Stardate 50732.4
(DS9) "A Simple Investigation"
(DS9) "Business as Usual"
(VGR) "Before and After" — Stardate 50973
(DS9) "Ties of Blood and Water" — Stardate 50712.5
"Good Night, *Voyager*" (VGR short story, SNW)
(DS9) "Ferengi Love Songs"
(VGR) "Real Life" — Stardate 50836.2
(DS9) "Soldiers of the Empire"
"Fiction" (VGR short story, SNW)
Historians' Note: Story is set after the Doctor gets his mobile emitter in "Future's End" *(VGR) but before Seven of Nine joins the* Voyager *crew in* "Scorpion, Part II" *(VGR).*
***Marooned* (VGR #14)** — Stardate 50573.2
(VGR) "Distant Origin"
(DS9) "Children of Time" — Stardate 50814.2
"I, *Voyager*" (VGR short story, SNW)
(VGR) "Displaced" — Stardate 50912.4
(DS9) "Blaze of Glory"
***House of Cards* (NF #1)**
• 2353 — [M'k'n'zy backstory]
• 2363 — [Soleta backstory]
• 2371 — [Selar backstory]
***Into the Void* (NF #2)** — Stardate 50923.1
***The Two-Front War* (NF #3)** — Stardate 50926.1
***End Game* (NF #4)** — Stardate 50927.2
(VGR) "Worst Case Scenario" — Stardate 50953.4
(DS9) "Empok Nor"
(VGR) "Scorpion" — Stardate 50984.3
(DS9) "In the Cards"
"Change of Heart" (DS9 short story, SNW II)
***The Dominion War #2: Call to Arms . . .* (DS9 episodes noveliza-**

tion) — Stardate 51145.3 (stardate applies to later events in the book)

Timeliners' note: This novelization adapts the DS9 episodes "Call to Arms," "A Time to Stand," "Rocks and Shoals," and the first portion of "Sons and Daughters." The book concludes in early 2374.

The Dominion War #1: Behind Enemy Lines (TNG)

Historians' Note: This novel begins soon after the fall of DS9 to Cardassian control late in 2373, as described in The Dominion War #2: Call to Arms . . .

2374

(VGR) "Scorpion, Part II" — Stardate 51003.7

The Dominion War #3: Tunnel Through the Stars (TNG)

Historians' Note: This book ends in early 2374, several days after the end of "Sacrifice of Angels" (DS9).

The Dominion War #4: . . . Sacrifice of Angels (DS9 episodes novelization) — Stardate 51145.3

Timeliners' Note 1: This novelization adapts the second portion of "Sons and Daughters," and the DS9 episodes "Behind the Lines," "Favor the Bold," and "Sacrifice of Angels."

Timeliners' Note 2: The 69923.2 stardate given in the book was adjusted to fit the Dominion War timeframe.

(VGR) "The Gift"—Stardate 51008

"The Healing Arts" (VGR short story, SNW II)

Day of Honor (VGR episode novelization)

Timeliners' Note: References to Day of Honor #3: Her Klingon Soul *occurring one year ago are inaccurate.*

- 2355 — [Pages 1–24]
- 2373 — [Pages 25–34]

(VGR) "Nemesis" — Stardate 51082.4

(VGR) "Revulsion" — Stardate 51186.2

(VGR) "The Raven"

(VGR) "Scientific Method" — Stardate 51244.3

The Captain's Table #4: Fire Ship (VGR)

Historians' Note: Story is set immediately before the events of "Year of Hell" (VGR).

- 2374 — [Framing story]

"The First" (TNG short story, SNW)

"Reciprocity" (TNG short story, SNW II)

Historians' Note: The story is set sometime during the Dominion War.

- *c.* 4 Billion B.C. [Framing story]

(VGR) "Year of Hell" — Stardate 51268.4

(DS9) "You Are Cordially Invited . . ." — Stardate 51247.5

(VGR) "Year of Hell, Part II" — Stardate 51425.4

Planet X **(TNG/X-Men)**

Historians' Note: Story is set shortly after "You Are Cordially Invited . . . " (DS9).

(DS9) "Resurrection"

(VGR) "Random Thoughts" — Stardate 51367.2

(DS9) "Statistical Probabilities"

(VGR) "Concerning Flight" — Stardate 51386.4

(VGR) "Mortal Coil" — Stardate 51449.2

(DS9) "The Magnificent Ferengi"

"Bedside Matters" (TNG short story, *Amazing Stories* **#601)** — Stardate 51401.6

Timeliners' Note 1: The 52501.6 stardate given in the story was adjusted to fit a timeframe before "Message in a Bottle" (VGR).

Timeliners' Note 2: Data's and Dr. Crusher's uniforms in the story's picture are not indicative of the uniforms in use in the story.

(DS9) "Waltz" — Stardate 51408.6 to 51413.6

Martyr **(NF #5)**

• 1873 — [Ontear backstory]

• 2354 — [M'k'n'zy backstory]

(VGR) "Waking Moments" — Stardate 51471.3

(VGR) "Message in a Bottle"—Stardate 51462

(DS9) "Who Mourns For Morn?"

Far Beyond the Stars **(DS9 episode novelization)**

Historians' Note: Sisko has visions that chronicle the childhood of Benny Russell (July 1940) and his life (October 1953).

(VGR) "Hunters" — Stardate 51501.4

(DS9) "One Little Ship" — Stardate 51474.2

Fire on High **(NF #6)**

The Q Continuum **(TNG trilogy:** *Q-Space* **(#47),** *Q-Zone* **(#48),** *Q-Strike* **(#49))** — Stardate 51604.2

Timeliners' Note 1: The 500146.2 stardate given in Q-Space *was too high, so we decided to drop one digit and rearrange the others to make the stardate fit shortly after "Message in a Bottle" (VGR).*

Timeliners' Note 2: On page 249 of Q-Strike, *Picard reflects on the recent entry of the Romulans to the Dominion War. This is inconsistent with the fact that at the time of this trilogy Betazed has not yet fallen to the Dominion, an event which indirectly led to the Romulan entry to the war ("In the Pale Moonlight" [DS9]).*

• 5 billion years ago — *Q-Space,* Young Q backstory

• 2.5 billion years ago — *Q-Space,* Teenage Q backstory
• 1 million years ago — *Q-Zone,* Q backstory
(VGR) "Prey" — Stardate 51652.3
(DS9) "Honor Among Thieves"
(VGR) "Retrospect" — Stardate 51679.4
(DS9) "Change of Heart" — Stardate 51597.2
Double Time (NF comic)
Historians' Note: Story starts after the framing sequence of The
Captain's Table #5: Once Burned *and ends shortly before* Double Helix #5:
Double or Nothing.
• 2352 — Calhoun at age 18
• 2368 — Shelby and Calhoun backstory
(VGR) "The Killing Game"
(VGR) "The Killing Game, Part II" — Stardate 51715.2
(DS9) "Wrongs Darker Than Death Or Night"
(DS9) "Inquisition"
Spectre (TNG hardcover)
Historians' Note: Story is set shortly after "Message in a Bottle"
(VGR).
Dark Victory (TNG hardcover)
Historians' Note: Story is a direct sequel to Spectre.
• 2375 — Second half of book takes place shortly after *Star Trek:*
Insurrection.
(VGR) "Vis à Vis" — Stardate 51762.4
(DS9) "In the Pale Moonlight" — Stardate 51721.3
(VGR) "The Omega Directive" — Stardate 51871.2
(DS9) "His Way"
(VGR) "Unforgettable" — Stardate 51813.4
(DS9) "The Reckoning"
"Seventh Heaven" (VGR short story, SNW II)
Historians' Note: Story is set some time after "The Killing Game, Part
II" (VGR).
(DS9) *"Valiant"*
(VGR) "Demon"
(DS9) "Profit and Lace"
(VGR) "One" — Stardate 51929.3 to 51932.4
Pathways (VGR hardcover)
Historians' Note: The framing sequence for this book takes place a little
less than a year after Seven of Nine joins the Voyager *crew.*
• 2289–2371 — [Tuvok's story, Chapter 14]
• 2349–2371 — [Neelix's story, Chapter 10]

• 2350–2371 — [Chakotay's story, Chapter 2]
• 2350–2371 — [Kim's story, Chapter 4]
• 2358–2371 — [Torres's story, Chapter 6]
• 2365–2371 — [Paris's story, Chapter 8]
• 2370–2371 — [Kes's story, Chapter 12]
(DS9) "Time's Orphan"
(VGR) "Hope and Fear" — Stardate 51978.2 to 51981.6
***Seven of Nine* (VGR #16)**
• 2369 (approx.) — [Prologue]
"Dorian's Diary" (DS9 short story, SNW III)
Timeliners' Note: The story starts 43 days after "Valiant" *(DS9), through 53 days after the episode. Thus, we decided to place it just before* "The Sound of Her Voice" *(DS9).*
(DS9) "The Sound of Her Voice"
***Millennium* (DS9 trilogy: *The Fall of Terok Nor, The War of the Prophets, Inferno*)**
• 2369 — *The Fall of Terok Nor,* Immediately before "Emissary" (DS9)
• 2369 — *Inferno,* Immediately before and during "Emissary" (DS9)
• 2375 — Just before the end of "What You Leave Behind" (DS9)
• 2376 — *Inferno,* Epilogue, several months after "What You Leave Behind" (DS9)
• 2400 — *The Fall of Terok Nor, The War of the Prophets,* Twenty-five years after 2375 (runs through December 31, 2400)
• Limbo — *The War of the Prophets, Inferno*
(DS9) "Tears of the Prophets"
"Ninety-Three Hours" (DS9 short story, SNW III)
Timeliners' Note: This story contradicts "First star to the right . . .".
2375
(DS9) "Image in the Sand"
Timeliners' Note: This episode is set three months after "Tears of the Prophets" (DS9).
(DS9) "Shadows and Symbols" — Stardate 52152.6
(DS9) "Afterimage"
(VGR) "Night" — Stardate 52081.2
(DS9) "Take Me Out to the Holosuite"
(VGR) "Drone"
(DS9) "Chrysalis"
(VGR) "Extreme Risk"
***Death of a Neutron Star* (VGR #17)**
(DS9) "Treachery, Faith, and the Great River"

(VGR) "In the Flesh" — Stardate 52136.4

(DS9) "Once More Unto the Breach"

(VGR) "Once Upon a Time"

"The Monster Hunters" (VGR short story, SNW III)

Historians' Note: Story is set after "Once Upon a Time" (VGR).

Battle Lines (VGR #18)

(DS9) "The Siege at AR-558"

(VGR) "Timeless" — Stardate 52143.6

(DS9) "Covenant"

Star Trek: Insurrection (TNG movie novelization)

Timeliners' Note: There is also a Young Adult novelization available.

Preserver (TNG hardcover)

Historians' Note: Story is set some time before the siege of Cardassia in "The Changing Face of Evil" (DS9), and immediately follows the second half of Dark Victory *(TNG hardcover).*

  • 2400 — [Epilogue]

(VGR) "Infinite Regress" — Stardate 52356.2

(DS9) "It's Only a Paper Moon"

(VGR) "Nothing Human"

(DS9) "Prodigal Daughter"

(VGR) "Thirty Days" — Stardate 52179.4

(DS9) "The Emperor's New Cloak"

(VGR) "Counterpoint"

(DS9) "Field of Fire"

(VGR) "Latent Image"

(DS9) "Chimera"

(VGR) "Bride of Chaotica!"

"The Best Defense" (DS9 short story, SNW III)

Historians' Note: Story is set after "It's Only a Paper Moon" (DS9) and before "What You Leave Behind" (DS9).

(DS9) "Badda-Bing Badda-Bang"

(VGR) "Gravity" — Stardate 52438.9

(DS9) *"Inter Arma Enim Silent Leges"*

(VGR) "Bliss" — Stardate 52542.3

"Gift of the Mourners" (VGR short story, SNW III)

(DS9) "Penumbra" — Stardate 52576.2

(VGR) "Dark Frontier" — Stardate 52619.2

"When Push Comes to Shove" (VGR short story, *Amazing Stories #595*)

(DS9) "'Til Death Do Us Part"

(VGR) "The Disease"

(DS9) "Strange Bedfellows"

(VGR) "Course: Oblivion" — Stardate 52586.3

(DS9) "The Changing Face of Evil"

(VGR) "The Fight"

(DS9) "When It Rains . . ."

(VGR) "Think Tank"

(DS9) "Tacking into the Wind"

"An Errant Breeze" (DS9 short story, SNW III)

Timeliners' Note: This story spans from the middle of "Tacking into the Wind" (DS9) through "What You Leave Behind" (DS9).

(VGR) "Juggernaut"

(DS9) "Extreme Measures" — Stardate 52645.7

(VGR) "Someone to Watch Over Me" — Stardate 52647

***Section 31: Shadow* (VGR)**

Historians' Note: Story takes place before "Equinox" (VGR).

(DS9) "The Dogs of War"

(VGR) "11:59"

***What You Leave Behind* (DS9 episode novelization)**

***Double Helix #5: Double or Nothing* (TNG #55)**

• Late 2369 — [Prologue]

(VGR) "Relativity" — Stardate 52861.574

"Second star to the right . . .", ". . . and straight on 'til morning"
(TLOD short stories)

Historians' Note: Story is set just after "What You Leave Behind" (DS9).

• 2374 — [Flashback] Just after "Tears of the Prophets" (DS9)

(VGR) "Warhead"

***I, Q* (TNG hardcover)**

• December 31, 1999 — [Pages 44–50]

• 2170 — [Pages 124–125] Set "several centuries ago"

• 2364 — [Pages 41–44] Set immediately after "Encounter at Farpoint" (TNG)

***Equinox* (VGR episodes novelization)**

Timeliners' Note: This book novelizes Part I of the episode, which is set in late 2375, and Part II, which is set at the beginning of 2376.

• 2375 — The prologue takes place about a month before the main part of the story

• 2376 — [Part II]

***Gemworld* (TNG duology: #58, #59)**

Timeliners' Note: Gemworld #1 states Reginald Barclay is on the Enterprise, but "Pathfinder" (VGR), set in 2376, mentions Barclay was on Earth for almost two years.

n-Vector **(DS9 comic mini-series)**

• From this point onward, only one television series remains on the air. The ordering of episodes of *Star Trek: Voyager* will therefore revert to production sequence.

2376

Diplomatic Implausibility **(TNG #61)**

Maximum Warp **(TNG duology: *Dead Zone* [#62], *Forever Dark* [#63])**

Timeliners' Note: The events of Maximum Warp *take place in the weeks between Chapter 9 and the Epilogue of* Diplomatic Implausibility.

The Quiet Place **(NF #7)**

• 2375 — [Riella backstory] Takes place six months earlier

Dark Allies **(NF #8)**

• 2356 — [Si Cwan backstory] Takes place twenty years earlier

(VGR) "Survival Instinct" — Stardate 53049.2

(VGR) "Barge of the Dead"

(VGR) "Tinker Tenor Doctor Spy"

Excalibur **(NF trilogy: *Requiem* [#9], *Renaissance* [#10], *Restoration* [#11] hardcover)**

Historians' Note: Stories span about six months. The three books take place simultaneously.

(VGR) "Dragon's Teeth" — Stardate 53167.9

(VGR) "Alice"

(VGR) "Riddles" — Stardate 53263.2

The Belly of the Beast **(SCE eBook #1)**

Fatal Error **(SCE eBook #2)**

Hard Crash **(SCE eBook #3)**

A Stitch in Time **(DS9 #27)**

• 2319–2369 — Garak's youth at Bamarren through his arrival at *Terok Nor*

• 2374–2375 — Just before "Tears of the Prophets" (DS9) through just before "What You Leave Behind" (DS9)

• 2375–2376 — Just after "What You Leave Behind" (DS9) through present

Interphase **(SCE eBook duology: #4, #5)**

Avatar **(DS9 duology)**

Historians' Note: Story is set three months after "What You Leave Behind" (DS9).

Cold Fusion **(SCE eBook #6)**

Invincible **(SCE eBook duology: #7, #8)** — Stardate 53270.2 to 53291.5

Historians' Note: Invincible, Book One *is simultaneous with* Avatar, *and* Invincible, Book Two *is simultaneous with* Cold Fusion.

(VGR) "One Small Step" — Stardate 53292.7

(VGR) "The *Voyager* Conspiracy"

(VGR) "Pathfinder"

Section 31: Abyss **(DS9)**

The Riddled Post **(SCE eBook #9)**

Gateways #3: Doors Into Chaos **(TNG)**

Gateways #4: Demons of Air and Darkness **(DS9)**

Gateways #5: No Man's Land **(VGR)**

Gateways #6: Cold Wars **(NF)**

Timeliners' Note: Gateways *Books 3 through 6 all occur simultaneously.*

Gateways #7: What Lay Beyond **(all-series hardcover)**

• 2268 — [TOS story] Occurs immediately after *Gateways* #1: *One Small Step*

• 2275 — [*Challenger* story] Occurs immediately after *Gateways* #2: *Chainmail*

Gateways Epilogue: *Here There Be Monsters* **(SCE eBook #10)**

(VGR) "Fair Haven"

Divided We Fall **(DS9/TNG comic mini-series)**

(VGR) "Tsunkatse" — Stardate 53447.2

(VGR) "Blink of An Eye"

(VGR) "Virtuoso" — Stardate 53556.4

(VGR) "Collective"

(VGR) "Memorial"

(VGR) "Spirit Folk"

(VGR) "Ashes to Ashes" — Stardate 53679.4

New Worlds, New Civilizations **(anthology)**

Historians' Note: Federation news reports set after the Dominion War.

Timeliners' Note: Story must take place after stardate 53693, since the Bersalis III firestorms (from "Lessons" [TNG], stardate 46693) take place seven years after that episode.

(VGR) "Child's Play"

(VGR) "Good Shepherd" — Stardate 53753.2

(VGR) "Fury"

(VGR) "Live Fast and Prosper" — Stardate 53849.2

"Black Hats" (VGR short story, SNW IV)

(VGR) "Life Line"

Dark Matters **(VGR trilogy: *Cloak and Dagger* [#19], *Ghost Dance* [#20], *Shadow of Heaven* [#21])**

• 2354 — Telek R'Mor's timeline
(VGR) "Muse" — Stardate 53869.0 to 53918
(VGR) "The Haunting of Deck Twelve"
(VGR) "Unimatrix Zero"
2377
(VGR) "Unimatrix Zero" Part II — Stardate 54014.4
(VGR) "Imperfection" — Stardate 54129.4
(VGR) "Drive" — Stardate 54058.6
(VGR) "Critical Care"
The Genesis Wave **(TNG hardcover duology)**
• 2376 — Book One, Chapter 1 — Six months prior to bulk of story
(VGR) "Repression" — Stardate 54090.4 to 54101
(VGR) "Inside Man" — Stardate 54208.3
(VGR) "Body and Soul" — Stardate 54238.3
"Welcome Home" (VGR short story, SNW IV)
(VGR) "Nightingale" — Stardate 54274.7 to 54282.5
(VGR) "Flesh and Blood " — Stardate 54337.5
(VGR) "Shattered"
Star Trek: Borg **(TNG interactive movie audio adaptation)**
Historians' Note: Framing story is set 10 years after the Battle of Wolf 359 and six months before Stardate 54902.
• 2367 — [Backstory] Takes place during the Battle of Wolf 359
• Limbo — [Q and Furlong's discussion]
(VGR) "Lineage" — Stardate 54452.6
"Return" (VGR short story, SNW IV)
(VGR) "Repentence" — Stardate 54474.6
(VGR) "Prophecy" — Stardate 54518.2 to 54529.8
(VGR) "The Void" — Stardate 54553.4
(VGR) "Workforce" — Stardate 54584.3 to 54608.6
(VGR) "Workforce, Part II" — Stardate 54622.4
"Shadows, in the Dark" (VGR short story, SNW IV)
(VGR) "Human Error"
(VGR) "Q2" — Stardate 54704.5
(VGR) "Author, Author" — Stardate 54732.3 to 54748.6
(VGR) "Friendship One" — Stardate 54775.4
"Iridium-7-Tetrahydroxate Crystals are a Girl's Best Friend" (VGR short story, SNW IV)
(VGR) "Natural Law" — Stardate 54814.5 to 54827.7
(VGR) "Homestead" — Stardate 54868.6
(VGR) "Renaissance Man"—Stardate 54890.7 to 54912.4
Endgame **(VGR episode novelization)**—Stardate 54968.4

• 2393 — *Voyager*'s original homecoming

• 2403 — Future sequences

Timeliners' Note: This novel takes the Voyager *story beyond the end of the series.*

c. **2948**

(VGR) "Living Witness"

Timeliners' Note: The year was calculated from information in "Personal Log" (VGR short story, SNW IV).

c. **3000**

"Personal Log" (VGR short story, SNW IV)

Historians' Note: Story takes place 27 years after the Emergency Medical Hologram Backup Module left Vaskan/Kyrian space.

• *c.* 3004 — [Next Log] Four years later

4367

"I Am Become Death" (TNG short story, SNW II)

Historians' Note: Framing story is set 2,000 years in the future of TNG.

• 2367 — Sometime prior to "Brothers" (TNG)

And the human adventure is just beginning . . .